BCID 284
www.bod

Falling Awake

Charles J Harwood

Charles J Harwood

This novel is entirely a work of fiction. The names, characters and incidents portrayed in it are the work of the author's imagination. Any resemblance to actual persons living or dead, events or localities are entirely coincidental.

First Published © 2011 by C J H Publications under the original title
Domestic Bliss
Cover design © 2011 Rachel Shirley
ISBN-13: 978-1468141931
ISBN-10: 1468141937

All rights reserved

The Right of Charles J Harwood to be identified as the author of this work has been asserted in accordance with the Copyright Designs and Patents Act 1988 Section 77 and 78.

No part of this publication may be republished, stored in a retrieval system or transmitted in any form or by any means without the prior permission of the copyright owner.

This book is sold subject to the conditions that all designs are copyright and are not for the commercial reproduction without the written permission of the copyright owner.

To Ruth and Christine

Chapter 1

THIS was the closest Gemma had ever felt to being raped. Sounds that only came with effort: grunting, puffing, wheezing plus other such involuntary omissions; the smells: stale tobacco-suffused perspiration, cheap cologne, overpowering her and causing her to squint.

Violator Number One bore a mask of indifference betraying but a smidgen of righteous satisfaction by the thin seam of a mouth as he effortlessly hoisted her mahogany bureau from its habitual resting place beneath the stairs: her mother's wedding present which had been delivered to her house soon after Gemma and Liam had returned from their rained-out honeymoon in Teignmouth. Her John Lewis gold-plated wall-clock had ticked its final tock here, her collection of signed crime novels would never be read here and her oak five-piece kitchen table had received its final tattoo of coffee stains here – or so Violator Number One had decided.

Violator Number Two was thumping about upstairs. Gemma dare not imagine. She did not bode well her chances of a hidden stash of gold jewellery, her plasma TV or of her laptop from evading his greasy paws. Please God he would leave Ben's room untouched, there was nothing there of any value – well not to these violators anyway.

Violator One was negotiating her bureau through the narrow doorway. His unlaced trainers, his knuckles and the grizzly pate of his head were all she could see. Gemma remained where she was, rooted to the alcove wall that separated the kitchen from the living room in her modest mid-terrace. And why was she standing in defensive pose, arms folded across her midriff and feet planted squarely upon the floor? Such a stance may have ruffled a rude queue-dodger or teenagers commandeering the swings but at this point in time, such a pointless and futile posture would yield the same outcome had she faked a panic attack, offered her guests a cup of tea of jigged the Riverdance.

Violator One scuffed his knuckles against the doorframe. He gave another grunt. Gemma experienced a surge of gratification. No doubt he would win his objective. That bureau would find its way into the black shiny hearse-like van that obstructed her view of the elms across the road as surely as the gravity affixed her to the floor. Never had Gemma felt such a convergence of destiny. She could delay it, she could twist the truth, she could make lame excuses, but those men would always find their way through her front door eventually.

And the ugly truth was, it appeared they had the right. Gemma had stumbled across a cluster of official-looking envelopes stuffed in the bin. The ugly truth was, the contents were likely few of many of its kind; the apex to an iceberg of demands, final notices and such letters with large red print. Not only that, but Gemma had learned that a notice had been added to the house deeds to the name of Colby and Vernon, a firm of solicitors two hundred miles away. Colby and Vernon acted for a third party who now held a considerable share to the family bricks and mortar. Their powers to enforce a sale to release her now little equity hovered over her like a scythe. And how had she reacted? She had reacted in the manner of an animal scared into submission. She had ignored the signals. She had discarded one of Liam's doodles hidden away in the glove compartment of their old Audi displaying a black shape resembling a nerve cell for its tendril offshoots that had given her the creeps. She had pretended the doodle was just a doodle. She had evaded the subject of Liam's late night phone calls and unexplained absences. She had stuck her head into the proverbial sand and made the childish hope it would all go away.

The bailiff, or whoever he was, had made the convincing argument that she had no right to keep them out. The house was also theirs and they could break the door down if need be. Gemma felt certain the courts would never allow this, yet her resolve crumbled. She simply wanted to get the ugly business over and done with. She let them take what they wanted with the tiny consolation Ben wasn't here to witness these events.

The bureau breached the door and made its way out into the drizzle. Gemma retained her defense pose, for all it was worth as Violator One made ballet steps to the back of his van, his broad, square torso making easy work of the task. His white, baggy T-shirt proclaiming his other one was a Porsche flapped in the breeze. His friend padded down the stairs with a smaller load, but more valuable to the pound, to join his colleague. They exchanged words, the bureau slowly entering the van's rear. Gemma wondered what other assets languished inside. Had these men made a round trip? Perhaps she was subject two or three on today's agenda. Tears condensed onto the inner rims of her eyes and with it a salty taste. Gemma seldom cried. She told herself these were tears of indignation rather than self-pity. The image of the two burly men blurred anyway. Ben had been spared the sight, thankfully. Gemma had scooped up his scrawny yet compact form from his lunch bowl which had rested upon their now missing kitchen table. His arms flailed, his fork plied with noodles barely meeting its destination and a guttural complaint '*Muuuumm!*' had pushed up his throat. The bowl had flicked to the floor where it now rested and Gemma had dragged him complete with crutches through their narrow porchway up the short hedge-lined path, sharp right and to the next house up where she had rammed an identical door with a bare fist.

Patti, her brick-faced neighbour etched by sun and briny gales at sunny Blackpool and a habitual ciggie had glared upon the sight of Gemma and her vertically-challenged son, incredulous.

'Please…' Gemma's plea came out a moan. The creases around Patti's eyes ironed out revealing paler skin, making Gemma think of starfish.

Patti gave a complicit nod that seemed to aggrieve at the other too, whether the upper class or the bureaucrats though Gemma had barely exchanged a word with her since moving in to Southsbury six years ago. And what did Patti imagine she was in on? Present circumstances granted little room for proper cogitation. Gemma was simply grateful Patti was willing to take Ben for the next crucial moments.

And as Ben cast Gemma one last look of bewilderment, magnified by his spindly reading glasses and his crutches had clattered to the floor, Gemma's ears had picked up the sound of her destiny: the low and deliberate thrum of a transit, almost inaudible in its efficiency. Gemma did not look back. She did not look ahead. Her sights remained to the ground as the moss-lined slabs passed beneath her. Patti's door clicked shut. Ben was inside. He was gone and that was all that mattered.

Had her husband Liam not strayed onto the badlands that was some nameless moneylender, unlisted in the phonebook and slippery in the eyes of the law, Gemma felt certain she could have kept her front door unbreached. Perhaps she still could if she hadn't been so blissfully uninformed at this point.

The thugs had rammed their fists against her door in a never-ending salvo when they were done with words. They meant what they said; if Gemma wanted to save her door from splintering from its moorings, she would have to let them in.

Before she knew it, her abode had become the scene of wanton looting, shadows jerking, floorboards thundering and that's when she made the parallel between the present situation and physical violation.

She fondled her mobile but refrained from calling the police. Her sights shifted towards the window as a flash of sunlight caught the headstocks of her Ashton guitar canting over the shoulder of Violator Two. A splinter of indignation rocketed through her gut, up her sternum and lodged into her throat. The intensity of it almost made her knees buckle.

Her Ashton, the guitar her sister had brought her three birthdays ago had initially lain redundant before Gemma had picked it up and reacquainted herself with the twelve year old who discovered most pop classics consisted of three chords in a chosen scale: firsts, seconds and fourths. Marley, Dylan and McCartney, it seemed had conjured the most latent chord combinations so no two constructions sounded anything like one another. Gemma had just moved onto other chords before discovering the meditative properties of fingerpicking and began to wonder why she had allowed such a passion to give way to the rigors of adolescence, married life and motherhood.

Her feet shuffled to the door without conscious awareness. The van's open rear door obscured Number Two from sight. Number One's feet clunked up her stairs. Gemma drifted towards the porch as soon as his footfalls took a pause at the top. Gemma kept moving, the narrow mining houses floating by the periphery of her vision. Number Two was still loading the back of the van. The hems of his jogging trousers scuffed against the floor. One foot disappeared onto the platform within the van. Gemma maintained her approach, anticipating the other foot to follow. The remaining sole shuffled against the patchwork of tarmac. Hardware thudded against the inner wall of the van. The foot shifted sideways. Gemma eased into a sidle. Another clatter and Number Two gave a grunt.

Waltzing Matilda staccatoed from his mobile. It cut off in mid-waltz with an 'Aya.' The second foot made its slow journey up onto the platform to join its counterpart.

Gemma made a graceful u-turn and spotted the headstocks of her guitar protruding from the racking within the inner wall. A multitude of other possessions cluttered the van's maw: a lawnmower, camping equipment, golfing accessories, a piano, chest-of-drawers, suites, a dismantled greenhouse, and was that a harp? Her coffee-stained kitchen diner, her leather suite and bureau had been pushed into a corner. But these did not concern her and neither did the harvester of these possessions, parking the posterior of his grubby gym pants onto the table and prattling into his mobile.

Gemma grasped the upper neck of her Ashton and slid it quietly from the racking. She pulled its belly towards her as though she were about to serenade present company with a song about unearthing unrealised forbearance, a change of heart and perhaps lull him into pardoning her husband for his financial misdemeanours and leave here minus her things. Present company barked into the phone, 'You takin' the piss or what?' and Gemma doubted he would appreciate any such lyrics from a minor key.

Gemma dismounted the van and made her way towards the end of the terraced row. Curtains were shifting now: Tall Trevor in number 73, Twitchy Dave in number 67, Serial Patio Cleaner in number 36 and brick-faced Patti. They and perhaps a few others were watching a woman in jeans, slippers and a pyjama-top ferry a guitar from the back of a black repossession van and pad towards the paper shop at the corner. She no longer cared about her mid-terrace down Newton Road. Minus Ben and her stash of memories, what was it but a series of rooms, interconnected by a landing, identical in layout to all others here? Those men could take the fixtures but they could not take the roof, dismantle the walls or unscrew the windows from their frames. Their looting was but purgation, a scrubbing away of things that were not really hers anymore and a means of gaining a fresh view and a new beginning. These fanciful notions took hold; her only purchase and flimsy sanctuary from the black reality. Yes she would strip the wallpaper, lift the carpets and unpeel the paint. She would squat in her small patch if need be; Gemma had no intention of exchanging her roof for any other, least of all some mildewed guesthouse or hostel on account of two greasy violators.

Gemma moved swiftly around the corner. Azhar's shop was closed until two. The ice cream banner squeaked in the breeze, reflecting her bleak prospect. Gemma kept moving toward an undefined destination. Bollards flanked a tree-lined thoroughfare to a playing area. Frustration bubbled in her chest. The cubbyhole beneath Azhar's counter would have been preferable. Azhar said hello to everyone and clucked about the state of his allotment. Wind, frost and drought had been a contributor to Gemma's overrunning schedule numerous times but Azhar's affability made this excusable. Azhar would have sheltered her Ashton. He would have nodded eagerly with that open smile of his and not asked questions. Instead, Gemma was making inroads to a cluster of swings where Twitchy Dave's sons idled. Dave's nickname, attributed to his facial tics, seemed to bother him little although Gemma never used the tag to his face as some of the neighbours here did.

Gemma made cautious approach, not wanting to draw attention. She settled upon a dilapidated bench clutching her guitar like a desperate busker. The swings squeaked, the radio prattled and the wind tousled at her hair. Had the black van done with its glut now? Had the men unburdened the front of her house of their big hearse no wiser for the missing guitar? Gemma wasn't so sure. Since finding herself in this strange terrain, she no longer knew what the rules were. Liam's disappearance had highlighted how pitifully little she knew about what he did during the day. It wasn't until last week that she had forged the courage to pick up the phone and seek advice from Debt Terminal Limited, a contact she had read about in the library.

'What is the size of the debt?' Julie, her designated case leader had asked.

Gemma had paused, words lodging in her chest like bricks. Liam's black doodle capered in her head. Nausea drizzled through her gut. 'I don't know,' she lied.

There had been a loaded silence. Perhaps Julie was waiting for Gemma to add something. Julie's voice had adopted a soft cadence. 'Who are the lenders, Annie?'

Annie was the name Gemma had given during the preamble. Gemma suddenly wanted to end the phone call. She wasn't ready. Not yet, she couldn't….it was too much.

Julie maintained her soft, professional tone, picking up on Gemma's hesitation. 'I know this is difficult for you, but you need to establish who the lenders are and the amount loaned. The good news is that lenders must be registered and regulated by the FSA and you have considerable powers and rights. But private lenders are a different matter. The first thing you need to do is to check out the name of the lender to see if they are on the Public Register and you need to establish the size of the loan.'

Gemma knew at that moment that the lender or whatever they were would not appear on any such register or even if they had a name.

Julie's voice came again. 'Annie?'

'Yes?' Gemma's syllable could not have been smaller.

'Annie. This is a crucial first step. You must establish these facts. When you do, someone from my highly-trained team or myself here at Debt Terminal Limited will be here to take your call anytime between eight and eight on workdays.'

Terminal. The finality of the word created the sensation of her stomach constricting to a tight ball and winching up to her throat. The insistent squeak of Twitchy Dave's kids on the swings exacerbated the sensation. *Debt, death, debt, death, debt, death.* Gemma had ended the call there and then.

Gusts ferried broken syllables across the park and she knew who was about to join them. Gemma shuffled towards the bin and pushed the guitar belly-up into the inner grating hoping it might offer concealment. The lower barrel caught the grating with a squeak. Gemma knit her lip and up-ended the guitar. One of the boys turned and watched. He nudged his brother and together they took in the spectacle. Gemma worked the headstocks this way and that like a witch stirring the world's biggest brew. She caught the boys' eyes and the Ashton protested with a tuneless ricochet. Gemma conveyed a small frown that signalled this scene did not warrant an audience. The older boy, Tommy, averted his gaze but not in the manner she'd hoped. Again, he nudged his brother and Gemma discerned the sounds of approaching footfalls. She released her guitar from the clutches of the bin, scuffing the fretboard. She turned, nestling the wooden belly into the crook of her armpit. The headstocks spun in the direction of the two men like a machete. If only. Number Two would get it before Number One. Instead, deep-set raisin eyes drew to her deliberate motion. Gemma hesitated. His flat, broad features caused her eyes to linger, not so much to the contours of his face but by their proportions; not male, but artificially butch. Soft down sprouted above his or her lip; a sad assemblage of follicles supposed to represent a moustache. He/she saw Gemma's look. The woman, Gemma decided, slowly extended her arm, palm flattened and supine. She beckoned sharply by flexing her knuckles. Gemma could make no sense of what she had seen or of this gesture. Gemma's clasp tightened around the belly of her guitar.

The transsexual's accomplice remained in her shadow. He lit a cigarette and took a pull as though this were all part of a day's work. Gemma's earlier splinter of indignation gave another jab into her sternum. How could he just stand there and light up when presented with the sight of someone in disintegration? The woman gave another abrupt motion, this time with her wrist. Gemma knew that running was futile. These violators may take care not to land themselves an assault charge, but they would corner her, they would wait her out and it seemed they cared little about the passing of time. Gemma was as trapped in this open parkland as she would have been down a cul-de-sacked alleyway.

The violators waited, the swings' squawks abating with the wind. Gemma untucked her guitar from her armpit, without unfastening her gaze from the woman's raisin eyes. *Debt, death.* One last death knell.

Gemma grasped the neck of her Ashton and extended the guitar in their direction. Number Two took a step towards her. Gemma remained by the bin. Violator One took another drag and flicked ashes to the floor. Those raisin eyes gave a small blink and she inched forward. Gemma raised the barrel of her guitar above her head and drove it ground-wards, straining all the tendons in her shoulders. Gemma took caution to strings whiplashing by gently closing her eyes. The rosewood belly met concrete in all frequencies from a sonic boom that oscillated against the soles of her feet, the spitfire crack that rent the air in a static discharge to the buzzing scream of the trebles as the strings warped against a newly-acquired hinge-joint midway up the fretboard.

No sooner had this macabre cacophony fade out, did Gemma take second aim, driving her limb extension upwards and groundwards in pickaxe motion. A fountain of splinters surged from the breach and showered her upper arms. The strings crooned, hissed and screeched. Base E snapped and coiled about her feet. Third and fourth aim split the belly, the headstocks now decapitated and lying at her feet. D, G and A now joined base E, detached and coiling in spasms. Wooden darts peppered the dilapidated bench and the barrel made one last complaint in a bizarre acoustic boom that made Gemma think of a piano bouncing down the stairs.

Raisin Eyes had not unfastened her gaze from Gemma's throughout. Her expression remained immobile yet one lower eyelid harboured a depression, that hadn't been there before. Her friend merely powdered the ground with more ashes.

The boys watched transfixed. Gemma stepped forward as though no one were present and calmly collected the detritus that had once been her sister's birthday present and inserted the components into the bin: fretboard first, concertinaed barrel next and finally the headstocks. The guitar now fitted perfectly within the confines of the grating.

The two violators seemed not in the least putout. More ashes showered the floor and dog-end followed. Raisin Eyes lowered her arm and shrugged her shoulders. They turned and retraced their steps through the leafy thoroughfare.

Chapter 2

THE two violators had done a thorough job. Just as well Gemma didn't care for soaps or quiz shows, although Ben would miss Horrible Histories and Doctor Who. Not only would they have to make do without transmitted pictures but sounds. Every radio, CD player and her Ipod gone. The violators had pillaged the garage at the rear of three bikes, a lawnmower, power tools, Liam's rowing machine, exercise bike and other gym equipment. Her bedroom now resembled a fifties bedsit, housing only her bed and a chest of drawers. Her built-in wardrobe thankfully was unmovable and provided ample storage space for her now few possessions which consisted mainly of clothes and toiletries. The looters however had taken her jewellery, her signed book collection, a dresser, two lamps and hair straighteners. Her laptop would be sorely lamented, although the thing was getting temperamental. Gemma had the foresight to delete her financial particulars on archives as well as backup. This she did after her search history had mysteriously been deleted shortly before Liam's disappearance. Liam liked to borrow her laptop like he did most things of hers. His habitual line, 'That's why you're called Gem, 'cause you are,' gave hollow solace. The house had also been looted of her guitar books, software, Ben's playstation, her leather suite, glass coffee table, corner unit, steamer and several other mobile kitchen appliances. They had even left the loft ladder down having taken Ben's Lego kits, jigsaws and scores of other kids' games some Ebayer would find a dream.

Ben's room looked the same, consisting only of his bed, a dresser and movie posters. Gemma knew the value of her stolen goods would hardly cover the debt, being merely second-hand. Only one article would pay off whatever the loan had been.

'We're not going to lose the house are we?' Ben seemed to pluck the words right out of her brain.

Gemma was sitting on the tiles of her kitchenette, legs spread out and Ben beside her. His crutches flanked him. She forced her lips into a cocked smile as though Ben's question were ridiculous. 'No...of course not, Ben.' The empty room enveloped her words and swallowed them whole.

Gemma would have performed the knee-jerk ritual of her mother when faced with a crisis and put the kettle on, but did not want to see if it was still there. That would have been one seizure too many.

A draft tendrilled its way around her ankles and teased at her nape hairs. Ben detected the air movement too but he remained beside her, possessing the unerring maturity for his twelve years not to speak.

Gemma kept her eyes to the door and slowly moved to stand. The black hearse glinted in the mid-morning sun. Unlaced trainers and oil-stained T-shirt emerged from the hallway and squinty wall-eyes pressed upon hers. He forced his syllables through polyped vocals, probably through smoke. 'You need to tell your 'usband his account is frozen with immediate effect.' A piece of paper came from nowhere and floated onto the windowsill. His tobacco-stained finger sported a gold ring.

Gemma couldn't help herself. 'Sleep well, won't you?'

Violator One barely paused. He rummaged into his breast pocket for a notebook and pen. He scribbled at length. 'You may think my kind repulsive, Miss.' He licked the nib of his pencil and continued. 'But I seen a side of human nature that'd make me seem like the Fairy godmother.' He tore the page out. 'People'll do anything for money. Your old man's no different. His disappearing act says it all. I mean, who'd leave his missus and his kid like this?' His sights landed on hers and it grew intent. 'You'll learn you're no different either.' He proffered the piece of paper. Gemma's mouth bunched. She didn't move, but this didn't seem to bother Violator One. 'You were quite a spectacle back there. Spunky. It'll be the making and the saving of ye. A mate of mine, Phil is looking for something like you. It's good money. You'll earn your stuff back in no time.' The man deposited the scrap paper on top of the first offering. 'Only it wasn't me who told you, understand?'

Try as she might, Gemma could not unbunch her mouth. His suggestion had the effect of a freshly-squeezed lemon pressing upon her tongue tip. 'Get out you filthy bastard,' she uttered hoarsely.

The man gave a slow blink and left quietly.

The piece of paper on the windowsill informed her that the thousand pound set-up fee was now 'discharged.' A header bore the name of Colby and Vernon, embossed and motiffed with a fern leaf and exhibiting a large scribble at the bottom. Gemma restrained the impulse to throw it away as she might need it as evidence. For what, she wasn't sure. She had already made the decision not to call the police for fear that Liam may end up in prison. She couldn't do that to Ben and she couldn't do that to Liam's parents, who had always been good to her.

Gemma spent an hour on the phone anyway. She'd given up on Liam, who seemed to have withdrawn himself from all modes of contact, and not her parents, who lived two hundred miles away in their retirement home in Cornwall. Not even Julie, but Liam's dad, Terry. Terry had become her lifeline when Liam went astray and his dark, gravelly voice never failed to reassure. Terry would take tomorrow off and visit first thing in the morning with some things prepared.

Fuelled by the dearth of her guitar, Gemma expressed her umbrage via letter towards these so-called solicitors who had endorsed this pillaging. She had made the decision not to involve the police, but she wasn't taking it lying down. Her venting took momentum, her language morphing into a frenzied tirade. She had suffered infringement of rights, trespassing of property and abuse. By the time she had finished, her head felt tight and her mouth dry.

Gemma gathered herself before she ventured into the garage to fish out a mildewed patio table and two deckchairs. She set them up in the kitchen. One of the legs kept popping out of the socket and Gemma had to take care not to jar the table whilst walking by. Gemma confounded herself that she was able to administer such tasks with little sentiment or tears. She reasoned that Liam's previous financial aberrations had prepared her for this moment, immuned her in some way. Gemma gave the table and chairs a once-over with Dettox. She couldn't sit in the deckchair for long for the piping at the front created pressure sores on the backs of her thighs. Heaven knows how Ben must be coping.

Gemma made herself prepare tea and she made herself boil water in a pan for a brew. Yes, the kettle had gone. Her stomach protested at the thought of depositing food into her mouth or of imbibing tea that appeared to have an oil spill. Ben sat quietly as Gemma dished out beans on toast. The chairs squeaked bleakly. Ben continued to appraise his dinner without picking up his cutlery. Gemma mustered the will to gather up several beans on a fork and show Ben by example that she was willing to eat, sleep and do the same tomorrow in spite of the unseen forces that threatened to snatch this tiny patch of land from beneath them. She paused and took a small mouthful. Ben continued to stare into his dinner.

'Mum, what's an audition?'

Poor Ben. Was he about to engineer a fantastic plan to save the house that equalled the chance of success as a lottery win?

Gemma's voice came forlorn. 'It's when an actor or dancer performs for a part.'

Ben seemed to consider this. 'Like on the X Factor?'

Gemma nodded slowly.

'I see. So when the audience is watching you, that's voyeurism.'

Gemma's next portion paused in midair. She slowly looked at Ben.

'I was told that you could earn bucketfuls doing voyeurism. We could save up and go the Disneyland Paris.'

Gemma slowly lowered her wrists to the table. 'Ben, where did you hear that word?'

Ben shrugged his shoulders in response to the edge in Gemma's tone. 'I found that piece of paper in the bin. I thought it was one of dad's stupid bookies so I called it. I've always wanted to tell them to get stuffed.'

Gemma dropped her cutlery with a clatter. 'Oh, *God...*'

Ben's eyes fastened to hers in an attempt to reassure. 'It's Okay, Mum. It was just some guy talking about a show. He said they have a performance every night and you have to wear a special outfit and a cat mask. I could make you one if you like. Mrs. Potts is good at helping me with stuff like that. You'd look cool.'

Gemma floundered with discomfiture at how such words could be misconstrued by an innocent boy. She opened her mouth to speak when Ben ventured a wry grin.

'Patti could keep an eye on me while you go to the show – she won't mind. And Gran'd be thrilled you got yourself a nice job dressing up and performing for voyeurism. It's better than all the boring jobs people do round here.'

Gemma gritted her teeth and extended her hand. 'Give the piece of paper to me.'

Ben's face flushed. Quietly, he dug into his trouser pocket and proffered the piece of paper. Gemma seized the offering and did a thorough job of screwing it up.

Ben seemed perturbed and hurt. He took to his feet, groping for his crutches. He made a small puff of effort and lurched from the table.

Ben did not appear again that evening. His beans on toast stiffened and dulled on his plate as did the remnants of hers. Gemma disposed of both dinners in the bin. Without transmitted culture, the four walls were indeed bleak. How did people cope without music, chat shows, the internet, comedy, the news? Sounds from another quarter commandeered – the wind skimming over the chimneypot, the traffic whisper, the floorboards creaking as the house settled down.

She still had her phone, her heating, running water, basic food and a roof over her head. She had read somewhere that four-fifths of the world population did not possess a computer or a TV. A large portion of this figure did not have clean running water and still millions of others were homeless. In those eyes, she was lucky. Even in her present situation, she retained her position as being near the top of the world's wealth and privileges. She only wished she could feel that way.

Gemma trudged upstairs to check on Ben. His partially-open door disclosed a darkened room. He was in bed apparently asleep.

'Ben?'

Ben did not reply.

Compunction at her harsh words earlier stung, and he had his father's absence to contend with too. How would such actions be comprehended when Ben reached adulthood? Gemma daren't imagine, but a fear of desertion came to mind, insecurities, relationship issues. Gemma had tried to protect Ben from the truth surrounding Liam's other disappearances in the past, telling him his father was away on business. It hadn't washed this time.

'It's some bookies, isn't it Mum?' he'd said a couple of days ago. Gemma wished it was as simple as that. 'Yes,' Gemma had replied. 'I'm afraid so.'

Ben's eyebrows had puckered furiously. 'Why doesn't he just stop? It's easy really. Just don't do it anymore.'

Ben's simple philosophy crushed her. 'You are right, Ben but some people…' Gemma groped for the right words. 'They can't help it. They just can't. You dad needs help. And until I know where he is and what he's got himself into, no one can do anything.'

Ben's furrow had lingered. He blinked slowly, taking this in.

'Don't worry, Ben,' Gemma tried to soothe. 'Your dad's safe. I know he is.' She kissed the top of Ben's head. 'And he loves you. He loves you to bits.'

The nonchalance of Ben's shrug was brutal. He collected his crutches with a clatter and made his way to the kitchen to fix himself a sandwich. Gemma had watched troubled. Ben had not asked about his father's whereabouts from that moment.

Chapter 3

GEMMA had used an alias when talking to Julie because of the truth. And the truth was uglier for the parts she couldn't see than for those that she could. Recently she had begun to realise how little she had seen since marrying Liam.

Liam had always been an activist, unlike his pool-playing passive, and dare she say it, dead-end hangers-on; his fervour and passion had initially attracted her to him. He seemed to possess everything her family lacked: the finger on the pulse, so to speak, the word on the street and the confidence to win or lose. He knew that property investment in Albania would yield wealth in mere months, and sure enough, a rash of investors made millions in time-share; Liam had the foresight to buy dividends in a local radio station and make a few thousand himself. And he advised his best friend, Steve on purchasing a plot of land for driving experiences, a venue where Joe Bloggs could be Mansell for the day, go-kart, quad-bike or drive a tank.

Liam possessed a nervous energy that made any venture seem irresistible. Sometimes this spilled into living the life and *having*. He loved *having*: cars, bikes, the latest gadgetry, racing gear, the smartest Iphone. His quest for having verged onto the tacky, such possessions, she thought would find its way onto tomorrow's carboot. She wished he wouldn't indulge Ben on such things though she conceded in fear of being branded a boring and imperious mother. She didn't like the garbage smell of candy and burgers on Ben's breath after Liam had taken Ben out to Steve's track, and she didn't like Liam's computer games intent on annihilating foes in the most creative and ghastly ways.

Liam was the perfect consumer and one Gemma suspected motivated by filling something. A void? A missing out on something? A fear of death? Gemma had sometimes glimpsed a disturbing fever in his eyes when something caught him, and she knew she could do little to withstand this force. Their marriage had faltered shortly after Ben's birth when Liam found himself laid-off from his job and saddled with the responsibilities of being a dad. A torpor had infested him, each nappy change, feed and household duty seeming to sap his vitality. He would spend his days watching daytime TV and surfing the Net in his Homer Simpson T-shirt and pyjama trousers. When Ben reached six months, it had come to light that Liam had run up a three thousand pound debt with an online betting company. Liam's dad intervened and coerced him into counselling, rehab and a job helping his friend at Barnstow garage. It was at this point that Liam's dad had disclosed that Liam had fallen foul of betting several times since his teens and each time, his parents had bailed him out.

Gemma had felt cheated by this. How come this information had evaded her until now? She had a son and a house. Would Liam learn from the past or was his tastes for fluttering ingrained into his subconscious? She hoped Liam would have the strength to resist the insistence within him. Failing that, a steady job might deter him or keep him focused.

Gemma no longer minded Liam's absences from the house. She could no longer bear to watch him play the domestic animal and prowl in circles, resentful at the walls that apparently entrapped him. She let him go out there, strive, to *have*; to work, to fill his life and experience a payoff in a more principled way.

How wrong she was.

When Ben had reached six, Liam had got into a venture restoring old cars at the garage. He overspent on spare parts, travelling across the country to complete his project. When it came to sell, the recession hit and he lost thousands. With the market stagnating, Liam found himself valleting cars to make ends meet. He ended his shifts early and took to bed. Two days after a weekend trip to Stratford to celebrate her birthday, he went missing. For two weeks, Gemma lived as a single parent, not knowing his whereabouts or even if he was alive. Liam's dad stepped in again after getting reports of sightings from the police in Brynton Sands, a resort north of Chapel St Leonard's skirting the Lincolnshire coast. *The east coast?* What was he doing there?

Gemma and Terry took the two-hour jaunt to The Wash, a coastal delta under constant erosion from the North Sea. The whole area was infused with an ancient briny smell that embraced the doomed cliff-facing cottages. Gemma bitterly wished she hadn't accompanied her father-in-law on the trip. If only she could unpeel the memories like an old skin, unsee the sights and unhear the sounds. Gemma squeezed her eyes shut whenever a sliver of it threatened to pierce her brain.

Gemma had returned adulterated. She no longer understood the world she lived in. Things were not arranged as she thought. Another world had presented itself, an underworld that threatened to engulf her old established belief system. Gemma did the only thing she could. Deny it. Time was a great obscurer. She would go back to the normality and the routine, where people assumed roles, where she felt secure and adhere to the old rules and she would continue to lie to Ben about how the world operated.

Liam spent thirty days in a psychiatric hospital after his return. Once the counsellor was happy that the antidepressants had taken effect, Liam was discharged to spend a few weeks at his parents'. Terry kept an eye on him by accompanying his son to his work at the garage. Liam seemed changed. The turn in his life had indeed seemed to shock him into being the dad Ben deserved.

Liam got in touch with his old friend Steve and partnered up in the driving experience business. He loaned money from the bank to buy an Aston Martin to test the track with.

The following year was a walk on the high-wire with Liam's chancing. But it paid off and the loan was paid back. Not only that, Liam had made a healthy profit and he treated the family to a holiday in Majorca.

Gemma decided to pay a visit to Steve's track one day. Liam conjured his usual sales-talk, even to his own impressionable son, selling him an idea, a dream, the memory of the sort of dad all his friends would envy: confident, exciting, adventurous. Liam tousled the top of Ben's prickly hair. 'Wouldn't you like to drive one of these one day, little fellah?' he'd asked, though the recurrent tendinitis in Ben's knees made this unlikely. His voice could hardly be heard beneath the roar of an Atom. Ben merely nodded, his lenses reflecting a cumulus sky.

Ben accompanied his father to the track each Saturday afternoon but Gemma suspected Ben went to please Liam rather than to please himself. 'Why don't you come Mum?' he asked one day. Gemma made the usual excuse about housework, but in truth, Liam's venture had begun to lodge that old foreboding in her chest. She wished he wouldn't. Why couldn't he just settle for a normal life like everyone else? Why couldn't he just do the nine-to-five at Barnstow garage?

Gemma got the notion of dust-balls gathering beneath her bed and powdering the air at night. She started leaving the window open even when frost threatened. Scum gathered between the bath-taps and the tiles every month or so due to soap and dust. Removal had been a routine operation before. Now it seemed imperative she excavate every iota, using Liam's cotton buds to ensure thoroughness. Suddenly the house seemed to cosset opportunities for dust to congregate: the tops of the kitchen wall units; the curtain railing, the cubbyhole above the back door. Every little community would bloom from the cracks in the walls and reach out tendrils to become larger communities. Gemma dusted twice a day yet the notion of unseen dust persisted – dark dust she would forever overlook. An odd concoction of despair and false assurance crept within her. Gemma took care not to look too hard or she would find. Her domestic province seemed on condition; the parts she couldn't see had unknown proportions and seemed to be slipping away from her.

Liam took to answering his mobile in the next room. He'd come home late with no explanation. Their dusty old Audi had abruptly become unavailable due to a faulty carburetor. Only the day before, she had come across Liam's doodle secreted within the dashboard; a black, distorted nonagon shape infilled with soft graphite. The doodle looked to be executed carefully, every outline shaded to airbrushed smoothness, akin to a nerve cell or jellyfish, yet resembling nothing meaningful. Liam took to doodling during phone calls or such abstracted moments, but were usually swirly lines echoing a phone number or a tear in the paper. The black shape was different for it seemed to represent something significant. Her discovery remained unvocalised for her suspicions Liam had been using her laptop in secret. She'd booted up, signed in and waited for the security screen to load and that's when she'd noticed the search history had gone. This spurred her to log into all her bank accounts, change the pins and delete all records of her sign-ins from the files. She felt guilty for what these actions implied.

Her fingers tremored as she signed into their mortgage account not knowing what she might find. Right on cue, each installment went in from Liam's bank account. Gemma's relief was not complete; something did not sit right. She ferreted for her mobile and dialled Liam's number knowing full well she would get no reply again. She dialled Steve's number. Steve answered after barely two beats in his usual affable tone. Steve always habituated a preamble on how business was doing, the weather or the price of fuel. Gemma wanted to cut it today.

'Can I speak to Liam?'

Steve's hesitation uneased her. 'He's not here.'

'Oh…'

'Hasn't been here for over a month. Didn't he tell you?'

Gemma swallowed a tight feeling. 'Tell me what?'

'He opted out.'

Gemma remained silent.

'Said he had other stuff to attend to. Not surprising really, but that's Liam for you.'

Gemma closed her eyes and assembled an even tone. 'Yes, of course. I forgot. I'm sorry to bother you, Steve. I'll get back to you once I've spoken to Liam about this.' Gemma cut the line before Steve could say more.

Gemma returned to her laptop to log off when she noticed a scroll down facility on her mortgage screen that hadn't been there before. She scrolled and an extra entry presented itself: a notice to the credit of Colby and Vernon. Gemma didn't understand what she was seeing as first, the words merging into one another. Her brain simply demanded what this extra paragraph was doing there. Had she signed into the wrong account by mistake? Was this an admin error? Had to be. A phone call would clear this up. But Gemma had the bad feeling this was not an admin aberration. Staring at those words, Colby and Vernon, she had the sensation of spotting an intruder in her house, in her kitchen, her bathroom, her bedroom, only to be informed that the intruder had every right to be there and she could do nothing about it. How had Liam done this without her consent? Why had the bank allowed this? And where was he?

Gemma Googled the name, Colby and Vernon. Several results came back: a firm of solicitors based in Hull. Their slogan had been 'The Power to Make Things Happen.' They specialised in administration, property law, insolvency and credit control. *Credit control.* She could only guess what that meant for her: seizures, debt collection, bankruptcy proceedings. According to the literature, such matters can be a costly and stressful business for any party to deal with. Colby and Vernon are able to step in to advise, support and administer to 'make things happen' with a range of options.

Gemma did not hesitate. She jotted down their number and gave them a call. She underwent the recorded message route 'Thank you for contacting Colby and Vernon, your call may be recorded for training purposes.' Gemma had closed her eyes, drummed her fingers, depressed the appropriate keys before a soft, Geordie accent had husked down the phone line. 'Hi, this is Aimee of Colby and Vernon. How may I help you today?'

Gemma explained the situation and Aimee listened without comment. Gemma began to wonder if Aimee were still there. 'Hello?' she said.

'I'm here,' Aimee informed her.

Gemma could sense she wasn't going to get far with this woman. 'Can I speak to someone who may be able to answer a few questions about the situation?'

'I am your most suitable point of contact,' Aimee informed Gemma, much to her dismay.

'What does this all mean?' Gemma asked.

'The notice has been put there to alert a third party if the house is to be put for sale. The third party may then take the appropriate action to collect money owed once the first lender, usually a mortgage company has been paid off.'

'A third party?'

'That is correct.'

Gemma was getting more frustrated with this woman. 'Who is this third party?'

'We act on behalf of certain companies who require guidance in law in matters of money lending and debt collection, and therefore…'

'I'm sorry, perhaps I hadn't made myself clear. What I asked was *who is this third party?*'

'As I was just saying, Mrs. Greene, we act on behalf of certain companies in legal matters relating to debt collection and we are bound by confidentiality not to give out information of that nature.'

Gemma's face flushed. 'But this is my home!'

Aimee had no comment.

'This isn't fair. How can some *third party* just creep its way onto my property deeds!'

'I am very sorry for your predicament, Mrs. Greene.'

Gemma doubted that very much. Gemma closed her eyes for the freefall. 'How much was the loan for?'

Aimee became silent but for soft tapping sounds and then Aimee husked down the phone again. 'It seems your husband applied for a secured loan two months ago to the amount of seventy thousand pounds.'

Gemma's fingernails burrowed into her palms until her flesh burned.

'Hmmm'

Gemma's eyes snapped open. 'What is it?'

'It seems a setup fee for a thousand pounds is outstanding.'

'Setup fee? What for?'

'I am unable to view that sort of information.'

'This isn't right. Liam would need my consent, wouldn't he? My signature? That notice cannot be put on the property without my consent.'

'It seems your name does not appear on the property register, Mrs. Greene.'

How could it be that Aimee was telling her that black was white or that the sun set in the east? 'Yes it is.'

Aimee it seemed was done with this call, perhaps overdue a lunch break. 'You will have to discuss this matter with your husband, Mrs. Greene.'

'He's gone missing,' Gemma blurted.

Again, Aimee had no comment.

Gemma decided she didn't have a comment to Aimee's non-comment, and sat out her silence, see how far she could go.

Aimee's voice finally husked its way up the line after seemingly an eternity. 'Then I am unable to help you further on this matter today, Mrs. Greene.'

Gemma slammed the phone down.

A minefield of mental snares awaited Gemma after checking in on Ben. It began with numbers. Carer's allowance for Ben, child benefit, tax credits, her wages from her part-time job. Could she claim more benefits until Liam showed up? Could she claim legal aid? What if Liam never returned? Without any financial contribution from him, how was she going to live? Could she get this third party off her property deeds? And if she couldn't, could she still live here? Could she make these lenders wait for their money until she decided to sell? And what rights did they have to enter her property – yes, *hers,* not anybody else's? For Ben's sake, she had to get Liam's name off the title deeds.

Colby and Vernon. Her throat became dry and her stomach clenched into a tight ball as it had done so when cornered in the park. She needed money. Even if this Colby and Vernon had no right to do what they have just done, she needed money quickly for whatever was in store.

Gemma barred any conjecture of Liam's state of mind when he had signed over his share of her property. That would ultimately lead to what she had seen in Brynton Sands and she couldn't dwell on that. Chain thoughts tore through narrow channels she could no longer control. It came to the same thing. What was the setup fee for?' What had cost Liam seventy thousand pounds? Liam's black nonagon doodle cavorted in her head. Gemma wasn't sure she wanted to find out its significance. Without knowing where Liam was or even if she would ever see him again, she equally feared she may never find out.

Chapter 4

PIGEONS have been roosting in his mouth again – or so it felt. They took flight depositing their feathers and bird dandruff a microsecond before his eyes fluttered open. And it seemed a microsecond had gone by since the performance had ended. A clinically square room enclosed him. The bed in which he lay no longer welcomed his form. The mattress had gone sour, it had gone off and its very fabric seemed to prod at his spine. He lay still anyway, staring at the ceiling, the contours of his body rigidly straight and echoing the rectangular platform beneath him. The ceiling exhibited a soupcon of shadows defined by a streetlamp just out of view of his window. Most would have found this ambient blend of light and shadow relaxing and perhaps engage the subconscious to create pictures from it. He didn't. He despised that half-glow because he had spent hours looking at something that never spurred meditation or the lower levels of consciousness. The self-professed insomniac, curse them, may have stared at it for a couple of hours once or twice a week before dropping off, and Luke had learned long ago that most self-professed insomniacs were simply not. Insomniac, that is. One must endure paltry sips of oblivion in a grinding replication until the days merged into one another. And why did these *tourists* profess to know what it was like? Thank God sleep clinics exposed them for the tedious subjects they really are: affliction-seekers looking to define their existences: Well, sleep state misperception would be their only endowment, or the clinician's more poetic term, paradoxical insomnia – the belief the subject has less sleep than was actually the case. Sadly the clinicians had confirmed Luke's fears. A sleep report that revealed anything but: condensed delta waves and a morsel of REM, amounting to no more than three hours' slumber per twenty-four hours during the entire assessment period – a night's sleep to equal the average afternoon nap. They had diagnosed him with chronic faulty sleep onset and inefficient sleep retention – psycho-physiologic insomnia, a ticking of all the boxes. Luke underwent diagnostic tests for heart irregularities, Parkinson's disease, restless leg syndrome, sleep apnea and many others. All came back normal. The staff asked him how he functioned in the day. Luke didn't know what to say. He just wished he could have worn this accolade like a mayor parading a gaudy chain; for people to *see* he was different. Instead he was expected to perform as everyone else who enjoyed the full compliment. Still going strong after a sudden onset five years ago. He likened the decline of his sleep to the evaporation of a desert pond after a flood, his mind like the doomed fishes within, shirking further from the shrinking banks in a quest for fresh water, or in his case, oblivion. Ultimately baked beneath the sun, the fishes suffocated slowly in a thick mud. Similarly, his brain, starved of sleep, withered beneath the continual glare of consciousness with little room for escape.

Luke slowly pivoted his head to the clock which informed the hour was 3.10. Well, he'd had worse. He drew his tongue over the roof of his mouth to dislodge the dandruffy scum. He lifted the baked-potato that was his head and massaged the cracked goose-eggs that were his eyes. He prized his eyelids open and his window came as a blurred shape, as did the window opposite. The performance had gone as expected. A few moves he hadn't seen before, his binoculars had misted up once or twice, but he barely gave it a thought once the thing was over.

Luke had heard about the letting opposite two years ago after Christian Lovett from accounts had confided he could see right into the flat across the courtyard. He had spent many-an-hour watching female students parade half-naked between the living area and the bedroom, cooking, grooming, watching TV, dancing with childish ditziness and abandon. Christian had offered Luke his flat when he got transferred to London. He had obviously supposed a fortyish insomniac divorcee had nothing better to do with his cavernous nocturnal hours than to leer at scantily-clad females young enough to be a daughter of his. Luke took the lease, by which time, male students had moved in. Luke spent his nights reading the entire works of Dan Browne for something light. Christian had telephoned him a month later on the pretext of querying a client's account.

'How gives the insomnia?' he guffed. Christian obviously hadn't realised his waifs had been replaced with the hairier, brawnier kind.

Luke sat perfectly still, squeezing his pen between forefinger and thumb.

'Well?' Christian prompted.

'Good,' Luke uttered.

'Good?'

'Yes. Very good.'

Christian's voice thickened. 'I told you.'

Luke took to spending more time at the flat, returning to his capacious detached in Berkham only to check the post, entertain friends (a seldom occasion now) and to do some work. The study, located at its heart and lacking windows, made him feel like a termite. The whole place had an oppressive feel since his divorce from Alison six years ago. Having no life forms to buoy the fabric or the air within, the house had grown heavy. Luke had the notion that the structure would subside into the ground. He would return one day to find it all swallowed up, revealing only the Georgian chimneypots and the rose-tiled gables.

Since taking on the second residence, Luke had come to realise how little he needed to perform the tasks of the day. The house had become a repository for things forgotten. The flat had become a remote but his most active quarters. To-ing and fro-ing was an unconscious process of gathering essentials, toiletries, books, laptop, a portable, clock, an aerial photograph of Warwick and his suits. A small fridge-freezer, the bed and several kitchen utensils were his only purchases.

Luke read McEwan's *Amsterdam* until the streetlight fizzled off. He then undressed and stepped into the shower, welcoming the bombardment of hot needles. He barely gave thought to his right hand lowering to his groin to caress the soft mounds of flesh which were already responding. He closed his eyes. An act that easily fitted a category containing eating, shitting…or sleeping, made it all too clear that this was all the mating dance amounted to: a brief transfer between craving and fulfillment before it all started again. Last night's presentation of flesh would have normally brought him to this point, but Luke did not particularly need such visual support to do what he needed to do. The act was automated and his mind blurred. His muscles stiffened yet his face remained slack and the needles continued to pelt. The roar of the shower filled his ears and changed pitch; steam whispered against his throat. Slowly he exhaled and opened his eyes. The anti-mist mirror reflected his face. He'd meant to remove it after taking the lease and never got round to it. The shower screen split his face in two, revealing only his right side. His right eyelid was slightly thicker than the left, giving that side a sly and leery look. At this moment, he could excuse an observer for describing that look as predatory. How confounding was it that the degree to which a pupil is obscured by an eyelid could make the difference between shock, surprise, nonchalance and conceit?

He killed the shower and stepped out. After breakfast and a shave, Luke cast a discerning eye through his wardrobe. In spite of this so-called progressive society, few outfits still commanded like the suit. Black, midnight-blue or charcoal tailored to the millimetre. All his suits were the perfect blend of cashmere, cotton and silk. Cheap suits aggrieved him as much as dog-mess finding its way onto his shoes. Such cheapness aspired and never could. He hated trousers that rode up the shins to reveal ghastly socks, he hated baggy trousers that scuffed against the carpet, he hated jazzy, 'funny', novelty or cartoon ties, he hated cufflinks of the aforementioned categories, he hated jackets riding up the back or narrow at the shoulders, he hated silver, cream and pastel – and as for suits worn over T-shirts and sneakers, well that's just being ridiculous.

Luke enjoyed the whisper of his dark blue silk tie against his collar as he positioned the knot snugly against his neck. His mobile sounded. Luke did not hasten. He deliberated with his tie-adjustment until the knot sat centrally at his collar and then he made a straight saunter for the table. He picked up. 'Yes.'

The person on the other end paused at this economy. 'Luke?'

'Yes.'

'Hiya, Phil here.'

Philip's camp-lilt and over-familiarity always made Luke balk. Luke waited.

'Just checking how stuff went last night.'

Luke gave a small frown. Surely Philip didn't take the trouble of calling at this hour just to ask the opinion of his silly little operetta? 'It went as expected,' Luke informed him.

'I was thinking about making some adjustments to the arrangement. Not that I ain't happy with it already. But how would you feel if we did away with two subjects and have just one?'

Luke sensed Philip was hedging. 'Why?'

Philip didn't seem to hear the question. 'One subject could be the definitive in what you're lookin' for. Just think of what people get up to on their own, when they think no one is watching?'

'Like reading?'

Philip clucked. '*No.* Y' know what I mean, Luke. Somethin' a little…minimal, intimate…saucy.'

Luke felt no desire to help him out.

At which point, Philip's angst finally got the better of him. 'For fuck's sake, the bitch has just decided to up and take a Law degree.'

Luke remained silent and Phil took it as a license to carry on. 'It seems she's suddenly too good to go flaunt her assets anymore. What I'd like to ask is why she's suddenly too good now after taking easy cash to parade her cellulite around? Fuck me sideways if she would have got past the doors of the seediest strip bar!'

Luke closed his eyes wearily at Philip's carping. Philip had the gift of creating his own soap opera impromptu featuring himself.

'I told her,' Philip was carrying on. 'Once you quit, you quit. You can't bring your fleshy cheeks back here. Bloody Law degree my chafed backside! She's got as much chance of wearing that cap and gown as I have of flying through your window right now in one.'

Luke opened his eyes to eradicate the image. 'Which one was she?'

'The Cat.'

Luke made it policy he was not informed of the participants' names. 'Hmmm.'

'It's a blessing is what I say. We don't need *her* anyway. Perhaps if I wrote a routine for one, it would tighten things a little, make it more dynamic.'

'When is she leaving?'

'End of next week.'

'Postpone for a replacement.'

Philip floundered at Luke's pithiness. 'Are you certain? Why don't you think this over first?'

'I don't need to.'

Philip fell silent a moment. 'Look. I'm gonna need time. Finding the right candidate is always tricky. It could ruin the whole arrangement if we get the wrong girl.'

Poor Philip spoke like a grandeurising playwright producing a Shakespearean play for the Globe. He surely wasn't. 'I have confidence in you Philip, 'Luke said and hung up.

Chapter 5

THE flat opposite had become vacant in the July as it always did. The landlord, a burly, grizzled man placed timer switches in the sockets to make it appear occupied. A cleaning lady paid a visit as did a maintenance man. Luke watched him test the electric sockets, check the fire alarm and repair the runners in the sash windows.

Luke made a query about the flat in the letting agency: six Templeton Court. The year's lease had been sold subject to contract. Something in Luke made him ask the price. The letting agent explained the lease was a fixed sum regardless of occupancy. Luke said he would outbid the price if he could buy the lease now. The letting agent advised Luke to consider before making a rash decision and recommended alternative cheaper leases within the area. Subject to contract, Luke pointed out, meant what it said, and until the contract had been signed, the flat was available.

The letting agent could not argue with this and invited Luke to take a look that afternoon. Luke was grateful the letting agent was a man of few words who saved the sales talk. Luke declined a guided tour and went in alone. The flat was described as an open-plan, chic loft apartment. A breakfast-bar partitioned the area into a living space and kitchen, both overlooked by a large window. The walls were painted magnolia and the floors, laid with mock oak. Minimal furniture of a two-piece leather suite and a glass dining set gave the flat a spacious feel.

Luke wandered into the bedroom, a square space like his own containing a bed frame, wardrobe and a whitewashed glow from an ample window. The bathroom, a blank canvas of neutrals had recently been modernised. Plastic flowers and a sun-bleached Monet print failed to disguise a clinical undercurrent. Luke knew he would sign the lease without further question.

The letting agent took the deposit and shook Luke's hand when the deal was done. 'When do you plan to move in?' the agent enquired.

'Oh, I have no intention to,' Luke informed him.

'A sublet, perhaps?'

Luke dragged his eyes across the room for the last time. 'Perhaps.'

The agent gave a confused frown.

The apartment remained empty and the rent payments came out of Luke's account like clockwork. Luke found himself staring out of his window and into the windows opposite. An enclosed courtyard separated them, a distance of perhaps sixty feet. He had checked out Christian's claim that none of the other flats in Templeton Court could see into number six and found it was true. His own, number twenty, was unique in this respect, his and six being on the second floor and both facing the courtyard.

Christian from accounts made an impromptu call on another pretext Luke couldn't recall and waited for him to get to the point. 'How's the view these days?' he asked.

'Rather static. The flat is empty.'

'Of course. The summer term. September will be worth the wait – not long to go.'

'I bought the lease,' Luke announced and regretted the admission as soon as it emerged.

Christian's tone upped a notch. 'You bought the lease?'

Luke got up and walked to the window. 'It was subject to contract.'

Christian failed to contain his fervour. 'Do you plan to…to…vet the students?'

Luke hesitated. 'I'm not quite certain what I plan to do with the flat yet.'

'I see.'

Luke could almost hear Christian's tongue emerge from his pale lips and linger there. 'I have a meeting scheduled at the Blackfriar's Inn,' Christian said. 'A client needs guidance on setting up an account for overseas transactions. I could do with some assistance. Perhaps I could pop up and go through some figures with you.'

Luke knew perfectly well Christian had no such meeting scheduled. 'This month's rather full.'

'Of course.' But Christian retained a granule of fervour. 'Perhaps later in the year, then.'

'Perhaps.' Luke ended the call before Christian could wheedle his way back in. Why hadn't Luke foreseen this manoeuvre? Luke resented Christian interfering with his private affairs. Did Luke ever invite himself up to see Christian's parading students when this flat had been his? No.

Luke took the ten minute drive to the Chrome building in the Prospect Business Park a mile outside Warwick. A ten-storey plexi-glassed building with a top that resembled a cigarette lighter occupied the Registry of Mergers within its upper five floors. In pigeonhole style, the rabble that processed the post, correspondence, data input, finance and IT inhabited the lower two floors. Middle-managers who facilitated teams, piloted and implemented new procedures, occupied the floor above. The lawyers took the fourth floor. The area managers and the Registrar of Mergers, his own appointment, enjoyed the spacious top floor with its sweeping skylines of Warwick, Leamington, Stratford and Kenilworth. Luke cut Dvorak and parked his black

Jaguar in his designated spot and strode to the back entrance reserved for CEOs. Rabbling mothers and jabbering tots making a stream for Jellybeans onsite crèche was a splash of cold water to the eardrums in the wake of Dvorak's *Carnival Overture*. Luke forestalled his sights from the vermin, their miasma of disorder and grubbiness. It seemed this corner of society was intent only upon imposing their expertise in hair lice, rashes, allergies, snotty noses, asthma, tantrums and such remedies to treat them, to the point of violation. And worse, grievances that kept the union working overtime. Thank God he had this entrance to himself.

Luke entered the glass doors, took a sharp left past the lifts and towards the stairs. The ten-storey climb never failed to provide a kick for the circulation and ensured aural hygiene from small-talk. The encroaching footfalls a flight above warned him today was not going to be one of those days. The footfalls hastened towards him and Andrew Chapelstowe, coordinator of correspondence, snagged him with his sights.

'Mornin' Luke. I thought I might find you here.'

Andrew waited for Luke on the corner riser dressed in a Hawaiian shirt, jeans and an appalling case of acne on his neck.

Luke drew level with him and offered a formal nod. 'Good morning Andrew.'

Andrew's eyes shifted in that irritatingly casual way meant to convey rebellious energy checked only by this 'gap' job.

We shall see.

'We have a bit of a crisis situation. I've just got off the phone to Theresa and had to make some last minute changes.'

Luke waited.

'Robert Doumbia has called in sick. Gall stones. Won't be in for a month. We need a stand-in to discuss the Milliband contract with Dr. Sui's secretary on Thursday.'

'What about Derek Johns?'

Andrew shifted again. 'No can do. He's tied up with the Montgomery agreement.'

No can do? Luke eyed the volcanic crusts on Andrew's nape. 'You'd best consult Cerys. She has my diary.'

Andrew plucked out his notebook from his back pocket. 'No problemo. I have just taken the liberty of consulting Cerys a moment ago.' He proceeded to flick through.

Luke watched him, his right eyelid dragging over his pupil. Sly, leering, predatory. Perhaps. Luke had a clear view down the back of Andrew's T-shirt where established boils were whiteheading. Why did creatures like him have to exist in this world in place of others? Why did precious resources, time and space have to be allocated to those who contributed nothing but a test of tolerance to others for their sheer ignorance? Luke's face fell slack like it had done so during his task in the shower this morning. He inserted his tongue between his teeth without opening his mouth and let it rest there. He envisaged raising his right hand, fingers together and flexing forward, and administering a sharp jab to the back of Andrew's neck sufficient to launch him into a pin-wheel down the stairs. Luke could almost hear Andrew's bones clattering against the concrete and something snapping with that high whiplashing sound. Luke had heard that whiplashing crack before. He had heard it many times, had felt the fissure beneath smooth flesh. Nothing quite replicated the sound of bones cracking, particularly the fragile kind.

Andrew had done with his flick-through and was talking. A sheen of sweat dewed Luke's brow. He didn't wipe it on his sleeve or a tissue, but allowed the moisture to evaporate into the cool draft.

Andrew turned, his mouth still moving, this mundane quandary causing his eyes to glaze over. 'You could free up May seventh by shifting that finance meeting to the following Wednesday.'

Luke's eyelid remained heavy. 'Perhaps.'

Andrew hesitated. 'Maybe you should confirm it with Cerys.'

Luke said nothing.

Andrew shifted on his feet and bounded back up the stairs. Luke would let Andrew discuss the matter with Cerys. He could discuss it as much as he liked. In the meantime Luke would engage his mind on his earlier hypothesis of bones cracking on the stairwell before continuing on his way.

The top floor opened out into a hexagonal lobby segmented by four glass offices, a reception desk at their hub. Still life oils by the Clare brothers spiced the sporadic terracotta walls. Luke anticipated the privacy of his office where he could stare at the skyline and sup coffee from his cafetiere. No such luck.

'Luke! Glad to have caught you.'

Luke turned to find Derek Johns' flabby form in attendance. The trousers of his shiny suit sagged at the knees and his shirt strained at his midriff. 'Has Cerys spoken with you?'

Luke could detect Derek's officious tone. 'I saw Andrew on the stairs.'

'Oh, good. Can we take it in here?' Derek shifted aside to indicate Luke first.

Luke could hardly believe the man's audacity. Why did he feel it necessary to discuss the Milliband merger in his office? Luke was only too aware of how Derek operated. Derek was a covert bully motivated by sloth, delegating unsavoury tasks to the unsuspecting and reserving the cream for his pandering favourites. Only recently, Derek had acquired the responsibility of coordinator for the IT Security Implementations Team in London, which entailed lots of meetings, hours out of the office and basically doing very little. That s not to say Derek didn't drop a few 'buzzwords' as he prated on about the duties of an IT security coordinator. He would look good, sound good and appear progressive to the powers that be.

Luke backtracked and stepped into Derek's cluttered domain. Luke averted his gaze from Subways' wrappers littering Derek's desk.

'Please be seated,' Derek said.

Luke refrained from clenching his jaw. He deposited his cache case next to the chair and sat. The suspension grated and collapsed a notch. Luke's knees braced in response. Derek didn't sit in his own chair as Luke had expected, but on his desk. Luke was conscious of the physical disadvantage Luke now had, his eyes drawing level with Derek's crotch.

Derek interlocked his fingers and rested them upon his lap. 'I thought it only fair I should brief you on the Milliband-Claybourne merger myself.'

Luke resented Derek's spin that he was doing Luke a service.

'I have arranged Cerys get the files and prepare the contract template. I have informed the chief of the firm, Dr Sui and he is quite happy to go through the contract with you; he is looking forward to meeting you.'

So Dr Sui had been informed before Luke had.

'Robert sends his regards and hopes to be joining us again soon. His wife said only this morning that Robert feels lucky he works with such supportive colleagues and wishes us all well.'

Luke deliberated with his response. 'I take it Cerys will be released from your service whilst I am working on this merger.'

Derek had the paradoxical ability to widen his eyes and furrow at the same time. Luke enjoyed the moment. 'Release Cerys?'

Now it was Luke's turn to clasp his fingers together.

Derek's chuckle burst forth in powdery spitfires. 'Good one, Luke. You had me there!'

Luke's smile sat wrong on his face, feeling more like a sneer. Derek had always resented Luke's position of chief overseer of mergers and often made barbed jokes that he could do Luke's job standing on his head. In reality, Derek wanted to attend the sumptuous functions himself and hobnob with the loftiest directors, get drunk and bore them with anecdotes about *the Excalibur*, his sailing boat on the south coast. Luke watched Derek's belly continue to lurch, the fabric of his shirt straining. Luke could easily cover the distance between them in a heartbeat. Luke's fingers were flexing right now, itching to engage in some squeezing. His index fingertips would meet at the back of Derek's fleshy neck and his thumbs would burrow into the protruding gristle that was Derek's windpipe. Luke would watch Derek's eyelids vanish into his sockets, having furrowed his final furrow. Luke would tango Derek to this chair, the chair with the faulty suspension and the backrest that threatened to pivot him backwards at any moment. Luke would hardly break a sweat as he watched Derek's jowls collapse back to his ears. And Derek's dying image would be Luke staring back at him, his lips pursed in exquisite apathy. And when Luke was done, he might be seen striding from Derek's office, his suit immaculate as of the instant he had adjusted his tie this morning. Luke would continue his duties in the suit he slay Derek, confer with Cerys, dine on grilled sea-bass with Jersey royals and asparagus, finish with a refreshing Chablis at Andre's, clear his inbox, amend the contract template and draught a letter to Dr Sui. All whilst Derek's beloved chair wore his crumpled form like a hat.

Luke eased himself out of the seat with a creak his smirk fading. Derek's voice followed him out. 'We may discuss the finer points over a coffee later.' Luke did not pause on his exit.

Luke returned to his office, blessed, he reckoned with the best views, looking north over unblemished greenbelt towards Kenilworth. Only by looking down through the glass would the sights encounter the car park and the gatehouse. The rest was a patchwork of ever-muting receding green.

Luke prepared himself a coffee and booted up his laptop. Cerys approached the glass door and tapped lightly before entering. She clutched a batch of letters, her gait punctuated with a small bob. 'Mr. Forrester, I have Robert Dhoumbia's files.' Cerys was unaware of this little curtsy. A postgraduate sporting black eyeliner and a choppy haircut, she probably never banked on curtseying to anyone not too long ago. Luke disliked the formality he seemed to instill in people. 'Please, it's Luke. Leave them on my desk.'

Cerys deposited the stack next to the laptop. She paused, turning. 'Me and Theresa were relieved to hear we were working on the Miliband contract with you, Mr. Forrester…er…Luke.' She knit her lip. 'Just wanted you to know.' She turned and traipsed to the door before leaving.

Cerys' remark left him speechless. Of course, what she meant to say was that they were relieved the contract hadn't ended up on Derek's desk. Who could blame them?

Luke sipped his coffee and leafed through the correspondence. Luke could instantly see this was no straightforward affair. Both Miliband and Claybourne possessed sleeping partners, subsidiaries and overseas parties. He scanned the list, the black print clawing into his retinas. The five-hour sleep deficit was already anchoring his brain beneath a smothering fug. Mid-morning was always the worst. Right now, his head was being dragged through ice-floes that were anything potentially apprehending. Sights and sounds pressed snugly against his skull where a membrane should be. Luke imagined the buffer to be soft, thick cotton wool. He could tell just by looking at people that all experienced the world from the shelter of this membrane. Luke's was tattered, thin and threadbare, and years of abrasion were wearing his skull away. He perceived his right cranium to be thinner than his left. Luke touched his forehead as he often did, to assure himself that perception and reality did not accord.

Luke cast his sights over the documents. This amalgamation seemed pretty dry: financial advisers, insurance brokers, insolvency practitioners and legal firms. Equally dry names like Niall Cotton, Nelson Redfern, The Brewer Society.

Amalgamating companies released huge funds for reinvestment and growth. Services could be offered at competitive prices and once other similar companies were priced out of the area, the corporation had freedom to make huge profits.

Much of his task was tedious – the checking that all the parties concerned had signed the deeds, that the dates tallied and to ensure link deeds had been lodged should any company undergone a name change or an earlier merger. Still, this was only a small part of the service. The main package was the ceremony itself, to be held in some corporate hotel, a meal, a shaking of hands, some speeches and a gaff or two: a marriage with all the trimmings. Luke performed a search of the concerns to provide a talking point during the summit.

Images of board meetings, switchboard staff and smiling partners grazed his weary eyes. The usual claims: 'Find a cheaper quote and we'll match it.' 'Consolidate your loan for easier payments; we'll' do the rest,' 'Suffered a loss? We'll make them pay.'

Luke decided to explore the last claim and found anecdotal contributions from so-called customers

'Stuart from Gloucestershire lost 2mm from the tip of his finger and received over 2k damages. "It's been a nightmare experience," he said. "I've lost something that can never be replaced, but the money has gone some way to getting my life back together."

'Mary from Wiltshire says, "I suffered trauma when I was miss-sold a stolen people-mover. I lost my deposit and didn't think I could get it back. But when I bought my case forward, I got 1.5k. The money has enabled me to buy another vehicle, although I can never trust another dealer again. It has scarred me for life.".'

Bile prickled the back of Luke's throat. Scarred for life? These stupid people with their idiot faces were actors, tourists who didn't have a clue.

'John from Sussex says, "I slipped whilst getting out of a leisure pool and gouged my leg. I had fifteen stitches and couldn't sleep for a week, but I got over 2k."'

'Consider your loss too small? You have more rights than you imagine, so think again. We'll make them pay.'

Luke took offence at 'John's' reference to insomnia. Luke had read enough. He sipped his coffee but the bitter taste did not dislodge the bile from his throat. Such overuse of the terms, 'scarred for life' and 'couldn't sleep' slighted the true meaning for the sake of a sales pitch. Luke clicked on the homepage and saw a picture of the chief, Barry Brewer, a Captain Birdseye clone for his full jowls, beard and cream suit. Luke wanted to punch him.

Perhaps a post on Luke's blog, *The Corporate Friend* was nigh. Luke wasn't into blogging in the way it was intended. His was simply free webspace to laud selected candidates in his own special way. Luke's preamble read:

'This blog celebrates quality within the private sector. I invite you to bestow positive comments upon my special selection of contenders.'

Facebookers and Twitters had linked to his blog, saving him the bother and from revealing his identity. He'd even been Stumbled a few times. He had written thirty posts in four years. A third of his posts attracted no comment; half or so, mediocre interest. Six had become 'sticky' to the search engines, acquiring a long thread. Four of the subjects featured had lost their jobs afterwards. Luke couldn't recall the reasons he had blogged about them in the first place; perhaps a suit violation, a supercilious expression, slicked back hair, sales spiel or a bullish arrogance.

Luke entitled his post: 'Praise to Barry Brewer of the Brewer Society.'

For the main body, he wrote, 'I am in awe at the bastion of Mr. Brewer of the abovementioned corporation. How does he win such handsome compensations for victims of injuries that might otherwise be derided as insignificant? I wish I knew his secret!

'His slogan, "Suffered a lost? We'll make them pay," suggests a pledge of valour to these casualties. In particular, my heart goes out to the contributors of the sad anecdotes on his website whose lives have been irrevocably damaged by the unscrupulous.

'Where would we be without the likes of Mr. Brewer and his associates? Money would remain with the greedy, that's where. These injured parties would suffer in silence and despair without anyone to fight their case.

'And Mr. Brewer seems such a nice fellow, with a face you can trust and good tastes in suits.

'*The Corporate Friend* invites you to bestow positive comments upon Barry Brewer.'

Luke's sights brushed against a long and capitalised comment on another post ladled with exclamation marks and profanities. He published his post and signed off.

Chapter 6

BEN sat on the deckchair staring down at his cornflakes. Gemma was certain a new day would have brought a new mood. She was wrong. Gemma inserted Ben's sandwiches into his lunchbox and paused. 'Your granddad's coming today. He's got some nice things to put in your bedroom.'

Ben didn't respond.

'Have you remembered to take your anti-inflammatory tablets?'

Ben shrugged.

Gemma couldn't remember when her racing brain had finally yielded to slumber last night. She had awoken too groggy to care that the clock proclaimed that it was now almost eight. After what she'd gone through yesterday, Gemma seemed to have lost all sense of urgency. She zipped Ben's lunch-bag and deposited it into his satchel. 'Listen, Ben. About your dad...' The words died in her throat. What was she about to say? Don't worry, your dad's coming back? He's safe somewhere and is thinking of you? Gemma was no longer certain whether Liam's mind had tipped into that black void again, and at this moment in time, if a thread of rationality had survived.

Ben gathered his crutches and lugged himself from the patio-table to go upstairs and brush his teeth. Gemma watched, her throat aching. Ben's cornflakes had gone soggy. She slowly cleared the table and spooned the dregs in the bin. Soon after,

Ben's footfalls trudged down the stairs. Gemma made her way to the door where his alabaster complexion initiated another ball in her throat. Gemma proffered his satchel which he took. He opened the door.

'Ben...I've been thinking.'

Ben's eyes met hers, his irises like jade glass.

'Perhaps you should go ahead and make that cat mask for me.'

Her words awarded her more than the desired effect. Ben's eyes lit up and his left cheek puckered. 'Really?'

Gemma nodded, suppressing her bewilderment.

'Cool.' He took the satchel from her and made his way out to catch the school bus.

Gemma watched, despondent. Of course, she had only uttered those words to get this reaction. Ben enjoyed making things. No doubt he would view this undertaking as something more than the usual Airfix, paper Mache or plasticine renditions. This was something special, a project that impinged upon the adult world and which could make a difference to their lives. Gemma would let him make the mask, gush at it, go out for a couple of hours on an evening and pretend.

She could pretend.

Gemma had already planned to contact her friend Alice who worked in the Cypress Care Centre. They always needed night staff and Gemma feared she would need as much money as she could get her hands on. She could work evenings and pretend to Ben.

Gemma dabbed an eyelash from her tear duct and found her eyes wet. She wiped the residual moisture onto the heel of her hand.

Just as expected, Terry arrived in his blue transit soon after nine. Terry, a slight, wiry ex-con, bore a vague resemblance to his son, having bristly silver-blond hair and eyes of pewter. Terry had the same nervous energy as his son, but maturity, experience and possibly his term inside had tempered it. Gemma never asked about this period of his life but Terry's wife, Vera confided soon after Ben's birth that Terry had orchestrated a string of robberies and looks back upon his former self with disdain.

Terry got straight to work, hoisting a small TV, a leaf table, kitchen chairs, entertainment unit and a conservatory suite into their designated places. This was followed with CDs for Ben, mobile kitchen appliances, including thankfully, a kettle. Terry gave Gemma a brief hug when he was done. He smelled of soap and tobacco. 'So sorry about what's happenin' Gem.' His gravel-voice reverberated through her chest from where her pulse took a small surge.

Giddiness arrested her when he released her. Gemma promptly made tea. Terry cleared his throat and sat.

Moments later, she joined him at the table savouring tea that no longer tasted of aluminum. Gemma noticed Terry hadn't touched his and was chewing his lip. 'I…er…appreciate you not callin' the police on this.' He alluded to her new belongings. 'And I'm sorry 'bout the quality of the stuff. I wanted to make sure that if those bastards return, the seizures wouldn't even cover their fuel.' He gave her a level gaze. 'I'm tellin' you, they ain't proper bailiffs. They had no right comin' in here. No right.' Terry pursed his lips. She could see he wanted to say sorry. Sorry for whatever his son had got himself into this time.

Gemma slid her hand across the table and patted the back of Terry's. 'I'm glad you're here.'

Terry shrugged this off, never comfortable with sentiments. 'I didn't see the signs this time. I thought I knew Liam better than that.'

Gemma slowly opened her bag on the table and took out the folded receipt the men had left yesterday. She gave it to Terry. He donned his glasses and squinted at the print.

'I haven't figured out what this setup fee was for,' Gemma said. 'My only guess is that it had something to do with the

Aston Martin Liam had bought a few months ago. Perhaps the venture fell through and he couldn't finance it anymore. It seems he might have gone to some grotty moneylender again and got stung.'

Terry was still scrutinising the document. 'A dispute over money should always go through the courts and there's no evidence of that in here.'

Gemma refrained from telling Terry that she had spoken to Julie from Debt Terminal about this.

'If you ain't got the money to shell out, there ain't nothing those bastards can do.' Terry folded the paper and pushed it away. 'Perhaps you should go through the courts, get a fair hearing. Until Liam shows up, they can't demand a penny off you. If there's any fairness in the world, Liam could get into one of those IVAs, y' know, where you pay off only what you can afford. I can keep an eye on him, make sure he sticks to the agreement.'

Terry's words instilled despair and she was certain Terry felt the same. Liam had done this too often and he had gone too far this time.

'Terry, there's something you should know.'

Terry's pewter eyes appeared more silver than ever, almost begging her to tell him there wasn't more. It was too late to back out now.

'A notice has been put on the house. It seems whoever these people are have found a way of claiming an interest in it. I had no knowledge of what was going on until recently and it seems…'

Terry was still watching. He hadn't blinked; he'd become a creature caught in headlights bracing for what was about to hit him.

'My name isn't on the house deeds.'

Terry did not show any reaction. His eyes remained starkly silver. She blundered on. 'I'm scared, Terry. Really scared. I don't think Liam is ever coming back this time and I'm scared for the future. For Ben. I keep thinking about how all of this is affecting Ben. And I've come to a decision.'

Gemma averted her eyes from the blast of Terry's forthright gaze and uttered the words that were long overdue, the words she had needed to utter since that day in Brynton Sands six years ago. 'Things aren't going to work out for us, Terry. I'm going for a divorce.' Gemma's hands kneaded to fists beneath the table. 'I'm going to get Liam's name off the house deeds somehow and I'm going it alone.'

Silence palled over the table like a thick blanket. Gemma closed her eyes.

Terry's gruff voice broke the silence. 'I'm sorry Gemma. I'm really very sorry.'

Gemma felt certain that Terry had not divulged the full story to Vera, his wife of their experience in The Wash, just as Gemma had not mentioned it to her own sister, Isabelle. The secret she and Terry shared should stay in the dark. Gemma wished not to analyse, verbalise or try to make sense of it, because it never could. Doing so would bring this other-world closer to her world. She couldn't bear the thought of the two worlds colliding.

Gemma and Terry had endured a four-hour journey to Chapel St Leonard's, having been stuck on the A47 tailback. Gemma had received a call from the police at 4am about a sighting. Vera, Terry's wife had taken Ben to school that morning and Gemma had packed lunch for herself and Terry. Terry's compilation of sixties country bolstered the tension as did their conversation centering on Terry's business as a landscape gardener and on Ben. The turquoise sheen to the sky signified the beckoning coast. Every dip in the landscape pledged a blue horizon. Gemma experienced an unsavoury blend of nostalgic anticipation and dread. Gemma nibbled at her cheese sandwich and her stomach balked. She deposited it in the bag.

Terry cut through Brynton Sands after a crawl through Chapel St Leonard's. Tourists streamed through narrow streets flanked with gift shops, candy stores, penny arcades and patisseries. Gemma was perturbed to see so many lumpy people here; backs of knees that puckered, muffin tops, bulbous armpits. Terry opened his window to ventilate a sudden stuffiness from the bright facades reflecting heat into the cabin. Gulls screeched. Gemma watched an assembly frantically dissect a discarded pastie. The smell of burnt onions commandeered and was followed by strawberry slushies and deep-fried doughnuts. Gemma glimpsed Brynton pier, a pink and blue construction jutting a quarter-of-a-mile out to sea. Terry nosed his blue transit into a parking space opposite the pier's entrance.

Gemma glanced at Terry confused. 'Where are the police?'

Terry's tanned profile was set. 'I told 'em I'd take it from here. Didn't want to be wastin' no police time on a grown man who's lost his way. I'll find him soon enough.'

I said it all. Terry had tried to deter Gemma from accompanying him on this jaunt. But Gemma felt responsible for Liam in the same way as a parent. It seemed the role of wife and mother overlapped in many ways and she'd become a matriarch to both her husband and son.

Gemma followed Terry out of the van where the sun drilled onto her scalp. They entered the Plaza Arcade and the gloom briefly rendered her blind.

Several fanfares prickled her ears rolling out the same seven-note turnover. Their repetition latched onto her brain and she knew those seven notes would play out in her head for the rest of the day. Aged yeast and carpet dust snagged her nostrils and she squinted to see.

Pinball and fruit machines lined the walls. A blurred sentinel attended each. One cranked a lever, initiating another seven-note play-out. Terry took no heed of this and continued to the bar next to penny falls – glass boxes housing thousands of coins upon moving platforms.

Gemma's awareness converged onto those shiny coins to-ing and fro-ing. An edifice, she was certain would collapse onto the lower platform and spume from a wide slot below the glass top. And yet, when the platform had made its trip, the edifice defied gravity.

Its attendant, a wheel-chaired woman, inserted another coin. The coin flipped sideways and vanished between two coin mounds not making a difference.

The edifice continued to move. Nothing had changed and yet Gemma was revisited by the same conviction the coins would topple over. Only when she blinked did she realise a stupor had detained her. She continued to the bar, the coin mounds no longer captivating her; and there lie the vital difference: Liam would have approached those penny falls right now and perhaps coax Ben into joining him.

Only briefly had Gemma ventured into these places when dating Liam and had attended a fruit machine herself. On watching her coin vanish into its greedy maw without so much as a clink, Gemma restrained a powerful urge to give the monolith a violent shove. Liam had merely laughed at her frustration and told her she'd get used to it. Gemma didn't want to get used to it or even give it a chance. How could such a pastime satisfy someone? She'd believed Liam partook in flutters to socialise, as some people went to the pub or played bingo. Gemma had given it little more thought, not expecting her husband to give up his diversion if it involved but a few pounds of his hard-earned cash now and again.

Terry was talking to the bartender and flashing a photograph of Liam. The barman shook his head and continued wiping his glasses. Terry beckoned to Gemma to follow him to the rear doors which lead to the pier itself. The sun blinded her again and the afternoon became an onslaught of candy-colours, barging youths, carnival music and hotdog smells. On exiting a casino where punters played blackjack and poker, a used condom stuck to her shoe. She flicked it away.

'He's here,' Terry uttered beside her. 'I can feel it.'

The sun had begun its descent now and the sea breeze ferried the stickiness from her spine. They traipsed across the beach where Gemma spotted a lone Punch and Judy periscope flapping in the breeze. There was no sign of its puppet-master. Gemma always hated Punch and Judy, even as a child. She hated the violent slapstick, the grotesque characters and the supposed humour. The seediness, she feared, touched upon an unseen reality, of how relationships can turn rancid over time and in secret. Liam wouldn't have seen her point of view, asserting that it was harmless fun kids had enjoyed for countless decades. Liam had always favoured the croc.

Terry telephoned Vera on his mobile to fill her in on the day. Vera, a small woman who scarcely left the house, would never have made it beyond the M69. Her comfort zone seemed to have shrunk with age, her world consisting of home, her flower arranging and her voluntary work for Scope. She possessed a fierce will when she wanted and Terry seemed to gravitate around it. When his account had satisfied her inquisition, they ordered fish and chips at the seafront bar. Cartoon Mr. Chippy's missing eye kept vying for her attention during Terry's conjectures on Liam's whereabouts. She was grateful a young, tanned teenager in beach shorts bounded over to them. 'Hey, are you that fellah looking for that missing bloke?'

Terry lowered his plastic cutlery. 'Yeah. You seen him?'

'No but my mate has. He saw this guy in town playing blackjack, early, like. When me mate came back that evening, the guy was still there in the same seat. Looked kinda spaced-out. My mate just made a joke about him playing the epic and this guy gets nasty, rears at him. The bouncer had to drag him out. Me mate saw him at closing time checking in at one of those guesthouses next to Doughy Jim's.'

Terry took to his feet. 'Do you know which one?'

'No, but there ain't many there. You wouldn't have trouble finding him.'

Terry thanked him and left his fish dinner untouched. Gemma followed.

Doughy Jim's had closed for the day and the guesthouses opposite had yet to illuminate their frontages. In the encroaching dusk, she could make out their pastel shades. Terry mounted the wrought iron steps to a porch dotted with cat figurines sporting bowlers. The reception inside smelled of old leather seats that had been sat on for hours. A skinny man with a dewlap paunch was chalking tomorrow's menu onto a display board. Plastic strips suspended at the doorway clattered in a draught. He glanced up at their approach. 'Good evening,' he breezed in a southern cadence. 'Welcome to Broadlands Haven. How long will you be staying?'

Terry went straight to business, explaining the reason for his visit and showing him the photograph. Gemma noticed the wall behind the reception desk sloped outwards towards the top and ended in a protruding box shape – like the end of a coffin. Gemma couldn't rid the notion that a body was walled up inside.

Terry, it seemed had got the affirmative and was already making his way towards the stairs. Gemma realised her heart had surged to a pelt and she made a move to follow.

Terry firmly stopped her. 'How 'bout you waitin' here? I'll go get Liam and then we can get home.'

Terry continued through the doors leaving Gemma bewildered. The man at the desk gave Gemma a small smile before he continued chalking. She loitered by the door, the room falling silent except for the man's scribing. Squeak, squeak, squeak. She turned and her vision was engulfed by a large print of a grinning cat, goggle-eyed and hat akimbo.

Gemma drifted from the poster and towards the hall door. The squeaks continued. The hallway beyond labyrinthed to a landing of three accessways. Gemma grasped the newel post and boarded the stairs. The thick pile muted high-frequency sounds reducing the chalk-squeaks to chirps. Gemma continued upwards, her eyes fixed onto the central accessway. Inch by inch, more of the ceiling opened up to her; coving chipped in places and harbouring inaccessible dust. Gemma drew level with the landing which led to a panel door. The door bobbed in a draught. Muffled sounds could be heard on the other side. A faint shitty smell wafted towards her. Her stomach braced. She advanced upon the door instilled by a morbid compulsion. Penny falls, Mr. Chippy's missing eye and cats in bowlers muddled in her head. Her vision seemed to have pushed forwards, revealing more of her peripheral vision, the door at its centre.

Gently, she pushed the door aside. The smell of shit overpowered her and her mouth drew downwards. Liam lay sprawled on the floor, his flies undone and his T-shirt smeared with sweat and grease. Terry was clasping him from behind and rocking him vigorously. 'Come back to me, Liam. You come back to me.'

Liam snarled, 'Get off me, Da!'

Terry's persuasion softened into small utterances inches from Liam's ear.

The jaundiced stench wasn't the worst part. Neither was the graveyard of half-eaten burgers rotting next to Liam's figure lolling like a dope addict. The worst part was Liam's eyes. What she had seen in his eyes was so alien, so strange that all thought processes seemed to have vaporised in her head. Only afterwards when her sensibilities had recovered did the word *feral* come to mind. Her trance brought on by those pennies in pendulum action didn't come close. Neither did her brief encounter with Tetris or Bejewel which caused her simply to self-castigate for allowing such squander of time and a sort of heavy dampness in her head. Admittedly, she even craved that gratifying sensation of matching rows cancelling each other out with a flicker and a stuttering chorus. But this obsession was as fleeting as her trance in the arcade. Liam's present episode didn't seem to possess that off-switch, even when it came to eating or relieving himself. Liam's glassy eyes bore no reason. Only upon his next fix. His huge black pupils stared into a void. A void of flashing lights and several-note fanfares playing out over and over. One more hit. Just one more hit.

Terry turned on sensing a presence. His expression hardened. 'I told you to wait downstairs! *Get outta here!*'

Her feet would not respond. The carpet pile seemed to have sucked her feet into place. Terry turned away just as Liam's eyes passed over hers. He didn't see her. At that moment, Gemma meant nothing to him. She was nothing.

Gemma reeled inwardly at that look. She backed off. Her eyes stung. Her knees tottered.

The passageway seemed to have narrowed, the floor a hundred feet down. She floated back to the stairs, her torso disembodied.

The squeaks had stopped. On re-emerging in the lobby, she saw the man had completed his task and was displaying the chalk-board behind his desk. Soup of the day: mushroom; main course: lasagna with chips, new potatoes or mash; sweet trolley: lemon cheesecake, fruit sorbet and 'smiley cookies' for kiddies.

Gemma wandered back to the seafront. The tide had come in and the sea lapped impassively against the great bulk that was the pier. Punch and Judy's periscope had vanished like a ghost. Perhaps it had washed out to sea.

Gemma waited in the back of the van. Terry never bothered to lock the doors, believing the interior contained nothing of value anyway and used only a steering lock. Terry and Liam finally emerged from the shadows. Gemma could see as they neared that Terry had cuffed Liam under the eye; a dark graze smeared his left cheek. The van jerked as both took the front seats. No one spoke. During the two-hour journey home, Gemma was only aware of the back of Liam's head pitching with each gear change. Liam didn't feel hers anymore.

Perhaps he never was.

Chapter 7

TERRY had quietly let himself out of the house without drinking his tea. Gemma would have forgiven Terry for never wanting to see her again. She would have forgiven him for being disappointed in her.

Gemma's sought diversion from her mission to salvage the house – anything to erase their last conversation from her mind. And the guilt. Not for her husband, but for Terry. For turning her back on his only son.

On Julie's advice, Gemma applied for legal aid. Gemma spent half-an-hour on the phone to Geary's Solicitors and John Geary himself had informed her that the marriage certificate, being a party deed, protected her interests in her half of the property. By lodging the relevant documents at the Land Registry, her name on the property would be reinstated. Gemma could apply for a divorce on the grounds of desertion, but keeping the house meant buying Liam out. However, whilst Liam was missing and not contributing towards child maintenance, Gemma could claim a portion of his half by informing the CSA. The matter of Colby and Vernon's notice was not so straightforward; getting the notice taken off depended upon the identity of the lender and the reason for the loan. But Terry had been correct in saying 'those bastards' had acted unlawfully and should be reported to a regulatory body. Furthermore Colby and Vernon's third party had no right to instigate such seizures or of hounding her, as the debt was not strictly hers. Gemma could live peacefully in the house for as long as she wished and the third party could do nothing about recouping the debt until she chose to sell.

Gemma made the decision that day she would never sell the house for as long as she lived.

Geary drafted a letter to Colby and Vernon, using her former diatribe as an outline. Geary formally demanded the identity of the third party and the particulars of the loan. The letter closed with the caution, a regulatory body will be informed once the third party has been established.

A wall of exhaustion hit her once she put the phone down. She collapsed into one of the cane chairs Terry had brought round yesterday and closed her eyes. In spite of the progress she'd made, the matter of the money kept plaguing her. How was she going to manage as a one-parent family? Could she realistically live here? There was so much to do. The conundrum of tasks impossible to complete without a prior undertaking befuddled her like a maze without a beginning or an end. Her cognitive thoughts might as well be coated in toffee and she couldn't find a way clear.

Gemma came-to at the sound of Ben pushing his spare key through the front door. She groggily pushed herself up from the chair.

Ben entered with a breeze. 'Hi, Mum.' He shoved his crutches in a corner.

'God, Ben, I'm so sorry. I haven't even prepared tea yet.'

Ben didn't seem to mind. 'He grabbed a cookie from the jar in the cupboard. 'Did you call that number?'

Gemma lumbered to the kitchen still recovering from a bad case of head-rush. 'Number?'

Ben took a bite. 'Y' know, that number written on that piece of paper. You were gonna call it.'

Gemma's brain-fog slowly cleared to the harsh reminder. Reluctance to lie to Ben jabbed in her chest. Gemma smiled grimly. 'Ben. Listen.'

'I've started making the mask today and it's looking good. Mrs. Potts has been asking me about it.'

Gemma's thoughts regrouped. 'Has she?'

'But I haven't told her about the show yet. I wanted to wait until you got the part, which I know you will.' Ben crammed the rest of the cookie into his mouth and walked off.

Ben possessed an unbudgeable tenacity when he wanted. Never a difficult or demanding child, he had exhibited this boulder of will regarding inexplicable things. Last year, Ben had created a metropolis of sand and bricks in the garden. When Liam had cleared it, thinking it was rubbish, Ben most emphatically told his dad to put it back. Liam thought Ben was joking; Ben daggered his dad with oversized eyes made stern by those rectangular frames. Ben was not joking.

Ben watched his dad replace the rubble before Ben deliberated for hours over the finishing touches. Ben partitioned off his metropolis with string. When Liam came home from the garage, Gemma overheard Ben instruct his dad, 'See that string there? That string means you can't go past.'

'I hear ya, little fellah,' Liam breezed through, half-listening.

But Ben hadn't finished with his dad yet. 'That string means you can't go past. Not even to cut the grass or nothing. And see that plank of wood there?' It seemed Ben now had Liam's attention. 'Don't touch that plank of wood, even if I've moved it. It's not to be touched.' Gemma spotted Ben the next day taking photos of his metropolis.

Gemma couldn't always discern the artistic value of Ben's creations; some didn't resemble anything in particular and did not exhibit deftness of hand. His drawings, montages and models appeared incomplete, like concepts.

'Why don't you finish that painting?' Gemma asked Ben, appraising a rendition of a forest containing a door in the sky.

Ben replied flatly, 'Just 'cause it has white spaces, doesn't mean to say it's not finished.'

'Some might disagree.'

Ben scowled. 'What would be the point of filling in white spaces if the painting says everything I want to say? That'd be like painting by numbers.'

Gemma encountered that impossible tenacity again. She couldn't argue with that. Heaven knows how he was going to take the news about his father, the divorce, the debt, the menace of repossession why his granddad wasn't going to visit anymore. Should she let Ben live out the fantasy that his mother was going to perform dance routines for VIPs in a cat mask he had made? Was it so wrong that Ben shouldn't create his own metropolis that could shelter his world from the cold reality? Gemma could no longer see a reason not to.

The idea she was preserving Ben's inner world compelled her to share a lift with Alice to the Cypress Care Centre that weekend. Each task drifted to the next before Gemma found herself donning a polyester uniform, latex gloves and a hairnet. Gourd-faced Mavis gave her a short demonstration of how to stack crockery into neat piles after receiving a blast of sterilising steam from the conveyer belt. The trick was to keep moving. Allow plenty of room on the stacking table or the oncoming crockery will have nowhere to go and the machine will have to stop. Mavis made it quite plain that stopping is not a good thing. Stopping is a criminal offence at the Cypress Care Centre and is punishable by a kick to the shins, so to speak.

The noise was deafening. The polyester uniform made her back itch and the steam made her eyes run. Just a couple of pounds an hour in return for backache and a streaming nose. Gemma must have been crazy.

'Get a move on, will ya!' Mavis hollered from the other end as she fed more dirty dishes into the slotted conveyer belt. Gemma made haste, yet the crockery kept bunching up. It seemed Gemma didn't have a talent for stacking crockery. The latex gloves were slippery and rendered her hands to flippers. Gemma slipped a glove off. And then it happened.

One minute the latex glove was there, and then it wasn't. Gemma couldn't understand how it could have vanished right before her eyes. She canted her view, mindless of a cluster of plates coming her way and spotted a slot harbouring a drive belt. A latex sheath protruded like a condom and was gone.

Mavis's voice came again. 'Oy!'

Gemma spurted into action, grabbing a stack of plates and her fingers recoiled at the heat. The plates slipped from her grasp and cascaded to the floor with a crash.

The drive belt died in ever descending octaves.

Mavis marched over, her face like thunder. 'What in Christ's sake was that, *Gemma*?'

Gemma was speechless for a moment. 'I…I'm sorry. I must have…' Gemma decided not to mention the glove.

'What, girl?'

How could this battleaxe be addressing her like some stupid little urchin? Gemma's eyes drew half-mast. 'Drifted.'

Mavis waited for Gemma to add something, which she didn't. Mavis's eyes alluded to the mess. 'You can clear that later. Go over to the pulverizer. Stella will start you off.'

Gemma took one look at the steel cylinder, and the back of her throat balked. A heap of dirty dishes piled with leftover shepherd's pie and apple crumble waited to be scraped off into a small opening that sucked and rotated in turn with a grotesque gurgling sound.

Gemma did not care whether Mavis or Alice was watching. She cut across the kitchen, unsheathed her remaining glove and strode out.

A cluster of care workers stood smoking and moaning in the balmy evening. Gemma propped herself against the wall and pushed her hand into the pocket of her jeans.

She uncrumpled the piece of paper and looked at it.

Chapter 8

LUKE made a point of not touching himself during the performance. The ebb and flow of arousal obscured the ever-mounting burden of wakefulness. Ten till one, for him were the most brutal of the day. What were they but the advent to long and bleak tedium where most people had access to obscurity if they needed? Visual caresses of thighs, bums, ankles, necks and hairlines had made redundant those benzoes and their ghastly relatives long ago. After popping every sleeping pill in the doctor's proverbial cabinet, the next day would jaundice him with that same nauseating fatigue whether or not he had been mangled through the vile coma they induced. And as an extra, they left a plastic taste in his mouth. Only cannabis came close to diverting him like the female form but was still not sleep. Yes, flesh tones were definitely worth keeping his eyes open for.

Three weeks after buying the lease to six Templeton Court, Luke had contacted Philip Meakin. Philip adapted scripts and choreographed scenes for the local Amateur Dramatic Society in Berkham. Luke had met Philip through Alison; both possessed a declivity for the aesthetic and both thrived on theatrical catharsis. Berkham Civic Centre would not have reached its heights without Alison's person-ability and Philip's vision. Alison designed and made costumes; Philip gushed over them. They did a lot of gushing together. Alison did a lot of things with a lot of people; Alison instilled an empathic response; it wasn't just her talent, wit and democracy, it was *her*. People flocked around her, volleying for that something she exuded – vivaciousness? Luke was certain she'd had plenty of offers. The company she kept included equally-talented, funny, off-the-wall people; attractive people. For some reason, she kept returning home. She kept remaining married. To him.

Philip had disliked Luke on sight. Luke was everything Philip aspired not to be: dour, stuffy, repressive, and as Luke had overheard Philip put it once, '*Soooo* unflamboyant!' Despite four years having transpired since her emigration to Canada to marry an architect, Philip would get misty-eyed over her and lament, 'Fuck, I *so* miss her. Ali was funny.'

But Luke's impromptu phone call after long years of silence had merely bought out that familiar guarded tone Philip never used on Alison and reserved only for Luke.

'Oh, er…hi, Luke. Haven't heard from you in a while.'

Philip's lofty formality thinly veiled the imminent demise of chit-chat.

Luke brushed this aside having shared many stilted silences with Philip in Alison's absence. Luke coughed. 'Yes. I've been…er…busy.' Luke refrained from mentioning the divorce.

A pause and Philip clucked. 'So…how's the cat?'

The chit-chat, it seemed, had thinned to parchment. Felix incidentally had died at the grand age of sixteen, but Luke reserved the news. Luke cleared his throat again. 'Do you still work at the theatre?'

Philip couldn't help himself. 'To wet every eye in the house is my never-ending mission.'

Luke closed his eyes momentarily and got to the point. 'I have a project that might be of interest to you.'

Philip's silence conveyed Philip's belief Luke wouldn't have a clue what interested him.

Luke continued. 'Since the divorce, I've moved into a flat in Warwick. Templeton Court. You might know it.' Philip did not fill Luke's silence. Luke knit his jaw, ploughing on. 'The bedroom overlooks a courtyard and straight into a flat opposite. And...er...well, I bought the lease on that one too.'

Philip made it plain he thought Luke had lost his wits. '*Ooookaaaay*.'

'This is where you come in, Philip. When I look out of my window, I wish to see something unfolding through the window opposite.'

Philip paused. 'So I er...what exactly?'

'Put an arrangement together.'

'You mean you want me to choreograph some routines for you?'

Luke couldn't have put it better himself.

'With a couple of...shall we say visually aesthetic ladies?'

'Something like that.'

'Pardon me, but why don't you just rent out some porn and wait it out with tissues?'

Luke floundered at Philip's vulgarity. 'Because it's not the same.'

Philip fell silent. It seemed he agreed on that point.

'I shall compensate you and the subjects, of course.' Luke paused. 'So long as you treat this with utmost discretion. The fee will reflect the hours at which I wish the performances to take place, being unsociable.'

'Oh. What sort of hours?'

'Between ten and one. The flat is available at any time of course, for the purposes of preparation and anything else you might need.'

'Christ, you must have a chronic case of insomnia. What sort of thing did you have in mind?'

Luke's jaw tightened at Philip's throw-away remark about insomnia and decided to let it go. He wouldn't have realised or understood. 'I'm not entirely certain.' Luke knit his lip. 'Nothing gauche, nothing tasteless or tacky or where everything is made...*obvious*. I want something soothing, sensual; I want a routine that gives me plenty to look at but leaves something to the imagination. But not their faces. Their identities are something I wish not to know.'

Philip's silence was one of cogitation.

'Are you up for it, Philip?'

'I got some ideas,' Philip uttered in a far-away voice that told Luke he was beginning to take this commission seriously.

After a further two weeks of silence, Philip contacted Luke for a rendezvous at the high street coffee shop to obtain the spare keys, to discuss the finer points and to reminisce. Four years had barely touched him; his skin still wrinkle-free having received habitual applications of face creams, although his brow furrowed rather more readily now; his lithe form forever dressed in silk shirts and low-slung tight trousers. His care-free breeziness may disarm at the other's peril, for barbed cynicism often lurked beneath. Luke noticed Philip make his own observations. Luke perhaps had not worn so well.

On the damask tablecloth, Philip had deposited his script. Luke kept his eyes from it, glancing instead at the menu. Once the coffees had arrived, Philip did not mince words. 'I just need to know before I commit myself to this.' Philip fixed Luke with his china blue eyes. 'You ain't gonna surprise me with anything at the last minute, are you?'

Luke poured milk into his coffee. 'Such as?'

'Y' know. Fetishes, bondage, sadism, sexual humiliation?'

Luke refrained from looking to see if anyone had overheard. He lowered the jug. 'Don't you think, Philip, that I wouldn't have mentioned that sort of thing to you before now?'

'Okay,' Philip dead-panned and made a note. 'And you ain't got no objection to skin type, tattoos, piercings?'

Luke could feel his colour rising. 'No.'

Philip made another note.

'But no tongue piercings.'

Philip exuded an inconvenienced sigh.

'And no ghastly tattoos you might find on a convict. Skulls, daggers.'

'But you don't mind the colour of the ass.'

The room seemed to hush. Luke's reply came out stiffly. 'No.'

Philip made one last note before closing his notebook and raising his brows. 'Just makin' sure. You never know.' He pushed the script towards him. 'You wanna take a look?'

Luke's sights brushed against the plastic folder tethering a stack of A4 sheets. The front page presented the title, 'DOMESTIC BLISS.' Luke didn't move to touch it. His sights shifted away. 'Surprise me,' he muttered.

Philip replaced the faded Monet print with Japanese lithographs. Tiffany lights and globes superseded tungsten bulbs and fluorescent tubes. Art Deco figures embellished empty corners and maroon drapes adorned the sash windows after seemingly an age.

Luke was aghast at what light can do: the simple act of placing blue filters at one end of the room and red at the other eliminated harsh corners and dead spaces. The rooms no longer appeared rectangular, but shapes undefined. Although mostly obscured from view, Philip had added silk cushions, a Persian rug and a rouge counterpane. The project, it seemed, had certainly taken a grip on Philip, every detail deliberated over in pursuit of a particular effect.

The flat remained static for a period and then another change would present itself; the shifting of a light-stand, the repositioning of a chair, the addition of two large houseplants. And then it happened.

The previous shutter-snap of sleep had been brutal and now seemed remote. Luke couldn't even read without the words jumping about or taunting him with shrouded meanings. The TV had ferried him through the small hours with only the dreaded chasm of wakefulness to grind him to smithereens before consuming him from inside out. Twenty hours later, Luke was sitting at his window, laptop open and investigating dormant accounts from previous clients. Movement at the periphery of his vision drew his eye. The moment he turned his head, everything fell away and the view before him locked his eyes in a snug embrace.

A pert female form clad in a silk sequined bikini was reading luxuriantly on the couch, a leg canted to one side and her head resting on the inside of a crooked elbow. Her lithe form emanated weight, heat, an occupancy of space, like a jaguar at rest in a tree. God, the potential of her caught his breath. She wore a theatrical mask – a vixen? It didn't matter. The prop was tasteful, unobtrusive and typical of Philip.

A second form emerged from behind a houseplant. Why hadn't he spotted her before? This one wore a dainty cat mask from where blue-black hair cascaded in lazy curls. Her long limbs tapered to an hourglass waist that made her appear to lope on stilts. Cat gathered up her dark, silky limbs into a huddle and crouched at Vixen's feet. Vixen was unresponsive, apparently engrossed in her book. Vixen turned a page, almost in disdain. Cat lowered her head and grazed her pink-lipsticked mouth against Vixen's thigh. Even from here, Luke could imagine the soft resistance of flesh, like an organic cushion. Vixen continued to read. It seemed Cat would need to do more to rouse Vixen's interest.

Cat rested her mouth onto Vixen's calf and made a long track of kisses towards the back of vixen's knee. Luke's chest took a jolt. Almost in response, Vixen's compact breasts rose and fell. Cat prized the book from Vixen's hand. Only then had Luke realised he was still sitting at his laptop, fingers poised in midair and in full view of the two females.

Luke refrained from leaping from the window and killing the lights. With smooth precision, he closed down his applications, each window complying with agonising deliberation. He logged off. Luke groped for the light switch. The room fell into darkness except for a pink glow on the wall above his bed. He almost dare not look. The agony of it obscured the grinding hours for an instant. Luke savoured that moment like a thirsty stork taking long sips at the water's edge. He closed his eyes and allowed his anticipation to creep over his body.

He lowered himself at the window and took another look.

From a dark vantage point, the skin colours leapt out at him. Shadows did not exit, only a blue fill-in glow that described inner thighs, backs of knees, throats and navels; an opposing red glow caressed protrusions: bottoms, lips, breasts and knees. The contrasts of colour on flesh brought to mind Matisse's nudes. Luke had to hand it to Philip; for a supposed gay, he seemed to know exactly what pleased the eye of the heterosexual male.

Domestic Bliss suspended time, obliterated Luke's conscious state: Matisse's semi-nudes stroked, caressed, tasted in a slow pendulum of giving and receiving. They fed each other strawberries on the kitchen floor, they massaged body oil onto each other's backs, they combed each other's hair, they kissed each other's feet.

And when it was over.

When it was over, the drapes closed, the lights died and Luke's muscles had grown stiff.

Chapter 9

A HOBNAIL boot had hoofed the inner wall of Luke's skull until his eyes fluttered open at the same unearthly hour. The same soupcon of shadows on the ceiling and the same birdcage taste on his mouth greeted him with baleful mirth. Well, he hadn't expected *Domestic Bliss* to cure his insomnia. But his mounting desire during the performance had indeed flattened those three hours to nothing, where before, he would have been staring at the ceiling counting the minutes. And he had been wise to detain his climax until the end. Luke knew only too well that giving in too early would reduce the performance to a mere pleasantry that would fail to divert him from the imminent tedium between lights-out and breakfast.

Who'd have thought such self-control could have such uses? He had his upbringing to thank. His father having never cried in his presence conveyed the belief that Luke himself should never allow his emotions to commit such betrayal. His mother, having succumbed to cervical cancer when he was three could provide no counterpoint. Only after his father's death of a stroke ten years ago had Luke realised such a stern demeanour concealed a fear of intimacy. It seemed his father served punishment with greater ease, particularly whippings for petty delinquencies. His father never acted out of rage but through a misguided corrective undertaking. He had taken particular issue with Luke's lazy indolence at the onset of his teens, waiting for the opportunity to subjugate such disrespect. All it took was the careless damage of a costly pair of trainers. Each lash had clawed into the tender flesh at the back of Luke's thighs where a singing heat had screamed loin-wards towards a ganglion of nerves initiating the sensation of a tightening reef knot. He'd wanted Luke to cry. His father had committed himself to the task and couldn't go back. But Luke had pinched his lip between his teeth until blood streamed down his chin. Luke won his objective. He had not shed a drop and the belt had sagged like a dead snake at his father's side, just like his father's pride. Luke had seen the belt for the last time that day.

Somehow, this self-possession seemed to have seeped into other aspects of his life, like roots sucking up a septic pool and causing leaves to wilt on unconnected branches: his inability to voice such afflictions to Alison; to look upon those given to emotional fits with discomfiture and inconvenience. What does one say in such situations? Luke would prefer to push himself beyond physical limits few could bear than to find himself in such company or to submit himself to such states of mind. For that very reason, Luke had declined cognitive behaviour therapy for his insomnia. He loathed the idea of 'talking' his way through his troubles. In fact the whole system of treatment for such afflictions suggested a self-indulgence of the most wallowing and repugnant kind. Tai Chi, Feng Shui, reflexology, Ayruveda, Reiki, acupuncture, Shiatsu, music therapy, aromatherapy, herbal remedies appealed little more. And yes he had been guilty of trying them all.

He knew about noise and light pollution, electromagnetic fields, geopathic stress, EMFs and sleep hygiene. It did not matter if his bed faced north, south or west; if he eradicated wireless gadgets from his room, or if he painted his walls blue.

But Luke had found his own self-help system: preparatory measures for Philip's next installment of *Domestic Bliss*:

binoculars, knee-rests, a selection of music CDs, an occasional nip of Southern Comfort at his side.

Luke learned quickly that music changed the mood of the performance as surely as Philip's choice of lighting; funk made it look sleazy, jazz made it appear contemporary, fusion made it look progressive, blues made it look melancholy and classical gave it exuberance. Mozart, Tchaikovsky and Bach incidentally, gave the cheesiest routines credence, and Philip had devised a few. Luke learned to his own cost that his medley must overlap the closing stages of the performance. As Vixen was massaging Cat's abdomen and Luke was working towards his own climax, Tchaikovsky's *Dance of the Swans* had ended abruptly, allowing the TV's tinny emission of *Only Fools and Horses* theme tune to commandeer the airways. Vixen's massaging appeared to work in tempo with the cockney croons, giving the performance a comic spin. Luke's erection died swiftly and irrevocably.

Philip centred his routines upon prosaic domestic scenarios; cooking pasta, watering the plants, dusting the shelves, vacuuming the living room, the post-tiff make-up, making the bed, ironing the sheets, scrubbing the floors and grooming, grooming, grooming. Luke did not care if forms swapped masks or what the masks depicted, although Philip's preference for Cat and Fox grew more evident. Cat had coffee legs one day and mocha the next; Fox's saffron waves had transmuted to gold strands the following week. Their outfits became arbitrary, whether they wore silk bikinis, scanty chef's outfits or frilly tutus. Luke only cared about how the bodies moved, the forms' occupancy of space, what they did to each other, how they touched each other, their roles in *Domestic Bliss*.

Ten till one became the fulcrum from where the other hours revolved. The rest of the day was but a bleak and featureless landscape by definition. Luke anticipated this most benign killing of time. Yes, that's what it had become: a killing of time of the most humane order.

Philip kept coming up with the goods. His two subjects, Fox and Cat continued to turn up at the same time to caress his wretched eyes with their soft grace.

Domestic Bliss became the slumber his actual slumber refused to be. Luke fancied that he had cheated sleep; that his three-hour trance was like pseudo-sleep. Could he make the claim that he was sleeping six hours now, instead of three, an amount that bordered on normal? The idea did not buoy him as it should. A man could survive without food for longer than without sleep and *Domestic Bliss*, sadly was a mere frill Luke wished were more. His actual source of sustenance was one without redeeming features: filthy water for the thirsty, rotting meat for the starving, and in the case of sleep, a functional three-hour coma interposed by the sensation his skull had taken a sledgehammer. How could he cheat something that could drive him insane if it took further umbrage and serve up ever measly portions?

It had happened before. A day without sleep had turned into two and then three. His sleep had deserted him completely for seemingly an eternity, taunting him, prodding him further into the hellhole of endurance that went beyond his father's beatings.

In his most desperate hours, Luke had spent the day at the gym, rowing, running, cycling and swimming, counting each stroke, just like he counted the minutes, and as he had pulled up for air, he had seen his father sitting in the spectator stands as clearly as the lifeguards. He wore his usual crisp open-necked shirt, his broad, dark face exhibiting its usual detachment and his eyes concealed by shadow.

Luke's derangement did not stop there; it had manifested the sleep-state in his mind as a solid form, could feel it, smell it, knew how it felt, was omnipresent, yet it remained just out of reach. Cotton fleece of organic colours shrouding consciousness; pinks and beiges. The fabric would spring to the touch as though air existed between delicate layers. But his consciousness possessed no such buffer from the reality around him. The reality was scraping at his head, making his eyes water and his skull to quake.

How he envied those who took sleep for granted – babies did it with such perfection; toddlers did it in public and in any position they happened to drop.

The agony had ended in the brutality he had anticipated: a snapshot of oblivion on his bedroom floor. He had no recollection of how he got there. He didn't care. At least he was able to black-out at the crucial time. Luke refused to consider what the episode suggested: that his sleep would continue to dwindle to a vanishing point where sweet oblivion would desert him forever.

He knew what continual wakefulness was like. It's taunting had tipped him into the abyss beyond sanity, where reality and dream-state merged. Such a state of being was for him an unknown hell that held no beginning or end.

Luke glanced at the corner of his bedroom and the sight burned him as though for the first time. Each time was like the first. Luke did not remove the display. Luke deserved to see, even though he carried the image around inside of him. Luke deserved everything in his life. If only his father was still alive. He would have deserved his wildest beatings. Instead, Luke had to find his own mode of penance. And when the time came, Luke would do the deed he had to do.

Chapter 10

THE question kept rebounding in her head. *My God, what are you doing?* Two days after calling the number on the crumpled piece of paper, Gemma was disembarking the bus at Temple Corner and walking down a quiet street towards a block of apartments. The person who had taken her query had a breezy, pretentious; overly-gay cadence embrittled with an edge that warned he is not to be messed with. Gemma envisioned a fat tranny trussed in a frilly shirt and burgeoning leather trousers presiding over young girls like a pimp.

Before even asking her name, this 'Phil,' had put her straight on a few things: the commission is to be treated with utmost confidentiality. Applicants must observe and maintain this discretion throughout. Any evidence to the contrary will acquaint the applicant with Phil's 'bad side.' 'And believe me,' he'd chipped, 'you don't wanna see my bad side.'

His next question had surfaced so unexpectedly, Gemma thought he had hiccoughed a syllable.

'Age.'

Only when the silence stretched out did Gemma realise Phil was awaiting a reply.

'Er…th…twenty-eight.'

A pause. 'Describe yourself in twenty words.'

Her thoughts staggered at this forthright expectation. 'Er...I'm...er...five-six, hazel eyes, slim to medium build, brown hair.'

Another pause. 'Hmmm.'

Gemma knit her lip, unable to rid that infernal image of a fat gay cogitating in a big leather chair.

'Not the most remarkable image comes to mind. Any tattoos? Body piercings?'

Gemma was still recovering from his previous remark. 'No.'

Phil decided a rendezvous necessary to 'check her out.' He reeled off a property address, the conditions of work, the pay, and was gone.

At that moment, Gemma had made the decision not to go. What else could it be but something seedy? A trading of her body little short of prostitution? The money said it all: three hours per night that equated to ten hours' pay at the Cypress Care Centre. She was almost certain the money would be cash, and that there was plenty more if she was willing to work for it.

And now, after apparently rejecting the idea, she was entering a modern apartment block and making her way up the stairwell. Gemma imagined young professionals occupied the leases; jasmine air freshener spiced the air and potted plants dotted the hallways. And like the occupants, she was a free agent. She could take a look, listen, and if something didn't appeal, she could leave, her pride intact. And Phil's bad side could go lump it.

Muted voices echoed from the upper landing. She paused at the bottom riser and looked up. The door to six Templeton Court stood just proud. Trepidation crept inside and goose-rashed up her arms. A free agent, she reminded herself and forged on.

Gemma gently pushed the door which slowly revealed an open-plan apartment. Some might say classy. Large windows on one side overlooked an enclosed courtyard sheltering evergreens. Tall, Art Deco-style barstools flanked a pine breakfast bar. A two-piece leather suite demarked a living area although the place didn't have a lived-in look. The red and purple satin cushions were too puffed-up, the mock oak floor too shiny and the ornaments too corporate. The Japanese etchings depicting idealised naked women bathing in basins left her cold. The apartment's overall appearance smacked of a man trying to give it a woman's touch. Gemma would have taken down the heavy drapes and replaced them with lightweight cotton curtains, and what was the deal with red and purple satin? Such an overused attempt at decadence didn't always convey and was heavy on the eye.

Gemma backed into the hallway on second thoughts, but it was too late. A woman stepped into view and directly in her line of sight. The woman's nonchalant appraisal brushed against Gemma's. Unfettered, she rested her palms onto the windowsill behind her and crossed her long legs. Her silver strappy shoes clopped. Gemma had never seen such long thighs. The combined effect of her short black lycra skirt and those stiletto shoes would deter any mesomorph from standing near her. Her fake lashes almost completely concealed her eyes, but Gemma could tell by a faint frown that she was bored.

The voice gave another utter from nearby, a separate room, perhaps. She could tell by the affected lilt that it was Phil's. Gemma made a tentative step inside. Leather polish and pine air freshener caught her nostrils. Phil guffawed and then kept saying, 'Yeah, yeah.' His form lingered at the doorway between the kitchen and the dining area. He seemed young and wiry. He wore a black silky shirt and tight jeans. So much for the fat gay. His gelled salt-and-pepper hair peaked over his furrowed brow, smoothing to a peach. Gemma could tell he had noticed her presence, but did not look at her. He continued to prate into his mobile and inch his way towards the breakfast bar. He roosted upon one of the barstools like one about to order a gin and tonic, and rested his shiny shoes onto a crossbar. Gemma could see now that Phil was older than she had first thought – perhaps in his mid-thirties. The woman had not moved from the window. Her lips puckered to no one in particular.

'Uhuh,' Phil continued 'Uhuh…yeah…uhuh. Uhuh. Okay.' And then the call had met an unprecedented demise. Phil delicately placed his mobile onto the breakfast bar. He seemed to enjoy the attention he was receiving; he seemed to enjoy making people wait. 'Okay,' he muttered. 'Let's see what we got.' He pivoted on the seat with startling agility and stopped at Gemma. The sudden force of Phil's stare took Gemma aback. His small pupils suspended without blinks had the effect of drill-bits. What was she supposed to do? Was she supposed to say hello? Smile? Turn away?

Slowly, Phil's scrutiny fell into a gaze – at nothing in particular, or certainly not her. He slipped from the barstool and approached her. He strolled past her. The woman seemed to take no notice of this. Perhaps she had seen it all before.

Phil approached the couch and adjusted one of the silk cushions so that each was perfectly aligned. Gemma couldn't help a bemused smirk. She forced her lips to a thin seam. Phil backed off to inspect and to clock his tongue. Gemma had to force her lips harder.

Phil clicked his fingers at the woman and Gemma's bemusement instantly soured to disdain. Small wonder the woman crossed her arms, pretending not to hear him.

Phil barked, 'Charlene.'

Charlene tossed an insolent sulk and rolled her eyes to the ceiling.

Phil pointed to Gemma. 'Over there.'

Charlene responded with deliberate delay, sauntering towards Gemma in pendulous clops. She stopped a few feet away, her posture in classic passive-aggressive; hips canted, arms defensively crossed and her mandibles working on a stick of gum she'd concealed until now. Gemma was all too aware of their height differences, Gemma being a head shorter; their clothes similarly contrasted; Gemma dressed down, as opposed to Charlene's 'up,' opting for a blue tracksuit which she believed to be practical attire for auditioning moves. And their countenances. How mousy Gemma must have seemed next to Charlene's porcelain visage, not to mention Charlene's razor straight mane against Gemma's choppy auburn cut. And what does Gemma do with her arms, her legs? Standing in front of Phil like a police line-up, these extensions felt as natural as prosthetic limbs. She crossed her arms, uncrossed them. She restrained an urge to fidget. Charlene stood as motionless as a rock, except of course, for her mandible workout. And all the while, Phil's drill-bit eyes were shifting from Charlene to Gemma. And back again. A thousand questions teetered upon Gemma's lips. She parted them slightly about to ask. Phil's scrutiny settled upon Gemma again. She closed her mouth. Gemma could feel her neck and chest reddening; she imagined the flesh enclosing her windpipe pulsating, surging until her skin blotched over like it sometimes did when she was nervous. God, if Phil so much as said a word about it…

Phil's eyes narrowed slightly. 'Hmmm…A little…' He paused, searching for the right word. He twirled his upper lip. 'Suburban.'

The word took her by surprise. Was that intended to be flattery or insult?

'Nice bone structure though.' Phil nodded. 'Reminds me of Blondie.'

As soon as Phil was done with his visual critique, he gave Charlene an approving little nod. 'I like the blouse, Charlene.'

Gemma knit her mouth and looked up to Charlene's lofty countenance; Charlene's grudging little simper vanished as abruptly as a kingfisher divining beneath water.

Phil did not seem to take notice. He blinked slowly. 'Jean, this is Charlene, Charlene, this is Jean, and I'm Phil.'

Gemma raised her hand. 'Er…My name's Gemma.'

Phil turned away and drifted towards the window. 'Whatever.' He pivoted again, seeming to enjoy how his shoes squeaked against the floor. 'So, let's cut to the shit. What can you do for me, Jeannie?'

For the countless time, Phil had stumped Gemma for an answer. Putting her on the spot seemed to satisfy him in some way. Gemma glanced at Charlene for clarification or some sort of assurance. God knows why. The woman maintained her rock-stance, letting everybody know she was not in a charitable mood.

Phil's voice took on an edge. 'Come on, you ain't here to fill in my tax return. Tell me what can do for me.'

Gemma stared blankly at Phil. Yes, she'd had a brief stint at traditional dance at the Studio Dance Centre in Warwick, but this was before Ben came along. Gemma certainly didn't think this 'commission' required more than a little agility and a willingness to show a leg; at this moment in time, she didn't know whether to strip off or do the Rumba.

Phil groaned at Gemma's confusion. 'Okay, let's try another angle. Charlene, do your thing on the couch.'

From her reaction, Charlene appeared to have a hearing problem, delaying in her response to the point of ignorance.

And then as though the message had merely been delayed in its transit to her cerebral cortex, she decided to straighten up and saunter towards the couch. Her fingers flexed. From there, she abruptly assumed her role, resting her buttocks and her hands upon an armrest and arching her back. The strands of her hair teased against the small of her back. Demurely, she raised her knees, one higher than the other and pointed her toes to the ground. A shoe dropped to the floor in sultry delay. She closed her eyes. The fabric of her skirt then received a thorough massage as her hips gyrated. The motions were slow and erotic. She parted her lips as one about to receive a grape. Gemma was convinced herself that Charlene was on the fringes of an orgasm. The movement seemed to radiate from her hips throughout her body, her hands and her feet, swaying in response to an energy source in Charlene's centre. And then Phil's voice cut in.

'Okay.'

The illusion vanished as abruptly as Charlene's simper earlier. Charlene dismounted the armrest and straightened up, her face restored to its former bored nonchalance. She donned her shoe and strode over to Phil.

'Okay, Jillie.'

Phil's address had become incomprehensible in the wake of Charlene's apparent ecstasy.

'When you are ready *please*.' Phil's tone finally pierced Gemma's stupor. Her eyes snapped to Phil's and panic tightened her gut. Charlene was now standing beside him, head cocked and arms crossed. And then the question in her head rebounded with ever more insistence. *My God, what are you doing?* Gemma took an awkward step towards the couch. She was all too aware her sneakers would not permit Charlene's perfect *en pointe*. Her baggy tracksuit made her look more like a PE teacher. Thank God the elasticated waist concealed the small pot that had refused to budge in post-pregnancy, despite the most rigorous Pilate.

Gemma placed her canvas bag on the coffee table and sat upon the armrest. She knew straight away her buttocks occupied more space than Charlene's compact peaches had. And she knew before craning her head, that her body lacked the poise, grace and control required to emulate Charlene's moves. The arch ended at her neck; the rest of her spine refused to follow suit. A steel rod seemed to have been inserted into each vertebra, rendering her spine about as flexible as lead piping. Gemma didn't place her palms onto the armrest, she *planted* them there, her knuckles turning white and her graceless biceps trembling. And no, rolling the eyes further upwards did not encourage her back to arch further; looking up and back only made her eyeballs ache. Gemma became aware her centre of gravity was shifting. Her hand slipped from the armrest, and grappled for purchase. It was too late. Gemma toppled backwards onto the couch. Her shoulders connected with those infernal silk cushions with a soft thud. At that moment, she wished the mock oak floor would open up and swallow her whole.

Gemma recovered as best she could, meeting Phil's disapproving eyes.

'Christ, if I'd wanted to get myself a sack of spuds, I would have gone to the grocers!' He rubbed the side of his head. 'You've never done this stuff before, have you?'

Gemma was speechless at his remark. *A sack of spuds*?

Phil turned away. 'What a fuckup.'

Phil's turn of phrase automated a physical response Gemma could do little to control. She took to her feet and snatched her bag from the coffee table. 'Who the hell do you think you are, speaking to me like that, you...you disrespectful pig!' Gemma shot a look at Charlene whose mandible had paused in mid-motion. 'I must have been crazy coming here. What was I thinking?' Gemma's trainers squeaked as her legs pistoned across the polished floor. All she needed now was the perfect alignment between veneer and rubber sole to propel her foot skywards and her buttocks ground-wards to complete her humiliation. Instead, Phil's voice surprised her from behind.

'Hold on a minute.'

Gemma stopped short of the door and turned. Her cheeks were still flushing.

'I could make this work.' Phil's face had taken on that cogitative gaze of earlier. Charlene watched him; her gum had yet to receive its next workout. The centre of her brow furrowed. 'We could go for the complimentary liaison.' He glanced at Charlene. 'Charlene, you are the starlet, the celestial. You provide the glamour, the glitter. You are *La Diva*.'

All of a sudden, Charlene's brow ironed out and her lashes lowered to the point of hauteur. Phil turned to Gemma. 'Jeannie, you are the homemaker. You are the earth. You maintain the frivolity of the starlet. Every Diva needs maintenance; lots of it and you fit the bill.'

Gemma could feel her expression harden. 'You mean like a scrubber.'

Phil didn't hear her. His eureka moment had transported him to a plane reserved for the endowed, poets, artists, *himself*. He let forth a little chuckle. 'You two are practically married.'

Charlene's eyes hardened to grey flints. The moment Gemma looked her way, Charlene averted her gaze.

Phil clapped his hands and gave them a little rub. 'The Starlet and the Earth. This is great stuff!' He moved swiftly to the window to where a plastic folder rested on the sill. She hadn't noticed it before. 'Okay, girls, it is time to congregate if you please.'

So, it seemed Gemma had been taken on. Gemma retained vigilance and the solace she could still walk away if she wanted. The job could be easy money if it merely entailed a few provocative moves. She could only hope.

Slowly, Gemma stepped towards Phil and Charlene. Phil had picked up the folder and was huddling it against his chest. Without looking at her, he announced, 'Charlene knows the drill, so I'll explain this only once, so pay attention.' He turned and looked out. 'This place just so happens to have some special features. For one, each room faces the same vantage point.'

From here, Gemma could see the courtyard was enclosed on all sides, the complex occupying a hollowed square. It wasn't much of a view, the window faced north and the bulwark opposite permitted little light, except perhaps in winter. A cluster of saplings in blossom offered some visual relief. In a few years, they might provide a more aesthetic screen. Phil continued in his nonchalant tone, 'You'll be performing a late night duplet for a client who'll be watching from that window.'

What window? Gemma could see no particular window except for obscured glass on the ground floor; unless he meant the sash window partially obscured by a cherry tree opposite. The curtains were half-open. It must be.

Phil went on. 'As you can see, this place overlooks an enclosed courtyard, so no one else gets a view up here.' Gemma noticed Charlene was not looking out. Her nose was turned up.

'You'll also notice there ain't no nets in this place because hiding is prohibited. *Pro-hib-it-ed.* And whilst you are on duty, observe the cardinal rule.'

Charlene's mouth mocked Phil's words in perfect synchronicity.

'No looking out the window.' Phil paused for emphasis. 'Feel free to include every room in my little *operetta*, but no deviating from the script unless it enhances the theme. The kitchen is my personal favourite. It's got *so* much potential.' Phil decided one of his random moves overdue and wandered into the next room. Gemma watched, perplexed. Charlene appeared not in the least so, resuming her mastication and staring into space. Gemma, couched into taking the initiative, walked into what she gathered would be the bedroom.

Gemma stopped dead at the doorway. A king-sized bed dominated the area. The counterpane, plaid in pink and purple and sequined in satin, appeared anything but for sleeping in. Small pillows in navy and mauve dotted the headboard. Phil was fussing over the drapes, making sure the gathers were symmetrical. Phil backstepped, nodded and drifted over to where Gemma was standing. He fondled the plastic folder he'd been huddling and unsheathed two wallets.

He proffered one each to Gemma and Charlene, who now stood together. 'Read 'em, study 'em, rehearse 'em 'til you know the moves in your sleep. I'll make some adjustments for the new theme. Any qu's?

Gemma still hadn't taken her wallet. 'Why is there a bed here?'

As soon as the question emerged, Gemma knew she'd asked the wrong kid. Phil was giving her one of his dismantling stares. Charlene's lips tightened and she emitted a tiny snort. Her eyes shifted away. 'I…I mean, you said on the phone that we perform for a voyeur across a courtyard. That's it.'

Phil urged her to take the wallet. 'Read the script, Jillie.'

Charlene made it obvious her cough was not a genuine effort to clear her throat.

Gemma took her copy and Phil walked off. Charlene proceeded to flick through. The pages within appeared to exhibit widely-spaced typescript broken into small paragraphs. Charlene paused and contributed her first words since making Gemma's acquaintance. 'Oh, God.' Croaky and nasally some might confuse with sexy. 'She continued to read. 'Fox kneads the dough. Fox stands behind Cat and embraces Cat. They knead together. Cat moves rhythmically with Fox. The kneading notches up. Fox slides out her tongue and traces the nape of Cat. Fox mashes the dough. They keep moving together. The kneading becomes frantic. Fox turns. They nuzzle.'

She tossed the script onto the bed. 'The wanker's contribution to erotica is like Pete's chippy to the culinary world.'

Gemma opened her copy, all previous thoughts dispelled. More of the same presented itself. Gemma didn't know whether to feel despondent or relieved. Scenes entitled, Making Fairy Cakes, Having a Soak, Time to Whip the Cream and A Good Lay merely reinforced Charlene's view. And it seemed she would have to get intimately acquainted with someone who appeared to have the emotional depth of a snail.

Gemma slammed the folder shut at the scene where: 'Fox teases the whipped cream from Cat. Cat sprays the cream over her chest. Fox proceeds to lap it up.'

It isn't sex. Well, not strictly speaking. No exchange of bodily fluids, no risk of sexually-transmitted diseases, no condoms and not a male in sight. She didn't even have to bare her privates. Scanty-wear would take care of that.

What was the alternative? Gemma had done her share of menial jobs for misers who barely paid above the minimum wage. She would close her eyes and imagine it was Liam, think of the money. Raisin-eyes' words came back to haunt her. *People'll do anything for money.*

It's not sex.

And at that point, Fox shattered the silence. 'Well, Cat, do you have a talent for baking bread, or what?'

Chapter 11

PHIL contacted Gemma later that week to fill her in on some changes he'd made to the script. From his tone, he'd assumed she'd been through it.

'The Chopping Board scene needs refinin',' he'd said. 'but I'm sure you know that.'

Gemma let him believe what he liked. He carried on without pause. 'I've been thinkin' about this complimentary theme and I'm suggestin' you take a submissive role within the action sequence. I mean, I don't want you to draw eye-level with Charlene and you certainly don't look down on her. Keep it low and understated. And that includes focal points. No sparkly jewellery, no fancy nail-art and no frilly lace. That's Charlene's job.'

Gemma couldn't help herself. 'Do you want me to dust?'

'Dust?'

'I have a spare dustpan and brush.'

This made Phil think. 'You know, you could have a point there.' And he was gone.

Gemma didn't employ the full-length mirror. She knew her body had seen better days. But she knew how to play up her best points: her small waist, her pert breasts, her sculpted legs. The cellulite on her rather full thighs could be concealed with cream and her small pot flattened with a discreet corset. She could wear stilettos to make her legs appear longer, but suspected Charlene would do the same and negate the effect. No matter what she did, Charlene was younger, taller and her womb had certainly never been occupied. But then, had it not been for their disparity, Phil's little 'duplet' would not have worked.

Gemma had no allusions the moves required of her could probably be achievable by someone twice her age. But owning the moves was different to simply doing them. Gemma knew she had to relearn self-possession of the body: the breath, the centre and balance. Strength and agility, she hoped she had in sufficient supply.

A sun salutation warm-up routine had taken care of all. Gemma inserted herself into this traditional yogic sequence whilst waiting for the kettle to boil.

She stood in prayer position, feet together. She exhaled and reached skywards, leaning back. Vertigo unsteadied her. She breathed out, bending forwards at the waist. A snowstorm obscured her vision. Her toes, once within reach, seemed to have retreated an inch in the past ten years. The snowstorm cleared. She lowered herself into the plank. Yes, she could remember that yogic tag, but had she omitted a move? She flexed her knees and brought a foot forward. The back of her neck wasn't having any of it. Down to the cobra. She pushed against her palms and eased her shoulders upwards. Her tendons ached, her wrists trembled. At that point, she lost the will.

Gemma put the pasta on, made herself a cup of tea and sat in the walled garden at the back of the house. Ben's feet whispered over the grass. He sat next to her. 'Did you get the part?'

Gemma nursed her teacup. 'They're going to call me.'

'I've almost finished the mask. I've even worked through my lunch break.' He ferreted through his satchel and lifted out what at first appeared to be an erotic South American artifact. Fish-shaped eye sockets atopped a silver pert nose. Idealised pixie ears sprouted from the brow; each feature was lined with intricate weave designs upon a coffee-coloured base. The mould ended at the jawline, allowing exposure of the mouth and chin, adding a classic theatrical theme. 'I based it on a Venetian cat design. None of the others looked quite right. The area around the eyes needs a little work, but it should be finished by tomorrow. Mrs. Potts is real pleased with it.'

Words eluded her. Teachers always took to Ben and his matter-of-fact sincerity, at times confounded at his dedication to a particular project. She hoped Mrs. Potts would save the friendly inquisitions if she ever saw her.

'Go ahead. Try it on.'

Gemma's voice seemed to come remotely. 'Oh, no. I couldn't.'

'Don't be silly, Mum; it's what it's for. Anyway, I want to see if it fits.' Ben had a point and she wouldn't blame him for feeling slighted by her reluctance. Gemma picked it up. The mask was as light as foam, yet as sturdy as plastic. A Velcro strap had been looped through a slit at each side. Gemma turned it over in her hands. Ben had lined the inside with muslin. 'How did you make this?'

Ben shrugged. 'It was easy really. Shredded paper mixed with glue and stuck over a mould.'

'Paper Mache?'

'Not exactly. The secret's in the technique. I used tissue paper, not newspaper and shredded each piece real small and mixed it to a fine paste until it was smooth. The mould is worked in thin layers. Each layer perfects and strengthens the last.'

'But how did you…?'

'The mould? The art teacher had a dummy's head. I used Clingfilm and Vaseline to stop it sticking. Once I'd moulded what I wanted, I did the rest by eye. I found out that a mould can be made to look like any animal you want so long as you get the design right.'

Gemma was still admiring the fine detail around the eyes, which looked to be adorned with metallic paint.

'Don't tell Mrs. Potts, but I had to scalpel out the eyes and the outline shape of the mask. Scissors would have ruined it.'

Gemma didn't register his words, trying to dispel from her mind the mask's true purpose.

'Go on, Mum. Try it on. I want to see if it fits.'

Gemma sighed heavily and did so. The mask felt light and snug. She adjusted the straps at the back, but she could see Ben's eyes were already transfixed upon her new appearance. 'Wow.'

Gemma awarded Ben an intent gaze. She skewed her head. That did it. Ben clapped his hands over his mouth and let forth a chuckle. Gemma skewed her head the other way. Another ripple seized him. 'Oh, God, you're beginning to freak me out!'

Gemma took to her feet and lunged towards him like a Ninja warrior.

Ben staggered to his feet, forgetting his crutches. Chortles gusted from him as he darted to the further end of the garden. She took after him, confounded he could move so fast for someone hampered with Baker's cysts at the back of his knees. Ben's chortles augmented into hearty guffaws Gemma had not heard for a long time. For a while, she had forgotten about her petition to divorce, her first mortgage default, and the word 'repossession.' Gemma knew it would always end too soon.

The next day, Gemma received a reply from Colby and Vernon, not via Geary, but to her directly. In true Aimee style, it was unhelpful, slippery and addressed few of her questions.

'Dear Mrs. Greene,' it had opened, 'we are sorry for the issues you have raised in your previous letter. Your complaint has been referred to our team leader who will look into procedural aberrations. Please be aware, this point has been reached after our clients have made repeated attempts to resolve the matter of the outstanding debt. We are sorry the means by which our recovery team undertook seizures from your property. We do not advocate such behaviour or methods, and do not represent who we are. We have informed our agent of our standing on the matter and invite you to take our recovery team to court.

We will of course advise the individuals concerned should you decide to take this action. Please be aware of the costs this is likely to accrue and the likelihood of small yields not to mention added stress. As we understand, such costs would be undesirable to you in your present situation.

As to the matter of the identity of our client and the purpose of the loan, this, we regret to inform you is strictly between your husband and our client in accordance with a signed document of confidentiality. To maintain this, we have purchased the debt from our client and therefore the debt is now an issue of ourselves retrieving your husband's share of the property. At present, we are advising our clients on this matter and will be in touch again soon. I am sorry I am unable to assist you further or to answer all your questions at this time.

A copy of this letter has been forwarded to your representative.

Yours faithfully,

The recovery team.'

Aimee seemed to have devolved into this recovery team. And Gemma had been around long enough to know credible jargon when she saw it. The vulnerable and the under-informed may have bought it. Gemma wasn't so sure about a few points – this right to confidentiality, for one. It seemed she would have to shell out considerable legal fees and possibly take them to court to establish if they were bluffing, and for what? It seemed Colby and Vernon had deflected the large stuff onto the small: the recovery method and Aimee's customer service. Gemma was sure she would win her case, only to find herself no closer to this grubby third party or of getting their notice taken off her property deeds. Gemma could see dead-ends closing in on her.

With the divorce pending, she was only too aware of their advantage. This third party was regrouping. She could feel it without having to read the letter. And what did she have? In two more defaults there would be no house for fight for. In fact, she could see Colby and Vernon buying her out, and the way she felt at the moment, she would happily give the curtains a good soak in gasoline and watch the house go up in flames first.

She placed the letter into a folder containing her other correspondence relating to the house. She looked out. Patti was shuffling on her short legs, The *Daily Mirror* tucked under her arm and a fag perched on her lower lip. One of Dave's kids and another boy were kicking a ball against the front of Dave's house.

And what was Ben's mum doing? She was setting herself apart from the despair etched upon these people. She was going out in a glitzy outfit and a theatrical mask to a place nowhere near here. She was doing her part in suspending Ben's belief. Who could blame him? Who could blame him for clinging onto this illusion?

Chapter 12

GEMMA read Phil's script on the bus enroute to Templar Avenue. Phil wanted to meet up at Annabel's Stage Attire before going through the moves at the apartment. Her eyes skimmed over the action scenes with objectivity and distance; moves, sequences, the placements of limbs, suggestion and manner around themes. That's all they were. Such a perspective made the read more palatable, although some of the sequences made her wince.

She had prepared Ben's tea early, informing Ben that Patti was checking on him later. A litany of duties ensued: don't answer the door to anyone else; her mobile number is by the phone; if anyone asks, she is working nights at the care home. Don't forget the tablets and don't wait up.

Ben stopped her before leaving. 'Don't forget your cat mask, Mum.'

Gemma paused at the table. Phil would have a thing or two to say about it; he would have his own collection. Well, Ben needn't know if Phil got his own way. She picked it up before kissing him on the top of his head and leaving.

The bus juddered on its crawl up Kenilworth high-street. Gemma stepped off opposite the chemist, passing dusty frontages and turning at The Terrace, a narrow alleyway she never knew existed until Phil had described it for her.

Annabel's was a narrow shop crammed with carousels of outfits short of obstructing the gangways. The checkout was obscured by long dresses suspended from the ceiling. Such a profusion of fabric seemed to rob the light from the shop. Charlene and Phil were already rifling through glitzy outfits at the back.

Gemma had never ventured inside a fancy dress shop in her life and the wares immediately seduced her attentions. A carousel dedicated to Halloween themes – Dracula, the Mummy, Pumpkin Man and Spiderwoman. A neighbouring carousel to fairy themes, balls and proms; another for mocking professions, nurses, policemen, chefs; the exotic: Pharaohs, Greek Gods and movie heroes. Pet costumes snagged her eyes: a dog Dracula outfit, a cat princess tutu. She lifted out a dog Batman costume: straps attached to mini batwings. Her other hand latched onto foam rubber of its own accord. The more she lifted it out, the more the costume burgeoned from the carousel. Effect stretch marks, cellulite and varicose veins swarmed her vision. Gemma became dimly aware of someone approaching from behind. The fat suit swept briskly from her vision and was replaced with Phil's implacable gaze. He proffered a cat mask. 'Try this on.'

The mask was lined in pink silk and edged with silver fuzz. The effect was sexy and chic rather than feline.

Gemma didn't take it. 'I won't need that.'

Phil's proffering grew forceful. 'Course you need it.'

'No I don't. I already have one and it's better than that.'

'You've got one?' Phil affixed her with one of his glares one might expect if she had told him she was going as a gimp. 'Don't fuck with me, Jeannie, put it on or I'll have a tantrum right here.'

Charlene was already attending a full-length mirror, her lip puckered and a sequined bikini at her side. Gemma donned the mask. The effect would have sufficed a ball in a formulaic way. Phil wasn't even looking, but fingering scanty outfits nearby.

Gemma had prepared herself for her commission by bringing a small arsenal of cover-stick, creams and a corset. Phil plucked a brown parlourmaid's outfit from the rack. 'What size 're you?'

Gemma's eyes hooded at the sight of it. 'Twelve.'

He took it to the counter. Gemma slipped off the cat mask and cast it onto the counter next to her outfit. She walked away.

Phil took them to the flat in his retro-mini, crooning along with his equally retro-music: Spandau, Erasure, Yazoo, and wailing to 'give a little respect.' Her heart had taken a surge as the reality of what she was doing began to sink in. Was this how stage-fright felt? Did some people fixate upon this thrill in the manner of one about to face a fear, whether it be danger, humiliation or gambling in excess of the pot? Liam's feral eyes flashed in her head. She blinked the thought away. Liam hadn't entered her mind in over a week. Already he was shifting towards the domain of old schoolteachers, ex-boyfriends…her ex-in-laws, and she had consigned all concern for his welfare and his whereabouts to Terry.

Much to her shame.

Once in the flat, Gemma headed straight for the bathroom. Charlene remained at the doorway, chatting with Phil. She made it quite plain she was a pro who was in no hurry.

Gemma sat on the edge of the toilet in a silent and static panic. She had unsheathed her jeans but could find no way of taking the next step. Moves? Sequences? The placement of limbs? This earlier analogy seemed more like a force-feed of vapid delusion. Her thighs looked more like doughy stumps, her feet sinewed and veined; her wrists tapered too abruptly from chunky forearms. She felt like a troll and probably smelled of beef stew. Had she brought mints? Did she have enough eyeliner?

'Jillie?' Phil's tone conveyed his urgency to get on with a quick rehearsal before curtain's up. Only half-an-hour to spare. No amount of time would have been enough.

'Jillie!'

'Okay!'

Gemma sprang to her feet. She grabbed Phil's plastic bag and slipped into the two-piece pinafore. The low cut granted ample view of her cleavage. No comment on that and no comment was good. The low cut emphasised her small waist. In spite of Phil's intended effect the outfit made her feel curvaceous, shapely. Her hands trembled as she applied eyeliner and affixed false eyelashes. Thank God she didn't have to worry about the freckles smattering her nose; the mask would hide those. But no matter what colour she used, her eyes always ended up looking matronly – handy if she wanted to perturb an officious chauvinist, but not for this occasion.

She applied glossy lipstick and lip liner. Phil was ramming at the door now. 'What the fuck are you playing at, Jillie?'

Gemma gritted her teeth. She disengaged the lock and entered the dining area. Phil was already walking towards Charlene who had donned her sequined bikini and looked suitably glamorous. Gemma eyed Phil's cat mask on the breakfast bar. 'Let's get on with it,' he seethed, not far away. Gemma finally completed her look, adjusting her mask until it was level. When Phil turned and saw Gemma ready, he looked as close to a myocardial infarction as anyone ever could. The furrows on his brow flattened out and his eyes burrowed into her from shadowed brows. 'That's not the mask I gave you.'

Gemma did not move or respond.

Phil's eyes shifted from hers and back again. Gemma was uncertain if this was due to her matronly eyes, the mask or her non-response.

'Take it off.'

To comply or not raced towards her and yet the galvanizing air shrouded her in inertia.

'I said *take it off!*'

The moment had come and gone. Phil could go have his tantrum, his infarction or whatever, but Ben's mask wasn't going anywhere. Gemma experienced grim satisfaction.

Phil's expression tightened. He knit his lip to a thin line and stormed out.

Charlene was watching from the door. Her face bore its customary immobility, but the shadows around her eyes suggested a slant. She turned away.

Chapter 13

THE dark can look at you. Gemma's spine tingled right now. A moment ago, the follicles on her forearm had bristled up one by one. As the night advanced upon the windows, the sensations intensified. Gemma envisioned one pair of eyes; a laser beam of scrutiny that burned into her flesh irrespective of objects or of Charlene obscuring the view. Would these sensations obtrude upon her role-play had she not known someone was there? True, she had glanced up in response to someone gazing at her at times, but at this moment, the resistance to look had got the better of her again. What was she expecting to see but black?

Charlene was reclined upon the counterpane, goddess-like and awaiting Gemma's application of lavender oil. The ambient light made her appear more resplendent. Phil had not returned; Charlene had flatly stated she did her own thing anyway and deviated from Phil's previous script. Rehearsals administered by control-freaks robbed the performance of spontaneity and sexiness. Apparently.

Techno-funk trickled softly in the background. Gemma sat at Charlene's feet, grappling with the lid. Oil had oozed onto her fingers and she couldn't find purchase. Charlene expertly appeared relaxed, but Gemma knew she was getting impatient. The lid slipped. Gemma inclined the bottle, gooseflesh pimpling her forearms. She pinched the midriff and a little oil spurted out. Charlene slowly presented her Fox demeanour – a suede mask with pert features, each contour edged with glass studs. Her expression was indecipherable. What else was there to do but to proceed with the massage? Gemma's muscles plasticized. Another tremor. Another move afflicted with jerkiness and imprecision. She pooled a little oil onto her palm and rested it against Charlene's thigh. A gecko tattoo emerged from her thong. Gemma averted her gaze momentarily. At least it wasn't pubic hair.

The smell of lavender spiked the air. Gemma gently slid her hand towards Charlene's bottom and made small circular strokes. Lovingly and erotically, so Phil's script had instructed. Gemma didn't feel any such thing. She tried; she kept stroking and the dark kept daggering at her nape.

Charlene's Fox head nuzzled into Gemma's neck. 'Move up the bed,' she uttered.

Gemma stiffened in mid-stroke.

'For fuck's sake skip this part and do my shoulders.'

Gemma otched upon her haunches and proceeded to do so.

Charlene slipped effortlessly into her role, her head sweeping back and her saffron locks cascading between her shoulder blades. Strands whipped Gemma's cheek skewing a false eyelash. Carefully, she prodded it back into place and resumed her massage, each stroke feeling incidental. Charlene closed her eyes and licked the contours of her plump lips in indeterminate appreciation; Gemma was squeezing more oil onto her hands. Charlene's shoulders inclined towards the window. Of course. Wasn't that the real reason Charlene had asked Gemma to move? To provide this voyeur an unobstructed view of the glitzy fox? The window. It was all about the window.

Fox's manoeuvre wasn't in Phil's script. Fox and Cat were supposed to interact in equal measure. There could be no master without the servant and no celestial without the earth. Charlene had decided she could do without either. Gemma doubted the voyeur would even notice. He (it had to be) was probably too busy salivating over Fox's silky thighs and gyrating hips. Cat's stilted attempts at maintaining the celestial in the background would undoubtedly remain unnoticed.

At that point, Charlene decided she needed a foot massage and kicked off a glittery sandal. Gemma dutifully attended at her heels. She was supposed to kiss her feet at this point. Feet weren't her thing, no matter how clean, manicured or sweet-smelling. Gemma brushed her cheek against Charlene's instep and this seemed to suffice. She proceeded to glide her cheek against Charlene's ankle.

Ben's cat effigy snagged her attention in the reflection. She'd almost forgotten. The sight reassured her. Gemma could do this. She could attend, serve and maintain just the way Phil wanted, so long as she got a wodge of notes at the end. She would treat Ben to a trip to Disneyland Paris once she'd bailed herself out of default territory.

Once the massage was done, Cat stirred the cake mix and they vied for the spoon. Fox got the lion's share, of course. Cat plied cream onto the fairy cakes and served an unimpressed Fox. Cat would have to do more to earn Fox's affections – perhaps some gooseberry jam or the grooming of hair. The window opposite prodded at Gemma's nape again. She didn't look. The climactic bed scene beckoned. Charlene assumed the lead.

The silk sheets undulated beneath Charlene's arching back. She raised a leg and pointed a toe. Gemma traced her fingertips along the ridge of her shin. Charlene emitted a hitched moan. Gemma flinched; had she smarted at a fingernail? Charlene's shins appeared as silky as before. She continued to writhe on the bed, arms akimbo. Gemma rocked back on her heels unsure of what she was supposed to do at this point. Charlene's moans grew in magnitude. Her knuckle grazed the gecko's tail. Two crooked fingers emerged. They teased the reptilian limbs. And then slowly, Charlene's fingers disappeared into her thong.

Gemma couldn't believe what she was seeing. Was Charlene fleshing out the parts Phil's described as 'make it sexy,' 'ladle it on,' and 'engage your fantasies?' Gemma glanced at the window – the black rebuked. Gemma squeezed her eyes shut. She leaned forwards, fingers splayed and they landed upon Charlene's thighs. Charlene continued to moan and undulate. Gemma's contributions again felt pointless. She might just as well be dusting the plants.

Charlene kicked off her other sandal, missing Gemma's head by inches. The succulent sounds of Charlene's exploratory fingers robbed Gemma of exasperation. Gemma's hands flexed. She couldn't. She couldn't do this.

Gemma decided to render herself invisible. She was good at doing that – had done so as a defensive tactic if one of Liam's friends had bestowed unwanted attention upon her at the Silver Spoon.

Gemma retreated. She drifted through the living room, behind the plants and disappeared into the bathroom.

The walls merely muffled Charlene's groans. The voyeur of course wouldn't be able to hear, but Phil had insisted they 'let it all out' audibly as well as kinaesthetically. An authentic performance was then assured as well as a client who could propel himself into the action.

Remote sex.

Charlene's cries ascended in pitch. Each forceful exhalation pulled together in a never ending string. Gemma clapped her hands over her ears; her feet oscillated with the sounds. God will it end? She closed her eyes.

After seemingly an eternity, Charlene's cries collapsed into the techno funk's baseline.

Gemma waited before letting herself out.

Charlene had already taken off her mask and drawn the curtains. She poured herself a glass of water and sipped. She deposited the glass on the bar with a rap. 'God, I was on fire tonight. I'll bet his cock erupted.'

Gemma took off her own mask to bare her distaste. 'You don't know anything about him.'

'I don't need to.'

'For all you know, he wasn't even watching.'

Charlene strode to her bag of day clothes. 'Oh, he was watching all right.' She cast a smirk and proceeded to change.

Phil's mini was already waiting outside. Charlene and Gemma entered quietly in the backseat. He said nothing about the scene earlier but he stopped in town instead of her house to express his gall. She had a fifteen-minute walk home and it was gone one am. Phil dished out two envelopes containing cash. At least both appeared the same in thickness. In this context, master and servant have equal pay. 'How'd it go?' He directed the question at Charlene.

'Fine,' Charlene intoned matter-of-factly. Gemma felt convinced Charlene would save the rest for Gemma's absence.

Phil didn't turn his head. 'If I find out my client is less than satisfied, I'll make a deduction from tomorrow's night's pay.'

Gemma groaned inwardly. Tomorrow night. And the next. And the next. Did she have the reserves to earn enough to make a difference to her situation? She let herself out and trudged the mile home.

Jaundiced light pooled onto the living room carpet, the only illumination in the house. Ben had already gone to bed. With compunction, she went up and gently kissed his head. Ben sat up, his eyes like polished jadestones. 'How did it go, Mum?'

Gemma nodded wearily. 'Good. Really good.'

'Did the audience like my mask?'

Gemma smiled. 'They loved it.'

'Bet you got a standing ovation, didn't you?'

Gemma's smile could barely hang on. She nodded again.

'I wish I could see the performance. Do you think I could?'

Gemma's smile was slipping. 'It's a private viewing. VIPs only.'

Ben's face beamed. 'Cool!'

'Get to sleep now.'

Ben dutifully settled himself back in and Gemma straightened up his blanket.

Gemma made cursory appraisal of the envelope's contents before going to bed. No great surprises, but the money would accrue at a pace no noble profession she was able to do could match. She hid the cash behind the electric meter under the stairs.

Could she see herself in the same way again? It wasn't sex, but had she prostituted part of herself? Someone she'd never met knew intimate details of her body: a burn scar on her right inner thigh, a mole at the apex of her left breast, a birthmark near her bellybutton. Her body wasn't her mind but Ben was. The disparity between his fantasy and the sordid reality repeated upon her like acid reflux. Ben had yet to learn about the brutalities of life. She was perhaps as cruel to nurture his fantasy.

She wouldn't tell him. Not ever. She had to preserve his impression of her in his mind.

Gemma blinked and moisture balled at her tear duct. The moisture made a slow rivulet down her cheek. She blinked again and closed her eyes. Suddenly, her limbs felt as heavy as sandbags and she was grateful. She was grateful to escape the guilt. Sleep would transport her from it.

Sleep was a form of forgiveness.

Chapter 14

LUKE lay within a myriad of mirrors, each plane trained upon a memory or a thought which was then reflected back on him tenfold. Every time he closed his eyes, floodlights brought out each reflection in lurid detail. He couldn't reduce the glare. He couldn't stop his thoughts oscillating.

Tonight was going to become one of those nights. Sleep had shrivelled within the glare and would not be making an appearance.

He would have preferred the pigeons. Please God, he wasn't approaching an episode. The last thing he needed was to pay his penance. But to forsake another night's sleep was more unbearable.

Philip made a brief phone call on how things went last night and an excuse to grouse. 'This fuckin' new girl's been gratin' on me big time, and I've had reports she's been taking a piss-break when she feels fit. Just give me the word and I'll dock her pay.'

Luke reclined in his swivel seat, irked already.

'Until someone else shows up, Luke, we're stuck with her. In the meantime, I can only apologise in advance for her behaviour.'

Luke could barely conjure the will to respond. 'Pay her,' he'd gruffed and ended the call.

Luke hadn't been too enthralled himself. This 'cat' kept glancing in his direction, an act not entirely new. Other girls had committed the same offence until the role consumed them. Her eyes were too distinctive, too knowing. She might just as well be sitting in the room next to him. Philip's *Domestic Bliss* was perhaps getting threadbare after some months now; Cat's guardedness exposed the fantasy for what it was – a panto. And it seemed this diversion scratched every part of him but the itch. In the third act, Luke dare to do something he'd never done before – pour himself a large scotch and watch a rerun of *Coast*. The binoculars unmanned hung despondently from its mount.

And now, an eternity later, he stood in his capacious office looking out, only he couldn't see a thing. The reality continuum was still pressing against his cranium and the buffer had eroded away. Features slipped from meaning, just as words eddied mirage-like. He could detect no textures of life. Only a bleak wasteland edged with the ever encroaching tendrils of something that wanted to consume his sanity. To switch off. God, to switch off. If only. Never had he felt so…*weary*.

His laptop was open, windows pinging. He sat at his desk; Google waiting. He typed in 'Humane ways to end your life.'

He stared at the words.

He closed the window.

Luke opened the case files on the Milliband Merger. Words like fishes, even simple words slipped away. He blinked. Fragments emerged through a thick cloud. His head pounded. He gleaned the words again.

Luke pulled himself up and strode out of the office. He would forego the cafitiere today and opt for a revoltingly industrial brew from the drinks machine. Perhaps anti-freeze or detergent would spike his bloodstream and pull him out of this fug.

He entered the alcove area, grabbed a plastic up and inserted change.

He turned sensing a presence nearby. Cerys was standing at the sink exuding a generous glob of phlegm into David Leek's coffee. David's cup was distinctive for its slogan: 'I got rat-arsed, what's your excuse?' David was Derek's yes-man, a Malteser-headed proprietor of a personalised number plate: DAV 5X. Luke had noticed David delegate work that wasn't his to delegate and Cerys had worked overtime as a result.

Once the phlegm had made its transit into David's cup, Cerys looked up. Her expression froze. Luke had never seen anyone stop so abruptly. The moment could have been freeze-framed.

Luke waited for his coffee-fill before lifting the cup and returning to his office.

His plan seemed to have worked. A scolding mouthful later, and the words came into focus. Luke spent the morning consulting an online handbook of clause entries. Each clause would initially appear the same, but crucial differences regarding an omission of a word or the addition of a sentence had huge consequences upon the resultant agreement. Luke ensured every likelihood was covered: the share of the assets if a subsidiary liquidated; formal procedures if a contractee was found to have a criminal record; copyright ownership of the amalgamated company logo; even the powers over a dispute regarding the colour choice of the office walls.

Luke went through each entry carefully before making his selection for the contract. He would have to discuss the finer points again with Dr. Sui before the summit.

From his correspondence, Dr. Sui seemed of open and noble disposition. Such greasiness of the Brewer Society could only profit from this amalgamation. Luke saved his document into draft, closed down his applications and signed into his blog.

It would seem his latest post on Barry Brewer had attracted some attention. One person had commented: 'What the fuck is this shit about Brewer? He only represents dodgy people who cheat the system. My company nearly went bust because that bastard kept getting people to lodge injury claims against my services, which I shall not disclose to protect my identity. I had no complaints for twenty years until he came along.'

Another commenter had added: 'Brewer's a crook who twists the law and plays on the ignorant.'

And for closure, someone had countered: 'These comments are most unfair! I have no complaints about Mr. Brewer's services and comments like yours should be taken down for slander. And you, *Mr. Corporate Friend*, I know what you're playing at. I'm going to find out who you are if it's the last thing I do!'

Luke sipped his coffee. Could it be that Captain Birdseye himself had paid a visit and made that last remark?

Luke decided to reply. He simply put, 'Perhaps.' He signed out and took another sip.

The glass doors whispered. Cerys entered, her face red and her gaze lowered. 'Mr. Forrester.'

'Good morning, Cerys.'

Cerys did not move. 'I…I feel I need to explain what you saw earlier.'

Luke waited, reclining in his seat.

'I…I don't want you to think I do that thing you saw because I don't. Something came over me. I'm not excusing myself or anything, it's just….I've been under a lot of pressure recently and Dave Leeks has been…' Her eyes brushed against Luke's and darted away. 'He's been pestering me, criticising my work and asking me into his office for petty reasons.' Her voice grew hoarse. 'Please don't tell anyone what I did.'

'Luke pinched his pen between thumb and forefinger. 'I am unsure of why you need to explain yourself to me, Cerys.'

Cery's cheeks purpled. Her lips fluttered. 'Because…'

'So far as I am aware, you were simply making coffee.'

Cerys's brow furrowed.

'Perhaps if you made his coffee more…*cappuccino*, he might be more appreciative.'

Words evaded her.

'Perhaps if you encouraged everyone else to do the same, he might consider making his own coffee in future.' Luke gave her a small smile. He imagined it to be ghastly.

Cery's expression did not indicate so. A complicit smile coloured with bewilderment made a bizarre mix. She cleared her throat. 'Yes. I'll bear that in mind.' She hesitated, perhaps for permission to leave or some similar vocal closure. Luke felt no need to say more. She left quietly.

Luke decided at that moment to hack into the account of one Derek Johns, Coordinator of IT Security Implementations Team. It might add longevity to his plans for Mr. Brewer and provide a little poetic justice. Luke knew Derek's username was Derekenterprises. Why the enterprise part, he wasn't sure; was it an entrepreneurial spin or a claim to Star Trek obsession? The password part, of course, was his only impediment, but that didn't faze Luke. Derek was out of the office, leaving Luke ample time to cogitate at leisure.

Derek had a dog, Hercules. Being a tiny shiatsu, Derek thought the name indicative of his humour. Yes, Derek liked to flout his pompous wit to make any unwilling participant feel ennobled and part of the Derek fanclub. Pity his imagination possessed the same rigidity. Up to that point, Luke had spent the afternoon sketching a mindmap of Derek's tedious life. Hobbies: boating, *Excalibur*, his dogs, covert foxing, possibly *Star Trek*. His wife, Elspeth, poor soul. His two sons, Gareth and Montague. Haunts? The South Downs, the Ashby Canal, the White Stag. Luke explored all avenues, mixing numbers into letters.

How very Derek to use a dog's name above his wife's or the children's. He signed in. Derek's Gmail account appeared dormant, perhaps favouring his company email. Luke doubted that Derek would even notice his blogger account had been activated. But then, so what if he did? Luke transferred ownership of *The Corporate Friend* to Derek.

After completing his task, Luke wondered if Derek's beloved Hercules provided the portal through Derek's work login. The system's requirement to change the password per thirty days may cause a little hitch, but then, people here tended to tag a number at the end to resolve conceiving an entirely new code. Luke discovered Derek had done the same. Thirty-four times since Hercules' birth.

Luke took a little time-out with another coffee before logging into Derek's work account and infecting one of Derek's document templates with a virus. Derek would soon encounter the problem tomorrow morning and get his yes-man to redraft. Mr. Leeks will be occupied for some time over the coming months.

Chapter 15

HOURS stacked up and reality forced a runnel of grit through his senses depositing granules behind his eyes. His mouth was dry; everything was too loud and too bright. And he knew sleep would be deserting him again.

Luke knew better than to try the old remedies; the mere thought of such attempts brought a ball of desolation to his throat. The old fear there was something systemically wrong with him revisited. The specialists had assured him evidence lacked to the contrary; the body would eventually cutout, for sleep was vital to live. Live or exist? If this was existence, he would rather not.

Luke poured himself another scotch and adjusted the focal plane. Mozart's *Clarinet Concerto in A* charmed his eyelids to a gentle close. When he opened them, Fox was perched upon a high stool looking resplendent in her turquoise bikini. Cat, clad in a scanty chef's outfit, was stirring what appeared to be butter cream in a bowl. She looked thoroughly pissed-off.

Luke drummed his finger on the sill. Cat assumed her role, yet vigilance cloaked her eyes. The notion of her awareness of him persisted regardless of where her sights fell. He couldn't do the business with her 'watching' him. The reason couldn't be defined. Cat no longer looked his way – it wasn't that. The cat mask admittedly an odd choice for Philip, was more decorative than sexy but this was immaterial. Her eye makeup? Fox took the prize for such definition, so why not Fox?

Cat seemed a little older than the other candidates. The way she skulked in the background spoke of cynicism fostered by life experience. She couldn't lose herself like Fox – perhaps that was it. Fox possessed elegance and chic; she wore her role as a starlet who knew nothing else. Cat was…potent, edgy; she loitered as a creature trying to camouflage and failing miserably. Pissed-off. He couldn't keep his eyes off her.

Cat extended the butter cream on a wooden spoon for Fox's evaluation. Fox licked the spoon and turned away.

And there it was again – Cat's hooded gaze. She stirred the cream awkwardly. Was the butter cold? Luke could detect clenched teeth behind the lip-gloss – she had a full mouth with a prominent bow. Her solid arms worked the mixture and worked the mixture. Luke wondered how Cat's forearms felt right now with the muscles engaging beneath her brown flesh. Most men would probably find the clutches from such arms difficult to escape from. He imagined her kisses to be firm, hot, like her compact form.

Cat proffered Fox the cream again. Luke wished Cat hadn't stopped mixing the cream just then. He could have watched her muscles flex a little longer. Fox extended her tongue and licked the spoon but Luke's eyes remained on Cat's arms, in repose yet implying feminine strength, like a housemaid in a Caravaggio painting. Another spoonful. Fox decided the cream was sufficiently creamy this time and her lips lingered at the spoon. Cat attended with that pissed-off expression of hers.

Why was Luke's right hand hovering at his zip at this point? With the performance an hour yet to go, the move was unwise. His fingers brushed against his penis which was already erect. Luke closed his eyes and exhaled slowly. He waited. Never had abstinence felt so difficult, but gratification at this moment would cost him greatly. The old argument presented itself: what else was there to transport him from the continuum of wakefulness without the craving?

Luke opened his eyes. Cat was groping for the body lotion on top of the fridge. Her index finger brushed against the label, causing the bottle to rock from its perch. The bottle nosedived towards her. Cat grappled with a grimace and in a blink, the bottle nestled safely within her clutches. Such a reflex defied belief. The bottle should have smashed to the floor. With anyone else, it would.

Fox was already awaiting Cat's body massage in the bedroom. Cat disappeared from view as she drifted between windows. Luke anticipated her reappearance in the bedroom. Cat stepped in and mounted the bed beside fox. Luke could comprehend Cat's compact form moulding the bedclothes and depositing a pool of heat. Luke wondered how long Cat's body-print would linger in her absence. Luke's viewfinder stumbled onto Fox's thighs, flawless like a Barbie doll. Why had such a visual treat been forsaken until this moment? Phil's Diva surely deserved the focus of his attention; her feline grace, her glitz. Fox implicitly understood the erotic pace the male spectator needed; she had the moves, the timing and the suggestion. Fox, like all others before her had teased his eyes with implications and promises. And the end never disappointed him. Cat's movements did not possess these undercurrents.

Cat's dark hands came into view. Her fingers slicked oil onto Fox's thighs. Luke licked his lips. He never tired of these flesh tones. Cat's wary gaze now out of shot enabled Luke to take the familiar route and watch smooth flesh upon smooth flesh. Fox could now carry him through the next hour; Fox would fend off the dreaded night, so long as he trained his viewfinder upon her.

Luke could almost hear the purr of satisfaction from Fox's sleepy countenance. Her gazelle-like form rocked gently beneath Cat's pulsing strokes. Cat paused to add more oil. She leaned over Fox's back and spread her hands – hot hands. Luke could see down Cat's cleavage. He ventured her aureole to be terracotta in hue. Would her smell equal the richness of her pigment? He trained his viewfinder onto Fox's posterior, rounded and pert. Cat's hands reappeared again. As though an obtrusion, Luke shifted his viewpoint away. And then he saw it. A scar nestled high in Cat's right inner thigh. He zoomed in. A crescent-moon shape, the mark had dimpled, suggesting perhaps a burn mark. The disparity between smooth and scarred tissue captivated him. Its location would be difficult for Cat to see or she would have used concealant. When had she last been aware of it? Was he one of a handful of people who now knew of its existence? Fox had a tattoo in a similar place, but Fox was highly aware of this embellishment; Fox had used every opportunity to flaunt her little gecko during her routine. Cat's mark was not one to flaunt – a brownish stain that blotched out at one side. The scar bore unadulterated evidence her body had been lived in, a heritage to her past and which etched out her existence. He imagined she would have been discomfited at the notion of such a scar being visible. His visual probe would have caused her form to close up and shut down like the shadows over her eyes.

Cat's skirt partially obscured the scar in shadow as she shifted across the bed to massage Fox's shoulders. Luke wanted to nestle into that shadow and graze his upper lip against the ridge of her scar. Would the burred edge tug gently at his lips as though wanting him there, needing to be kissed, perhaps the first ever kiss for being passed off as an aberration? Would she make a sound? Would she splay her fingers through his hair and hold him in place, her arms in repose as earlier? Would she surrender that hooded look of hers for eyes half-closed?

Cat's other thigh brushed gently against the scar. With a little more pressure, his mouth could flatten that ridge, only to spring back on release, poised for another kiss.

And another.

And another.

Never enough.

Luke lay on his back, sweat dewing his brow. The pink glow flickered on the wall opposite and Mozart played out his concerto. Luke couldn't bear to watch Philip's sleazy pantomime any longer – What more could it now offer? And what did the night have in store for him now except the usual reruns and a bottle of scotch? Until the pigeons reacquainted themselves, he couldn't even read his book *Amsterdam* without the words capering about.

That wretched Cat.

He should have stuck with the Fox. Fox didn't pull so obtrusively at his vision. Fox slicked past like warm milk. She did not apprehend him in such a chaotic manner. He had no one to blame but himself.

Care must be appropriated that Cat does not become an issue. Luke had decided since the divorce never to let another female burrow into his head. Yes, he'd had an affiliation or two in the past six years. The whole business of relationships was a mire of contradictions, mind games, word-play, flirting. Melody Cottrell, for one; a large-boned team-leader who exalted in her bigness – her form, her desk and her voice – had made her move soon after his divorce absolute. Melody and her borderline personality disorder decided sexual chemistry required jealously, conflict, frantic grooming and noisiness in the bedroom. Luke tired of her and abstained from returning her calls. Melody humiliated herself in a bottle of Diamond White with her power friends at the office to prove she was about to undergo a Renaissance. Apparently, 'wankers like him were weak and couldn't get it up for strong, independent women like her.'

Luke flattered other female colleagues whose eyes flickered his way; he continued to act the wanker Melody described and dropped them once he'd seen their bed and only a wasteland of word-play remained. Strange he seemed to attract women on the incline. Was he merely viewed a challenge for female counterparts to conquer for his status, his height, his reticence, a code to be cracked? To mould?

Alison's memory had now hardened, inhabiting a part of him that no longer felt real. And Luke preferred it that way. He wanted not to miss, single-out or to wonder.

Luke would speak to Philip about this Cat. With no one to replace her, Luke understood Philip could do little about her. But Luke would suggest ways of making Cat conform with the others; a body to captivate and to forget, without leaving so much as a vague after-print.

Chapter 16

A BLURRED moon came into focus. Was it a moon? She blinked the image clear. A clock face slashed in two; quarter past nine. Gemma's brief panic subsided. Today was Saturday. Thank God. Her body's inertia felt wonderful. She never wanted to move again. She closed her eyes, the prospect of spending this evening pampering Fox a distant concern. God she was sick of massaging Fox's buttocks. Gemma felt certain she knew Charlene's body more intimately than her boyfriend, Mark, a lanky guitarist who showed up now and again to pick her up. His black mop of hair failed to conceal his furtive smirks. The idea of two scantily-attired females engaged in caresses more than his juvenile brain could handle. But reality was far from the fantasy. Massaging taxed her arms, as did blending the butter cream, spoon-feeding Fox and dusting the plants. And all whilst Fox just lie there or sit there like an overgrown baby. Gemma wanted to spank her – and not in a sexy way.

Gemma had paraded her wares for a week now and still could not get used to the window with the eyes. How did Charlene immerse herself within the celestial realms as though the window did not exist? Gemma decided such a lack of inhibition was a gift.

And no word from her voyeur – only a regular cash sum. She now had enough to pay this month's mortgage installment. Just another two payments and the final demands would stop.

The doorbell downstairs sounded. She lifted her groggy head from the pillow. Was that the second chime? Gemma crawled out of bed, pulled on her dressing gown and peeked out of her window. Terry's blue transit surprised her outside. She pulled the opener and spotted Terry waiting at the door. She called down as discreetly as she could. 'Just give me a minute.'

Terry's head jerked up. He gave her the thumbs up. Gemma found Ben's bed already empty. She castigated herself.

Gemma washed, dressed and hobbled downstairs. Ben had already let Terry in and they were both sitting at the table sipping tea. 'Morning, Mum,' Ben chirped without lifting his gaze from a magazine spread out on the tabletop. Terry offered a little smile and slurped his tea.

Gemma's smile surfaced stiffly. What was Terry doing here? Had he forgotten their last conversation? 'Ben, I'm so sorry about this morning.'

Ben waved this off. 'It's okay, Mum. I'm not such a spaz I can't dress and feed myself.'

Terry exuded a gravelly laugh at this.

Gemma poured herself a cup and joined them. 'It's a nice surprise to see you, Terry. How's Vera?'

Terry saw through this pleasantry. 'She's still flower-arrangin' and she sends her best.'

Gemma nodded watching him. Terry's eyes darted to the window behind Ben. She could see Terry was trying to retain a light atmosphere in the presence of Ben. Had Ben asked about Liam in her absence? What did he know – if anything? Compunction singed at the notion Liam might be dead. This could not be so, for the police would have informed her. Please God, Terry hadn't dropped by to beg her to take Liam back.

Terry's gruff voice cleaved the silence. 'I hear you've been working hours at the care home.'

Gemma glanced at Ben who was still reading his magazine. Ben, good with secrets and promises, excluded himself from the conversation by design.

'Yes,' Gemma croaked and cleared her throat. 'Just a few evenings a week to help make ends meet.' She continued to watch Ben, confounded he hadn't brought up the subject of his father. 'Ben's been really good about this, haven't you, Ben? Patti next door keeps her ear to the wall in case Ben needs her.'

Terry's silver eyes finally settled upon Gemma's. 'Ben can come round ours now and again if it helps.'

Ben glanced up on cue. 'Can I have a play around in your workshop?' Terry's tool shed, the size of three garages had all modes of equipment to make anything from treehouses to birdboxes. The interior was a litter of half-completed projects and experiments.

Terry beamed at Ben. 'Course, you can, so long as you don't touch the power tools.'

Ben gave Gemma a sardonic grin. 'I'm sure Mum wouldn't mind.'

Gemma repaid the smile in kind, but noticed Terry's had thinned to a tight seam.

Terry turned in his seat. 'Me and Vera clubbed together and got you somethin'.' He reached behind him. Gemma hadn't noticed the object propped against the wall until now. Terry lugged the gigbag by its handle.

Gemma pushed herself from the table and approached.

'We weren't too sure about your preferences but I noticed yours had a cutaway and you ain't too keen on nylon strings.'

Gemma pulled the gigbag towards her and unzipped it. A pristine Tanglewood nestled inside. The cedar glided beneath her touch. The strings enticed her fingers. Ben now stood beside her. 'Where did you get it, Granddad?

'We ordered online. Came today.'

Gemma's words came out unsteadily. 'God, Terry, you shouldn't have done this.'

'Well, it was Vera's idea really. It's a shame what happened to the other one.'

Gemma hadn't admitted she'd trashed it. Terry believed the Ashton had been confiscated by her looters. Isabelle basked in ignorance. Her sister always remained in ignorance. Like their mother, she tended to flap and lecture in crises. Since Gemma had married Liam, Isabelle and her parents had become increasingly ill-informed on Gemma's life, none of them liking Liam from the start and their distance had developed into an unspoken rift. Gemma's pride had stopped her from telling any of them about her present situation or about the guitar. They would collectively vilify Liam's name and she wasn't going to admit they might have been right on some points.

Ben had taken the guitar from the gigbag and had rested the cutaway against his undersized knee. His fingers caressed the strings at random. Unfretted, a soft thrum stirred the air – tuneless yet soothing. Gemma could see Terry wasn't listening to Ben's efforts. Gemma didn't like the mode of his preoccupation.

Her words emerged quietly so not to draw Ben's attention. 'Has there been any word on Liam?'

Terry coughed and moved casually from the table. Ben gave no sign he noticed, but he did. Ben's skinny fingers continued to pluck, his face expressionless and his sights to the floor. Gemma felt like a dirty sneak moving from Ben's earshot in this way, but feared the words he could overhear. Terry convened with her at the back door.

Once in private, Terry didn't mince words. 'Liam's stayin' at a hostel in Bristol.'

'Bristol?'

'He understands your reasons for divorce and he says he'll go along with it. It pains him so, but it seems a clean break is the only option.' Terry paused to allow a moment for Gemma to absorb this information. 'He says once he gets his life back together, he'll do his best to pay maintenance for Ben. The CSA don't know his whereabouts yet, but he plans to buy a flat down there and start afresh.'

A stone of obsidian grazed against her throat. If Liam had been standing here now, she would have pummelled his head to the ground. And did he plan to see Ben again, she wondered? What about Ben? What about the mess he's left behind? Such plausible words only a coward would utter. Liam's essence no longer close by was more identifiable for what it was. The maintenance would never come easily from someone with no fixed abode and no job. Gemma had no faith that Liam would ever commit himself to this promise. Liam could never commit to anything.

'He's in a mess, as you can imagine,' Terry continued and avoided her eyes, perhaps reading her expression. Was the guitar an atonement? 'I feel like throttling the sod meself, but he's my son and I have to do what I can for him.'

Gemma's face felt hot. She glanced at Ben who appeared engrossed in his fingerpicking. Ben had the right idea. Ignorance was indeed bliss. Her eyes met Terry's again. Her next words emerged quietly. 'This debt of Liam's, the seventy-thousand pounds. What was it for?'

Gemma could see Terry had prepared himself for her question. His silver eyes darkened and remained steady. 'One of his stupid ventures that didn't work out. You should know him by now, Gemma.'

Terry rarely called her Gemma, preferring Gem. She searched Terry's seamed face. His eyes had become difficult to read, his eyelids having lost elasticity, partially draped over his irises. A smudged scorpion tattoo protruded from the sleeve of his T-shirt. Gemma's persistence to an ex-con suddenly seemed unwise. Terry, strictly speaking was no longer her father-in-law and she wondered about his loyalty to her. But where did this leave Ben?

Her eyes remained on his anyway. 'Liam must have told you the reason for the money.'

Terry's right eye ticked. 'Gemma, there're some things that are better left unknown, for Ben's sake.'

'Did you pay this visit just to inform me you have to withhold information from me?' The words came out more harshly than she had intended.

The rims of Terry's eyes flushed. 'I came 'cause I wanted to see me Grandson and I was hopin' to keep communications with his mother.'

Gemma turned away, a hot ball of shame ascending her throat.

Terry's hand brushed against her arm in an awkward attempt to console. 'Look, Gem, both Vera and me want to keep in touch with you lot here. You still part of the family so far as I'm concerned. Whatever Liam's got himself mixed up with is just by the point. I want you to get Liam's half of the property as much as you do. Go get these hounders off the deeds and the rest will take care of itself.'

Gemma closed her eyes and the black nonagon capered about beneath her eyelids like a jellyfish. She opened her eyes, turning slowly. 'Everything you say makes sense, Terry, but I need to know what Liam's got himself mixed up with. This greasy third party is intent upon taking the house from me. They're not giving up. I had a letter from their solicitor.'

'Gem, listen to me.' Terry's pallor had become pasty and his expression was flat. 'You know I've done things I regretted, stuff that got me inside. I got mixed up with things too. It takes away your pride, you lose all dignity – it makes you a lowlife. I know I'm not the best advertisement for being noble or honest or nothin', but I am tellin' you the truth here when I say I don't know who this third party is. I don't even think Liam knows, but I will tell you that the seventy grand was for something that makes me feel sick to the core. I don't want you findin' out what it was for because I don't want Ben ever findin' out.' Terry's skin looked like parchment. 'I want him to grow up without anything more to burden his poor heart about his father than his desertion. We family now. You, Ben, Vera and me. And I'll tell you something I'm ashamed of admitting, but the truth is often ugly. Liam doesn't deserve you. I seem to have brought forth a loser who doesn't know when he's got something worth fighting for. Sometimes, I wish he'd do somethin' to get himself sent down. Then he'd see himself as I see him now, and feel the shame that I feel about him.'

The kitchen fell silent. Ben's guitar sounds had stopped. Terry closed his eyes, suddenly aware of how easily he could have been overheard. He turned. Over his shoulder, Gemma could see Ben had gone. The headstocks rested against the wall as it had done so earlier. Terry cast his eyes down, trying to contain his anguish. 'Excuse me,' he uttered and stepped away. A moment later, Gemma watched him perch himself on the patio steps smoking a spliff. Gemma decided to speak with Ben once Terry had gone.

The phone trilled. Gemma answered and in a blink wished she hadn't.

'Jeannie?'

She glanced at Terry who was still smoking outside. 'Oh, er…hi.'

'My client got an issue with a mark on your thigh.'

Phil's words permitted no room to regroup her thoughts. Such a matter-of-fact tone obscured his meaning for an instant. 'Mark? What mark?'

'You gotta mark on your right thigh? Sorry I didn't get to you earlier about this. I've been workin' backstage at the Riverside Theatre all week.'

Gemma suspected Phil enjoyed name-dropping his precious theatre venues. But still. Proof her voyeur existed. He'd made himself known as a creature's movements beneath water, leaving ripples but no sight of the cause. 'I was burned when I was three. What do you expect me to do about it?'

'Look. He no-like. *Comprende?* Get rid of it or somethin'.'

Gemma glanced at the window. She could no longer see Terry. 'What if I wore a longer skirt or a maxi?'

'And why don't you put on some tights, a blouse and a cardigan and do some filing. This ain't a day at the office, Girlie; this is eye-feed for a peepin'-Tom. Do you get me drift? Get some concealant or something.' And Phil was gone.

Umbrage arrowed at her the moment she put the phone down. How dare some sex-freak voyeur pass judgment upon her physical appearance? She forbade any imaginings of the optical equipment at his disposal. Only a powerful zoom would make something so ensconced visible from across the courtyard.

'You okay there?' Terry had let himself through the back door. The evenness in Gemma's voice came with much effort. 'Just the care home checking they have cover for tonight.'

Terry nodded, waiting for something. She could smell faint tobacco smoke. He gruffed. 'Sorry about that outburst earlier. I think perhaps you and Ben need some time alone to talk things over.' He knit his lip. 'I'll let meself out.'

Gemma pocketed her hands to curtail the fidgeting as she spoke. 'Terry, there's nothing to apologise for. You're just doing your best for Ben and me.' The words came out awkwardly. She was never good at these things. 'I'm really touched about the guitar and Ben needs to see his grandparents. He needs some stability in his life.'

Terry shuffled on his feet as she spoke.

Gemma wanted to ask him about Liam's doodle but remembered his warning earlier: some things are better left unknown. 'I wish Liam the best,' she found herself saying. The words sounded hollow. 'I hope he finds his way for your sake. But I will do what it takes to protect Ben and to keep this house, even if it means finding out the truth about Liam. Whatever it is that he's done, it won't change the fact that you and Vera are his grandparents and I would like you to keep on seeing him.'

Gemma could see from the way Terry averted his face he wasn't good at these things either. The silent interlude did not agonise, but provide respite. She wanted the silence to stretch out. She wanted their discourse to end there.

But then Terry half-whispered, 'Don't dig too deep, Gemma.'

His words caused her fingers to writhe in their pockets. Terry's eyes retained that flat look of earlier as he looked at her. 'I'll keep in touch.'

He opened the door and let himself out.

It was at that moment she noticed a letter flicked side-on to the skirting board. She didn't investigate until Terry's van had moved off the kerb.

The letter from John Geary Solicitors opened with a brief recap on their previous meeting, present state of affairs and a two-paragraph summary of a further letter they had received from Colby and Vernon. Gemma preferred to read the copy letter unadulterated first. She skipped the first part.

'…our client, not being a registered lender or indeed a business power, cannot be regulated by a governing body as you mention in your previous letter. The agreement between Mr. Liam Greene and the third party is a of personal matter insomuch as one made between individuals in a classified manner. Such a capacity falls outside of this influence. As the agreement is clearly set out, signed by the parties concerned and witnessed by Mr. Colby himself, the contract is bound by law. Since Mr. Greene has violated the agreement, he has lost his share of the property assets to the amount of £70,000, in accordance with the clause within…'

Gemma reverted to John Geary's letter, which offered nothing more than the closure, 'If you wish to proceed with this matter, please do not hesitate to call, but fees may apply.' Gemma wanted to see this agreement, but suspected the notice of confidentiality would get in the way.

So, that's it. Liam had borrowed money from a private individual – not a lender. A private individual who could be anybody. A friend? A relative? A work colleague, perhaps? How could such a scumbag hide outside the radar just by being a 'mate'? To remain hidden, like a burrowing tic in the skin. A high street lender would have been preferable. Gemma tried to think. Someone at Steve's track? The garage? The Silver Spoon? Liam knew countless people, many of which seemed unscrupulous, seedy. The pub landlord, Carl Crank, for one, who habitually hijacked her evenings out with Liam with private chats behind the bar – his greasy comb-over and stinky breath. Steve's mechanic, Jim Todwell, rakish and shifty, his eyes like ball-bearings could never sustain a gaze for long. But who was she to assume the guilty party was a mate of Liam's, a shifty-eyed mechanic or even a man? Wild guesses would only foster red herrings and paranoia. Perhaps Terry had been right. Don't dig too deep; don't waste time finding out who or why.

Gemma made a weary climb of the stairs to speak to Ben. The notion of dark dust in the house had plateaued somewhat but the residue was ready to burgeon out and congregate as soon as the conditions were ideal. And Gemma suspected the dust wouldn't remain static for long.

Chapter 17

BEN had snuck out leaving a note 'Gone to Zack's. Will be back for tea.' Zack shared Ben's obsession for cycling over a stack of ramps Zack's dad had set up in the back garden. She'd told Ben countless times not to careen over them Zack-fashion with the intention of hovering in the air. Ben's frequent bouts of tendinitis rendered his muscles and reflexes like putty. But to stop him trying to be like other boys seemed a crueler fate.

She would talk to Ben about Liam as soon as he came back. Ben's advent to teen-hood was dragging with it shards of cognitive reasoning. She could no longer dress up and sugar-coat the cold hard truths about his life. Ben could feel cheated or deprived. Perhaps telling him straight, as one adult to another might put right her complicit evasion with Terry earlier.

Gemma returned to the bedroom after lunch. She closed the bedroom curtains, gathered a face mirror and a bag of makeup. She undressed to her underclothes and reclined on the bed. She hadn't seen her scar since God knows when. Being an inch below her crotch and midway between her buttocks and pubic area, the scar was mostly inaccessible to the eye. Strange how many areas of the body were mostly invisible to the owner: the bottom, the back of the head, the spine, the armpits. The front of the body, mostly the face commandeered one's self image. In this respect, the existence of a mole or freckle on the spine or shoulder-blade could remain oblivious to the owner for a lifetime. Perhaps she had been fortunate the location of the burn was mostly unseen to her.

Gemma switched on her lamp and took a look through her mirror. Not a pretty sight. The shape and texture of a half-eaten biscuit, the scar tissue had retracted during healing leaving a raised edge at the top segment of the crescent. The burn had never paled as the doctor had predicted, but darkened to a sort of bruise, fading to yellow at the centre. The day she had acquired the brand was a memory of contorted pictures and testaments. A day out at Weymouth beach. Ham sandwiches? Mum was berating Isabelle for decapitating her ice cream cone against the beach steps on the way up to the front. Some kids had abandoned a burnt out beach barbecue. Covered with sand, the oddity provided a suitable curio for a three-year-old. Gemma remembered her toddle, her mother calling from somewhere. Dad was buying Isabelle another ice cream. Gemma squashed her fingers into the sand and fell onto her posterior in a way only toddlers know how. Gemma didn't remember the causal pain, only the aftermath – the discomfort weeks later. The barbecue had been turned on its front, the disc-shaped base still hot hours after the cuisine had been served. Mum often lamented, 'If only you hadn't been potty trained so early, a nappy could have kept your bottom unblemished.' Gemma wondered years later if nappies were inflammable. If not then perhaps Gemma had been lucky her bare flesh had alerted of this heat so quickly.

Gemma hadn't needed skin grafts. The skin specialist had prescribed creams to keep the skin supple during healing. Mum made her wear cotton mitts to stop her from scratching.

Sensation in the area had vanished over time. So had her awareness of the scar – except for an occasional snag of nylon against the raised edge when she pulled on underwear.

Looking at the blemish now, Gemma experienced a concoction of grief and distaste. Grief for her former self; the days when afternoons stretched to the horizon, when everything seemed to reside in the sky, and when clouds were mountains. And distaste that some creep had ogled at and taken issue with her imprint. On account of a long hiatus of non-observation, not even from Liam, the 'creep' had somehow made her scar his. Every time she thought of the scar, his grubby feedback would overlay the original memory. Gemma had reasoned the unsociable hours of her work to be the basis for the handsome pay. But now could see that things like these were closer to the mark. In many ways, her body *was* her mind.

Gemma got down to business to curtail the seeds of resentment. Dwelling on Phil's words would do no good and she had a job to do. She mixed a powder puff of tan and a little rouge. She knew before applying the mixture that nothing would hide the scar. What could hide a raised edge except for the cosmetic equivalent to polyfiller? So far as she knew, nothing like that existed. Gemma applied the tint anyway. Even the slightest mismatch made the area appear dirty. Gemma tried to blend the edges out with progressively more tan. The area looked like a botched-up skin graft. The colour wasn't so much the problem. Even a perfect colour match would not hide the scar. The problem was the raised edge. Phil's oblique lighting would show it up like the teeth of a canyon at daybreak.

Gemma pushed her paraphernalia aside. The afternoon was slipping away. Desperation was setting in. Gemma cogitated without direction. If the depression could not be filled, could the ridge be flattened? Tights with a lycra blend might help. Gemma cleared the bed and ferreted through her drawers. She was in no short supply, being part of the dress code at the practice. One pair provided a subtle effect, being a close match to her skin colour and low in denier. Her voyeur might not notice. Gemma decided not to put them on until this evening in case she laddered them.

Ben had stuck himself in front of the TV with a cheese sandwich by the time Gemma had come down. 'Hi, Ben,' she tried to breeze.

Ben raised his eyebrows at her, his mouth too full to reply. He showed no signs of a troubled mind and this only troubled her further. Any opener on the subject of Liam was going to be awkward. She sat on the opposite chair, looking but not seeing the world's deadliest creatures on their small set. She watched Ben discreetly. The TV reflected blue squares on his lenses obscuring his eyes. 'Ben,' she ventured.

Ben did not stir. Was he too captivated to hear or had he pulled the shutters down? In fear of the latter, Gemma decided to commit herself. 'Ben, listen. I think you should know your dad's safe and he's living in Bristol.' The TV's soft intones did nothing to buffer the tension. 'He won't be coming back, but your granddad's going to do what he can to make things okay for us. You dad promises…'

At that point, Ben shrugged.

Gemma continued at a different point. 'Your dad and I are going to be divorced and I do think it's for the best. For us. For a clean break.'

Ben did not respond.

'Okay?'

The word came out squeaky and the moment was excruciating.

Ben finally replied nonchalantly, 'Yeah.'

Gemma gave her knees a small clap and made a desperate departure from a discourse she'd made a ham out of.

With her present hours of work, Gemma conceded Ben company two or three evenings a week. Zack was his preferred choice, although Amil and Felix seemed pretty responsible too. They watched films and larked in the back garden. Gemma set out clear ground-rules: the boys must leave by ten and Ben must be in bed by eleven. No damage please and always lock-up. This seemed small recompense for her evenings' absences, and the fear she would one day return to a burnt-out house haunted her. Her mobile remained switched on during *Domestic Bliss* despite Phil's telling her otherwise. In a few months' or so, Gemma would have the power to tell Phil to go massage Fox's buttocks himself.

Gemma left the house at the usual time to meet Phil as his designated pick-up point in town where he duetted with Annie about a 'thorn in my side.' Since her first evening, Gemma had adopted the bathroom as her changing room and Charlene didn't seem to object. She lingered at the door chatting with Phil.

Gemma changed into a particularly drab servant's outfit, even by Phil's standards – a grayish-fawn apron and leather boob tube. Gemma slipped on skin-coloured briefs before pulling on the tights. With only one pair to spare, she took extra care not to snag a fingernail against the fabric. She gathered up a sheath and in turn fed a foot into each. She pulled the tights up and donned another pair of briefs.

Using a small hand-mirror, Gemma appraised her upper right thigh. The lycra blend seemed to do the trick, flattening the scar. But would her voyeur accept such a covering? Well, her attire will at least show she'd taken on board his comment and made an effort.

Gemma emerged from the bathroom with a casual air she didn't feel. Phil was thankfully gone, but Charlene's eyes gravitated immediately towards Gemma's legs. She glanced away knowingly. Of what, Gemma dare not imagine. Phil was going to be pissed, perhaps?

Gemma pushed aside conjectures and got on with the routine: cleaning the floors. Phil's scenarios seemed to explore every avenue of humiliation and servitude to the point of slavery. And as for Charlene, clad in iridescent French knickers, a Bandeau top and strappy stilettos, looked as usual like one to be served.

Gemma scrubbed the floors as Charlene dropped sweet wrappers at her feet. Gemma arched her back, indeed cat-like and flaunted her posterior. Charlene flexed her knees demurely and gave Gemma an appreciative little pat. Gemma continued to scrub the floors. Scuffing hazards became a constant concern, particularly her knees against hard surfaces. Her tights seemed to be holding out, but there was considerably more scrubbing, grooming and a little romp on the couch in store.

With her role becoming an integral part of the day, like washing up or getting Ben ready for school, Gemma discovered her ability to switch off during *Domestic Bliss*. But the window with the eyes would always pull at her like gravity. Was he looking for the scar right now?

Low denier had proved to withstand everything Phil's script could throw at her. Cat, in unfailing fashion, earned Fox's approval in the end, took her place beside Fox on the couch. Gemma could envisage the two of them as a tangle of arms and legs – like a pair of cheetahs lolling in the Serengeti shrub, as Phil had put it. Charlene adopted a slow writhe, stretching her arms over the armrest of the couch. Gemma rested her head upon Charlene's breast and planted her palm against Charlene's clavicle. Gemma inclined her head. The underside of Charlene's chin obscured the window, which offered welcome concealment. Charlene enclosed Gemma's shin within the crook of her knee and brushed her hand against Gemma's shoulder. The finale was approaching and a lightness blossomed in Gemma's chest. Not long to go before lights-out and Phil's heavy drapes would once again obscure the window opposite. Gemma even closed her eyes in abandon. She glided her ankle against Charlene's. She kicked off a clog, an ugly black thing that accorded with her outfit; she flexed her knee. Resistance was abrupt and alarming. Gemma's eyes snapped open. A stud on Charlene's infernal stiletto had dropped anchor into Gemma's tights. But with her knee in mid-flex, her thigh muscles couldn't relax. Gemma tested the anchor with small knee pivots. Adherence was complete. Gemma knit her lip and lifted her head from

Charlene's breast. The black window scorched her. Gemma's head jerked back. Cramp burrowed through her muscle. The urgency to stretch the afflicted leg became irresistible. Gemma gritted her teeth. Gently, she pulled her calf towards the back of her thigh. The stud decided it was having a piece of Gemma's low-denier tights and the mesh separated with a long thin buzz. Gemma retained facial composure, but suspected she was looking increasingly resolute. Charlene twisted her head sideways until her breaths gusted over Gemma's hair. She hissed, 'Stop actin' constipated, for fuck's sake. What the matter with you?'

Gemma decided there was nothing left to salvage. She clenched her teeth and pulled her tights free. Another searing sound. Cramp shot groin-wards. She raised her leg to unlock her muscle and exhaled slowly.

Once the cramp had evaporated completely, the window with the eyes weighed in the centre of her mind like a fat toad on a lily pad. Gemma did not have to visually appraise the damage to realise a ladder had unzipped from ankle to thigh. If she flexed her leg again, her knee would emerge from within the netting like the tip of an icecap. Charlene's breaths no longer gusted; the bellows from which they came had fallen unsettlingly still.

Charlene's next words exuded quietly and with suppressed rage. 'Get on top,' she spitfired.

Never before had Gemma experienced such a keen desire to be someone else, somewhere else or to be another species. That houseplant would have been ideal.

Gemma complied by planting her hands on either side of Charlene and carefully rolling onto Charlene until they were abdomen-to-abdomen. Such a body position obscured the ladder.

Charlene nuzzled into Gemma's neck. Her breaths smelled of sage. Gemma credited Charlene yet again for taking precautionary measures against anything unpleasant in the physical intimacy department. Gemma's efforts were as exacting but perhaps less genteel, her campaign aided by industrial products and sugar-free mints.

Charlene's pains to prevent the studs of her stilettos from hinging onto the tatters of Gemma's tights permitted no grace or eroticism in the closing romp. Gemma secured her elbow into the cushion in a maneouvre more suited to a rugby tackle and the couch pitched. Charlene seethed through her teeth. Gemma aligned her pelvis with Charlene's and her elbows trembled. The couch pitched again. Charlene closed her eyes and turned away in resignation. All that remained was the window, now fully in view. Gemma did not look, but was fully aware of the black rectangle within the black window. And the eyes.

And at that moment, everything went black. The remote for the lights, forever beneath a cushion or between pillows at the locale of the final act made a more aesthetic close than the sight of a participant fumbling with the dimmer switch.

'*Jeeesus Christ*,' was Charlene's closing comment.

They dressed in silence once Charlene had closed the drapes. Gemma knew she had Phil's wrath to contend with but Phil didn't trouble her so much as her voyeur, evolving from a sad little old man to a tyrant, a Mafioso type from *The Sopranos* who dispatched anyone who didn't deliver per demand.

Chapter 18

PHIL wasted no time, calling at ten o'clock on a Sunday morning. 'He no-like tights,' he'd opened, 'especially the laddered kind.'

At least he wasn't screaming at her. 'I was trying to hide my scar.'

'My mother wears tights to hide her varicose veins.'

Gemma's mouth knit. 'Perhaps you might have a suggestion, since you work in the theatre.'

'This ain't no apprenticeship, Jeannie, you a big girl now. Use your imagination.'

Gemma didn't bite. Phil's caustic remarks were revealing themselves more to be a collection he dished out indiscriminately.

'Think about the eye,' he purred as though she were indeed his understudy now. 'What draw the eye? Strategic arrangements of focal points can create any effect you desire, rendering the unaesthetic invisible. You get my drift?'

Gemma didn't. His haughty advice merely signified an intimate understanding of his craft and an inability to make it understandable to the listener. Strategic arrangements of focal points? How could that make her scar invisible?

His purr came back – he had just imparted a nougat of advice, apparently. 'You think about it, Jeannie.' And he was gone.

Gemma didn't. She pitied his theatre troupe. What a wealth of reasons he must provide to bitch aside. Gemma would have plenty to contribute.

Ben wanted to resume the family habit of a fish and chip dinner at the Silver Spoon down the road. Gemma had refrained from such activities in the face of recent events. Her efforts to retain some normality in their lives became an objective with a price. The moment she and Ben had taken their seats within the dingy interior, fare served, the notion her grubby third party shared the lounge repeated on her. Twitchy Dave and his sons got chatting with Ben about last night's match replay on the TV, although Ben had no interest in football. Carl Crank was perusing today's broadsheet at the bar, his comb-over swathed in his usual grease. Liam's ex-work colleagues from the garage played pool in the corner. Glasses clinked and sports punters prattled on the big screen. Liam would have been standing at the fruit machine at this moment. Instead, the lights pinwheeled at no one in particular, and someone here probably knew why. Her hands quaked. The urge to squeeze her glass of coke into a mass of shards overwhelmed her. She needed the glass to cleave her flesh, to see the shock of crimson. Anything to detain the impotent rage that suddenly heaved inside. Ben continued his chatter and his finger-feed of chips, oblivious.

Zeeta, the district nurse from the practice entered with her friend. They approached with drinks. Seldom had Gemma anticipated the prospect of trivia and gossip as she did now. Gemma realised on her departure an hour later that his fish and chip routine had been their first without Liam and this was how it was going to be.

Gemma waited until Ben was upstairs before giving Steve a call. She had postponed her task, her stomach churning at the prospect she might detect an evasive air from him. Having known Steve for years, she would know immediately. For once, Steve's voice came clearly without background interference from the track. He offered his breezy preamble that indicated the same old Steve, but Gemma suspected he knew she had more pressing matters to discuss.

'Steve, you've probably heard about me and Liam splitting now.'

'Yeah, sorry and all that.'

'I was just wondering about that Aston Martin he bought.' Gemma grimaced as her query went underway. 'I'm sorry to have to ask about it, but do you have any idea what happened to it?'

'Yeah, sure. He sold it back to Paul from the garage. So far as I know, he got back exactly what he paid for it.'

Gemma sighed relief at the news. A lead to be eliminated. This satisfied her query and she could end the call.

But then Steve added, 'Liam had installed some extra features to it. My guess was to make it safe for the track. These two fellahs seemed behind it all. Paul was pretty mad when he got the Aston back – took him a week to undo Liam's handwork.'

Gemma paused to take this in. 'Men, you say? What men?'

'I dunno. Never seem 'em before. They spent the whole time chattin' with Liam at the side of the track. To be honest, I wanted 'em to buzz off. They didn't really seem interested in the machines. They just, well, hung around.'

Gemma contained her emotions and forestalled any interrogation. This approach could shut Steve down in fear he might end up in a witness box for some reason. Gemma feigned a care-free realisation. 'Yes. I think they might be some friends Liam met on holiday last year. Is one of them thinning on top? Sort of tall?' She hoped her guess might come close or convince.

'Skinny and flabby, if that makes sense. I dunno, about six feet, a high dome. Sort of Bobby Charlton without the comb-over. The other fellah was sort of short and toady, thick grey hair, low brow and glasses. They both wore suits. Looked shabby to me.'

Well that ruled out comb-over Carl. Gemma maintained her tone. 'It sounds like them. Did they make regular visits?'

'Just saw 'em the once. Ain't seen 'em since.'

Gemma was almost certain Steve had no involvement with Liam's final venture. A moment later, she ended the call, unsettled. The likelihood these fishy men had nothing to do with Liam's debt seemed unlikely. And staking out Steve's track in the hope of seeing them again would be futile. Liam was their reason for meeting up at the track; as Steve had made clear, these men had not been seen before or since.

Gemma suspected they weren't local, perhaps not of Liam's circle after all. But then, where did this leave her? All roads led to Terry's words yesterday: Don't dig too deep. At present, she didn't have anything to dig with.

Gemma trudged upstairs faced with the same cosmetic dilemma as yesterday. Had yesterday happened? Tights were out, but Phil's remark about focal points gave her an idea. Gemma foraged through her jewellery box which sadly had been stripped of her Parisian collection of filigree chains. Some of her costume jewellery was however elegant. Gemma lifted out a chain of silver plated weave. She unhooked the eyelet and arranged the weave around her right thigh. Bringing the ends in an inch made a snug fit but could pinch after a while. A garter would have been ideal, if she had one. Gemma made a mental note to buy one tomorrow. For now, her thigh chain would do.

Gemma took another dip for a charm – nothing too large, garish or cheap-looking. A heart-shaped locket immediately drew her eye; a black stone edged with quartz. She placed the locket against her scar. With careful positioning, her scar would be entirely concealed.

Her phone sounded downstairs. A moment later, Ben called up. 'Mum! It's that man from the show!'

Gemma dropped her jewellery onto the bed. She didn't much like Ben speaking to any employee of her voyeur. She raced downstairs. When she entered the living room, Ben was holding the earpiece towards her, his mouth cocked to one side. Gemma plastered on a smile in-kind. 'Go put the kettle on.'

Ben did so and Gemma's smile evaporated the moment he had gone. 'What now?'

'Jeannie, I'm gonna be workin' late at the Riverside this week, so Mark will be doin' the lifts again. You're gonna be leavin' half-an-hour earlier from now on.'

'Am I?'

Phil missed Gemma's sarcasm. 'Mark's gotta do a round trip for Charlene on the way to pick up some gigging equipment. You're to rendezvous at the usual place.'

'And do I get half-an-hour extra pay for the inconvenience?'

Phil tished. 'You could of course walk the whole way. That'd make it a whole hour without pay.'

Gemma held her tongue there. She still needed the money and the sum remained considerable. Gemma decided to have the last say. 'Fine.' And hung up.

Ben had surprised her with a brew at the table, his expression still bemused. 'That man sounds kina weird.' He gave a snort. 'Like a real eccentric. I'll bet he's got a big old country house full of dusty books and leather armchairs.'

'Gemma sat but did not lift her cup. 'I'm sorry, Ben, I've got to leave half-an-hour earlier this week.'

Ben joined her at the table and poured himself a cup. You must be doin' somethin' right, or they wouldn't keep asking you back.' He took a sip.

Words evaded her. At that moment, she saw an apparition of the man he was going to be. His oversized jade eyes conveyed a disturbing air of fragility and intensity. He nurtured a secret world he could not share with the boys in the estate. As his friends watched footie or gadget shows with their dads, Ben watched old musicals, variety shows or Carry on films. Enigmatic figures fascinated him; Peter Sellers, Kenneth

Williams; a documentary describing Bob Monkhouse's life and his vault of old TV show recordings otherwise wiped or destroyed had captivated Ben for weeks. Clad in his dressing gown and sipping his tea, Ben would have looked the part within his imagined country house with the dusty books and leather armchairs.

'What's the place like?' he asked.

Gemma knew Ben would eventually ask. His postponement merely spoke of Ben's growing anticipation of her revelation – an investment by the passing of time. 'Well.' She shrugged. 'I don't know really.'

'Is it a big stage? I mean, does it have spotlights and box seats and stuff?'

Gemma nursed her cup. 'Yes. Yes, it does.'

'Do many people get to watch?'

'No…just a few.'

'How many?'

Gemma scratched her chin. 'Well, it's hard to tell. It's…dark.'

Ben grinned. 'What sort of stuff do you have to do?'

'Er…' Gemma was floundering now. 'Routines. Just routines with another girl. A troupe. A dance troupe. Together.'

'Bet you're the prettiest of them all. I'll bet you are the one to wear the feathers.'

And he sipped his tea.

Chapter 19

LUKE'S reflection rippled as the lift doors to the Sheraton Hotel in Kensington slid open. He jutted his chin and adjusted his tie before striding into the Boardroom suite, a capacious lounge boasting period features from the Edwardian era. Modern innovations tastefully blended or enhanced, never competed. The deep red pile sprung beneath his shiny Oxford brogues. He spotted two Matisse prints amidst the elegant Post Impressionist collection – nudes spot-lit by rose-effect wall lamps that dotted the walls. Mendelssohn's *Song without Words* arrested his progress.

Waiters milled, attended and fiddled with bow ties, their expressions closed. Directors, chiefs, assistant-chiefs, interpreters, secretaries, deputies, their spouses, friends and colleagues discoursed. Luke imagined this mode of socialising to be ego-grooming. A complicit understanding between parties to alternate this preening and to keep their mandible joints greased. Some payoff must be sought, a portal into higher circles, perhaps, or simply a compliment or a little flirtation. Well, the Milliband/Claybourne foundations had cherry-picked one of the most sumptuous venues on the program to stage such intercourse. The Registry of Mergers offered a choice of locations from country houses to castles; from cruise ships to listed buildings, and even a dungeon to celebrate such a juncture. Luke likened the ritual elements of mergers to a marriage ceremony. The official signings and the shaking of hands equated the takings of the oath. Speeches? Well, the best man could fulfill that part. The rest spoke for itself: photographs, dinner, cutting of the cake, drinks – plenty of drinks and a concluding brawl-up which might be a disco or a live band. Being the merger overseer, Luke could have been the minister/registrar/vicar, although the actual merger had already taken place when the administrators had witnessed the director's signings in a drab office about a month ago. Luke's role often stretched to marriage guidance counsellor, as like couples in marriage, parties fell in and out of love and had squabbles and little grievances. Contractees often sought his advice post-amalgamation on the finer points of the agreement, to clarify indemnity clauses or distribution of bonus shares.

The celebratory part served as faff, show, pomp, an opportunity to name-drop, recommend, hobnob, creep, promote, mingle, head-hunt and perhaps bump into a celebrity or linchpin. Rarely on any other occasion did Luke ever hear more bullshit. At least it was a day out of the office, a free meal and an opportunity to do some serious imbibing himself. Dr. Sui, however, had taken a special liking to Luke for some reason, which was not conducive to losing one's faculties.

Luke plucked a tall glass of Chablis from a passing waiter and sipped. A large-nosed woman with a furry boa hooted amongst portly male spectators competing for the most garish cummerbund. Luke wasn't sure if the men were laughing at her, with her or vying for the best view of her ample cleavage, which appeared augmented. At the back, a dark, stately woman nursed her wine, a smile of condescension on her face. She wore a dark brown pantsuit that matched her eyes and which gathered at her tiny waist. Her sights brushed against Luke's and paused. It grew intent. Without taking her eyes from his, she sipped her wine.

The headwaiter announced that dinner was ready. Luke stepped aside and a huge spray of flowers engulfed his arm – springy ferns smattered with oversized carnation heads. Real as they were, the carnations appeared plastic and garish. Luke selected the biggest and pinkest of them all and pinched off the head. He inserted the stem through the buttonhole on his lapel. He gave this ridiculous decoration a little pat. Now he really felt like a guest at a wedding.

Luke took his appointed seat at the head table next to Dr Sui of the Milliband Foundation and Dean Claybourne of Claybourne Associates. Dr Sui's interpreter sat not far away, although why Dr. Sui thought he needed one was beyond Luke, as Dr. Sui's English was impeccable. Three other seats were occupied by chiefs of subsidiaries, but the seat of Barry Brewer remained obtrusively vacant. His name-card rested on the tablecloth like an epitaph. Dean Claybourne's hatched-head nodded in Luke's direction. His sights latched onto Luke's pink carnation.

Luke nodded in kind.

Dr Sui stood, prompting all guests in the room to do the same. He raised his glass in a toast. 'To mark a truly momentous day and the beginning of a long and prosperous future for everyone in Milliband and Claybourne.' His sip led by example.

For a small and wiry man, Dr Sui's voice conveyed well. Luke admired his silver suit few could carry-off and guessed it to be a Ralph Lauren. A noble and honest suit without a frill or crease in sight.

Dr. Sui did not sit. He alluded to Luke. 'And I think a toast is in order for Mr. Luke Forrester, our merger overseer, who has been exemplary in making this merger a most pleasant and smooth evolution.'

Dr. Sui raised his glass to Luke. Luke coughed and took to his feet. The weight of a sea of eyes bore into him, a blend of bemusement, scrutiny and suspicion. Dr Sui clapped and a ripple condensed into a hearty round. Luke planted his hand against his suit in a formal gesture and his hand landed on the carnation. Luke gave a little bow, smiled and sat.

They order. Luke fancied freshwater salmon, artichokes and new potatoes and perhaps pecan pie from the sweet trolley. Seldom had Luke seen so many utensils with which to dissect his food. Few took heed, the sounds of collective dining commencing. Luke found Dr. Sui to be the perfect dinner companion, charming, polite and an attentive listener – marks of a true cosmopolitan and skills in short supply within this quarter. Dr. Sui indulged in his research projects into herbology, the subject of his doctorate and a passion he found time for in spite of his work for the foundation. He asserted that safeguarding against rogue batches lies at the heart of accurate research. Without intending to, Dr. Sui had implied Barry Brewer in this remark. Dean Claybourne shifted in his seat, although on paper, he was not accountable for Brewer's little transgressions. Enclave companies often operated separately to the parent company. Luke's blog entry had sprouted a thread as tendrinous as a taproot. *The Corporate Friend*, it seemed, had hooked itself a stinky fish. Luke had forwarded the webpage via email to Dr. Sui, expressing his concerns. Dr. Sui's reply was brief, formal and troubled. Dr. Sui saw only the best in people and any evidence to the contrary was to him, a personal betrayal. If Luke had mentioned Brewer's name at the table now, Dr. Sui would have denied any knowledge of him.

Captain Birdseye would soon find himself an orphan within the business world – no one was going to want the smell of his fish on their fingers. Luke sipped the excellent Chardonnay as a little toast. Goodbye, Captain Birdseye. May troubled waters splatter your cream suit, evermore. Goodbye and farewell.

Claybourne expressed his agreement with Dr. Sui in a bid to dissociate himself from one who was no longer invited to Dr. Sui's party. 'It's been an absolute pleasure,' he'd continued. 'As smooth as a round of golf. Do you play golf, Mr. Forrester?' Claybourne's accolade had drawn the attention of his associates, all eyes of which were trained upon Luke's pink carnation.

'Well, I…'

'I insist we meet up, exchange some moves. My swing doesn't always measure up; seems to always pull left.' Claybourne skewered a piece of swordfish and snagged it between his teeth. He chewed noisily. 'Tell me, what you do when you're not coordinating mergers?'

The rabble at the table softened. Associates of both parties were now watching Luke with faint smiles. Luke's eyes grazed over Claybourne who had decided to postpone further dissection of his swordfish until Luke had responded. Luke's right eyelid dragged over. 'Well…I do have a cute collection of Ferraris.'

A general rumble of approval rippled over the table. Claybourne skewered another morsel with a knowing nod.

'I enjoy the theatre,' Luke continued, 'particularly the opera; the proms are greatly anticipated and I endeavour to attend the Albert Hall in person. I indulge in beer festivals too, as I have a passion for local brews; I love cricket, the arts, watching rugger on a Saturday afternoon…'

They were still nodding and Claybourne continued to chomp.

'I dabble in watercolours whilst listening to jazz or the classical guitar, it depends on the mood. I have been known to throw clay onto the potter's wheel and therefore have a collection of skewed pots. I go skiing in Austria every winter, fly-fishing in Coniston, Munroe hiking in Scotland, kayaking in the Pennines. And I love film, especially the silent era.'

An associate or two had stopped eating now and were tittering; smiles of others were spreading thin.

'Wine tasting in Bordeaux is a little vice of mine, but square dancing keeps me in shape. Pigeon shooting, classic literature, a spot of chess takes care of my mental reflexes, as does fencing.

But then again, if I am feeling especially wistful, there's always tossing.'

The table had fallen silent. Dr. Sui hesitated before leaning towards his interpreter for clarification.

Claybourne faltered in his chewing. 'Tossing?'

'Yes.'

The interpreter shrugged at Dr. Sui's inquisition and whispered, 'It is an English expression…er…'

A compressed wheezing fit filled the interlude, which to Luke sounded like an effort to die quietly. Bewilderment forestalled Claybourne's next mouthful. He quickly superseded this with an affable smile that implied he was in on the joke. 'Yes, indeed, Mr. Forrester. We are all busy people with perhaps, a little more on our plates than most. We deserve all our indulgences we can muster, and why the hell not?' Claybourne's eyes fastened to Luke's seeking some sort of token from him before closing the subject.

Luke didn't feel the need to add anything.

Luke wandered up to the roof terrace as the speeches went under way. How he lamented the palms of those who could not flee the clapping ritual. Well, that was the price of these things, he supposed. Tea-lights dotted the makeshift bar – weather-dependent, and this evening certainly accommodated. A balmy breeze ferried jasmine scent; a copper-smudge of sunset backlit the London skyline. He ordered himself a double-whisky and took a barstool. He sipped. Cat entered his head for the countless time today, which piqued him – Cat with her edgy loiter and her unerring awareness of him. She'd acquired a thigh chain to hide her scar. He hated it. The cheapness erased something that made her Cat; her potent occupancy of space, her lightning reflexes, her pissed-off expression – and what did a cheap-looking piece of costume jewellery contribute? The choice was as inexcusable as the bumbling romp with the laddered tights last week. But then, why should he care what she chose as an embellishment?

She was just *Cat*. He wanted to be rid of her. Watching her parade had a chaotic effect upon his mind – his eyes wouldn't stop sticking to her and even when she was obscured, he found himself looking for her. Such an affliction robbed his ability to pace himself throughout the performance, just like before. For this reason, he had done the business in the shower afterwards every time this week.

At least the pigeons had returned. He had paid his penance, it seemed. The sleep clinicians had proved themselves correct again; his body had shut down in the name of survival and he had awoken in his chair. A paper-thin buffer had been restored around his cranium, hardly one would call a shield – but then, paper-thin was better than nothing. He touched his brow to assure himself both sides were equal.

He cast a thought to Fox – a little pact to adhere to. If Cat should invade his brain, then Fox will follow. Equal thought for both. Favour none. He closed his eyes a moment and conjured the image of Fox's milky white skin and tapering limbs. And the way she moved – she certainly owned her body; she could replay a move with the highest precision. He opened his eyes.

The woman with the brown pantsuit was sitting at the further end of the bar. Had she been there all along? She sipped what looked to be martini from a fluted glass and watched him. She blinked slowly and the corner of her lip curled up.

Luke had no doubt she would pleasure his groin most exquisitely. By the cant of her head, she seemed to believe so herself. And what more could he hope for than sweaty fast-food sex in a hotel room, her bearing down on him against an Edwardian ceiling embellished with a small chandelier? At which point, a saboteur clambered into his head. Luke could picture her wearing that cat mask as he came. And then afterwards he could lie awake, listening to her soft snoring for the remainder of the night.

Luke raised his whisky on ice with a harsh clink. He followed this with a protracted leer that would have deterred the most hard-boiled hooker.

Apprehension immediately clouded her expression. She crossed her arms over the bar and averted her face. A moment later, she was gone.

Luke took the late train to Birmingham New Street before hitching a taxi to his flat. Few places depressed him more than stations and platforms at the late hour. To him, they were ghostly places that should no longer exist when people were at their homes or in their beds, except perhaps for people like him. Luke entered the flat exhausted but knew sleep would shirk him yet. He entered his bedroom and cast his sights over the closing sequence of *Domestic Bliss*. Cat was feeding Fox grapes. Fox parted her lips suggestively and allowed the grape to nestle between. Slowly the grape disappeared into her mouth. Cat watched impassively, wearing an Egyptian tunic and that infernal thigh chain. She plucked another grape. Unadulterated disdain surged through him. The pomp, the fakery of it all. It seemed he had not left the Sheraton – could he ever? And who were these people that served him? Yes, they did what he wanted yet he had nothing He could only watch and never be a part of anything real. Such a thin and cheap veneer of sleaze. Luke felt no wish to peek through the binoculars this evening.

He snatched up his bottle of whisky and flicked on the TV but internal sights and sounds invaded his mind; bones splintering, a joint displaced, flesh the colour of gesso chalk. How he wished his father was here right now to whip him. Whip him and whip him into oblivion, whip him until he blubbed like a big baby and let his father watch impassively.

But his father was no longer here to do this service. The lights opposite went out and that's just what Luke needed – to become invisible, even to light. Luke would do what he must do, just as he had done so numerous times before, to remind himself of what he was. He took down the aerial photograph of Warwick from the wall. Utter black made the ensuing task possible.

Chapter 20

JETLAG was an affliction that held little meaning to Gemma until now. Wasn't it just a commuter's disease, or a penance of the flighty rich that owned properties on all quarters? Gemma had little time for those who made public the mess-up of the circadian rhythm for such reasons. Dr Jacobs, at the practice for one – who regularly flew to Australia to study cutting-edge procedures in oncology. Didn't people like him just use jetlag as a license to make known they were well-travelled, worldly people who led hectic lives? Oh, the unfairness of it all!

Right now she would take it all back. Two am had become eleven o'clock. And right now, eight am felt like five. She hated that clock that said *time to get up*. Someone had piped glue between her eyelids and the roof of her mouth had taken on a scaly quality. Her stomach protested the most, demanding food late at night and then going on strike to the point of constipation until noon. How did Charlene cope with such a brutal daily routine for so long? She worked full-time in a shoe shop too.

Shamefully, Gemma had fallen asleep at her desk twice last week. No one had noticed but Gemma had to take vigilance between eleven and twelve. Whilst the chief practitioner was talking to her about a patient's files the swirly pattern on the wallpaper behind him appeared to be moving. She could feel her eyes going. The indignity of falling asleep whilst someone was talking to you – especially one Dr. Sheti Nedgati MB ChB BSc was a prospect Gemma could barely comprehend. If only she could be left alone – just for a moment, she could get through the day. Gemma went to the filing room where few ventured with the intention of having two minutes and found two had become fifteen. She returned with a stack of patients' files no one needed.

As her work ended at one, at least she could go home and have a kip but this second-hand sleep did nothing to clear her head or shake off her fatigue. The considerable savings ensconced behind the electric meter gave her no joy. She didn't even have the energy to go into town to deposit the money in the bank.

Gemma came-to abruptly. She shot up and head-rush slapped her in the face in a riptide. When the snowstorm had cleared, the clock's hands had shifted an hour. The light had changed and the stillness of the house indicated Ben had gone to school without waking her. She groaned.

Gemma decided to call in sick. The practice had enjoyed her constant service without a single sick day for over four years. Well, gastroenteritis demanded at least three days' recovery. Yes, diarrhea too. It must have been the chicken tikka last night. Yes, I will drink plenty of fluids and get plenty of rest. Gemma dropped the earpiece onto its cradle as soon as she had done with her lament and went back to bed.

She roused at lunchtime feeling a little better, but her new disposition did not last long when the dreaded sight of Colby and Vernon's cream-coloured envelope awaited her attention.

A brief letter, it simply said:

'…In light of Mr. Liam Greene's abscondment and our clients' surrender of the debt to us, we plan to enforce a sale of the property to release the necessary funds. We are at present putting our case together for the courts. You will be contacted again regarding this matter in due course.'

Gemma read the letter again in disbelief. How could they enforce a sale? The status quo she believed she had attained evaporated into smoke. Suddenly the assurances of Terry Greene, of John Geary and the general tenet the law protected the innocent victim pitched on sandy ground.

So this grubby client didn't like her status quo? Was the letter a ploy to give it a little shake, to make her panic, to squash her resolve? She had been right about the sediments of dark dust in the house. They were still there, waiting to congregate from the crevasses.

They were waiting.

Were they watching?

Gemma glanced to the window expecting to see a big black hearse outside again.

She screwed the letter into a tight ball and pitched it across the room.

She cried.

Like sleep, emotional catharsis made time meaningless. She let her reflexes take over. All rationality of thought remained suspended within a torrent of tears and spasms. The back of her throat hurt, her eyes stung and her lips puffed up. And within this so-called tight-knit community, she felt alone.

The collar of her dressing gown was saturated. She unpeeled the covering and wiped her face on the hem. In her baggy T-shirt and elasticated trousers, she probably resembled a pair of pillows. Gemma shuffled to the kitchen to make a cup of tea. She ought to ring her mother or her sister, but would regret the decision, knowing the conversation would veer to Liam – if only she hadn't married Liam. Gemma envied Zeeta at the practice who seemed to involve her mother in everything she did. They shopped together and even swapped clothes and makeup. As for Gemma's father, silly old fool cared more about his potting shed than anything else – and living in Cornwall, what could they do anyway? At this moment, Gemma believed John Geary and Terry to be her only real line of defense. The thought of her considerable savings behind the electric meter gave her some solace. Now that her mortgage payments were up to date, she would use the money to pay necessary legal fees.

Gemma clutched John Geary's previous letter like a tear-soaked handkerchief and made an appointment to see him next week – his only slot for a month. With her head now clear, something didn't add up. Why did Colby and Vernon purchase the debt? She wondered if this client of theirs was hiding more than their identities. Of course, she could choose to fight, but with what? She did not have an inexhaustible supply of money and she could lose the house to legal fees without any help from Colby and Vernon.

The phone sounded. Jerkily, she picked up.

Phil's voice drifted towards her. 'He no-like body jewellery.'

Phil's impertinence knocked her out of the preceding moment. She took a breath and visualised her impulse to punch his shiny forehead. A slow exhalation helped disperse the image. How could it be that Phil was saying *he no-like* again? Gemma thought last night's routine went well albeit the steam-iron sequence made her face red. But then, anything was better than scrubbing floors. 'You said I couldn't wear tights,' she uttered.

'The maintainer of the starlet does *not* wear jewellery.'

Gemma tried not to lose it. The money had become more important to her now than ever. She would happily wear one of Annabel's dog tutus if it made her voyeur happy and the money kept coming in. 'What about your lecture last week about "strategic arrangements of focal points?"'

'I've just said,' Phil griped, 'the maintainer of the starlet does *not* wear jewellery.'

'A garter, then. I'll wear a garter.'

Phil paused in thought. 'Nothin' fancy,' he asserted. 'Black or grey – and no gathers. Plain. Keep it plain.'

And then the tone flatlined.

Perhaps she should just dye a bandage black and use that.

Gemma found an unfussy garter not far from Annabel's – a black thing that sadly gathered at the top. Well, garters weren't meant to be plain. Her trip to town had cost her Ben's company at teatime. Gemma didn't have the gumption to apologise yet again for being an absent mother. Ben didn't seem to mind. He reiterated almost defensively, 'I've told you before, Mum, I'm not helpless. I don't expect you to do everything for me while you're doing that evening job.' She wished he didn't have to be so grown-up about it.

Mark and Charlene met her at the usual place in Warwick in his tatty Volvo transit stacked with amplifiers and a drum-kit. They mooched at leisure in the front seat as though Gemma wasn't there. Gemma entered the flat and dressed in a saucy baker's outfit. In Phil's kitchen scene, she worked the dough and worked the dough until her biceps knotted up. She took license to Phil's script, balling her fists and pummelled for good measure. Fox's hands emerged from behind as per-script, joined in the pummelling and as per-script, the pummelling grew frantic. But Gemma could not leave it there. The pummelling had become immensely gratifying. Gemma blessed the agonising cramp in her arms and found creative ways to disfigure the dough mixture. A crater here, a dimple there. Bobby Charlton without the comb-over now has no dome to speak of and his toady companion now has an even lower forehead. Charlene's false fingernail became a casualty of Gemma's 'friendly fire,' the polymer splitting in two.

'Fuck,' she spat.

At that point, Gemma stopped, her breast heaving.

Charlene and Gemma baked a perfect loaf, prepared earlier. And Charlene grudgingly accepted Gemma's peace-offering of marmalade solders. Charlene as usual relished these phallic creations with eroticism that verged onto the burlesque.

'He no-like knuckle fights.' Phil this time dished out this critique in front of Charlene at the flat the following evening.

Gemma conceded his point. 'I'm sorry. I guess I got a little carried away with the dough.'

Phil's expression did not change. 'Not at the price of Charlene's fingernail.'

'*False* fingernail.'

Phil was glaring at her. Gemma held her tongue.

Gemma spent the following evening cleaning floors for Charlene again. Penance, she was certain. Charlene had a vast collection of sweet wrappers this time, which she scattered to all quarters of the room like a hen feeder. Just when Gemma thought she had gathered every one, Charlene pitched another sweet wrapper. When Gemma was done, Charlene gave Gemma a pat on her posterior, sufficiently smart to make her eyes water.

Phil called the following day. 'Your outfit was creased at the back. And your hair was all messed-up.'

Gemme kept her tone even. 'Has the bastard made a list?'

'Oh, that didn't come from him.'

Gemma swallowed her indignity. She kept thinking about the money and the court costs. She took her usual route to the pickup point and found Mark's Volvo had already gone. The drizzle was gathering momentum and gusts whipped at her jacket – impractical attire for this change in weather, but not for the interior of a car she had been expecting. She had come too far now to turn back and fetch her waterproofs.

She raced to the bus station and waited ten minutes for the last bus to Templar Avenue. Phil couldn't blame her for this. Gemma seethed at Charlene. Gemma had her excuses ready. God, she was really going to drop Charlene in it for doing this to her!

Gemma fussed with her hair which frizzed up regardless. The rain had completely smudged her mascara and Gemma had bought only eyebrow pencil and false eyelashes to fix her eyes.

Gemma disembarked at the corner and trotted to Templeton Court. The lights on the top floor were already aglow. Gemma spurted the last hundred yards to the apartment block. Once in the stairwell, she grasped the newel post for a quick breather. The reflection on the glass doors presented one dressed for a shop at Sainsbury's rather than a participant in *Domestic Bliss*. The rain had flattened her parting and crisped up the ends of her hair. The overhead lights brought a ghoulish cast to the planes of her face and her carrier bag sagged within her grasp. Phil's housemaid's outfit must be a soggy and crumpled mess now. At least she had Ben's mask. Her little disguise had become her succor. With her cat mask on, she need not exhibit an expression she did not feel.

With *Domestic Bliss* already underway, Gemma could not ready herself in the bathroom, for her watcher would see her sneak in the background. This meant getting prepared in the foyer outside the flat. She bunched up her mess of hair and tied it in a pigtail. She stripped off to her underwear, backing into the shadows. Nimbly she skipped into her housemaid's outfit which felt damp at the hem. She crushed her day clothes into her carrier bag and then remembered the spare keys. She yanked her jacket from the carrier bag. Her snatching breaths echoed against the empty stairwell. She grappled for the keys which spilled from her jacket pocket onto the floor with a clatter. In automation, she lowered her hand to the floor and scooped them up.

She inserted the keys and pushed the door open. Charlene's usual sleaze-funk oozed from the stereo somewhere nearby and an occasional clop from those three-inch heels. Gemma remembered to don her mask – a close call, and dropped her bag by the door. She inched her way in. Gemma adopted a jaunty lope, purposeful and implying design. She would ease her way into Charlene's routine – a full body massage tonight, though how Charlene planned to this without Gemma's assistance

Gemma could not imagine, unless of course, she planned to pull that stunt with the gecko that first time.

Charlene's hair came into view. She was sitting on that high stool of hers, heels resting on the crossbar. Another figure emerged. Gemma stopped dead.

The second figure, a bottle-blonde, wore a cat mask – the cutesy generic kind Gemma had seen at Annabel's. The bottle-blond approached Charlene and grazed her hand against Charlene's shoulder. Charlene canted her head and allowed Cat's lips to caress her neck. Gemma retreated towards what little concealment the doorway offered. From there she could see how a new girl could change the whole routine. The blonde cupped Charlene's breast in her right hand, a liberty Phil's script had never permitted Gemma's 'Cat.' The new cat possessed creamy legs that terminated at white platforms. She wore a bikini top that resembled corals delectable yet not upstaging. Again, focal points deficient in Gemma's Cat.

As Cat's left hand landed on Fox's other breast and drew her closer, Gemma's vision blurred. Nano-pins pricked her throat and pushed down to her lower gut.

It wasn't that Phil had denigrated Gemma to ironing, changing the sheets, dusting the plants, massaging Fox, kneading the dough and scrubbing the floors – God, how she *scrubbed* the floors! It wasn't Phil's method of laying her off. It wasn't even the demise of her once lucrative source of income. She just felt so... *sullied*. The voyeur had taken something from her; he had passed off his assessment of her physical form and then cast her into the gutter like some used piece of meat. Gemma had bared her scar, her moles, her navel, her stretch-marks, her moves, albeit not so refined as Charlene's, her efforts, her expression, her interpretation, *herself*.

Gemma was certainly not cut out for this sort of profession, not like Charlene or those who worked in strip clubs. Don't take it personal, they'd probably say. Did they have a secret strategy, or were they fundamentally different in disposition?

She despised that black window with the eyes. Anything by association would be tarnished. If she discovered her voyeur had blonde hair she would loathe all blonde men. Ditto if he had brown eyes, went hiking, bred pigeons, went to Ascot or watched Wimbledon. Phil's condition that his client remains anonymous was perhaps beneficial to her state of mind. By the same token, Gemma made the promise never to establish any facts about Phil's 'client.'

Gemma retreated from the room and quietly closed the door. She rested her bare shoulder-blades against the panel. The wood felt cool against her skin. She no longer cared if a resident perchanced to spot a half-naked woman in a skimpy housemaid's outfit in the hall. What did it matter now anyway?

To salvage what little pride she had left, she fished out her mobile and dialled Phil's number.

Phil answered expecting Gemma's voice, as the caller's name was displayed on his phonepad. 'Yeah, er...Hi Jeannie. Sorry I never got to tell you. There's been a change in plan.'

'Evidently.'

Phil breezed over her caustic tone. 'Suzie's gonna be standin' in for a while Just to test the waters.'

'I see.'

'Look, it ain't like that.'

'Explain, exactly.'

'My client just fancies a change, that's all. He likes things just-so. He's the boss after all.'

'So, that's it. Sling your hook, then.'

'Look, he's been real patient with you. Consider yourself lucky you're still on the books.'

'I'm not on your books.'

'What d' you mean you're not on my books? I've got your name right here.'

'Someone by the name of Jillie or Jeannie is on your books. But my name is Gemma. Do you hear me? *Gemma.*'

She ended the call.

The rain had eased into a murky drizzle that permeated her jacket, her jeans and her shoes. An endless trudge later, her clothes had sponged up enough moisture to encumber her walk. Her socks squelched and her collar doused her nape. She barely noticed. An apathetic fog muted all thought except a meaningless meander. For that she was grateful.

Once home, Gemma toweled herself dry and changed her clothes. Ben had already gone up to his room as it was half-past-eleven. Ben was changing into his pyjamas when she knocked and entered.

He turned, a frown teasing his eyes. 'Oh. Hi, Mum. You're back early.'

Gemma sat on his bed. 'Ben, I'm sorry about everything.'

Ben pulled on his pyjama top without pause. 'What for?'

'For not being around when I should.' She faltered when she noticed a bruise on Ben's ankle. 'How did you get that mark?'

Ben fastened his buttons. 'What mark?'

'On your ankle.'

Ben lifted his foot like a flamingo in mid-strut. 'Oh, I fell.'

'When?'

'Last week in the kitchen. It's nothing. I just lost my balance; hadn't got hold of my crutches properly.'

'Why didn't you shout me?'

Ben sat beside her. 'You were upstairs getting ready for the performance. I didn't want to bother you.'

Gemma fell silent. Not once during her lamentation over her ravaged pride had Ben entered her mind; the sacrifices he had made. Her stupid pride, her stupid tenacity.

Ben broke the moment. 'Why are you back so early?'

Gemme's smile was grim. 'It's over, Ben.'

Ben's expression did not change but the lights in his eyes wavered. 'Oh…Why?'

Gemma shrugged to make light of it. 'These things just happen. They were looking for something different, that's all.'

Desperation crept into his tone. 'But I don't understand. You've come this far. You were doing good, they liked you. Perhaps if I made another mask, better than the last one…'

Gemma stopped him there. 'No, Ben.'

Her last words were brutal but necessary. Gemma could not encourage Ben's delinquent imagination if embellished lies become the result. Gemma patted Ben's knee to lighten the atmosphere. 'But this is good news for us because it means I can spend more time with you and I've saved enough money to pay the bills *and* take you out for a treat.'

Her words fell short of the effect hoped for. Ben nodded slowly. Gemma kissed the top of Ben's head, not knowing what else to say. Yet again, she proved her ineffectiveness when faced with such situations.

Ben had known no other world than Southsbury, Caester School, the club and the town. This might have sufficed for some, but not Ben. Ben needed an annex world to make this one tolerable – a world that promised something more: glamour, strangeness, opportunity. For a period, this concept-world had brushed against his; detained him from the realities of his father and their new situation.

Ben exhibited no sign that anything had changed the next day. He readied himself for school in his usual blasé fashion. But on tidying Ben's room that afternoon, Gemma came across a crumpled crayon drawing down the side of Ben's bed. She uncreased the paper to see a depiction of a crowded theatre. In the spotlight, a dancing figure in a cat mask pirouetted. The faces in the audience were indistinct, pink smudges. Only the central figure in a silver and gold leotard exhibited detail in the form of pencil strokes around the mask and the dappled outfit.

Gemma could not be certain how long she had stared at the picture, the scene embraced her. The crowd anticipated the figure's next move; a perfect performance as always. Gemma wished she could have been the figure in his picture. She wished Ben could be in the front row, watching her, applauding, joining her in this other world. Away from this one.

Gemma decided once she had flattened out the picture to take Terry up on his offer and have Ben for the night.

Chapter 21

THE new girl glided like satin across his vision – cool, soft, a little oily. She was exactly what he imagined he needed. Without a blemish and without substance, and dare he say it, bland. He experienced a cool serenity when she first appeared and a fanning out of visual channels, his eyes liberated from the old cat. The sequences engaged his senses gestalt, not in parts and without the old cat hijacking the whole thing. Intended or not.

Luke observed the new cat attired in a candyfloss kind of cat mask, glide her cheek against the back of Fox's hand. No longer a master and servant theme, Philip had adopted a glamour couple approach. The sequences suggested Fox and Cat mingled with the elite, led professional lives and enjoyed high culture. They supped wine from fluted glasses and draped one another in fine jewellery and kissed the adorned body parts. Luke watched like a tourist on the ideal beach, admiring the perfect sunset and sipping an ice-cold beer and fooling himself he wasn't bored. Luke drifted once or twice. Not in micro-sleep, sadly. He just drifted.

He climaxed watching a milk and cream entanglement on the couch at the end. No laddered tights and no fracas with the dough. Dependable Philip had delivered. Luke decided on a Motown soundtrack the following evening. Mendelssohn at times overly grand for a medley of pearl jewellery, tiaras, strappy shoes and what appeared to be supermarket plonk.

A cloud of umbrage had for some reason descended over him when he had taken up his station at his binoculars this time. Of course, he had his reasons, his sleep showing signs of wanderlust again. He'd had an hour last night and now his eyeballs were pincushions for a bed of nails. Milk and cream offered little reimbursement for such a brutal day. Always an insufficient tonic for a torment few could understand. And at this moment, torment didn't come close.

The new cat appeared on cue. Luke's mood darkened to petulance. Cat pertly made her way to the fridge and lifted out a punnet of strawberries. Fox emerged from behind the drapes and perched herself upon the breakfast bar, her lithe legs scissoring with grace. Oral sex with strawberries. Disdain as of the other night revisited him.

Luke tried to focus, to go with it. He had to. Music and a state of mind had proved effective in making any routine sexier than it actually was. Marvin's voice gave solace, an excellent choice after all. A ghetto lament moulded with such class. Luke's gut was putty in that man's voice.

Luke had drifted again and when he came-to, his eyes beheld a scene that punched between his eyes like a lobotomy. His blinking reflex had suspended; his glass of whisky-dregs dangled within his grasp.

A third figure had come out of nowhere.

At first, the figure could not be identified for a refusal to fit into any category his subconscious had constructed during his lifetime. The 'thing' burned into his retinas; a morbidly-obese man – a sumo? The thing was wearing the former Cat's mask. The out-of-proportion body affronted the human form, being too large for the head. Luke could barely stand to look at it. Fox and her new partner were still engaged in their strawberry oral-play upon the breakfast bar, their mouths closing in on a particularly juicy specimen and the prospect of lips meeting. But seeing that…that *thing* in the background commandeered his eyes and sucked all eroticism from the scene like planetary mass into a black hole. Of course, this usurper was his former cat, dressed in a fat man suit – piqued at Philip's bedside manner upon dismissing her.

A conglomeration of baked potatoes and that wretched garter stretched to breaking point on her...*its* right thigh wasted no time with its mission. The abomination strode with unnerving speed for one so big towards Philip's glamour couple. The new cat turned and her head pivoted backwards as though receiving a blow. The strawberry popped out of her mouth. This new cat and her creamy substance was no match for a stack of King Edward's. Her cherubic little mouth yawned a mighty rictus. Luke could hear her bubbling scream in his head. She leapt from the breakfast bar as though the Formica had tasered her like a cattle prod. The unfortunate new cat landed directly in the sumo's path where Sumo dutifully lurched her ponderous belly forward to administer a perfect belly-but. Fox's new devotee flew head-first onto the couch like a ragdoll where her fluffy little cat mask pulled awry. No reflex was quick enough. Her creamy form and her lopsided mask flapped from the apartment like a freshly-plucked hen.

Fox's demeanour, what he could see of it, exhibited one of incense rather than incomprehension. Luke had no trouble lip-reading her initial utterance, 'Fuck *me*!' when she had laid eyes upon her new potato-sumo-cat friend.

Luke plonked his empty glass onto the shelf with a harsh rap; a paltry outlet for his mounting infuriation. How could this wretched cat just invade his arrangement like this? Make a mockery of the precious few hours he had to distract himself from the hellish eternity of wakefulness? That wretched cat...that wretched bloody...*woman!*

Luke balled his hand into a fist and brought it down hard enough to make his whisky glass leap. He cared little for the needles that shot through his wrist. Luke strode across the room and killed Marvin whilst singing about 'what's goin' on.' Sorry, an insult to the eyes must never encounter the sublime to the ears. He grappled for his mobile knowing fully Philip had switched his off – Philip's infernal Riverside commitments! Not that Luke had cause to ring Philip at this hour before now, so why should Philip keep his phone on? Luke cast the useless thing onto his bed.

Luke's sights drifted to the window. A fracas was unfurling that made the dough-pummelling sequence the other night look like a cake decoration session. Luke resumed his station and peeked through. Fox in her two-piece glitter bikini, silver stilettos and tiara was being worked against the wall by the sumo like that dough the other night. Simulating sex. And from here, Sumo's member could clearly be seen; a small worm-like thing that sprung back and forth with each thrust. Sumo's balls dangled udder-like just behind this worm-thing, ensconced within folds of fat. And all while Cat gazed impassive upon her 'lover' from behind her static cat mask.

Fox's lithe frame could not resist the cut and thrust. Her tiara drifted askew. The maw on her face contorted; the strap on her bikini crept down to her elbow. With a grimace, she eased her form from Sumo's urgent embrace like toothpaste from a tube. Once liberated from the thing's clutches, Fox darted, bereft of footwear, to the bedroom; a pointless manoeuvre, Luke thought, as the exit was located the other way. Sumo was in no hurry. She adopted a pendulous lope, her arms swinging at her sides and her member flopping about like a skinned rabbit.

Fox pushed the door shut – an act of futility, as the interior doors (bar the bathroom) possessed no locks. Fox's willowy biceps surely stood no chance against those housemaids' arms snug within that fat man suit. And indeed, that sumo monstrosity with the small cat's head bulldozed through that door and the waif on the other side, as a bull against cardboard. Fox climbed on the bed. Sumo didn't seem to mind. She embraced Fox from behind, her huge manbreasts compressing against Fox's slender back and proceeded to pump Fox's posterior as a remorseless piston. Fox's tiara by now hung by a thread, oscillating with Sumo's motions like an insect on a spider's web. The fabric of Sumo's abdomen pleated up against the manbreasts in Sumo's endeavour to relieve him...*itself*, evoking a rubbery, squeaky sound. Please God, Luke would never hear it.

Sumo permitted Fox a small reprieve – to toy with Fox, as a cat with a mouse. Fox clambered over the bed screaming. Luke could hear the fury in his head as see her mouth contort.

Sumo pawed a bottle of body lotion from the bedside table. Luke could barely stand to watch. She gathered the small of Fox's back between the cloying folds of those sumo thighs. The skinned rabbit thing rested gently on top of Fox's upper back. Sumo squeezed lotion – a generous portion judging by the dribbles through her fingers. Lovingly, Sumo massaged Fox's back and shoulders. Fox's legs scissored furiously behind her. Sumo canted her cat-head as one not to be rushed. A full body massage apparently must be exercised scrupulously and with exactitude. Sumo took a generous portion upon herself, daubing her manbreasts, abdomen and thighs. She flattened her palms against the rubber and made circular motions. With such an ample body to cover, Sumo deliberated, ensuring no area would be missed. The oversized nipples on the manbreasts glistened proudly like glace cherries. And the bellybutton – a grotesque outer – like a walnut.

The nine baked potatoes with a cat's head finally dismounted. Fox squirmed herself from Sumo's cavern like a potholer burrowing from a cave-mouth. Fox appeared no worse for the onslaught of Sumo's ardour, writhing with renewed fury, her mouth contorting and her lipstick smudged. She skittered across the bedroom and fell through the door. For an instant, Luke could not see her, having been obscured by a partitioning wall. Sumo's sheer size meant she/it covered ground effortlessly before Fox could recover on the other side. Sumo gathered Fox's head, now on her knees, to her oily breast. Sumo patted Fox's head in a come-to-poppa gesture that reeked of depravity. As though Fox's humiliation weren't enough, Fox stumbled to her knees again. Luke closed his eyes an instant, the moment too agonising.

Luke opened his eyes to behold Cat-thing standing to attention in the centre of the room, arms akimbo in true sumo fashion, about to participate in a body lock. Fox's hand emerged from somewhere below. The fingers grappled for purchase on the breakfast bar, but being Formica, gave little joy. Fox's hand vanished. But Fox's tenacity was admirable. Her white-knuckled fingers seeking purchase from the kitchen table instead. Fox's head emerged jerkily from below. She looked ridiculous. Luke wished he'd abstained from the binoculars earlier. Her other hand soon followed. The muscles on her shoulder blades oscillated with effort as she heaved her body weight up, although Luke could see Fox's BMI wasn't the problem, for hers was like a bird. The oil on the floor caused the difficulty.

Fox anchored both elbows onto the tabletop and steadily straightened her pelvis. Once safely on both feet, Fox proceeded to walk her hands across the furniture as a novice in roller skates. Her eyes fixated upon the safety of the Persian rug which offered sufficient purchase for her slippery heels. Body oil dripped from her hair and slicked her arms. She seethed; Luke could see profanities spitfiring through her clenched teeth. Her tiara had deserted her as well as her composure. Once she had traversed the room, Fox snatched up her bag by the door and spun her head to hurl a constricted glower at Cat. Cat's posture hadn't changed, her sumo body squared up for action and her arms akimbo. Her cat face however merely watched dispassionate. As always.

Fox exited the apartment, seemingly without a sound, but Luke would bet the apartment shuddered as the door crashed behind her.

Cat now stood alone, her greasy fat man suit now more like a basted chicken ready for roasting. Luke's infuriation sat small and hard in his chest. *What now, Cat? What are you going to do now?*

At that moment, Cat's undersized head panned across the room and stopped at a point directly ahead. At him. She looked directly at him.

Luke drew back on impulse; his breaths caught in this throat. *The impudence of her!* Luke knit his lip to a firm line and curbed the urge to swipe his binoculars from the shelf.

Not until that moment had Luke considered the long-term effects of Cat's sumo performance. Could he ever watch *Domestic Bliss* again without being reminded of Cat's skinned rabbit gonads dangling between those sumo legs? The glace cherry man-nipples? The burlesque garter stretched to breaking point? And what about the anal sex simulation with Fox, the cut and thrust? Could Fox or any candidate like her divert him as before? Would *Domestic Bliss* forever seem a mockery of itself – for that cat?

Luke dare not think. He peeked through the binoculars again. Cat was still looking at him, her sumo legs astride and her arms akimbo. *What the hell is she doing, just standing like that?* The tight knot of frustration bloomed outwards from his chest, invading his lungs, his liver and his lower gut. Luke knuckled his binoculars, sending the eyepiece swivelling on its mount with a squeak. Perhaps he should go over there himself? Grab her by the elbow and storm her out of the apartment? But he could not stand the thought of that infernal mask staring impassively at him as he did so. And what if he unmasked her? At this moment such a deed was unthinkable. Her face, whatever her features would etch into his memory like a hot brand. No. He wished not to see further than the housemaid's arms or that scar. Forever, she would remain the cat that lurked in the background kneading the dough or scrubbing the floors.

And yet, Luke lowered his head to the binoculars again. The cat-thing was squat-thrusting on one leg. The other foot rested upon the chair and her arms were still akimbo. He could hear the rubbery squeaks in his head with each thrust. When she had done with her right leg, she swapped over and repeated. Another ten.

A tedious display, he thought, but then, she wasn't doing this for his entertainment, and the point was made patently clear. She paused to give her crotch a quick scratch before she progressed to forward bends. Two pillows conjoined by a pleat where an anus would have been presented themselves to him. Each pillow appeared to nod at one another as Cat's pelvis pulled up and down. Her garter strained with every bend. Cat, in reliable fashion, was not one for clocking off early. She made herself comfortable upon the couch and placed an order over the phone. She waited, her pendulous arms spread across the back of the couch in an overly-casual manner. Luke didn't get a view of the unfortunate delivery person at the door, but Cat had her handbag at the ready and compensated the person – Luke believed – with a tip. The sight of a sumo carrying a handbag would never leave him.

Cat returned to the couch embracing a pizza and a coke. Vexation surged through him again. So, she was just going to sit there and gorge a pizza at his expense? This was *his* time; *his* apartment. Cat unfolded a serviette and affixed the fabric to her oily chest as a mockery to such etiquette. The thing was still crooked. Box on lap, she lifted out a wedge and sunk her teeth into this Italian delicacy. Strands of mozzarella coiled down to her walnut-thing. Crescents of pepperoni flopped down to join its cheesy company. She flicked the bits away.

Luke could bear to watch no more. He took to his feet and paced the room. Philip was going to hear about this, by God! Morning couldn't come soon enough. Luke scanned the room for his bottle of whisky to refill, but the blasted thing seemed to have gone for a walk. What did he have left? TV, books, music, at this moment, all such orthodox modes of diversion filled him with despair, and now robbed of the one fix that came close to making his affliction bearable. The cat commandeered. She waited at the delta of all his senses.

What choice did he have but to wait out the end? Until Cat had done with her pizza and coke engorgement?

Luke took a last look. Cat's pizza box now exhibited a detritus of pizza rinds and flecks of cheese. She lifted her can of Pepsi and took a nip. On lowering the can, she dabbed her lips diffidently and crushed the serviette into a ball. She stood to clear away the rubbish, presenting him once more with the two dimpled pillows saying hello to one another. She pushed the rubbish through the flaps of a nearby kitchen-disposer. And then, as an encore, she turned, remote in hand and faced Luke. She cocked her leg as a parody of passing wind. With that she depressed the off switch. The lights died.

Luke's face fell into darkness. He knew by the tension in his facial muscles that he wore a stern expression – his lips pressed together, his temples clenched and his jaw set.

The attack came on ten minutes after lights-out. A delayed reaction like the onset of heartburn an hour after dinner or a raised lump the morning after an insect bite. In rational terms, a time to reflect after the event. Luke was brushing his teeth when a snapshot of Fox falling through the door pushed into his head. His diagram pitched, propelling toothpaste and spittle from his mouth onto the taps. How can someone fall through a door? Falling *through* something surely was defined by vertical motion, as a parachutist through clouds or a diver through water. Yet that's exactly what Fox did. She fell through a door.

He sloshed water over the taps once he was done but feared he might inhale water if he rinsed out his mouth. Fox kept falling through that door. Fox in her glossy lipstick, glitter bikini and her tiara.

And what did become of her tiara? Last he saw of it was in the bedroom when Cat was grinding away at her. The thing was swinging from her hair with each thrust. Perhaps the tiara was still on the bedroom floor. Philip said she prided herself on her props and would worry if such a valuable item got lost.

Perhaps Luke should return it to her.

Luke's windpipe threatened to seize up again. He decided to forego the oral rinse and return to his bedroom but he was making a strange wheezing sound. Fox was probably wondering where her tiara had got to, unless of course, she had contents insurance, in which case she could make a claim first thing tomorrow morning. She could report 'it got lost during an altercation with another colleague at her place of employment.' Luke's epiglottis rebounded in a long sequence that did not sound like his at all.

Philip would be mortified at what Cat had done to his arrangement. How could she make a mockery of his efforts? What an insult to his sensibilities for one of his performers to wear a grotesque fat suit and parade about with those...*man-bits* hanging out? Fox and her new company could be traumatised for life by what they had seen and then there are the physical injuries to consider. This is a health and safety matter, after all. Body oil and a mock oak floor must conspire to create the worst slipping hazard imaginable. Fox took quite a fall.

By now, blood was surging to his face; his epiglottis took another hammering, forcing every inch of breath from his lungs and squashing his abdomen into a tight ball.

And then there's the mess to clear up. Such a squander of body oil! Such wanton gratuity! And as for her pizza engorgement on the leather couch, spilling pepperoni everywhere! The disgrace of it! Think of the cleaning expense!

Luke doubled over in mute agony. Sweat and tears seeped through his skin. He clenched his teeth bracing for a momentary respite where he could take another breath before he blacked out.

Phil's *Domestic Bliss*.

Luke collapsed to his knees, his neck straining. His epiglottis continued to spitfire remorselessly in yet another cataclysm.

Not much bliss there.

Now was the time for his heart to expose defects or abuse, to give out on him. There was nothing left to give. The cat abomination had cocked a leg in farewell. She was done with her performance after gratuitous sex, a self-massage, a body workout and a pizza-feast. How *could* she! How *dare* she! No-one could show more wanton disrespect for a carefully-conceived arrangement by a theatre director!

At that point, Luke died.

Chapter 22

TEN thousand miles away, Luke could hear the Pacific boom. How could he hear something so far away? The moment his mind had propositioned the question, logic shimmered into a mirage. He could no longer make sense of or remember the question. The answer held no relevance. To what, he could not imagine.

Without realising, Luke had traversed the Pacific, a journey deep, lofty, perpetual, profound – and yet he had not moved an inch. The pillow cupped the back of his head, radiating warmth back from his scalp. Somehow this enclosure extended around his head, inside his head in a thick, snug and organic blanket, His mouth was dry yet the pigeons had roosted somewhere else. Washed upon the furthest shore, he slowly teased his eyes open. Below, to his right, a pale rectangle wavered into focus. His window. The sky outside was blue. How could the sky be blue when it should be reflecting the street lamp outside? He hadn't drawn his curtains last night – a ritual he did religiously to bar the light from his room. A slit of sunlight traversed his bed in the mornings, he knew. The light would have caressed his eyelids on its travels. And yet the light had failed to awaken him.

Luke didn't want to move, every muscle agreeable with the sheets beneath. A beautiful anesthesia moulded his face, his limbs spread-eagled, his boxer shorts on display and his shirt half open to show his abdomen, He had no memory of how he got here and he didn't care. Luke drifted in and out of stupor. Finally, he stretched slowly and pulled himself up. He glanced at the clock. Nine-fifteen. He stared at the numbers incredulous. His next thought was of his near-death experience last night before falling to his knees. The fat suit. The body oil.

Luke had awoken to a former version of himself, almost a stranger for the protracted time since his last acquaintance. Luke thought this former self was dead. The eyes from which this stranger viewed the world was the same and yet different. Today Luke could differentiate the irrelevant from the relevant – no longer bombarded by a sea of meaningless dirge that carved into his consciousness. He perceived only what he needed by some dredging-out system that hadn't been working for some years.

He could focus.

Luke touched his forehead. Of course, the anatomy always felt the same. He closed his eyes and drew his fingertip across his brow. The membrane was not tangible, but there. And both sides equal. The implications of what last night's seizure had triggered began to sink in. He hadn't lost his ability to sleep after all. The proof was evident. The indisputable fact buoyed him inside. It seemed he just needed the right stimulus. A release evidently but not any kind of release.

Luke had no allusions, recreating last night's response was near impossible. To make someone laugh as hard as he had depended upon a multitude of factors. Most comics had probably spent a lifetime trying to achieve what Cat had achieved. Yet again his thoughts returned to her and yet he did not even know what she looked like.

Luke got up, suddenly alert and his mind clear. He went into the bathroom. Luke caught his reflection, but his new pallor wasn't the reason for his arrest, but his right eye. More leery than usual, positively disdainful. His eye stared back at him in an accusatory fashion. Had that part of him taken umbrage to him for some reason? Admittedly, the moment he had awoken, guilt clung to him as one who had indulged in adulterous sex or someone else's privileges. Luke shirked from the most likely explanation for that feeling of facing his father when the belt was due. He wished not to face any such thing now. Not ever.

Luke picked up the phone and called in absent. He then called Philip.

'Who is she?' he dared ask Philip in the coffee shop the moment they took their seats by the window. Philip's eyes kept lingering over Luke, resenting the compliment he could honestly express. Yes, Luke knew he looked and felt better than he had in years, but Philip had bones to bear, and he hadn't mentioned the unmentionable yet. Philip pulled his chair up to the table with a grating sound. 'I think it's for your best interests that I never tell you,' Philip announced for Luke's own good.

Poor Philip and his haughty self-importance. 'I think I can decide that for myself, Philip.'

'Okay, for your information she's a desperate single *mom* who thinks a choreographed routine is just a few moves, y' know, a hand gesture here, a nod there, perhaps a fat man suit to *shake* things up a little.'

And there it was.

Philip glared at Luke. 'You have no idea of the mess I had to clear up this morning. Grease don't clean up easy.'

Luke tried to wave this off. 'I'll pay for the extra time and the inconvenience.'

Philip's look did not waver. 'That ain't the point, Luke. Foxie landed real hard on that floor y' know. She got a big bruise on her right buttock, and all 'cause that fuckin' cat went on the rampage with the body oil. You don't realise the health and safety inspectors could be called in if she decides to take further action. Those floors need lookin' at for tripping hazards.'

Luke stopped him with a warding off gesture of the hand. 'Please, Philip, I cannot discuss the health and safety issue right now.'

'But tripping hazards ain't no laughing matter, Luke. Foxie was lucky the injury wasn't more serious. What if she was wearing her stilettos at the time?'

Luke's voice grew firm. 'Please, Philip. Not now.'

Philip stared at Luke, his eyes as pale as porcelain. They narrowed. 'This ain't funny.'

Luke set his jaw. 'No, it is indeed a very grave matter that will need to be looked into. I trust that you shall deal with it, perhaps a fitted carpet with a grip underlay will solve the problem?'

Philip's eyes were still narrowed at Luke.

The beverages arrived and Luke sipped his coffee. Philip's eyes did not leave his. 'I think you have taken leave of your senses to want to know that woman. As my client, I am advising you to hear no evil.'

'So you are my adviser now?'

'She caused damage to the flat as well as injury and trauma to my girls. And for your information, she got referred to me by the doorman of the Funland Bar, y' know the strip club?'

'So, she's a stripper?'

'With those moves? You've got to be kiddin'. No. Dan clears stuff for repossessers when he's not bouncing at the club. He was commissioned to clear her house a while back, some fuckin' debt she got herself into. It just begs the question. Drugs? Gamblin', a fuckin' Gucci addict? She's just desperate. *Des-per-ate*. What more do you need to know?'

Luke had never felt more focused than he did at that moment. He stirred his coffee. 'Okay, Philip, so you are not going to reveal her identity to me. But if you can get her to come back, I'll pay you double. That goes for her and anyone who is willing to work with her.'

Philip for once was speechless.

'I don't expect you to like the idea, and I am not sure of how this is going to work, but it is something I feel I must do.'

Philip was still staring at Luke with that infuriating staged-exasperation. 'You bloody well *have* taken leave of your senses.'

'No, Philip. I am feeling quite sane.'

Philip could see that Luke was not to be deterred but could not help himself. 'Fine,' he said, not caring who overheard in the intimate surroundings. 'But I just can't wait to tell you, *told you so.*'

Chapter 23

PHIL'S voice grated up to her ear when Gemma answered the phone. She had expected Geary, Terry or the surgery.
Gemma didn't stop to listen. What would he say to someone who had donned a fat suit, shagged Charlene and eaten pizza on his precious couch? She was a psycho, obviously; she'd gone too far with Charlene, and his client was most infuriated. Gemma cared not to dwell upon that last point. Phil left a text message an hour later which she deleted.

The phone trilled again that evening whilst she and Ben were watching Myth Busters. Gemma deterred Ben from answering with the excuse salespeople often made calls at this time. She hoped the calls would stop. Okay, she *had* gone too far with Charlene; she'd suffered sexual humiliation and a bad fall. Gemma doubted Phil, her voyeur or his troupe would accept her apology and wouldn't blame them. The voyeur was her real target. Phil, Charlene and Suzie had just…well, got in the way.

The calls stopped the next day and Gemma dare take assurance. The whole unsavoury affair was over. And what had she learned? Well, exhibitionism didn't come naturally to her, that's for sure. She, borne from a sexually-oppressed mother and sister to a moraliser could never be like Charlene. Gemma had already breached the family code when marrying Liam. Gemma would take the secret of her short-lived commission to her grave.

Gemma ambled towards the window to establish if the post had come but could see nothing. Colby and Vernon's silence unnerved her as much as a communication. She unfastened the front door for a better view and drew eye to eye with Phil's pin-prick pupils. He had at that moment mounted her steps and was about to depress her doorbell. Automation took over. She shoved the door against him before Phil had a chance to speak.

'*Gemma!*' he squawked.

She kept pushing.

'Look, he's willing to pay you double. Just name it!'

The words bore no meaning to her. Gemma had made the decision to shut the door if he had told her royalty had called upon her services. The door was closing and that was that.

'*F'r fuck's sake, Gemma!*'

Gemma gave the door a hard shove. The lock engaged with a satisfying click. Gemma turned and rested her shoulder against it. Silence fell. She dare not look, not even through her peephole which Terry had installed two weeks ago. She could not bear to see any person or object that reminded her of *him*…her voyeur and how he'd made her feel. She would serve him no more.

Soon after her closing act in *Domestic Bliss*, Gemma had disposed of her fat suit and taken a taxi home. She promptly sorted through her belongings for items that reminded her of him and disposed of them too – her false eyelashes, her concealant, her corset and that garter. Lastly, she had gazed upon Ben's cat mask, the one prop that remained untarnished; her only shield and emotional stanchion. She decided against returning the mask to Ben in fear Ben would throw it away as he had done so his drawing. She carried the mask down with her and placed it on the table as a reminder to discuss it with him later.

Ben returned from school whilst Gemma was weeding in the back garden. Her small haven never failed to clear her head of cerebral pollution and the moment was too perfect to be sullied by the thought of seeing Phil's face at the door. She lamented that moments like these occurred too rarely these days.

Ben wandered in and sat on a deckchair.

Gemma teased up a tenacious taproot with satisfaction. She tossed the thing aside enjoying the soil bouquet – one of the reasons the garden lulled her.

'Mum.'

The smell that evoked new potatoes, autumn, minerals and the earth detained her from replying. 'Hi, Ben. How was school today?' Gemma set-to on a neighouring weed.

'You know that performance?'

Gemma paused. No doubt the sight of his cat mask on the kitchen table had brought this on. 'I've told you before, Ben, there are no more performances.' Her tone was unwarranted. Ben had not brought up the subject since their discussion last week. Gemma leaned back upon her haunches. She gazed upon him. Ben looked pale as usual and his eyes inscrutable behind his square frames. 'I'm sorry, Ben, I didn't mean to sound harsh. I brought the cat mask down because it made me think about the Three-D Design Club at the school. I think you should speak to Mrs. Potts about enrolling.'

Ben seemed less than enthusiastic about the idea, merely shrugging.

'Look, Ben, I know you think this…this show I was doing was going to solve all our problems and change everything, but the reality is different.'

'But I thought…' Ben's brow furrowed. 'Making that cat mask felt special, important, like I *had* to get it right.'

Gemma knit her lip, regretting the whole affair. She wished she could find some other way to fill the void she feared existed inside of him. Before Gemma could garner assuring words, Ben gathered his crutches and lurched to the house. Gemma watched with compunction. He was suffering a bad bout of tendinitis. His knees had swollen to puffballs. She hoped he wouldn't need another steroid injection – the procedure always spurred him to put on a brave face. She would request alternative therapy on his next visit to the rheumatologist.

'Hey, Ben!' she yelled after him in a tardy attempt to lighten things up. 'Go get that cat mask! I'll hang it in the hall!' Gemma resumed with dispatching her next weed, thrusting her trowel into the dirt which tended to be high in clay, drying out like concrete after every shower.

A shadow drifted over her. Ben probably needed some help with hanging the mask, the picture hook located some six feet from the ground. Her circular trench now complete, she grasped the dandelion head and pulled. Only then did she notice a pair of black shiny shoes five feet to her left. She stared at them stupidly. Releasing the weed, she slowly raised her head. Gemma knew nothing about suits but never had she seen one so immaculate. Dark grey; razor sharp creases only where creases should be. Otherwise the folds undulated like silk. Hair-thin stitching edged buttons, cuffs and hems which were discrete in themselves. She wanted to touch the fabric. She imagined her fingers would glide over the surface without resistance. Her eyes kept travelling upwards to a point where the sun blinded her. She dropped her trowel and shielded her eyes which did little to impede the glare.

The figure appraised her from a lofty position without moving. She squinted, words dying in her throat before she even knew what she wanted to say.

She lowered her heels and straightened her knees with a totter. The man's face remained dark – at first she thought he was southern European, but quickly discerned this was not the case. The skin around his eyes were pigmented with smudged shadows that radiated towards his cheekbones giving him a swarthy look, otherwise, his skin had a sallow but smooth complexion. Gemma's autumn collection of eyeshadow would have matched the hues around his eyes perfectly – perhaps a little amaretto blending out with a smidgen of coffee-tan. The skin being dark, made his olive eyes appear paler than they actually were. His irises had a dark tide on the outer rim, adding intensity to his gaze. The breeze teased a dark forelock over his squarish forehead, the sort that did a lot of thinking.

His voice was as dark as his suit, his words rolling from his tongue in a crisp yet proper manner. 'I didn't mean to startle you. The door was open. I called but no one answered, so I…er…well…'

Gemma was still staring at him stupidly. Her horror was coming at her like a tsunami in the distance. The tide had sucked out for miles. The thin blue line had yet to reveal the true proportions of the solid wall about to hit her.

The man searched her face, taking her in as she did him. She noticed one of his eyelids was a little lower than the other. 'I apologise for Philip,' he uttered. 'He is vulgar and has no etiquette. I would dispense with him if he wasn't so capable at what he does.'

Gemma could not respond to this admission. What was she supposed to say?

The man seemed to realise this. 'I'm, sorry. My name's Luke.'

And then the wall hit her. 'Oh, my God.' Her words slipped out in a whisper.

Ben's voice shattered the moment. His slender form emerged from the house behind Luke. 'Hey! Mum! Where did you say I should hang this?'

Gemma's eyes flicked towards Ben. Ben was standing on the patio steps holding up her cat mask. A hot and momentous ball-bearing rolled up from her gut to her throat. The heat radiated to her neck and scalp, setting every follicle on her scalp aglow. The ball-bearing continued to roll in her throat, rendering her speechless.

Luke turned on hearing Ben.

Gemma gritted her teeth. Released from Luke's scrutiny, she leapt about like a pogostick, making slashing motions with her hands and across her neck, mouthing empathically at Ben to get rid of it.

Ben simply watched her, confounded.

Whether Ben comprehended now or not was no longer of consequence. Luke had seen what Ben referred to and had probably overheard her earlier suggestion to hang the cat mask in the hall. Luke could only conclude that Gemma liked to engage her twelve-year-old son in what to do with the props she wore for sexual exhibitionism. Her cat mask, of course, should be hung in the hall like a moose-head for people to admire. She wished intensely that Luke wasn't looking at the cat mask right now. Please let the moment end.

And then Ben said, 'Who's that?'

Gemma's lips quivered but nothing would come. She could see by the inclination of Luke's eyelashes that he was still looking down at the cat mask. Why must his eyes dwell on the damned thing? Gemma experienced an inner release when his gaze finally shifted slowly upwards towards Ben's face. Gemma's words came at last with a croak. 'Ben, go inside a minute. I'll speak to you in a bit.'

Ben's inscrutable gaze remained on Luke. Ben complied, adjusting his glasses and pulling at his crutches. Ben disappeared into the house. When Ben had gone, Gemma turned her attention to Luke who had yet to face her. Seeing Ben with the cat mask had obviously confounded him. Similarly, the sight of this man in her garden continued to perturb her. His suit did not suggest sales attire, functions, the government, business or corporations – just him. He was the quintessential man-in-a-suit few men actually managed to pull off. Liam always looked a spiv in one, even on their wedding day.

Luke finally turned to her, his implacable expression unchanged but sweat now dewed his brow. Because of what he was, she made the unsavoury association with sex. She immediately banished the thought. Of course, in this suntrap, he must have been melting in that jacket. Gemma hesitated when she spotted movement at the periphery of her vision. She glanced across and saw Patti in the next door garden pegging out her washing. Patti's care-worn eyes instantaneously shifted to her pegging task. Gemma pretended not to see her, focusing once more on Luke. 'What are you doing here?' Her voice came out as a murmur.

Luke didn't reply because some inner turmoil prevented words from emerging; hardly surprising after what he had seen. Without looking at Patti, Gemma strode into the house. Luke followed her.

Once in the kitchen, Gemma visually scanned the living room for signs of Ben. The area seemed empty. She faced Luke again. He appeared tall at the doorway, the mining houses possessing doorframes just over six feet high. 'You've got a nerve coming here,' she uttered.

'I don't blame you for despising me.'

Gemma faltered at this concession. 'Your inclination is your business.'

'That's not why I'm here.'

Luke's intimate knowledge of her body began to permeate her mind. Those intense olive green eyes had pored over every inch of her, including her scar. This man had made her feel like a used piece of meat after watching her demean herself, scrubbing floors and grooming her starlet. Gemma regrouped her thoughts before they carried her away. To him, her commission was nothing personal and she was probably one of many; at least he had paid her well. Gemma adopted a nonchalant tone. 'Look, if you're that much into fat men, why don't you get Phil to consult his books and see if he can find the real thing?'

Luke was watching her seriously. 'I'm not into fat men.'

'Oh, so it's the sexual humiliation you're into?'

'No, but what you did the other night would have given an older man a coronary.'

This confounded her. Never had she considered the possibility that her ultimate performance would have comic value – least of all for him. 'Well…I'm…I'm *glad* to hear it,' she blurted, the irony falling short.

'And then I slept for eight solid hours.'

Gemma had a better retort prepared but his response had invalided the meaning. She felt like a passenger on an escalator that kept shifting sideways.

'Do you have water?' he asked.

Yet another unprecedented shift, but admitted he looked like he needed some. She took a glass from the drainer and filled the glass with cold water. She offered him the glass.

He took it and drank deeply. His left eye didn't close fully like his right, exposing a small area of white. She wondered if his expression right now was anything like his come-face. Did he look like that whilst she watched her and Charlene on the couch together or in the bedroom with the body oil? Gemma looked away disliking her thoughts. She wished he didn't have to enjoy his drink so overtly. Once he had finished, he put the glass on the sideboard. He removed the moisture from his mouth with the back of his hand.

'I'm sorry,' he muttered, much as I needed that, I would never have been so impertinent. What I was asking was whether you have water supply.'

Gemma frowned. Was he making fun of her? 'Evidently.'

'What is plentiful is always taken for granted.'

How could someone who she'd groomed herself to hate render her speechless like this? She merely looked at him, observing the autumn hues around his eyes.

'Imagine if one day, you turn the tap and unexpectedly nothing comes out. Maybe a trip to the shops will fix the problem, but everyone is after the same thing. The shelves are empty. Thirst begins to knock at your door. The next day arrives. There is still no water. You don't know if the supply will ever return. The thirst gradually intensifies. By evening, the sensation has reached a level you have never experienced before. Your quest to find water dominates your very existence. Everywhere you look, you are reminded of water. The need taunts you until it drives you insane.'

Uncertain of his point though she was, his supposition carried her into a disturbing realm she had little considered. Yes, she was guilty of taking for granted her privileges, her amenities and her standard of life.

'I have seldom had more than three hours sleep on any night for almost six years.' Not intending his revelation to emerge as a pivotal point, he continued without pause. 'Insomnia to the layperson is but two nights or so of sleeplessness every now and then. Perhaps to others it might mean five hours of sleep per night. To them it will not rob them of their identity or to give reality the feel of cold steel or to make them feel scooped out, detached. To me...' Luke faltered, seemingly taken aback by the force of his own words. 'To me, it is a prison sentence. For one night, however, you gave me a little reprieve. What you did gave me a taste of what it is to feel human again.'

Unease crept over her at the realisation he was expressing an intimacy. His affliction had seeped into his life like a lover. His insomnia had such reaches he owned it and it had moulded him.

His intent gaze caused her feet to shift like a dumb adolescent blagging her way out of detention. 'So...so you want me to perform some comedy act for your little peepshow all in the name of a good night's sleep?' She regretted the cheap remark the moment it emerged.

Her words sadly had the effect desired, causing him to blink slowly. 'No...I mean...that's not what I mean.'

He was still gazing at her, reconciling her face with the body that had scrubbed the floors, ironed the sheets and kneaded the dough for him.

'Are you the man Mum works for?'

Gemma turned abruptly to find Ben in the living room looking across at them.

''Cause if you are, Mum says she wants to do more performances for you. She really enjoys it. If you want me to make another mask, that's no problem. I enjoy making stuff.'

Gemma learned her ability to feel embarrassment was unquantifiable, blood prickling her neck and scalp all over again. She forced a carefree laugh that sounded grating, mirthless and flat. 'No, Ben, this isn't the man I work for and he is just about to leave.' Gemma tailgated this odd prating sound with an assured smile for Ben. Ben wasn't fooled.

Gemma walked to the front door signaling her visitor to do the same. She opened her door and waited for Luke. Behaviour protocols well-ingrained into him, it would seem, complied graciously. His hard leather soles swished across her carpet. Before leaving, he conceded a small nod, which thinly veiled regret and solemnity. Perhaps her move had been abrupt. Her voyeur had been anything but what she had been expecting. He seemed polite, well-spoken, nice, even, but people with such qualities were the worst, weren't they? A need to maintain her aversion to him roiled with pity and an admission he possessed physical magnetism.

She didn't trust him and she didn't trust herself.

Chapter 24

ENTERING her domain, he felt like an emperor seeing for himself how his country really worked for the first time – more complex, more tragic and more secret than he had ever imagined. Her modest dwelling enclosed the sort of fixtures he had seen through a charity shop window: scuffed edges, garish patterns, missing screws. And yet the place oozed pride to the point of defiance. Luke had three properties at his disposal and all three lacked what this one possessed: a heart.

He had meant to say something the moment he spotted her in the garden weeding, but the sight of her arms engaged in her task stopped him from speaking. He didn't want to be the reason to stop her. Within her own environment, her potency made sense. This was the place that drove her forward in everything she did; a modest territory but hers to groom however she wished – like at that moment, exhibiting dedication to a task he had never seen before. But it was more than that. She demonstrated a possession of self. Such a mundane sight as seeing a woman weeding the garden filled him with jealousy. Why hadn't she exhibited such love of her tasks during her performances? The question immediately invalid for what Philip had done: in his condescension slotting her into what he thought to be a fitting role for someone like her. No wonder the money hadn't tempted her. Sometimes, Luke could wring that man's neck.

Not until that point had Luke realised he had dreaded and anticipated seeing her face for the first time. He could discern she was not one to be caught off-guard easily. She had high cheekbones and a firm jaw; suburban, Philip had described her and Luke could see what he meant although Philip had failed to mention her hazel eyes, almond-shaped and ensconced in shadow, exhibited an inscrutable intelligence and, as in that moment, suspicion. She harboured secret thoughts. She was his pissed-off cat for certain.

As soon as she looked up at him presenting a sprinkling of freckles across her nose and bereft of lipstick, he felt oversized and overdressed. He wanted to rest his tongue against her naked mouth. Instead, he felt awkward in his suit within the suntrap of her garden. He began to feel hot. He sorely needed a cool drink but could not voice such an imposition since he had just trespassed onto her property.

His thirst retreated from his mind when he saw the boy. The boy was standing on the patio steps holding her cat mask at his side. This prop intended for sexual voyeurism might just as well have been a toy car or a robot for the way the boy held it. Luke could not bear to think of the times he had...*played* with himself whilst she wore that mask. Luke had the unsettling suspicion the boy had made it for her. At that moment, the sun singled him out. Luke felt ridiculous. And hot.

Slowly the boy filtered into Luke's consciousness. The boy, Ben, appeared to evaluate Luke intently. Few scrutinies probed like that of a child, and Ben took the liberty, as children typically do, of observing Luke. The sight of that boy flanked by his crutches in his oversized glasses and baggy polo shirt clutching that cat mask was to him sex and death. Now the sun had company in singling Luke out. The whole garden seemed to converge on him. Luke felt naked, exposed, yet rationality told him no one here could know.

Immediately, Luke could see that Ben was special – not like the grubby prepubescent rabble that evoked aversion borne from a sort of inverted jealousy. Ben was reflective, shy, rather like himself at his age.

Luke grazed his sights over Ben's bare legs, as he was wearing shorts. They were perfect. Like a colt – overly long with knuckled joints. Luke knew exactly how the flesh would have felt beneath his fingertips: firm and willowy – nervy. The bones enclosed would have been twig-like, no wider than the crossbars of Ben's crutches. Luke's sights drifted towards the soft flesh at Ben's thighs which were partially in shadow. The sight of smooth flesh stretched over bone brought a thrill to his chest. Intact. unblemished. Untouched.

Luke knew the force necessary to bruise his flesh, to make those bones crack with that high whiplashing sound. Hot splinters surged up his own legs to his groin. Luke's right knee twitched. Ben's spectacles lay on the floor lenses cracked. Luke squeezed his eyes shut to clear the image. He licked his upper lip and tasted salt. When he opened his eyes, his right eyelid dragged over.

She told Ben to go back inside before Luke had finished with his visual inspection. Ben's affliction impeded his reactions. Luke wondered how fast Ben could move if pursued. Would he get away as quickly as his male contemporaries? Luke thought not. For this reason, Luke singled Ben out as vulnerable. And she was blind to it.

Luke remained acutely aware of Ben's presence, even when Ben was out of sight in the house. And then for some reason, Luke had felt the need to divulge of his affliction to a near stranger after she had given him a much needed drink of water. Luke had always concealed his insomnia from people, a private matter like sex or a personal diary. Of course, Philip had deduced Luke's sleeplessness for himself, but the subject had remained an implicit understanding.

Gemma Greene. That was her name. This, Luke had determined from the bouncer at the Funland Bar. Luke's dress and clipped manner often made people bend to his will, consenting to his air of authority. The bullhead assumed Luke was from the insolvency service and included Luke in his banter as people often do about the weather. The bullhead remarked on the debtor's skill for guitar smashing. Not easily impressed by the things he had seen during his line of work, had to admit, the woman stuck in his mind. The discourse over and the bullhead no wiser, Luke learned Gemma's husband had deserted her with debts and the threat of repossession which explained why she had always looked so pissed-off during her performances. Gemma's present single status pleased Luke. He didn't want a man in her house.

But Luke had clearly made a grave misjudgment turning up at her house like that. Luke himself had come away perturbed and humiliated. She had expressed her wishes clearly to him. Luke felt he had no choice but to respect them. He could barely stand to look at himself anyway. Since the morning after he had slept the eight hours, his guilt had amassed. His leery right eye continued to direct a disdainful beam at him whenever Luke encountered his reflection. Luke knew his only escape from the sensation was to pay back for his blissful oblivion. And he knew sleep would desert him for the next twenty-four hours.

Domestic Bliss being suspended for the time being, Luke sat in his bedroom staring into space. A shadow reared within him. Ben's effigy flashed in his head. His image was so clear he could have been sitting beside him. All Luke had to do was reach forward to touch the unblemished skin on his thighs. But when he did so, the boy's legs became broken and blooded and a splinter of bone breached the flesh. The boy's smashed glasses and his crutches lay sprawled on the floor.

Luke could stand it no longer. He clambered onto the bed and unhooked the aerial picture of Warwick from above his bed. He did the deed. And again, tomorrow, he would hope the pigeons would return. When Luke was done, he was faced with a terrible truth: he was trapped between guilt and penance. If guilt reared, he had to pay. When penance had been served, Luke had to maintain the equilibrium by enduring the ice floes of consciousness crashing against his cranium.

Luke's reprieve now taunted him; he wished he had never reacquainted himself with what he'd missed. After three days without sleep, Luke had the sensation of being forced down an endless hill within a glass box. His body engaged in an eternal brace and his teeth clenched against the force of the tumble, could never experience the liberation or the release.

In his office, Luke drafted entries for his next commission: a series of recruitment offices in London. He touched his browbone: symmetrical as always but this offered little solace as anatomy did not always accord with inner functioning. Her garden flashed in his head again. He had taken her by surprise and yet she and her son had ultimately ambushed him. He was trapped within a decayed past and she, in spite of her situation, was free and her future filled with hope. Luke kneaded his brow and the back of his throat felt suddenly like rubber. He swallowed hard to rid the unpleasant sensation.

Luke saved his document into draft. He opened a new window and conducted a Google search of Colby and Vernon – names the Funland Bar bouncer had mentioned during their conversation. Luke found their website immediately.

A concern based in Hull that deals in property law, insolvency and administration, Colby and Vernon declared 'Debt collection can be a stressful business for any company to deal with. This is where we step in to advise, support and administer to, make things happen with a range of options.'

Colby and Vernon's tagline, 'The power to make things happen,' reinforced this closing statement which suggested to Luke this particular firm provided a plausible front for contortion of the law. Luke pondered what measures Geoff Colby and Brendon Vernon used to 'make things happen.'

The usual nauseating smiling sales team and corporate tops slithered by. Their literature declared: 'Unpaid debt not only costs the economy as a whole, but also the small business including individuals who do not always have the means or the resources to collect money owed. In many cases, the law errs on the side of the borrower who may use and abuse the system to shirk out of paying money that has been loaned, even if the funds are available. We are here to help such agents to get their money back.'

Colby addended at the bottom: 'My former business almost went bust because I was too generous and too giving. I have learned the hard way that a good business must also protect itself in order to exist. This is why I am here to help and advise others who find themselves in such a situation.'

For the benefit of the peruser, Mr. Colby had provided a personal page to show people he was a nice man really despite the premise for his company was taking money from people. A picture of Colby abseiling a mock edifice during what appeared to be a team-building day in the Cotswold's attempted to underline his humanity. Harnessed like a toddler, the portly man gave the photographer a little wave.

Luke clicked on the homepage to find the figures Colby and Vernon trimmed and pasted onto a white background. Colby's stumpy form commandeered, arms crossed and with a toady grin. His partner, Vernon, tall and stooped couldn't quite hit his partner's comic mark, his expression stiff. Who would attempt such a pitch for company specialising in debt collection? Luke thought they looked ridiculous – a comic duo like Morcambe and Wise. But of the two of them, Luke could see Colby called the shots.

As was often the case, Luke could find little else about these clowns on the internet, drawing little attention at this point. But guilty of misconduct or not, Luke thought Geoff Colby with his pink stripy tie echoing his bulbous nose interlaced with capillaries, deserved inclusion with his lauded corporates within Luke's blog.

Luke opened a new window and logged into Derek Johns' account and clicked into *The Corporate Friend*. He entitled his post: Hats off to Geoff Colby of Colby and Vernon. Such a title ensured anyone conducting a search against his name would see Luke's blog entry beneath his website on the SERPS pages like an unwanted leech, and suitably visible for anyone wishing to establish a more democratic view of Mr. Colby.

Luke wrote: 'Mr. Geoff Colby wins my admiration as one who campaigns for the perceived villain. Indeed, if I experienced the same difficulties as Mr. Colby with his former business, I would enlist the services of Mr. Colby himself to chase up the debt until the offender pays up!

'His slogan: "The power to make things happen," offers the unfortunate lender solid reassurance that Mr. Colby will use every means at his disposal to squeeze that money from those so-called shirkers! I hope I will never find myself in the position of owing money to a business or individual should Mr. Colby get enlisted. What a stalwart figure he is to our economy!

'And where does he get those ties?

'*The Corporate Friend* invites you to bestow positive comments upon Geoff Colby.'

Luke lifted an image of the comic duo and saved it into MyPictures. Luke then trimmed the image to exhibit only Colby's toady grin. Luke browsed for the image and affixed it onto his blog post. Luke's work was complete.

After a chat with Robert Dhumbia, a large Ugandan with the most unrestrained smile of the office about his recovery from his operation, Luke grabbed a coffee and encountered Cerys on her way out. Luke offered a formal smile. 'Off early Cerys?'

Cerys' smile was warm and respectful. Luke regretted the latter. 'Yes, Mr. Forrester.' She hesitated, almost adding something.

Luke waited.

She renewed her smile. 'Yes. It seems my work load has lightened up somewhat. I'm looking forward to putting my feet up in front of the TV for once.' Her eyes flashed with something Luke couldn't identify. 'I'll see you tomorrow, Luke. Have a lovely evening.'

Luke noted her shift of his address. 'Yes, Cerys. And you.'

Cerys went on her way. Luke made a little note to hack into Derek Johns' login later to infect another document.

Once back in his flat, Luke noticed through his window that Philip had fitted a wheat-coloured carpet in the living area. Luke did not anticipate his next installment of *Domestic Bliss*. Over three days now and sleep had yet to show itself. Luke switched on his TV. Perhaps he might find something funny. A hopeless expectation, he knew. A *Frazier* rerun offered his only hope. Luke sipped his scotch.

But Luke feared three days may become four. And four was unknown territory.

Chapter 25

GEMMA could not shake off her experience last week in the garden. Her voyeur had a face now and she knew his name. She could not un-know him. She wished she could.

She conjured a smile for fellow mothers as she filed into the school assembly hall. Ben's class was reenacting the events around the Great Fire of London. Ben had been given his first lines ever owing to his shyness and tendency to stutter when nervous.

Gemma sat on the front row watching Ben's class file in. A table and four chairs had been arranged on the podium. Mrs. Matthews, Ben's class teacher, ushered the children through the door. At last, she spotted Ben, lurching on his crutches. Once seated and his hands free, he glanced up and smiled at her. He gave a little wave.

Gemma waved in reply, conscious her elbow might encroach upon the airspace of a neigbouring parent. With more filing in, she had to bunch up. Gemma was lucky to possess a modest form.

As the room hushed, Ben's eyes shifted from hers to the person next to her. His smile lingered, taking on a formality. Gemma turned to her left in automation to behold Luke's long profile. He wore a different suit today, midnight blue with a dark crimson tie. Gemma faced front in a pivotal jerk. At that moment, the room hushed.

Though she could no longer see him, Luke's presence beside her pulled at every cell in her body. The pulse at her neck prodded against her skin. She could feel him lean in towards her, his suit whispering as he did so. Aftershave and a seashell aroma drifted over her.

'You have to help me,' he whispered.

Soft thermals teased the hair at her ear and neck. Gemma didn't move. She kept her eyes on Ben who was now diverted with taking his position at the podium.

Luke was still leaning towards her. 'I haven't had any in four nights,' Luke added.

Neigbouring mothers overheard and misconstrued. Tishes and grumbles ensued behind her. Gemma's jaw tightened as did her neck and shoulders. Sitting at the front and centre in retrospect was a bad idea. She seethed as quietly as she could, 'What do you expect me to do about it?'

Luke came back with the reply, 'The way I feel right now, I'd like you to punch me in the face.'

A woman coughed to Gemma's right. Gemma kept her sights on Ben who was soon to narrate. Mrs. Matthews took to the stage and greeted the parents. For the first two minutes, Gemma didn't hear or see a thing; Luke's presence hijacked her every thought.

Children dressed in period costumes opened the play. Ben, Leila and Zack stood to the side sharing a mike. Eventually, Zack informed the assembly, 'the fire started at a baker's down Pudding Lane. It spread quickly because the houses were made of timber and thatch.'

Now it was Ben's turn. Gemma straightened in her seat. Ben faltered as he stood. He lowered his crutches to the floor with a small clatter. Ben, not one to be rushed, cleared his throat and pushed his glasses up his nose. He grasped the mike and in a big voice, breathed, 'Samuel Pepys wrote in his diary about the fire. It burned for three days and three nights.' He exhaled into the mike in a hurricane. 'He buried his diaries with a lump of cheese, so that...' he paused, 'so that it would stay safe and he could eat it later.'

Briefly, Gemma forgot her surroundings. Ben only occupied the room. Her painted smile, once constrained relaxed and broadened, incorporating her teeth. She took a deep breath, watching Ben take his seat once more. Undersized re-enactors dressed as Samuel Pepys and a fireman were now doing their part.

Gemma shifted her gaze to her left, forgetting her company. She snuck a look at Luke. He was still facing front. The ball on his Adam's apple bobbed slowly. The fore-hair at his temple appeared damp despite the cool air conditioning in the hall and Gemma's back was feeling chilly. A bead of sweat detached itself and tracked slowly down the side of his face. He didn't move; he retained his scrutiny of the children in front. Gemma's former smile extinguished immediately. She forgot the old decree not to stare. She couldn't help herself. The bead of sweat rolled slowly down his cheek to his jaw line where closely-shaved bristle-stubs impeded its tracks. The bead flattened out and lost definition. Luke did not blink. The narrow gaze of his right eye appeared intent, predatory.

He was looking at Ben. Gemma could tell. His hooded pupil was trained directly upon her twelve year old son.

Gemma could not define the roil of emotions inside. At first, she felt nothing. Her rational side informed her she *should* hate him. Obviously. She had groomed her dislike for him already. It should be easy. But now her aversion had a different wellspring. She must make him into a pariah at the school, villainise him, humiliate him, report him.

The reality was different. Her emotions remained quiet, composed even. Hate wasn't present at this point. Ashamedly, she identified pity for him. Who would want to inhabit skin that harboured such impulses? If her fears were correct, she would hate to be him.

Forgetting herself, Gemma faced front. Mrs. Matthews was conducting a closing speech. Ben, like the other children was watching his teacher. A moment later, the children filed back to class. Ben glanced her way as he went. Gemma wished her smile felt genuine. She waved too frantically, causing Ben to look bemused.

Gemma did not look to her left. The parents on her right could not have moved quickly enough, although 'parents' wasn't accurate. Except for Luke, the audience comprised entirely of mothers. She and Luke were the oddity.

She embedded herself within the ordered melee, drifting towards the main doors. Luke was already waiting for her outside. How did he get there before her? She had no choice but to pass close by him.

'Why is your son in crutches?' he asked.

Gemma stopped in her tracks. Zack's mum was chatting with Twitchy Dave's wife not far away. Gemma turned from them to avoid being noticed.

Luke was still looking at her. 'I just wondered.'

Gemma didn't look directly at him. 'He had rheumatic fever when he was three.' There was more to it than that. Ben's immune system had taken umbrage to the soft tissue in his joints for some reason. The consultant said Ben's condition was not uncommon in children and he may grow out of it in puberty. Gemma hoped.

'He is a very special boy,' Luke stated. 'You are lucky to have him.'

Gemma daggered him a glare. 'I'd rather you didn't talk about Ben.'

Luke conceded with a nod but he did not take his eyes from hers. 'I realise it was wrong of me to turn up like this but something tells me had I turned up at your home again, you would have sent me off like last time.'

'Then why are you here?'

'I keep thinking about what happened the other night. When everything else has failed me from the ghastly benzoes to cannabis.' Luke blinked slowly. Gemma could see he wasn't exaggerating about his present state. The autumn hues around his eyes had acquired a bruised tinge, especially around the rims of his eyes. Gemma would have added a dab of cerise to her autumn colour-blend to match it. 'I want you to come back,' he added. 'I'll pay you anything you want.'

'And then what?'

'I don't know, perhaps you could surprise me.'

'Do you know how ridiculous you sound?'

'I fully realise how I sound but you have no idea what you have done for me, even if it was just for one night.'

'But what if it doesn't work? What if you don't even crack a smile after me and Charlene in a couple of stag suits have finished shagging each other to death in the kitchen?'

Had she just said that? Gemma glanced around to see if anyone had overheard. The troupe of mothers was now thinning out and thankfully Zack's mum and her companion had gone. When Gemma faced Luke again, her neck had reddened. Luke didn't seem to notice, his eyes trained on hers.

'You're right,' he said at last. 'It is ridiculous. A repeat performance is unlikely to yield the same result.' He coughed stiffly.

Gemma didn't know what to say. With a strained silence stretching, she glanced away. Luke didn't seem to understand unspoken protocols of eye contact his not leaving hers for a moment. 'But I have renewed hope,' he said, she suspected as a ruse to detain her. 'I am thinking of returning to the sleep clinic after some years. Perhaps they will run new trials for me.'

Gemma knit her lip. 'I am pleased for you.'

Luke detected her brusque tone. 'Philip tells me you are in some financial difficulty. I would like to show some appreciation. I could get you a decent job at the Registry of Mergers where I work. It pays well and the hours are flexible. You could take care of Ben.'

'I already have a job, thank you.' Gemma sorely hoped her face wasn't reddening too. His offer made her bristle inside. How could he take the liberty to dish out favours for something ulterior? She would feel obligated by someone who she pitied or despised. He was giving her the creeps but he was also getting to her.

'I don't expect you to like me,' he said.

'I find your manner…ingratiating.'

'Perhaps you could tell me what you would do with twenty-one wakeful hours every day. Believe me, reading has its limitations and TV can be such a trite culture.'

Gemma knit her jaw. 'This has nothing to do with how you spend your spare time. You do what you have to do. I did it for my own reasons.' Her jaw tightened and her gaze narrowed. 'I just pity you. Now please excuse me.' Gemma strode off before he could add something. She was perturbed to find her and Luke had been the only two adults left on the school grounds.

Gemma's phone rang that evening. Thankfully, Ben was at Zack's. She didn't answer. She didn't even establish who the caller was, preferring not to know either way. Luke had become a shadow within her. He had found access to a part of her she never knew existed and which Liam had never come close. This part of her enclosed her feelings for shame, embarrassment and fear of exposure. Ideally, a trusted person only should have the way in; someone benign and unlikely to abuse or hurt. But who had found his way there instead? Someone who seemed nice, considerate, well-spoken, immaculate, polite, creepy, ambiguous, predatory.

Gemma made the decision to get Ben a cheap mobile phone the next day; his first since Liam's departure. She would tell Ben to carry it with him at all times.

She would then make an important phone call.

Chapter 26

SHE'S got a car now: a battered Fiesta, dark blue. He watched an older man, a father-figure with a tattoo on his shoulder park the thing on the front of her house. Luke had been watching from inside his Jag out of sight next to a run-down off-licensee called Azhar's.

Tchaikovsky's *Serenade for Strings* detained his thoughts, an arpeggio causing his nape hairs to bristle. Gemma kept stalling the engine. The father-figure patiently demonstrated how to find the biting-point. The car lurched violently backwards. Smoke drifted across the road. Gemma had obviously got little rusty with her driving since her husband had left her destitute and without a car.

Ben emerged from the house. Luke straightened in his seat. Regrettably, the boy was wearing trousers so Luke couldn't catch a sight of his smooth legs. Ben pushed on his crutches and watched his mother inch forward in the car. The boy remained impassive, still. Luke volleyed for a better view but he couldn't risk being spotted, not after last week at the school. Watching Ben read his lines in assembly, his body yet to grow into itself, awkward yet graceful, Luke thought he was beautiful. And then a treacherous bead of sweat had given him away. Luke could have wiped it off but Gemma had already noticed. She had seen right through him, had done so ever since he had first ventured into her garden.

Ben's effigy came back to Luke's bedroom again last night. Luke put the TV at volume to offer distraction but those sights kept coming clear to his head: smooth then bloodied; perfect, then irreparable. No good closing his eyes, the imaged kept coming clear. Would his penance ever be enough? Luke massaged his eyes and took another look. He didn't want to leave but he was already late for work. Luke decided to return later and follow her if she took her Fiesta for a maiden trip.

Philip had new recruits for *Domestic Bliss*. His 'Foxie' ending her commission after her fall. Luke suspected injured pride was the real casualty. After three nights, Luke hadn't watched a single installment. Luke's customary sleep routine had returned: two or three hours per night now before a vicious knock to the head upon his awakening.

Luke had made a wise move with his blog entry, providing an opportunity to pay Gemma another visit – to see her. To see Ben. As soon as Luke entered the office, he logged on and signed into *The Corporate Friend*. Barry Brewer's post was still attracting attention. In response to Luke's last comment, 'Perhaps,' someone had put, 'Perhaps? What sort of fucking answer is that? Are you a fucking psycho or something? Fucking maniacs like you deserve to be held up for ridicule, so people can see what a headcase you really are.'

Luke didn't bother to read on, navigating away with a little smirk. Luke opened his post entry on Geoff Colby and found several comments already.

'You are a sick man, *Mr. Corporate Friend*,' the first contributor opened. 'A pathetic little nobody who takes potshots at successful businessmen and entrepreneurs to serve your own (no doubt, personal) failings. You have cost businesses and livelihoods. I am watching you, *Mr. Corporate Friend*. I have already alerted your server and they know about you.'

Mr. Brewer, perhaps, or possibly another casualty of his blog? Luke sipped his coffee. Rather bitter, he thought and read on.

'Re previous comment: Get over yourself. This is the age of free speech. *Mr. Corporate Friend* has done nothing wrong. He hasn't defamed, denigrated or committed libel. He has provided a platform for those brave enough to speak up about unscrupulous individuals in the business sector and of course to praise those who are honest and hard working. The voice of the common people has taken your "potshots." And to those who deserve it. *Mr. Corporate Friend*, keep it up!'

Which was followed by:

'Colby takes backhanders from bulldogs chasing up debt by using dodgy means. He twists the law for financial gain and he feeds plausible legal jargon to the innocent and vulnerable to squeeze cash from their purses. My mother lost thousands because of him. Our court case is still pending.'

And then someone had replied:

'You'll be lucky to get anything from that slippery man. He passes the buck, keeps using the excuse, "I am simply acting for my client." Even if the victim wins, Colby gains from dozens of others who don't win or fight back. That's how he makes his money: calculated risk.'

A fourth comment piqued Luke's interest.

'Don't no if I should say what happen to me. I lost my house because Geoff Colby told me I had to pay this man for something my son did. I don't no who this man is, but they say his identity is protected by a right to confidentiality. I didn't take it to court because I couldn't afford a solicitor and was frightened about what might happen to me.'

Luke decided to stir things up a little. He put:

'Oh, dear, I am most dismayed to hear these stories about Mr. Colby. Surely they cannot be true. Perhaps someone might like to elucidate on some of these stories so that I may evaluate my opinion of this figure.'

Luke signed out.

Some of her chords were indistinct but he picked out a series of minors and bars that could only be from The Beatles' *The Long and Winding Road*. He could not see her garden for the tall shrubs at the back but he could see an upper floor window and an opener slightly ajar. Luke guessed the window looked into Ben's bedroom but hers must be close by or he wouldn't be able to hear her guitar. She kept repeating the fourth bar, a chord transition he suspected was the problem, not that he knew about playing the acoustic.

Luke fondled a screwdriver in his jacket pocket. He drew his fingers over the drill-bit, before pinching the pad of his index finger against the point. Movement stirred him from the right. Two boys on bikes trundled by. Luke backed into the hedges and they paused at the garage frontages before continuing on their way. Luke eyed their retreat before emerging from his cover. Something hit his shoulder. Luke turned. A white blob oozed on his lapel. Luke's jaw tightened. The offending bird swooped over the garages. A hawk judging by the wingspan. *Cursed bloody pest!* Bird-mess was a devil to wash off! Luke would have to let the gloop dry to a powder before brushing it down with a soft brush. His suit might still need special treatment at the dry cleaners.

On his way back to his Jag, Luke took off his jacket and slung it over the backseat. He loosened his tie. Luke fished out his screwdriver and tossed the thing on the dashboard. Bach would have to wait; the bird-mess would have robbed all sublimity from his compositions.

Luke pulled up outside his flat to see a squad car parked next to his allocated space. Luke thought nothing of it. On his way up, jacket in arm, Luke encountered a police officer. 'Mr. Forrester?'

Luke beheld the young man's open expression and the sort of brown eyes Luke had seen on a cocker spaniel. Luke paused in his tracks. 'Yes.'

'Officer Davies from Warwickshire Police. Could I have a word with you?'

Luke's right eyelid dragged over. 'On what matter?'

'I think you might prefer to discuss this in private.'

Luke could see no one on the stairwell who could overhear, but conceded. Luke inserted the keys into his door and let the policeman in.

Luke led Davies into the living room where they sat. Davies took off his hat and cleared his throat. 'I'll get to the point, Mr. Forrester.' A cogitative tongue emerged briefly. 'We've had reports of sightings of you at Caester School recently which has caused some concern. Can I confirm that you had visited the school?'

Luke saw no reason to deny it. 'Yes.'

Davies appeared nervous – perhaps his first callout. The man fondled his hat like a pet. 'May I ask why you would visit a school if you have no children there?'

Luke appraised Davies. Words snagged in his throat. How could this be happening to him? Davies' question made Luke's skin crawl. Davies appeared to read Luke's thoughts. His gaze shifted uneasily. To him, Luke must appear an anal reclusive, tied to his job and concealing some sexual contortion. Gemma had done this; who else could it be? Luke shouldn't be surprised – especially after the impression he had given at the school assembly. Luke only wished someone else was behind this. Anybody but her.

Luke replied, 'I wanted to speak to a friend.'

'About what?'

Luke bristled at this intrusion. What relevance did this have to whether Luke was guilty of…of…*stalking* children or not? 'A private matter.'

Davies nodded. 'I understand an allegation of this nature can be very distressing for anybody, as in most cases, there is an innocent explanation. Our view is not to assume guilt straightaway. Reports like these from anxious parents or school staff are not uncommon. I note you do not have a police record.'

Luke didn't reply.

Davies gave a small nod. 'I'm not going to issue you a caution at this point, but if you are seen at the school again without proper reason, a caution will be issued against you.'

'I resent that.'

'It's just a precautionary measure, Mr. Forrester. You can understand that, can't you?'

Luke knit his jaw. 'Excuse me for a moment.'

Luke stood and took his soiled jacket from the back of the settee to hang it in the utility room to dry. On passing the kitchen, he encountered a man standing next to the fridge. Luke stopped in his tracks; his lower lip fell ajar.

Christian Lovett from accounts gazed back at Luke equally taken aback. Luke knit his lip and proceeded to the utility room where he draped his jacket. Luke then returned to the kitchen. Christian hadn't moved. Blonde, tall and rakish, Christian wore a silver suit interwoven with black threads and a narrow black tie. He looked like a quiz-show host. Christian would never be seen dead in a suit once, starting off as the union man – a militant thorn-in-the-side of CEOs and middle managers. Luke could see now that Christian had always aspired to wear a suit and be like Derek Johns or Robert Dhumbia. At this moment, he looked more like a weasel who had likely overheard the conversation in the living room.

'Luke,' he uttered with a smooth southern lilt tinged with an apologetic simper. 'God, I'm so sorry to catch you like this. I was just in the area and I wanted to…well, surprise you.'

Luke's tone was flat. 'You have my flat key?'

'Christian's apologetic simper intensified. 'I had spares cut when I used to live here in case I lost them. I relinquished the originals when moving out, but kept the copies.'

Luke took this in. 'I see.'

'I'm sorry, Luke. I thought, well, we could catch up on stuff. I bought us some beers.' He alluded to a crate of Budweiser's on the worktop. His voice died off. 'No one knows I'm here.'

Luke could see where this was going. 'Look…er…Christian, now isn't a good time to…*catch up*. Perhaps you could come the next time you are in town.' Luke made a mental note to have new locks installed.

Christian's grey eyes remained on Luke's. 'Yes, I can see that. You're in some sort of trouble.'

'No…no. Not really.'

Christian turned and detached a Budweiser from the crate. He flicked the cap and took a nip. 'Some bastard report on you?' He licked the foam from his lips. 'Y' know, if you need a character reference, I'm your man.'

Luke eyed Christian's manoeuvre. Christian, it seemed was making himself at home. 'Thank you, Christian, but that will not be necessary.'

Christian shrugged. 'Okay. Fine.' And he unslotted his midriff from the enclosure between the fridge and the cooker.

Luke lingered to escort him out. Christian went on ahead, but instead of turning right to the front door, Christian continued into the living room where Davies sat.

'Good evening, Officer,' he intoned in an overly informal way that made Luke recoil inside. Luke could smell alcohol in Christian's wake. Christian from accounts had spent the afternoon loading himself up with more than a few cans in Luke's kitchen, it seemed.

Davies turned, bewilderment crossing his face. He stood. Christian offered his hand. 'I'm Christian Lovett, a work colleague of Luke's.'

Davies accepted Christian's hand and they shook. 'Officer Davies.'

Christian placed his can onto Luke's sideboard not wanting Davies to see. Christian's yeasty aroma however betrayed him.

'Luke tells me there have been unsavoury allegations made against him,' he began.

Luke's sights centred upon Christian's nape hairs, where mousy curls teased his collar. Luke's face fell slack and his breathing steadied. So, it would appear Christian *had* eavesdropped upon the conversation.

Christian continued, 'I would like to assist in any way that I can – perhaps I can answer questions or offer relevant information?'

Davies smiled, overwhelmed at Christian's toadying. 'Well, anything you can offer, Mr. Lovett.'

'Well, actually, there *is* something that might interest you about Luke and which might prove relevant to your enquiry.'

Luke's right eyelid twitched.

'I am referring to the view through his bedroom window; it's pretty fantastic, by all accounts. Luke said he'd show me but as yet, he hasn't.'

Davies frowned at this.

'In a manner of speaking, Luke *is* into watching things, you see. He is very much into watching things, especially from afar, aren't you Luke?'

Christian turned and latched his grey eyes onto Luke's. Luke didn't reply.

'If you could let me stay and watch, I will tell Mr. Davies about the nice telescope you have in your room. I hear Venus is out tonight and it is going to be a dramatic sight, indeed, outshining anything else you can see around at this time of night.'

Luke's face was still slack. He opened his mouth and dwelled upon the word before uttering, 'Yes.'

Christian lifted an eyebrow, latching onto Luke's utterance before turning his attention to Davies. 'You see, the point I am making Officer Davies, is that Luke would touch any minor below the waist as much as my aunt Flo could hook herself up with Brad Pitt. He was happily married once, for God's sake. Luke's voyeuristic tendencies end with skywatching and I am very much looking forward to joining him this evening.'

The room fell silent. Officer Davies was nodding, his smile knit into a straight seam. 'Yes, well. Thank you Mr. Lovett.'

'Pleasure.'

And Davies was done with his enquiry for today.

Once Davies had gone, Christian remarked the flat had hardly changed. This meant Christian needed no guide to find Luke's bedroom. The weasel mauled Luke's mounted binoculars as though they were his and made himself at home on Luke's leather chair. He downed two more cans and prattled about his work at HQ. Luke did not join Christian at the window, but remained at the door.

'By *Christ*,' Christian whispered as the lights came on in the flat opposite, disclosing coffee and tan upon the couch. The new Fox and Cat were sitting on barstools, bare legs lithe and smooth and playing footsie with one another. But Luke watched no further. His attention instead focused upon Christian's frantic groping. Christian couldn't unzip himself fast enough, his cock already erect. He proceeded to pull on himself as a milkmaid on an udder. 'Oh, God,' he groaned. 'Oh, Good God.' He kissed the air several times. 'So fuckin' *beautiful!*'

Luke's right eyelid twitched several times. The screwdriver sadly languished in Luke's Jag but a ballpoint pen on his cabinet might do just as efficiently. A decisive jab to the back of the neck is likely to yield equally decisive results. Christian's demise will sadly arrive as prematurely as his ejaculation. Christian's forehead rebounding against Luke's mounted binoculars would be his ultimate sensation before his departure from this earth.

But worse was yet to come, for as Luke watched Christian's movements, he could see himself there, doing the same thing, many, many times before now. The sight sickened him.

Christian made snorting sounds through his nose. The performance had barely begun and he couldn't control himself. Christian's semen squirted dejectedly onto the waistband of his trouser suit in lazy pulses. Luke could taste bile at the back of this throat.

Luke wandered into the bathroom and tore off a length of toilet roll. He returned to the bedroom and offered it to Christian. Christian complained about the mess as he dabbed himself. Well, what else had he expected?

Luke let Christian sleep on the couch. Ladened with alcohol and sexually spent, Christian decided to retire then and then. He kept gushing about the display apposite and said he would like to pay another visit. He would even pay to watch if Luke let him. Luke hoped Christian wasn't going to make a nuisance of himself. Once the locks had been changed, Christian would have no choice in the matter.

Luke lay in bed staring at the ceiling throughout the remainder of *Domestic Bliss*. Luke decided to postpone the performances in light of Davies' visit but equally through seeing himself in Christian's despicable display.

Caester School was off-limits for now. But this did not bother Luke too much, for Gemma would soon have a reason to pay him a visit.

Chapter 27

GEMMA couldn't go through with it in the end. She telephoned the incident desk of the local constabulary. She spoke to a nice lady called Chloe. Gemma gave Luke's name and the place of his work and soon after apologised for wasting police time. Gemma could see where this could lead. How did she know this man? He paid you for sexual exhibitionism? How much did he pay you? Was it in cash? How long did you perform for him? What sort of things did you have to do in front of him?

Something would seep out. Tongues would start wagging and in a territory where houses were packed closely together, Gemma would never escape the rumours or the looks. Names would be called on the playground and Ben could learn the true meaning of voyeurism. Gemma couldn't do it.

Terry had surprised her with a blue Fiesta last week. He'd bought it from Barnstow's. Paul had got a good deal – previous owner, an old lady who kept it in a garage for years. Gemma had trouble getting used to the clutch, but looked forward to her first drive into town since Liam had gone. She came out of the house and found two of her tyres had been slashed.

Gemma had gone beyond tears. She stared at the puncture wounds, dumbfounded. Why would anyone do this to her? Reckless vandalism, she had to conclude, but such occurrences were rare here. She slammed her car keys on the table and informed John Geary she would be late for her appointment.

Gemma arrived at Geary's plush offices ten minutes late. She had to shell out a considerable sum to see him for half-an-hour. Helpful and informative though Geary was, the solution to her problem came down to the same thing: money. Money for legal fees, a solicitor and court costs. And sadly, her money wasn't inexhaustible; soon she would have to take a further loan and Gemma's share in the property would shrink further. Her grubby third party's interests would increase relatively. The reality began to hit. They had the advantage. For the first time since Liam had left, Gemma could see her house really slipping through her fingers. She and Ben were simply tenants in someone else's house and the third party could evict the pair of them. Gemma could see a future with hostels and guesthouses or at best a council flat. Her little back garden overgrown or dug over for someone else's tastes; her modest living room gutted and modernized, twelve years of memories erased.

Could she go back and serve her voyeur, if as he had claimed would pay her double or more? Could she use him to salvage her house knowing what he might be? The answer came back as a unanimous negative.

The milky sky had thickened and the air had grown oppressive. The bus journey home was long and crowded. The mass of bodies exuded moisture to saturation point. She resented that tyre-slasher.

Gemma got home and picked up the phone to call Terry. Vera answered in her usual faraway voice. Gemma never knew what to say to her, often coming away verbally fatigued after keeping the conversation going for the pair of them. What she and Terry talked about in the evenings, Gemma could not imagine. Did they talk at all?

'Can you give Terry a message?' Gemma said after the preamble with Vera. 'It's about the car. Someone's slashed the tyres.'

Vera dithered with her reply as usual. 'Oh, dear. When did this happen?'

'This morning.'

'Oh, dear.'

Gemma knit her lip. 'It's probably some bored kids. I'll have to keep it in the garage in future.'

'Yes, I think it's for the best.'

Gemma picked her nail. 'Yes. Right. Oh, and by the way, thank you for the guitar.'

'Guitar?'

'The guitar. Terry said it was your idea.'

Vera made a small sound. 'I'm not sure what guitar you mean, dear. It wasn't my idea.'

Sometimes Gemma didn't think Vera was the full ticket. 'Don't you remember?'

'Terry never said anything to me about a guitar.'

Gemma suddenly wanted to end the call. She made the excuse someone was at the door and said goodbye politely. She didn't like the deduction Vera had provided. Terry had bought her a gift. Terry. Not Terry and Vera. Terry alone.

Her phone trilled again. Gemma snatched the earpiece up, her thoughts still in disarray. At first the line was silent. Gemma thought someone had got the wrong number. And then he spoke.

'Gemma?'

The pulse in her chest took a surge and her mouth became dry. 'Luke?'

'I'm sorry to disturb you at this hour.'

Her lips hovered over words and refused to come.

He detected her disarray and took the liberty. 'I think I upset you with my visit to the school the other day and I wish to set the record straight to you personally rather than through the police.'

'The police?'

'Yes. I believe you reported me.'

Gemma's cheeks flushed. 'I think you're mistaken.'

'You didn't report me? Then how did the officer get my name?'

Gemma fell silent.

'It could only have been you, Gemma.'

Those words made her squirm inside. How could he talk to her like that and use her name as a cudgel? She kept her voice even hoping not to give her nerves away. 'No. I contacted the police but I did not actually report you. I withdrew the complaint.'

Faintly, she could hear Luke's breaths down the earpiece. 'Then someone else must have reported me but got my name from you.'

Gemma could feel him dragging her in. 'It's perfectly understandable in light of the way you behaved in the school the other day.'

'I am not what you think,' Luke said firmly. 'I came to the school to speak only to you – no other reason.'

Gemma closed her eyes. She wished he would just go away.

'There is one other thing,' Luke added.

Gemma didn't speak.

'I have a name you might like to look up.'

'I'm going to hang up now, Luke.'

'The name is Bertrand Biscuit.'

She put the phone down.

Half an hour after calling breakdown, a towing truck came and hauled the Fiesta to Barnstow Garage. Paul said he was fully booked for three days but would bring the car himself once he'd replaced the tyres. Well, she'd already lived car-less for some weeks now. What difference did three extra days make?

Gemma prepared tea for Ben and looked out for his school bus. She kept thinking about Luke's closing words on his phone call. Bertrand Biscuit. The name meant nothing to her. What relevance to her did this Biscuit man have? Gemma had the creeping sensation Luke was trying to help her. Gemma opted not to dwell on the matter for the distaste it bought. And if she had not reported Luke to the police, who had? Twitchy Dave's wife, Stacy came to mind. Stacy ran the Caester School Parents' Association and she grilled unannounced visitors regardless. Understandably in one respect, but she was also a bit of a stickler with Dave and tended to think all men were potential rapists. Surely seeing this stranger chatting with Ben's mother would have put to bed her suspicions? Then again, Gemma would not put it past Stacy to report Luke just for his behaviour during school assembly.

Gemma decided to 'bump' into Stacy if she saw her, get chatting. Gemma's theory may be way off the mark but Stacy knew all the goings-on at the school.

Terry's blue van pulled up outside. To that moment, Gemma had forgotten her conversation with Vera this afternoon. Gemma opened the door for him before Terry had pushed the gate open. Gemma returned to the kitchen to finish peeling the potatoes. At this moment, Gemma could not be sure she could look at him. Terry's gravel-voice which had for years offered reassurance and comfort, bought a tight ball in her chest.

'I got Vera's message,' he gruffed oblivious to Gemma's inner turmoil. Gemma continued her task, forcing a casual tone. 'Yes, can you believe it? I had to get the bus to town and was late for an appointment.'

'Some stupid hooligans, no doubt.' Terry sounded genuinely piqued on Gemma's behalf. 'Well, where is the old banger? I can sort it for you now if you like.'

Gemma's throat had become dry. 'I got it towed to the garage. I'm sorry, Terry. I didn't realise you were going to come up or I would have told Vera.'

'Tis no trouble.'

He was waiting for her to face him. Gemma would have offered Terry a cup of tea at this point but restrained herself. She wiped her hands and faced him. 'How is Liam these days?'

Gemma had come to realise she no longer wanted to know. Liam's name had become a deflector; safe ground like talking on the weather or about Vera. Terry seemed to see through her tactic, his eyes lingering. He sensed something was wrong.

'He's doin' fine now. I think he's pullin; through. He's got a job down there now and he's savin' some money. He's been asking after Ben. When he gets himself sorted, he'd like to come down visit him.'

Gemma's chest had been steadily tightening. An aversion to questioning Terry about the guitar gift rendered her speechless. Her sights grazed over the tattoo on his upper arm and a twisted scar on the back of his hand – legacy of a streetfight. Gemma knew as his brow furrowed over his silver irises that she would never confront him. Her gut told her such an accusation could never be unleashed to a father-in-law, ex or not. And he could deny it.

'I've met someone,' she said.

Terry's right eyebrow lifted quizzically. 'Oh?'

Gemma's heart thudded. 'Yes.'

'Who?'

Luke's face flashed in her head. 'Someone at work.'

Terry's expression did not change. 'Does Ben know?'

Gemma went to the freezer for a bag of frozen peas to break eye contact. 'Not yet,' she said.

The room fell silent. Gemma lifted out the peas and broke the seal. She poured a measure into a saucepan. She could feel Terry watching her. 'Well,' he finally uttered, 'it didn't take you long.'

Gemma gritted her teeth at his remark and decided to leave it. She flicked the igniter. 'Is he nice?' Terry asked.

Gemma balked at the question, the sort only her sister or mother would ask and which reinforced her suspicions. 'Of course.' With tea almost prepared, Gemma took the initiative before Terry could ask any more questions. 'I'm sorry about your wasted journey here, Terry. In future I will have to keep the car in the garage.'

Terry wasn't really listening but he took the hint. 'Yes, of course.' Terry stepped away from her. 'Well, I'd best get goin' since everything seems in order here.'

Gemma faced him with an open posture hoping to retain a morsel of how things were. 'You don't have to go yet, Terry. Ben will be here in a minute.'

For a man who forever had physical self-possession, he didn't seem to know what to do with himself. After a moment, he understood that Gemma was inviting him to act as Ben's grandfather. He raised his eyebrows and nodded. 'Sure. I'll stop a minute, say hello.'

Gemma did not concern herself Ben might mention Luke's visit to the house or the school. Ben wouldn't as before and being infuriatingly reticent, did not volunteer information anyway. As for Terry, he would never ask. Terry and Ben often said a lot without actually saying anything at all.

Gemma thought her relationship with Terry had reached a new plateau. He drank tea at the table with Ben and talked of Ben's project work for his Three-D Design Club: an inside-out model of a space station. He called his project, 'Breathing Space,' and talked of his creation as nothing more than a rocket made from toilet rolls or a house made from cereal boxes. Terry listened a little perplexed. Gemma was ashamed to admit she wasn't certain if Ben was ahead of everyone or a little autistic. Terry left the house before Gemma served tea. She could detect no tension between them at this point. She hoped Terry had made some mental adjustments.

Ben was thrilled with his mobile phone. Gemma had bought a basic Nokia model after speaking to Geary. She reminded Ben the service was pay-as-you-go and for emergencies only. She was certain Ben had other ideas. What a paradox Gemma had purchased a precautionary device for Ben against someone who had provided some sort of information that might be crucial to her. Pity she was unable to look up this Bertrand Biscuit since she no longer had a personal computer.

Her morning shift at the surgery grew more agonising, her workspace set up to prohibit surfing, a privilege consultants enjoyed. Though she could understand why, this gradist stipulation piqued her and suggested those of her standing could not be trusted or were less responsible. She finished early and took the bus to town. The librarian set up a computer desk for her. Luckily plenty were available, an infrequent occurrence. Gemma signed in with a designated password and opened a search window. She keyed in Bertrand Biscuit and cogitated for the first time at the oddity of the name, quaint yet faintly sickly. The proprietor perhaps relished the biscuit part, thinking up all possible puns, jokes and novelties that associated with a flat, sweet condiment. Did he have a biscuit-shaped doormat?

A Facebook page came up that divulged little since Gemma wasn't a 'friend.' Biscuit lived in Suffolk and since retiring as a machine fitter, renovated old furniture. Gemma clicked upon an image on Biscuit's wall to enlarge. The fuzzy snapshot revealed a round-faced man with a low brow; squashed up features atop a broad chin; a pudgy face that could easily be caricatured. Biscuit attended craft fairs and was proud to be a valued guest on the *Antiques Roadshow* where his Spode collection caused quite a stir. Gemma bet Bertrand had volunteered his name to the unsuspecting antique expert for a guff. But what did this have to do with her?

Gemma clicked upon a second photograph further down the Facebook wall showing a picture of Bertrand Biscuit with his brother, Teddy. Though again, the image was indistinct, she could see Teddy was taller and lankier than his brother. Teddy sported a high sun-burnt dome, the contours of which reminded her of a butternut squash. Both men wore short-sleeved plaid shirts and similar paunches slung low over their waistbands, although Bertrand's was larger than Teddy's. The image had nothing more to offer and yet Gemma's eyes kept gravitating over Teddy's face. Something about the arrangement of his features kept nagging at her. Gemma refreshed the page and typed in 'Teddy Biscuit.' No Facebook this time but a small website served by Wordpress about Biscuit's personal enterprises. Biscuit, a retired cobbler now renovated sailing boats in his capacious workshop. An image overkill of boat models, not real boats irritated her. Some of his handiwork looked botched, the lettering skewed or colours poorly-matched. His website offered little information and was difficult to navigate round.

She enlarged an image of Teddy at work on his *Northern Lady*, a small rigger. Seeing his face again brought the sensation of beholding the same puzzle from a different angle. His high dome, this time, brown and freckled was fringed with straight flaxen hair that teased his shoulders. Gemma had already made a possible connection between Steve's 'Bobby Charlton without the comb-over' and Teddy's image but something else scuttled the outer perimeter of her conscious thoughts. Something alerted her to a presence, but when she looked, the presence had gone. It was Teddy's face. She's seen him somewhere before. The answer kept slipping around like a bar of soap from her fingers: his simian, downward-sloping brown eyes that gave him a dopey look; his long crooked nose that echoed the downward slope of his shoulders. His entire torso appeared to slip onto his waistband as an inverted triangle. Gemma stared at Teddy's image for long moments. The man's face had not imprinted her memory recently; that she was certain. A childhood memory, perhaps? A friend of her parents? A once-regular of the Silver Spoon or friend of Liam's? Gemma had mislaid Ben's christening bracelet four years ago. She had last seen his engraved locket in her bedroom. In her quest for recovery, Gemma had stripped the room. She never found it since. Similar hopelessness advanced upon her now as she looked at Teddy's face. Gemma closed the window.

On the way home on the bus, Gemma made further connections. The violator who had provided Gemma the crumpled up piece of paper with Phil's phone number could have spoken to Phil about her situation, and of course, Phil knew Luke. Had Luke provided the name of her grubby third party?

Gemma feared she may find herself obligated. Luke was waiting in his courteous fashion. He was waiting for her to prepare her response to his tipoff.

Paul turned up with her Fiesta a day earlier than expected. The garage being a mere ten minute walk away enabled him to leave the truck behind and drive the car up himself. A slight, wiry man with permanent grease on his face or neck and equally a man of few words, he approached Gemma's steps without a greeting. Gemma suspected he had more to say to Liam when they used to meet up for a drink at the Randolph down the road.

'Whoever did your tyres meant it,' he uttered.

Gemma didn't like how that sounded. 'Oh?'

'Never seen nothing like it before. Slashed clean through. Whoever did that made damned sure that car weren't goin' nowhere.' Paul glanced at Gemma. 'Has any of your neighbour's cars been attacked?'

Gemma shook her head disliking what the word 'attacked' implied. 'No.'

'Well,' Paul uttered, 'it don't appear like some random vandalism to me. I'd keep an eye on it.'

Paul moved to leave when Gemma remembered her previous conversation with Steve. 'Paul, before you go, can I ask you about the Aston Martin you took back from Liam?'

Paul burrowed his hands into his jeans pockets and shrugged.

'Steve told me Liam had made safety modification. What sort of things did he do?'

Paul scuffed his soles against the curb. 'The full works,' he uttered. 'Crash guards, impact bars, manual override on windows, fire-retardant on seats, pilot harnesses, that sort of stuff.'

Gemma didn't understand the entire litany but she got the picture. 'What was the safety features for?'

Paul shrugged again. Paul was an out-of-sight-out-of-mind kind of person. The Aston Martin now fixed and sold off, no longer concerned him. Gemma wondered if Liam fitted the same category.

Gemma paid Paul for the tyres and filled in an insurance claim form once he had gone. After three days, Luke still hadn't called. Gemma couldn't bear it. She could never be released from him until she could get the answers she needed. Not surprisingly, Colby and Vernon had officially set the date for the court hearing for next month. Gemma couldn't believe this was finally happening. She awoke in the small hours after coming-to with a jolt. Someone was hiding beneath the bed, arms extended and about to pull her ankles from beneath her. The first thought she had upon awakening was of Teddy Biscuit. The sight of his dome-head made her think of being walled up in a house where no one can hear you scream. He was the man who made scratching sounds in the night, the man with one eye poked out and with an insanely wide, teethy grin. Gemma shot out of bed and gagged dryly in her hand.

Chapter 28

LUKE had become her lonely secret. She could not even bring herself to ask Phil for Luke's phone number – not that Phil would want to speak to her again after the way she had shovelled him from her doorstep like a sack of coal. Not surprisingly, Luke's number was 'withheld' on her call-memory.

She left a note for Ben: she had to leave early for work. His cereal, packed lunch and ironed uniform were on the table. His mobile phone was in his bag.

Four am was a lonely time too. Her drive to Templeton Court was marked only by passing street lights. With little need to alter speed, the effect was tunnel-like. Was she moving at all? Despite the warmer afternoons, a chill at this hour misted up her windows. Tarnished rose tinged the easterly sky once she had turned into Templar Avenue. Gemma had no intention of entering the northern limb of the court where Luke's flat must be located; she would rather draw him out somehow.

From the roadside, Gemma could not be certain which window was his – the central courtyard could not be accessed from here but being the only resident likely to be awake at this hour, only he would see her signal. She pulled up next to a black Jag, so that her headlights faced the flats. She killed her engine, completing the darkness. She then flashed her headlights three times. Her hands were shaking. She waited. Residual light had entered the windows; ceilings had flashed into view through slits between curtains, but of course the front of his flat must comprise the living room. Would he be lying awake in bed or would he be sitting at the front? She flashed three times again.

Gemma waited. Her hands became still. She poised herself for a third rotation when a square of jaundiced yellow punctured the gloom – an upper room. She waited.

A tall figure in a trench coat emerged. She could barely stand to look at him. What did this attire conjure to mind but flashers, stalkers, weirdoes and perverts, especially on him? Of course, the idea was found-less. A chilly morning as this hour would call for such an overcoat and many considered it smart or apt. Before long, she could discern his footfalls crunching the gravel. She got out of the car. The frosty air caught her breath.

Before Luke had the chance to speak, Gemma had a few words of her own. 'So, Phil's told you about my impending repossession, has he? Mr. Bailiff is evidently one for Chinese whispers.'

Luke's head appeared dark and looming in the poor light but his voice retained measure. 'Philip has told me next to nothing and I have done my own digging.'

Gemma knit her lip. 'I don't trust you.'

'I understand how things might appear and I don't expect you to.'

Her eyes now adjusted to the gloom could make out Luke's features more clearly. His pallor was ghastly; the pores around his cheeks appeared enlarged and the autumn hues around his eyes had turned to winter. He looked, doomed, sinister and wretched, but which conversely added to his magnetism. Gemma focused her thoughts with effort. 'I think this Biscuit man is after my house.'

'So you have looked him up?'

'*They*. Bertrand has a brother, Teddy. I've seen him somewhere before but I can't remember where.'

'It will come to you.'

'I can't stop them. Their solicitor is taking the matter to court. I can't afford a solicitor of my own. The house is as good as theirs.'

Luke had not taken his eyes from hers. 'And yet their solicitor deems it necessary to keep their names hidden.'

'What are you saying?'

'Write to this Bertrand's solicitor by name. Tell him you know who his clients' are and state their names. Tell him you intend to go to the press. Whether you actually do or not is up to you. Tell him you will hold nothing back. You will tell everything.'

Gemma scowled. 'But I don't know anything.'

'Tell this man you know everything.' Luke's gaze remained steady and he gave a small nod. Gemma got the meaning; a tactic she had used on Steve from the track: to gain an advantage by the pretext of knowing something. 'Still not sleeping?' she asked.

Luke delayed in his reply. 'I'll live.'

A trite throw-away deflection she'd heard many times before, but from him held meaning that chilled her. She cared not to dwell on what living must be like for him. Was he still paying to watch his Fox and Cat oiling it up in the bedroom opposite? Gemma daren't ask.

She wasn't out of his clutches yet. Sometime in the future, she suspected she would owe him a further debt of gratitude, but gratitude did not buoy her at this moment. She relished in wanton brusqueness. 'I have to go,' she announced. She turned from him without giving him the chance to detain her. Gemma got in the car. Thighs planted on seat, she couldn't get away quickly enough. The engine fired into life. The damned clutch slipped again and she lurched backwards. She braked with a screech. Her cheeks kindled. Condensation obscured her view. She flicked the demistifier which roared like a train. Gemma slipped into first and moved forward. She could see him in her wing mirror, distorted by the convex glass. He looked like an oversized raven. He hadn't moved. His dark shape retreated as she approached the car park entrance, not moving only watching. The sight stuck with her for the remainder of the journey.

Ben left her a text to say he'd gone to school okay. At the surgery, Gemma had the odd sensation of possessing two minds: One focused upon collating case files for the chief practitioner Dr. Miles, the other upon the task that awaited her this afternoon. Gemma would send her letter FAO Mr. Geoff Colby before Ben arrived from school. His name in large print upon a dispatch sticker for the hard of seeing, (prepared and secreted from the practice's printer) may also cause his lunch to go down the wrong way. Her only concern was the contents of her letter.

'To Mr. Colby,' she began and stalled. She had no real proof either Biscuit were the identity of her grubby third party. Doubt clouded her. For all she knew, Luke had fed her some random names of which one had invoked disturbed thoughts and a distant memory. Why should she listen to a man who had paid her to perform sexy scenarios for his voyeuristic tendencies, particularly now that his true sexual leanings had come into question?

Her pen dithered over the page – as did that too familiar scythe over her house. What did she have to lose?

Gemma continued, 'I know who hides behind your 'right to confidentiality.' Your secret clients' names are Bertrand Biscuit and his brother Teddy Biscuit. I've met Teddy Biscuit before. I even know where he lives.'

Gemma stopped, astounded at what she had just written. She continued with mounting frenzy.

'Teddy owns a guesthouse in Brynton Sands called Broadlands Haven. It has pictures of smiling cats in bowler hats on the walls. It is situated near the Plaza Arcade lined with betting establishments and a huge casino – a perfect locale for harvesting people who like to play blackjack or penny falls now and again and with a little luck, someone who can't control the habit. Teddy Biscuit sits in the centre of this gambling hub like a fat spider on a web, waiting for his victims and when he finds someone suitable, he lays in wait before he stings. Only then does he enlist the services of his brother Bertrand to conceive proposals the victim cannot refuse. Their proposals are unethical and abhorrent. Between them they cheat people out of money, wreak havoc upon people's lives and destroy their sanity. And then they use you to play the legal system to shield them. I have little doubt you earn a handsome cut for you troubles.

'I know everything Mr. Colby and I am going to the press to tell all. I don't know how you can sleep at night sheltering these people.'

Gemma's hand was shaking when she had finished. The memory flashed at her: the weird coffin-shape of the wall behind his dewlap form, the scratching sounds as he scribed today's specials on his blackboard, the smell of sat-on leather that was probably stale sweat and leftover tomato soup.

That man must have cleaned up Liam's excrements along with the debris of fast food after Terry had cuffed Liam's cheek and dragged his son out. Biscuit had noted Liam's long stints at the casino opposite, watched Liam's despondent form lurch back to his guesthouse. And then Gemma's husband had obliged his details upon Mr. Biscuit's guestbook: Mr. Liam Greene, 33 Newton Road, Southsbury.

The connections Gemma made created a picture beneath a picture, one that had been totally obscured by the other. The cosmos under normal light as opposed to radio images came to mind. Objects exuding profuse radiation invisible to the naked eye dominated under the radio telescope – lurid, contorted. And now she could see the picture beneath the picture. She could barely breathe for such callous craft in a human being. She wanted to bring them both down, especially Teddy. But she wanted to do so without ever having to see them or speak to them.

Gemma wrote her final draft and then she sealed the letter inside the envelope and sent it. Had she leapt from logic to wildly possible? At that moment, Gemma didn't care but she would soon find out.

Chapter 29

HIS episodes were getting closer together. This month, he'd endured seventy hours without sleep on three separate occasions. No matter what he did, Luke could never repent enough. His guilt stacked up like an anvil cloud. Luke followed the boy from his house to a park nearby. Luke concealed himself behind bushes and watched Ben with his friends scooting on their bikes. Ben couldn't scoot so quickly, his swollen joints impeding him, but Ben didn't seem to mind. He laughed with abandon as his friend skidded off a hill and landed on his shoulder. His friend leapt up quickly none the worse. Ben would not have possessed the same agility. Turgid with fluid, his knees were ineffective. Ben did not have his friend's speed or that of a typical boy of his age.

Luke's father had made another appearance – on the roadside junctioning Templar Avenue. He was wearing his accustomed short-sleeved shirt, tie and black trousers. His sentinel form had swept past the periphery of Luke's vision on his journey from work, but was unmistakably his father. Dark recesses harboured small obsidian eyes about fleshy features, thick lips knit into a hard seam; unreasonable, obstinate, narcissistic. Luke's head had pivoted to that spot but the figure was gone.

The reality continuum abraded Luke's skull. Sights and sounds that may invoke interest, note or disregard in other people crashed against his skull. Shadows reached ever further outwards from the inner corner of his eyes like cracks. Luke kept doing the deed above his bed, his father gazing on in his usual brittle nonchalance. His father wasn't impressed. Luke could never do enough.

It was the boy. The boy had spurred this reaction in him. Luke could not get past, climb over, crawl below or avert his path from what he had seen and felt in her garden. Everything since his divorce seemed to lead to that point. Luke felt he had no choice but to go to that point by the use of whatever means necessary, however devious.

The Corporate Friend had given him what he needed; someone who knew someone or someone on the inside. A timid and short contribution, Anonymous had simply said,

'I know who this man is. I'm not supposed to reveal his identity but I can't keep quiet any longer. I haven't figured out know how he finds his victims. It makes me sick.'

It was just a matter of time and Luke was good at waiting. And now he had her, albeit in an obligatory fashion. She would have to call him, and she hadn't let him down. She wasn't too happy about doing so. She couldn't get away quickly enough; her car had almost stalled in her haste and then the clutch had slipped into reverse. She lurched backwards. For the second time this week, he lamented his inaccessible screwdriver. But she would have to call on him again.

She had to.

And again he would wait.

Derek Johns called a meeting to convey the HQs new implementations of the security systems. Derek enjoyed presenting his powerpoint, stressing the importance of hacking deterrence. Luke asked a token question about how this new system prevented such a breach. Derek described encryption codes and labyrinth layers. Luke learned a lot that day, and Derek was most accommodating. Luke would gain no further satisfaction if Derek had discovered someone had hacked into his login. Somehow, there was more poetry to Luke's deed if Derek never did.

Domestic Bliss was still suspended until Luke had the locks changed. Philip had been most inconvenienced at this, especially after the trouble he had gone to over the fitted carpet. The man would probably blow a fuse if he found out Luke had been speaking to his 'Cat' behind his back. The silly man liked to wield control over the most unreasonable things, but then, his irascibility was perhaps the secret behind his progression to chief theatre director and choreographer for several venues in Warwick as well as support playwright for the West End.

Luke didn't care much for mocha on buff or fawn on russet these days anyway. Luke had other thoughts to preoccupy his mind now as he did the business in the shower. Such lucid images Philip could never recreate on his *Domestic Bliss*. His sleep-starved brain must have slipped into another consciousness. As Luke climaxed, he had the sensation of disintegrating into splinter-shaped atoms. His knees could barely support his weight as his lower gut convulsed. His flattened lungs denied him a guttural cry to the point of asphyxiation. He feared his lungs would lose the parasympathetic response of inhalation. When Luke had recovered, he regained his posture. His half-closed eye regarded him through the mirror with that hateful beam. Next time, Luke would do a better job and use a club-hammer.

Chapter 30

THE instant Gemma had entered the house after completing her shift her phone rang. A John Cleaton from Mr. Colby's office had opened the phone call with a blunt northwest accent Gemma guessed was from near the border. Once establishing he was speaking to Ms. Greene, he pushed on the defensive. 'This letter you have sent us is full of speculation and wild fantasy.' He pronounced 'letter' as 'lettre' and protracted his vowels. 'There is no concrete evidence you have whatsoever that Mr. Colby has any connections with this Teddy and Bertrand Biscuit. Mr. Colby would never behave in an unethical manner to acquire money from individuals. I understand your husband Liam Greene has debts to settle which are tied up in your property and you deem it necessary to slander Mr. Colby with these accusations to get out of paying this debt.'

Gemma let Mr. Cleaton wind up his attack that included a pledge to employ a pool of well-informed legal specialists against her. Seldom had she felt more ready. Yes, she might not have concrete evidence of anything, but Colby didn't know what she had and she had nothing to lose.

'Fine,' she simply said and broke the line.

The phone trilled to life ten seconds later. A gritty more northern accent punched up the phoneline. 'How much?'

Gemma flinched at the force of this man's utterance. Was this Mr. Colby himself? Cool as she had felt, Gemma had not expected this. The line fell silent. Was he still there?

'I want my house back,' she announced to apparently no one.

A silent segue stretched out.

Colby's voice shattered the silence, seemingly inches from her eardrum. 'You will give your word you will take no further action?'

Gemma didn't rush in her decision. Let him wait. Colby's response teetered between a question and a statement. He liked to get his own way. The right thing to do was to go to the press, but with what? All she had was a bizarre doodle that would not stand up in any situation. She had no concrete proof Colby had any connections with Bertrand or Teddy Biscuit. She didn't even know what Liam had done to set her back seventy thousand pounds. Furthermore, Gemma was hardly in a position to campaign against these men as a single parent to a disabled son; she would fear reprisals.

She cloaked her response within a masquerade of power and a willingness to go to the press if she didn't get what she wanted. 'I want my house back,' she declared 'And I want full monetary compensation for all the things your looters robbed from my house and then I want you to leave me alone.'

The line cracked in response.

The line went dead.

Two days later, she received a letter from the bank. The notice had been removed. A week later, the courts informed her the case has been dropped. A handsome deposit had also been made into her bank account.

Exhilaration eluded her. Had she cheated her son and herself out of proper justice? Had she acted like the little person bottling out? Guilt clung to her like a shadow. The victims played on her mind, especially the victims of the future, the ones she could have saved. Was Teddy still watching, waiting for his next victim in his creepy little guesthouse?

The next day, Gemma saw Bertrand's photo on the TV. It was the snapshot she had seen of him on his Facebook wall. Gemma lurched forward and turned up the volume. Some woman from Yorkshire had gone to the press after stumbling upon a blog thread that revealed the identity of a man that had sucked her son into a 'bet of a lifetime.' Her son, a chronic gambler had lost thirty thousand after forfeiting a clause in the agreement for non-attendance. The report went on, 'Messrs Colby and Vernon had purchased the debt in order to wield the legal system and to conceal the identity of Bertrand Biscuit who was behind the operation.' The woman, a fraught sixty year old with liquorice-coloured hair said she'd lost her home to a man she neither knew the name of or the reason.

'Police are speaking to several other victims of the scam that involve life-threatening stunts. One victim had suffered sixty-percent burns, another had lost the use of his right hand. There are unsubstantiated reports of a death.'

The report concluded, 'Messrs Colby and Vernon and Bertrand Biscuit are being charged for obtaining money by dishonest and unethical means.'

Gemma watched eagerly but didn't get everything she was looking for. Where was Teddy in all this? There was no mention of Teddy in the report. She grappled for the phone.

Two hours later, Gemma was standing over the lip of Fell Reservoir, a disused quarry pit half a mile from Steve's track. An area of scrubland called the Keeps was hardly a place for dog walkers, riddled with sinkholes and sheer ledges. A disused quarry track meandered to the edge of the abyss one hundred feet down. The sheer scale made her eyes go funny.

Rainwater and underground springs now filled the pit, the reservoir having the visual consistency of a green-black metallic plate. A rap of the knuckles could have resounded with a ponderous gong. But judging by the sheer angle of the walls, a plummeting object would disappear beneath and never reach the bottom. Rocky spikes, on the other hand may menace inches below the surface. The walls of the pit reminded her of a cake-cutter giving the reservoir spiky edges.

Just like a contorted nonagon, a black nerve cell. Liam's doodle.

Gemma had punched Terry's number moments after the TV report. He had been expecting her. Gemma simply said, 'It was a dumb stunt, wasn't it, Terry?'

Terry had fallen silent. 'And there were two of them, not one. They were bothers: Bertrand and Teddy.'

'I told you, Gem, I don't know anything about them.'

'What was the money for?'

Terry's voice had thickened. 'I can't, Gem.'

'I know about the Aston Martin. Liam had installed safety gadgets to the works.' Tears seeped to the back of her throat. 'Was he willing to risk his life to leave Ben father-less and me a widow, and you childless for some cheap stunt? And for what? a couple of grand from a pair of buzzards?'

'Gem,' Terry's voice cracked. An ex-con who had wielded a knife and robbed banks as a teenager and who sported tattoos and scars on his arms let forth a sob.

Gemma gritted her teeth against breaking down herself. 'I need to know.'

Gemma approached the edge. She wasn't afraid of heights but the black contorted nonagon shape one hundred feet down a convoluted pit nauseated her.

How long had Liam carried that black weird shape inside his head, dreamt about it, hated it yet needed it to define his existence? What did he see as he stood at this very spot? Had he actually driven here to do the deed, under the gaze of his two spectres? Them standing there against a big sky like the pair of vultures? Were they vaguely amused at Liam's fear? Did they bring movie cameras? Did they do a high-five behind Liam's back? She could picture Teddy's tall, dewlapped figure and his shorter pudgier brother. Waiting. Sniggering. Getting bored. Or just waiting.

How near Liam had come to driving over the edge, she could never know. But Liam had already fallen down the pit in that room at Broadlands Haven at Brynton Sands. He had gazed down into the reservoir and saw himself there. At the bottom. Drowning. Perhaps he had wanted to die. To him, little else in life had meaning but the thrill. Even to feel guilt. Such a state of mind, she could understand now, permitted no room for her and Ben or for anybody else.

Gemma turned with a start. Only then had she become aware of the unnatural silence. Not a bird or even the breeze stirred the air. Even so, she had the creeping sensation of being watched. She coughed just to hear the sound. She kicked the gravel. She moved with composed speed to her Fiesta parked on the side of the track. An imaginary shadow loomed behind her as she neared the car. Once she had slammed herself inside, her heart exploded against her ribcage. She started up, her sights darting about, but the scrubland gave nothing away.

Her breaths settled once she had reached the A-road. Her mobile sounded with a sharp report that sent her heart into another pelt. She snatched it up and could not see who was calling and flung the thing aside. The trill continued until she reached the town. Ben was already home when she pulled up. He opened the door, seeing her get out of the Fiesta. Perplexity slackened his face. 'Has something happened about dad?' he asked.

Nausea coiled at her gut. She wanted to lie down 'Why do you ask that, Ben?'

'Grandma rang a few minutes ago to speak to you. She sounded…not right. I'm a bit worried something might have happened.'

Gemma's feet seemed to be floating beneath her. She did not look down in fear she might keel over. 'Don't worry, Ben, I'll go ring her now.'

Ben waited at her side as she picked up the phone. Vera answered promptly. 'Gemma, is that you?'

Even in panic-mode, Vera sounded as spaced-out as ever. 'Vera, is everything all right?'

'Well, I'm not sure. I think Terry's gone missing.'

Gemma was standing at the lip of the reservoir all over again. 'What makes you think that?'

'Well, after you had the phone conversation with Terry this morning about the news, he went out. I assumed to do some tinkering in his workshop. You know how he spends hours in there. I have to call him three times sometimes to get him to come in for tea.'

Gemma broke in. 'So…'

'When I checked on him later, he wasn't there. His van is gone. He's not at Trevor's and Ben has just told me he's not with you.'

'Perhaps he's just gone to the nursery.'

'He would have come back by now. He's been gone over four hours and he's switched off his mobile.'

Gemma tried to think. 'Did he say anything to you after I spoke with him?'

'Well, no. Not really.'

And then it struck her. Gemma tried to sound calm. 'Vera, I'm going to have to go.'

'Oh, er…'

'I'll explain later.'

Gemma cut the line more fitting for a rude caller than poor Vera but explanations would have cost valuable time. Ben was still watching her when she picked up the phone again. When the desk officer replied, Gemma asked to be put through to Lincolnshire Police. A moment later, she was informed a squad car was on its way to Broadlands Haven guesthouse in Brynton Sands. All Gemma could do now was wait.

The nausea in her gut coiled tighter every time she thought of what she had done: to save Terry from himself, she had to preserve Teddy Biscuit's repugnant form. Terry would have opted for the bare knuckle; a, jaw-cracking jab between the eyes. And once one had been unleashed, the dams would open for a reign of others. Teddy's flabby form would have stood no chance against Terry's brute force latent within his compact biceps for over thirty years. Biscuit's body would have hit the floor behind the reception counter like a mountain of blancmange. Terry would then latch onto his prey like a jaguar clutching a ponderous buffalo and set-to. And Biscuit's cat caricatures would have gazed on, grinning insanely as the room filled with the sounds of pummelled meat.

Her phone convulsed at half-past-eleven. Ben had been watching the television with her, waiting for news. When Gemma picked up, Terry's voice croaked down the line. Gemma gestured to Ben to reduce the volume. 'Terry, where are you? We've all been worried sick.'

Terry sounded remarkably composed and coherent. 'I've been a fool, Gemma, but you know that.'

Questions volleyed at her throat but Gemma pushed them down and waited for Terry to speak again.

'I was gonna do it,' Terry came back. 'You've no idea how close I came. I was gonna kill that fucker and laugh all the way home. I thought that part of me was dead and gone, but we don't change, Gemma, we just learn to…to make ourselves acceptable to society by whatever means.'

'Where are you?'

'On a country road just outside Chapel St Leonard's.' Terry gave a grunt of amusement. 'I saw the squaddies outside the guesthouse and guessed only you were behind it. You did the right thing, Gem. What good would I have done to meself, getting back in the slammer? It made me think twice.'

'Come home, Terry. I'll inform the police it's over.'

'This Bertrand fellah is all over the news here, but no-one's said nothin' about this Teddy. Not a fuckin' dickie-bird.'

Ben's hand brushed against her skirt. She pulled him towards her.

Terry continued, 'No-one's made the connection but you. I would never have seen it meself. The fellah was just some geezer whose guesthouse Liam stopped at years ago. He'd have slipped through for sure. We've gotto get him. Together we can put this bastard inside.'

A wall of resistance reared up inside her. She was emotionally exhausted after months of living in fear of losing her home and the last thing she needed was to face media attention and to attend police appointments. Above all, she did not want to encounter *them* in the process. She stroked Ben's cheek with her thumb. 'You don't need me to do that, Terry.'

'Are you kiddin'? You're crucial in all this. The police don't know it, but they need you more than anybody else. Their investigation ain't complete without you. You made a connection everyone else failed to see.'

Resentment coloured her previous resistance. Where was Liam in all of this? He had created the mess and he was somewhere in Bristol starting a new life of his own. All she wanted right now was to be left alone, to be at peace with Ben. 'This is your battle now, Terry. Yours and Liam's. You have all the information you need to bring this man down. I just want to get on with my life in obscurity and look after Ben.'

'I can't believe I'm hearin' this. 'His voice receded as though jerking away from the mouthpiece. He came back. 'I never took you for a…a coward.'

Gemma closed her eyes.

'This…this man almost killed my son – Ben's father. He played him for a cheap bet for money and for their own sick entertainment. You lead me to him and then you back off. You…you cop out on me!'

Gemma held her tongue. She could understand why Terry would feel angry at her but Gemma's decision was final. It felt right.

Terry's voice had grown ragged in response to her silence. 'Okay, Gemma, I hear you. I hear you loud and clear. I'll bring this man down without your help. I'll do justice for you, Liam and Ben just so you can be left alone to shack up with this new fellah you told me about.'

Gemma gritted her teeth. 'It's not like that, Terry.'

'I ain't no fool. I've been on this planet sixty-two years and you can't take me for a fool.'

'I don't think you're a fool, Terry. I think you will do what you need to do because you are Liam's father and you are a good man.'

Terry's breaths whispered shakily down the phone line. He seemed to struggle to convene his next words. 'Tell…tell Vera I'll be home in a few hours and not t' worry.' And he cut the line.

Ben stuck to her hip like glue as she informed the police she had heard from Terry and that he had cooled off and was going home. She was informed that an officer would remain at the guesthouse for the time being. Her earlier distaste revisited at the thought people and resources had been called to arms for the preservation of someone like Teddy and that she, Gemma had been instrumental.

She lowered the phone after speaking to Vera and experienced a silent purgation inside. Clutter and weight had suddenly gone, leaving a white plateau behind. She did not welcome the feeling as a weight off the shoulders. This cliché was too pretty. Hers was bleaker, more of a wilderness. But the whole ugly episode was finally over. Gemma had imagined this moment to bring tears or laughter. But expressing emotion was the last thing she wanted to do right now. She simply said to Ben, 'Your granddad's coming home and everything is going to be all right.'

But Ben looked up at her and simply said, 'Can I go to Zack's house for tea tomorrow?'

Ben's mundane request in the wake of what had just happened confounded her but spurred a smile. 'Of course,' she said. She kissed him and Ben loped slowly to bed. Ben possessed none of the Greene physical agility or fieriness. He would not have understood why his granddad would want to hit anyone. But then the likes of Terry made things happen. What more could a force like Terry's need than to put someone like Teddy behind bars? Gemma suspected he might soon discover he needed no-one to fulfill his purpose. He would brandish Liam's name as the core of his cause but every hearing, every testimony and every inquiry would yield personal gratification. Gemma had provided the quarry. Terry would do the rest. He would pursue Teddy by legal means. And he would win.

Gemma hoped that one day soon, Terry would come and share his experiences. But a dark shadow loomed over the prospect. None of this would have been possible without Luke. He had been behind everything. She had a debt of gratitude to pay and Luke was waiting.

Chapter 31

TWITCHY Dave's wife, Stacy was two spaces ahead of Gemma in the supermarket queue. Gemma wanted to ask but couldn't bring herself to. Every time the question on whether she had reported Luke to the police reared in her throat, her pulse surged and her neck blotched red.

Stacy paid for her goods and went on her way. On shifting forward, Gemma spotted a news item on the lower front page of the Birmingham Post bearing Bertrand's name. She snatched a copy from the shelf and paid for her goods. Gemma ambled to the side of the gangway and read.

The article, *Bertrand's Betting Scam finds a Brother* began with a recap of the story so far. Gemma's sights latched onto the second paragraph: 'Terry Greene of Kenilworth tells how a connection between Bertrand and his brother Edward aka Teddy Biscuit had been bought to his attention after recalling how his son, Liam had stopped at Teddy's guesthouse in Brynton Sands on the Lincolnshire coast. "My son had a breakdown after his gambling habit got out of control there six years ago and this Teddy saw it all," says Terry, sixty-two. "It seemed too much of a coincidence that my son would get caught up in this betting scam masterminded by the brother of this guesthouse owner. Teddy was our only link to Bertrand and I will keep fighting to prove beyond a doubt that Teddy was gleaning out potential victims from people stopping at his guesthouse. So far as I am concerned, he is as guilty as his brother."

'With more victims and witnesses coming forward, the case is likely to go on for some months.'

Gemma was vaguely aware of the sliding doors opening as she neared the exit. She glanced up to meet Stacy's watery-blue eyes beholding a permanent surprise. 'Gemma? Ben's mum? I owe you a big, *big* apology.' Cherry gum radiated from her breath as she spoke.

Gemma was rendered speechless by Stacy's direct gaze and forceful entreaty. She patted Gemma on the shoulder as a fellow mother to another upon a common mission. 'I reported a friend of yours to the police. You know what I'm like, health and safety to a fault, and if that is my only vice, I hold my hands up right now. I just thought he was acting suspiciously at the school until I saw you talking to him during assembly the next day. I am so...*so* sorry. Please accept my most humble apologies.'

Gemma floundered at what Stacy was saying. 'You saw him the day before?'

Stacy's eyes did not blink. 'Yes. He was talking to Ben during lunch break through the fence railings. They seemed to have quite a chat, them two. I would have said something to you but I've not seen you on your own until now. I must say, he's quite a well-turned out young man, very distinguished. I hope there are no hard feelings, Gemma.'

Gemma felt railroaded by this woman. 'Well...er...no.'

'I'd love to chat but Dave's waiting in the car. I'll see you around the school.'

And she was gone.

Gemma tucked the paper beneath her arm and strode towards the car. She decided to speak to Ben after school before taking any action. She stopped dead when she spotted a black Jaguar coupe two rows from hers. Why the sight of this car would cause such a jolt, she could only guess but she had seen one like this parked outside Templeton Court before she had last spoken with Luke. She looked about, lowered her head and peeked inside: immaculate, as expected, chestnut leather seats, a suit jacket draped over the backrest, a clutch of CDs on the passenger seat; Mozart, Beethoven, Mendelssohn.

Gemma backed off. Though the evidence fitted, she took the logic many people drove around in black Jaguar coupes with such items within. The alternative was unthinkable. She returned to her Fiesta.

Ben's school bus could not arrive soon enough. Until then, Gemma diverted her thoughts by digging over the rose patch. She almost showered herself with dirt when her mobile started up. Gemma wouldn't look at it. Her arms were shaking and her chest lurched. The trilling kept on. She cursed beneath her breath. She clenched her teeth. The phone kept on. And on.

Gemma recommenced with digging the dirt now for the sake of digging. The trowel hit a stone. She gouged the thing out and the small rock pinged over her head and rebounded on the garden path.

The trilling stopped. Gemma closed her eyes. Blood squelched against her eardrums.

'Bloody creditors, eh?'

Gemma opened her eyes and looked across. Patti was standing against the party fence, her considerable forearm draped over the building post.

Gemma's breaths were still lurching. 'What?'

'I said, bloody creditors, eh?' Patti jerked her head in a complicit fashion. 'I assume that fellow in the suit was one of them.'

Gemma wasn't sure what to say, but Pattie didn't seem to concern herself over this. 'My brother-in-law lost his business ten years ago. Liquidators stripped him clean. It takes a certain kind to do that sort of thing. I reckon these people suffered some sort of trauma that splits their psyche in two: one half does the job; the other goes home to their families. Guilt. That's what it is.'

Gemma felt obliged to an offering with little to give. She slowly stood and dusted herself down. She attempted a smile. 'Yes. I suppose so.'

The creases around Patti's eyes ironed out, revealing again skin relatively untouched by the sun. She gave a little nod, apparently pleased at the opportunity to exhibit empathy for Gemma's situation. Gemma allowed Patti to believe such empathy had given solace. At this moment, Gemma wished Patti had got it right.

Gemma entered the house to see if Ben's bus had arrived and found Ben's school bag already at the kitchen floor. The bus must have come early. Ambient soft rock punctuated with fanfares trickled from the living room. Gemma stepped towards the alcove and saw Ben without his crutches standing on a balance-board in front of the TV. The screen itself exhibited an interactive snow-boarding trip down an idealised Alpine slope. Ben's arms spread eagle-like and his knees pivoted as he braced for a particularly steep causeway. He appeared to glide upon an air cushion, the muscles in his calves and thighs, never seen before, twitching and spasming with effort. Once the ground had leveled out, Ben turned, sensing her presence behind him.

'Hey, Mum!' he cried. 'Look what came in the post today!'

From that instant, Gemma didn't hesitate. She lurched towards the TV and ferreted for the wire. She pulled the plug. The guitar riff died at a discord along with the flickering pictures. Quietly, she gathered the wire up to the plug and disengaged the terminal pins. She pushed the coils and the Wii remote into the packaging box. The Wii player followed suit. At this point Ben had dismounted the balance-board. That too went inside. Gemma then dragged the box through the kitchen and pushed it out into the side passageway. A glassy resolve had formed in the centre of her chest once she had returned to the living room. Ben was standing in front of the TV, perplexity and pique pushing his eyes into the recesses of his brow-bone. From there, his irises appeared more grey than green.

Gemma showed she was not fazed by his look. 'Why didn't you tell me he'd spoken to you?'

Ben's expression did not change. 'Who?'

Gemma knew he was being contrary. 'You know who.'

'There's nothing much to tell.'

Gemma crossed her arms. 'What did he say to you?'

Ben did not answer, seemingly on a curfew against her cross-examination after she had ruined his game.

'Answer me, Ben.'

Ben's brow furrowed, affronted by her tone. 'You never told me not to speak to him.'

'Well, I'm telling you now.'

'Why? He was just saying hello.'

'Stacy across the road said he was talking to you for quite some time. How long did he need to say hello?'

'He was just asking about my legs, that's all.'

'Did he touch you?'

Moisture glistened on Ben's lower eyelid. His lip trembled. Gemma gritted her teeth at her demand to know. 'I said, *did he touch you?*'

Ben's grey eyes remained on hers. 'No.'

Gemma closed her eyes in monumental relief. When she opened them, her vision had blurred. She blinked the tears away. At this point, Ben found the resolve to argue his point. 'He was just being nice.'

Gemma moved close to Ben until she could see a small mole on one of his irises. 'No one is nice, Ben. Do you understand me? *No one.*'

His voice tremored. 'Mum.'

'I've told you enough times, never to speak to strangers.'

At this point, Ben turned away.

Gemma made the most despicable decision of her life after preserving Teddy from Terry's wrath: not to inform the police about Luke. The fact remained he was the ultimately the reason she and Ben still had a roof over their heads. They still lived here and she still intended to preserve her secret about *Domestic Bliss*. She was still obligated. She was still 'his'.

Gemma prepared tea in silence. Her feelings towards Luke had tendrilled through ever deeper canyons inside her, especially during her final battle to get her house back. Stacy had described him as well-turned out and distinguished. These descriptions were fitting. He had physical presence and a warped kind of magnetism. She wished she could jettison the part of her that responded to the way he looked at her as though no one else existed. She wished she could rid of the lucid picture of him she carried, the bleak winter around his eyes, his features ravaged yet made captivating by his insomnia. She wanted to lay a soothing hand upon his forehead and recoiled at the idea. She wanted to see his eyes close and his lips to land gently on hers. Her gut roiled. He had letched at countless women from his secret window. How tragic his person could harbour ever sicker fantasies than voyeurism. She desired, pitied, feared and despised him.

And he was still waiting.

Gemma served tea but Ben had other ideas, watching a news documentary she knew he found uninteresting. Gemma began to recant on how she had reacted earlier, treating Ben as though he was to blame. She lowered two plates of shepherd's pie on the table. 'Your dinner's ready, Ben,' she uttered.

Ben didn't respond.

'Come on, Ben,' she persisted.

She waited as he dragged himself from the armchair and slumped himself at the table. He squashed his cheek up against the heel of his hand. His other hand twiddled his fork in pirouettes until the metal clicked repeatedly against the side of his plate.

Gemma kept eating.

The clicking sound increased in frequency propelling peas to the edge of his plate.

'Stop it, Ben.'

Ben kept on twirling his fork with renewed force. Ben's behaviour dismayed her. Rarely had she seen Ben this angry. She had been guilty like most mothers of treating her child as a possession, to overstep boundaries other individuals had the right to preserve. But the advent to his teens may have already sprouted forth an annex labyrinth she would have no access to. She began to suspect she no longer knew all of him, or at least know only what he wanted. 'Ben,' she finally uttered.

Ben stopped and gave her a daggered look. 'That present was *mine.*'

Gemma knew any argument was futile. 'This isn't up for discussion.'

'It was mine. Luke bought it for me. You had no right to take it away from me. And you lied. He *was* the man you work for and that means he is not a stranger.'

The mere mention of his name sparked a bolt from her chest down to her legs. Gemma gave Ben a level look. 'Don't ever mention his name in this house again.'

'You hate men, don't you?'

Gemma's fork slipped from her hand with a clatter.

Ben's scowl grew more pointed. 'You never mention dad. It's like he never existed. And you never accept help from anybody. You just drive everybody away including granddad. You're not happy unless it's just you and me struggling against the world. Everything is boring and we're broke. And all you want to do is control me.' Ben pushed his dinner away. 'I hate you.' He staggered to his feet and lurched from the table.

Gemma couldn't move if she wanted to. She watched him trudge across the room and disappear upstairs.

Gemma knew a pursuit would push him further away. All reasoning and explanations would yield no response from him.

She stared at the TV without taking in the evening's entertainment. For the first time in a week, the news did not feature Geoff Colby's enterprise or his party. Ben was right. Since Liam had left, her world had grown smaller. She'd forfeited friends who would view her single number as a spare part. Paul and Kelly from the garage; Steve and Sharon from the track. Yes they would welcome her company if she showed up at the Randolph or the Silver Spoon, but too much time had elapsed and she feared the conversation would be stilted. Terry was her heaviest loss. She had got so wrapped up with saving her house and getting the divorce through, life had crept by. She had isolated herself including Ben. All she had left was her job at the surgery.

At eleven, Gemma went up. She noticed Ben's bedroom door was firmly closed. She approached and rapped gently. 'Ben.' Without a sliver, she could not tell if his light was on. She rapped again. 'Ben.'

Still no answer.

Gemma's stomach coiled tightly at the thought of Luke. She would have to face him. Only then could she release herself from him and pick up the pieces of her life.

Chapter 32

BEN'S empty breakfast bowl on the table on her rising warned her Ben wasn't through with his indignation. Ben picked up his satchel without looking at her.

'Let me drive you,' she said.

Ben turned and gave her a doleful look. He left the house quietly.

The practice was in jovial spirits as Zeeta had brought in a birthday cake and chocolate cookies. Even Dr. Miles had a compliment for her, praising her minuiting work and aside, expressed admiration for the way she had held up during her divorce. His sincerity did not abate the throbbing in her chest. She wondered if Ben would come home for tea or would he stop out at Zack's all night? She got home for lunch and flicked on the TV. A death connected with Colby's operation has been confirmed. Malcolm Treadwell, 37 died of impact injuries whilst scaling Rackwick Cliffs on the Isle of Hoy without safety equipment. Colby withdrew funds under an indemnity death clause which had been agreed between both parties. Vernon claimed he had no knowledge of what Colby was up to and would fiercely defend his innocence.

Gemma switched the TV off. She resented Luke's part in Colby's downfall; without him, there would have been more deaths, more injuries and more families shattered. Gemma had already made the decision not to contact Luke at his place of work, as this meant finding more out about his life. She wished not to know. She decided to turn up at Templeton Court tomorrow morning and employ her secret signal, much as the idea dismayed her.

Her phone sounded. Gemma paused in brewing a cup. She picked up and Luke's voice crackled up the line. 'I believe you have been trying to contact me.'

A violent riptide tore inside her. For an insane second, Gemma thought Luke had seen into her head. She feigned an abstracted tone. 'Maybe. I've been busy.'

'Hmm.' He seemed to dwell on something. 'Well, it occurred to me after our last meeting that I had failed to supply you my contract details. I am a private listing.'

She didn't like his 'hmm.' Did he not believe her?

Luke went on, 'and I think it unlikely you would contact me at work in light of things. Any matter you wish to discuss with me would be private.'

He was right. Sometimes she suspected she confused his courtesy for arrogance. 'Yes,' she said and silence drew out. He was still waiting. 'I do wish to speak to you in person as a matter of fact.'

'May I suggest a lay-by off the main road to where I work? There's a bistro called Andre's not far away. The trees offer screen but is not too…deserted.'

Gemma picked up on what he was implying and did not correct him. 'Yes,' she said. 'Now is as good time as any if you are not too busy.'

'I will clear this afternoon's schedule,' he said.

Gemma refrained from telling him not to put himself to such trouble. She ended the call.

Her twenty minute trip to the outskirts of Warwick was but a mental performance of present tasks, her mind otherwise unprecedentedly clear. She took a wrong turning and consulted her A to Z. She spotted Andre's, a taverna-style lunchery with tables outside. The lay-by almost crept past her until a black spoiler sparked sunlight into her eyes. She turned into the further entry. She stopped a car-length behind his and killed the engine. She appraised Luke's car quietly for a moment. She couldn't see inside; the sun blinded her and his rear window appeared to be tinted. In fact, the whole aerodynamic form appeared moulded from the same alloy but with a latent force inside – his.

She took the initiative and got out as there was little legroom in her car anyway. She realised on her approach that he could be watching her reflection in the wing mirror. Teeth gnawed at her ribcage. She promised herself this meeting with him would be the last.

The passenger door swung open. She paused and fingered her mobile in her bag should anything go wrong. She drew level and looked inside. He was already looking at her. Cool air-conditioning brushed her face; chestnut leather seats, a Mozart CD on the dashboard. She was now certain but said nothing. She sat beside him.

The pallor around his eyes resumed autumn hues; a combination of the small hours and poor light may have bought out his worst the last time she had seen him. His insomnia still embraced the colour out of him. He possessed freedom to move as anyone else, and yet he looked upon her from the dark side of a shroud. Still, immaculate as usual; clad in a sage green tie and a charcoal suit that flinted cobalt in the light. He or his car smelled of fern. And he appraised her with composure verging onto conceit. He proffered his card. She deciphered the name Luke Forrester and wished she hadn't. In automation, she slipped the narrow edge between her fingers, inadvertently brushing her fingertip against his. His flesh felt cool.

Quickly, she dropped the card into her bag. 'I think I should thank you,' she began stiffly and squirmed at how she sounded. 'Without your help, my home would be repossessed by now.' She omitted Ben's name from the equation.

Luke's premature blink signaled that her words of appreciation were unwarranted. 'I have been following the news,' he said. 'I take it this Colby man was holding you to ransom.'

Gemma was still aware of her fingertip. She fondled her bag strap. 'Yes. And I remembered where I had seen Bertrand's brother before.'

'Yet I suspect you haven't involved yourself with the police campaign.'

She cleared her throat. 'No.'

The car was too quiet. She wished he would put music on, even if Mozart was the sole option. He didn't seem to want her appreciation either, which confused her.

'That game I got Ben,' he said. 'It will help his coordination, strengthen his calf muscles. I hope you received the package safely.'

Gemma depressed her nail into her palm until it pinched. 'Someone saw you speaking to Ben at the school gates during lunch break.'

'Yes, of course.'

His admittance floundered her. She was about to volley a retort when something caught her eye. The fabric on a small fragment of his lapel orientated differently to the rest of his suit. The patch was invisible unless the light hit the fabric obliquely. The shape suggested a deposit from the sky, like a paint drip or bird-mess. He noticed her looking. She trained her eyes upon his.

But his eyes had hooded. 'I needed to ask Ben something in your absence as I doubt your answer would have possessed his candour.'

Gemma knit her lip.

'I knew the Venetian cat mask was not Philip's style. I can see now only Ben could have made it. I understand he did not realise what it was for. It makes me look rather a…bloody fool.'

Gemma knit her lip harder. The car fell into deeper silence. Will the cat mask issue ever lie?

He added quietly, 'Still, something tells me I deserved it.'

Gemma decided a silent interlude preferable to posing the question whether she had spoiled his *Domestic Bliss* forever. But another quandary took precedent. Was she paranoid or had Luke been evasive just then? Perhaps Luke *had* asked Ben about the cat mask, but he had also withheld the crucial part about his inquiry into Ben's legs. What reason could he have to ask about this part of Ben's anatomy except the unthinkable? Luke had not touched, but did he have a good look? The mark on his lapel drew her sights again. Yes. Bird-mess. Definitely. How gravely satisfying.

He spotted her clandestine inspection. She saw no point in confronting him about her sighting of his car at the local supermarket, or of whether he had followed her to Fell Reservoir. Her gaze met his, not wanting to rouse his suspicion that anything was amiss. But she could see something he couldn't. She could see through him. Luke could brush himself up, talk with that plumb in his mouth, win people's trust and respect, but he could never erase that mark. The mark on him that made him what he secretly was. 'I'm sorry you feel that way,' she said coolly. 'None if it was intended.' She drew her bag to her lap. 'Again, I can't thank you enough for what you have done for us both. I hope…' Her following words felt cumbersome. 'I hope the sleep clinic find a cure for your insomnia.' She knew Luke had detected her insincerity.

Luke said nothing as she got out.

Gemma entered her Fiesta and started up. This time, she double-checked she had not slipped the car into reverse. She released the clutch gently. She applied the gas similarly. The banger having accumulated quirks through mileage and abuse, conspired against her. Blue smoke issued from the pipe along with an oily smell. Luke's car, inert and majestic emerged from within the cloud. Gemma didn't care if she had arrived in a tractor. She was happier with the fumes and the clatter than his aroma of fern and the air conditioning. She gave the engine a little kick and juddered forward. She didn't look back.

As soon as Gemma got home, she had a shower. A habitual step-in-and-step-outer, she remained for minutes. She increased the pressure and the temperature until the water stung. She closed her eyes and lost herself within the thunder. Luke's face emerged clearly, his surrender to the cool drink she had provided – one eye partly open. Climaxing. She snapped her eyes open. The shower continued to thunder. The shower curtain, undulated: cream and corn, the ideal neutral on which to project meditative images. She would happily exchange hers for anyone else's in this street; Patti and her obsession with bingo, soaps and Blackpool; Stacy and her endeavours with the school; the more prosaic the better. For the first time in months, she wished Liam was here.

She stepped out.

Ben had left her a text as expected. He was having tea at Zack's and would be home late. She texted him back to say no later than ten.

She served herself a microwave lasagna that had lain in the cupboard since before Liam left. She ate two forkfuls and slung the rest in the bin. Since this afternoon, her stomach would accommodate no more than a cup of tea. At dusk, she donned her coat and walked to the playing field next to Azhar's. The sound of kids larking about grew more distinct as she cleaved her way through the thoroughfare. Since her last visit with her Ashton guitar, the hawthorns had closed in. Ahead, she could make out the grated bin that had been her Ashton's final destination. Nettles hugged the hedgerows and cypresses behind the playing area gathered deep shadows.

Ben, Zack and Amil were circling the swings in their bikes. Another boy was pushing high on the swing. Zack sped in front of the swing as the boy pendulumed backwards. Amil followed, waiting for the next backswing before pedalling forward. Gemma wondered at why boys of his age had to devise these games. Risk? Thrill? Peer pressure? Or just part of being a boy she could never understand? Now it was Ben's turn; he readied himself at the boy's flank. If Ben mistimed his manoeuvre, the boy would clout Ben hard enough to knock him out. The boy would never be able to stop himself. Ben pushed forward with perfect timing. Ben was evidently a veteran with this game, and likely equally-dangerous others. Gemma did not stop them. She watched from a covered spot. She let them be.

A dark shape pulled at her vision from the opposite side of the field. She glanced across. The figure was standing beneath the cypress trees next to railings. From here, he – as the stance suggested male – appeared to be wearing a long trench coat and was watching the boys. She wasn't sure if the figure had been there all along as his immobility had rendered him almost invisible. Gemma trained her sights upon the figure. So still was he, the shadow could have been part of the railings. He took a step towards the swings. Gemma's legs twitched. Blood surged through a narrow hiatus in her groin and down her legs. She wondered if the jacket beneath his trench coat cosseted a bird-mess imprint. She hoped so. She hoped the dark figure would take another step towards the swings. She wanted him to go all the way, to charm the boys with his creepy solicitations. Lasagna essence revisited the back of her throat. She restrained a cough. From here, he wouldn't spot her but he could hear her. The figure lifted a hand to his head and emitted a thin whistle. A black and white collie bounded over. The man strode away from the swings, plodding on short legs, a gait not indicative of Luke's.

Gemma exhaled at length and breathed easily. Paradoxically, she wished the man had been Luke: to have her fears founded; to expose him for what he was; for Ben to see for himself.

The boys were still eddying about the swings. Gemma backtracked through the thoroughfare and returned home.

She heard Ben enter the house at ten. She was on the upper landing at the time sorting through the washing. She didn't hear him come upstairs; but the sound of running water informed of his presence in the bathroom. Gemma carried the washing down to the kitchen and set the timer. She waited for Ben to follow but the house fell silent.

She went upstairs. Ben's door as yesterday was shut. She rapped and this time quietly entered. Ben was already in bed. He faced the wall; his head nestled into the crook of his elbow.

Her entreaty came out constrained. 'Come down, Ben.'

Ben burrowed his head deeper into his elbow. Like a butterfly closing its wings, Ben's eyelashes swept downwards to his cheek.

'Please, Ben. Let's talk about this.'

Ben didn't move.

Watching him barricade himself against her, she wondered what Ben had been thinking as he roller-coastered around the swings this evening. Did he not care if the boy on the swing had belted him? Would he not have cried for the pain of a father's desertion fare greater? Now that the reality had hit that his father was never coming back, did he blame her?

Gemma left the room quietly.

Chapter 33

GEMMA roused earlier the next morning to guarantee she shared breakfast-time with Ben, even if silence continued to divide them. Ben munched his cornflakes, his glasses reflecting the bay window opposite and concealing his eyes.

Ben scraped at his bowl. 'I'm going to Amil's after school,' he announced.

Gemma's chest hurt. 'Oh.' She took Ben's bowl. 'What time will you be home?'

'Depends on how I feel.'

'Tell Amil's mum I want you back by eight.'

Gemma knew this earlier time would not go down well with Ben, but tough. She was the sole parent now. She sealed the rubbish bag and opened the back door. The interactive Wii game was still in the side passageway. Her mouth twitched at the sight of it. To her, Luke's gift was but the catalyst to the disintegration of her relationship with Ben. She knelt down to crush the items further into the box for disposal when a small brown envelope caught her eye. She fished it out and unsealed the flap. Inside she found two tickets to go to Disneyland Paris. She entered the house.

Ben was putting on his coat. She breezed past him, brandishing the envelope. 'I see by these tickets to go to Disneyland Paris that you had a lot to say to him at the school gates.'

Ben afforded her a smouldering glare. 'No. I told him that *after*.'

Gemma scowled. 'After?'

Ben turned away.

Gemma remained where she was. 'You mean…you mean you saw him more than once?'

Ben had solidified to rock, his arms crossed in defense.

Her voice was shaking. 'How many times, Ben?'

She could see from behind him that his cheeks were flushing. 'How many times?'

Ben conceded with a murmur. 'Just twice.'

'Where?'

'In the park last weekend.'

So, he had loitered in the park as she had imagined; an oversized raven shielded by shadow. She wanted to grill Ben about every detail but knew she might just as well gag him.

Ben picked up his satchel and faced her, his mouth set. 'Can I go now?'

Gemma didn't speak.

Ben took this as a yes and gathered his crutches. He left the room.

She watched Ben mount the bus from her window. Everything behind her, inside her was dark and turgid. Everything outside was normality. The outside world was no longer accessible to her. The dark enclosed her.

Gemma went to the garage and reversed out her Fiesta. Only when reaching the main road to Warwick did she realise she hadn't informed the practice of her absence. She didn't care at that moment and planned to blag an excuse later. The volume of traffic at this hour caused little delay, all lights on green. In barely twenty minutes, she was passing Andre's and the lay-by where she had last met up with Luke. She kept her eyes in front not wanting to recollect. A half-mile further on, she turned into the Prospect Business Park. Glass frontages of all tints from turquoise to maroon reflected stark cumulus formations and a strobe of sunlight. Symbolic or arty installations dotted small roundabouts – a winged man, a Henry Moore influence, a quoit emulation. Fountains and plaques sporting names of corporations, mostly foreign meant little to her. She imagined these monoliths housed a virtual service to a global market. In her banged-out Fiesta, she was a country mouse in the Land of Oz.

She knew the moment she spotted the tall domed tower glinting copper behind a dandelion seed fountain she'd found her destination. A marble-effect plaque informed in minimalist italics the Registry of Mergers occupied this site. She pulled up on a grass verge near the gatehouse. She got out and clopped her way down a narrow tarmac track. She wasn't clenching her teeth and yet she had the sensation the roots were burrowing into her gums. She caught her reflection on the glass doors near the front and saw a woman bundled up to herself, her face a maze of harsh shadows. She kept walking.

Staff in similar aerodynamic alloy vehicles was filing through the barriers. Gemma walked by a big black man with a Cheshire-cat grin engaging with a young russet-haired woman with gothic-style eyeliner. The young woman noticed Gemma passing. Several other power-dressers filed through large rotating doors at the front. Gemma stepped in line.

The entry opened out into a large tea-coloured lobby with wall lights and huge windows looking out onto the car park and a tree-lined avenue. The marble-topped reception desk was manned by a careworn security man in a blue uniform and peaked cap. The man glanced up on her approach.

'Hello,' Gemma said quietly, 'I'd like to speak to Luke Forrester please.'

The security man nodded and lifted the desk phone. 'Right-ho, Miss. Can I say who wants to speak to him?'

Gemma thought she might sprint back through the rotating doors, dive through the influx of power-workers and throw up on the grass verge by her car. But the tone of her voice betrayed none of this.

'Just tell him it's Gemma and I will be waiting for him outside the main entrance '

'Sure, Miss, if you will give me a minute.'

He depressed the relevant keys and Gemma turned and strode out of the building.

Gemma backed up against a steel girder framing the doorway. The steel chilled her shoulder blades; the influx became a blur. Her mind grew still as though paralysed by icy water at the bottom of a deep pond. Likewise, her hands felt clammy, cold. She couldn't stop blinking.

'Ben needs to lose those crutches.'

His voice drew inches from her left ear. She turned with a start to meet Luke's haunted gaze. The breeze teased his hair at his brow but he did not blink. He was wearing his despicable trench coat in spite of the weather.

'Forgive me,' he added, reading her disorientation. 'I never use the main entrance. I've been watching you. Has Ben tried out his Wii fit yet?'

Gemma's hands shuddered. She pushed them into her jacket pockets. 'I see you've done well for yourself. What do you do exactly to earn yourself a private entrance?'

'I liaise between corporations in drawing up contracts and mergers. A sort of ambassador if, you will.'

Gemma's voice was shaking. 'It's always the same, isn't it? People like you sneaking your way into high places, leeching off people's trust.' Her voice was growing in magnitude and perusals behind him were gathering. 'Was that why you helped me get my house back? Did you think you could obligate me in some way, so that you could get what you were really after?' Her breath snatched. 'I've seen the way you look at Ben. I know you have been talking to him on the sly in the park. I saw your car at the supermarket near my house too. What were you doing there when it's nowhere near your neighbourhood? Hoping to see him, perhaps?' Her breaths shuddered. 'You see him as a weakling, don't you – easy prey? Children are so easily won over, aren't they? God, when I think of what I did in front of you. You make my skin crawl.'

Luke's eyes hooded over, his right one more than his left. Perhaps now she was seeing the real Luke: manipulative, callous and scornful of fellow human beings. The two colleagues who had been chatting by the gatehouse had joined a small congregation. Gemma couldn't stop herself. 'Well, I've given a lot of thought to what you said the other day about how a deficit of a basic need can torment you. Well, I hope you never sleep again. I hope you lie awake, tormented for the rest of your life. You creep. Keep away from me and keep away from Ben!'

Gemma fists quaked within the confines of her pockets. She strode away. She ducked her head as she made her way through the congregation. She trotted back to the gatehouse and to the grass verge. Once in the car she doubled over until her face pressed into the folds of her skirt. She did not throw up. She rocked.

Chapter 34

THE guesthouse taunted her with false exits. A narrow landing terminated at a delta. Doors on either side offered ever more choice. She had entered the building two or three turnings ago. The walls had shifted, an opening had closed, or was she mistaken? A further landing tapered to a wedged point. Scratching sounds stirred the air, almost indecipherable, yet all over. The walls oscillated beneath the palm of her hand. She retraced her steps and found the opening behind her had closed to a dead-end. The urgency to get out compressed upon her chest – every cell in her body screamed to get out. If she didn't get out, she could do nothing and *it* would happen.

Gemma did not come-to with a start. Capering TV images emerged gradually from a soup. Congealed saliva had created a seam between her lower lip and the fabric of the chair. Her head throbbed. At that moment, Gemma did not know the time of day or how she had got here. Her thought processes had been swathed in Clingfilm. She blinked her vision clear. Fragments punctured through: her drive from the Chrome Building; the dandelion seed fountain; passing between Andre's and the tree-lined lay-by. She could not recall pulling off the grass verge by the barrier or of pulling up outside her house. Had she put the car in the garage? Her memory could not confirm either way. She'd splashed her face with cold water soon after coming in, and then, nothing. *Ben needs to lose those crutches.* Everything flooded back.

She heaved her head from the arm of the chair. The bay window presented dusk. What this implied was incredible. She had sensed a protracted slip of time upon awakening but when had she blacked-out? The guesthouse detained her still. With all resolve, she unfurled her joints and pushed onto her feet. Gnats swarmed around her head. She waited for the blizzard fade-out to finally escape the clutches of the guesthouse miasma.

Gemma trudged to the kitchen, unpopped two painkillers from the blister pack and swallowed them with water. She shuffled to the foot of the stairs and called up. 'Ben!'

No answer.

Her surroundings shifted abruptly into focus. She returned to the living room and checked out the timer beneath the TV: nine-thirty. A brick materialised within her ribcage. She told herself not to panic. Ben was obviously still mad at her and was administering a mighty hoof against her new mode of authoritarianism. She crossed the lounge and picked up the phone. She knew before Ben's line cut to voicemail he'd switched his off. She scrolled through the contacts list on her mobile and dialled Amil's parents. His mother, whom Gemma only knew as 'Amil's mum,' informed Gemma in broken English that Ben hadn't arranged to visit Amil today. Indignation prickled her. So, Ben had decided to go off somewhere and make up a lie? She tried Zack's number. As expected, the same result. By now the brick in her chest had acquired razor edges. Gemma refused to consider the nauseating possibility yet. Ben had not gone missing after visiting a friend; he had gone somewhere else to pique her. Had he taken off to see his father? Terry came to mind. Despite their last exchange, Terry, would have informed her if Ben had shown up there. Luke's haunted eyes flashed in her mind. *He is a very special boy. You are lucky to have him.* Gemma kept scrolling though the contact list. Nothing else jumped at her. She tried Ben's number again. No joy.

Gemma switched off the TV and stopped dead. Ben's crutches were propped up against the side of the cabinet. He must have stopped by after school and left them there. True, Ben regarded his crutches unseemly for larking about at the park with his friends even if he needed them. Yet the sight of his crutches now held significance she didn't much care for. The nauseating possibility revisited with a prod. Ben was with...*him* at this moment...wasn't he? The deed may yet to have occurred or the deed may have already occurred, whatever the *deed* was. What was a race against time if she was uncertain if she was fighting against the future or another time frame? She begged that it was not the present or the past. Was her mounting adrenalin redundant? Her body refused to have it any other way. Her mind now clear and her tendons pulled tight, she strode to the door with increasing haste to check the night. She trained her sights up and down the road. No movement except for Stacy shutting the curtains opposite. Gemma's Fiesta was not parked out front; she must have locked it in the garage after all.

Gemma barged into the hall and grabbed her coat, keys and mobile. She rummaged around for Luke's card he'd given her yesterday. Hands shaking, she dialled. The number immediately cut to voicemail. Was he watching *Domestic Bliss* at this moment? Or was he doing something else? Her throat momentarily closed up. She spurted to the garage round the back with the aim of checking out the playing area before contacting the police. She found in her earlier dazed condition that she had neglected to engage the padlock. She raised the door with a clatter and knew before flicking the fluorescent tubing that something was wrong. Glass encrusted the floor; the bonnet displayed jagged reflections of the trees opposite and the body of the car did not recede into the shadows as her Fiesta should. She flicked the light.

A rind of teeth hugged the metal seals where a windscreen once had been. The actual windscreen had been pummelled outwards in one shattered piece and lay on the floor. The rear passenger window evidenced a neater job, the glass clean off. The bodywork had been chipped and dented around the windows. The passenger door handle, a casualty of the frenzied attack now canted at a forty-five degree angle. A front headlight dangled by a thread.

Gemma stepped towards the car, breath bated. Shards scored the cement beneath her feet. She looked inside. The interior was untouched except for glass dusting the passenger seat. Her lungs had taken leave of her body and had fallen down a shaft. The bellows resumed their remote respiration. Her shoulders felt tight; her hands trembled. Gemma unlocked the door and got in. The car rocked disagreeably. She rested her hands upon the steering wheel and stared out. The present, to her was vitality, not the future, not waiting. Waiting was passive resignation more repugnant than a trample over this broken glass in bare feet. She pushed the key into the ignition. The car clattered into life. He could have pushed a toothpick into the slot instead – a more proficient method to disable a car. But disablement wasn't his only objective it seemed, but to vent rage. Paul had been right: her car had been attacked. Luke, armed with something akin to a crowbar, had taken wanton aims. In his suit. Always in his suit; his expression steadfast, like the creases in the fabric of his jacket and his eyes unwavering. And he had emerged job complete. Immaculate.

She killed the engine. She got out and checked the rear. The exhaust pipe appeared clear of foreign objects but her two rear tyres had been minced again. He evidently believed her car had been disabled enough. Gemma got back inside and started up with the aim of releasing the clutch. With only one headlight, she could be mistaken for a motorbike. But what did she care? She was moving. She was moving in the present, and not waiting on something or someone. She would reach his flat in the time it would take to call the police and explain everything. The unthinkable option: waiting.

Without rear tyre suspension, the car canted backwards and quaked in the bargain. Without a front windscreen, an Arctic hurricane assaulted her. The engine deafened her. And on checking her mirrors, discovered he had removed her rear windscreen as well. On the main road, every passing vehicle flashed at her. A truck's horn blasted her eardrums. But Gemma regarded fellow motorists' wrath with detachment. She could not feel the wind at her face or the bone-shattering transit. At one point, she reached thirty-five. The Fiesta resented her right foot's resolute pressure, but the thing kept moving – in the present. Her physical discomfort detained unthinkable thoughts and the hell-hole of possibilities. She remained in the present; her only shield.

The wheels grated alarmingly as she veered into Templeton Court an eternity later. Self-censure pinched ever harder. Why hadn't she alerted the police after all? Her delusion of high focus had in fact been confusion. In her blind panic, she had not considered the possibility he may have taken Ben elsewhere. And even if Ben was up there, what if she couldn't gain entry? She spotted Luke's Jaguar and her mind fell still. She pulled up alongside it.

The wind at her face abated. The grating sound deepened to a series of clunks that concluded with an almighty jolt. Her single headlight died along with a shock of sparks on a rear wheel arch she'd just noticed through her wing mirror. Had the disc frictioned against the main road like a welder's torch all the way here? It no longer mattered. Gemma got out. His window at the top of the apartment pulled at her vision. She crunched across the gravel, her sights pinned to this dark rectangle.

She entered the building. The stairwell opened out ahead of her in identical fashion to its southerly-facing counterpart.

Disinfectant and jasmine invoked unwanted memories of *Domestic Bliss*. Why she had avenged him with her fat suit the last time, she could not at this moment recollect, but the reason would have seemed paltry now. She grabbed onto the railing with a clop. She paused and slipped off her shoes. She strode up the risers as silently as a cat. By the second flight, her strides had gathered momentum. Clover motifs on the walls raced by; stone-effect risers sped beneath her. Her lungs burned. She was going to a realm once unconceivable to her – she was going up to her voyeur's hide, the place from where a laser of scrutiny had seared the nerve endings of her arms, her abdomen, her legs, *her scar*. The upper landing pooled out into a nexus of three apartments. Two houseplants flanked a large window overlooking the car park. She knew without a doubt the white panelled door occupying the courtyard-facing wall fronted his domain. He had removed the bulb to his security-light, draping shadows over his entryway. Silence smothered her. She gazed at his door, fastened into place by a wall of resistance unforeseen. She had reached an agonising fulcrum between a mother's duty and approaching that other world, the world she had encountered at Brynton Sands, Liam on the guesthouse room floor, his eyes feral and his room stinking of shit. She was nothing to him. At that moment, she was nothing.

How could it be that she was standing here like this? Time was crucial. She had just endangered her own life and possibly the lives of other drivers getting here. And Ben's safety could depend on her alone.

Would she hear scratching noises on the other side? Would she hear something scratching?

She stepped forward, raised her hand to administer a knock. She stopped. Wood had been chipped from around the brass plate housing the keyhole. The imprint of an earlier housing could be seen beneath. Luke had changed the locks recently. But further indentations suggested someone else had tried to break in; scratch marks crisscrossed the brass plate itself. She lowered her hand.

Gemma stooped to drop her shoes to the floor and noticed a coin-sized splat of blood on the doormat. The blood had dried to rust, almost invisible against the fawn bristle. She couldn't tell if the blood was an hour old or a week, the stain having dried to a matt crust. The shape suggested a deposit from above, perhaps a nose bleed.

Gemma straightened herself. She raised her hand once more and grasped the door handle. She pushed down and forward. The door yielded to her will. A warm draft caressed her face. She wished the door had resisted. The world on the other side would have remained inaccessible to her, locked away and unseen. Gemma stepped in. Gloom detained her progress until her eyes adjusted. Another splat of blood blemished the tiled floor; atoll-shaped and black. She gazed ahead; a third splat of blood, a fourth. In poor light she couldn't tell if the deposits had dried like acrylic or smear easily. Her bare feet took a clear path to avoid finding out. Pointers to the other world abraded her as inverted enticement. But unlike before at Brynton Sands, she had no choice but to look. Two doors to her right passed slowly by. Gemma's sights remained ahead, upon a partially open door at the head of the hallway, the door that permitted a dusky glow from beyond. The indiscernible and the detectable had surpassed a threshold without notice but her ears were now unmistaken – a stir in the air – a sigh? Gemma paused. The air stirred again. But this time, Gemma did not stop. She followed the trail of blood markers towards the partly-open door. The sound grew more distinct; scribbling, an inscriber's whisper. The corner of a framed photograph propped upon a unit shifted into view. The scoring undertone insisted upon her eardrums. But Gemma was not here. The sights and sounds were being received via an inanimate device and she was not processing them. She was simply picking up the signal in a disembodied way. Her approach opened out the view of the photograph little by little: an image that formed the terminus of the blood trail – a picture of Ben. Ben, in his crutches and spectacles is standing in a garden Gemma doesn't recognise. Ben is wearing his school polo shirt and trousers. He tries to smile but the sun makes him squint. Ben's toothy grimace is frozen within the scribing sounds. Gemma stepped through the door and picked up the photograph. Ben morphed under the dusky light. His face is a little rounder than Ben's. His eyebrows more arched. A front tooth overlapped the other. This boy has freckles.

Blood flecked the glass on a background section that could almost pass as poppies. A red smear slashed his right leg. Such a blemish was unforgivable. The photograph had acquired weight, or her muscles had grown weak. She feared she might drop the picture. Jerkily, she lowered the photograph to the unit.

Now standing at the doorway of Luke's room, she could see out of his window, the source of the dusky glow. His right drape had been partly drawn across, but this did not obstruct the view. Her first impression was that of a diptych aspect, his window framing two sections of the adjacent apartment's interior: the living area and the bedroom. Steel binoculars had been mounted upon the windowsill below, the optical viewers trained upon the apartment. Gemma didn't have to peek through to discern the scene unfolding. Two women wearing matching silver bikinis were licking cake mixture out of a mixing bowl in the kitchen. Charlene and Suzie appeared to have tendered their commission, but present forms possessed Charlene's lithe grace and tapering limbs. And both sported idealised, elegant masks, just the way Phil had intended. The new 'Fox' flicked cake mixture onto the new 'Cat's' belly. Fox extended a finger and dipped into Cat's bellybutton. She licked the sugar mixture off lovingly. Cat grazed her long fingernails over Fox's shoulders and bared her throat. She raised a knee and drew her thigh against Fox's hip in stroking motions. Gemma had gender in common with these performers but that was all, her posture pulled tight, her body trussed in a duffel coat and her skin wind-parched. Watching them, Gemma had the notion the atoms in her body were closer together than the atoms in those women. She could never score her fingers in such feathery motions over Fox's shoulders, could never pivot her knee so exactly. Against Phil's pink and mauve diptych, Gemma was a black silhouette on the dark side, the spectator across the void. She experienced distaste, pity and loss.

The scratching noise stopped. This lapse drew her attention as a commencement of sound. Gemma turned her head and realised she had drawn level with the foot of Luke's bed. The room appeared grey in the gloom, the objects within equally Spartan: a bed, a chair, a unit, a small portable and a pile of books. Gemma stared dumbly at the scene in front of her. Luke was standing on his bed, his back to her. He wore dark boxer shorts and a loose shirt. In his right hand, he grasped a wide pencil. The drapes drawn on his side of the room rendered his form in shadow but she could make out a Pollock-style chaos of marks on the wall in front of him. The scrawl looked to be applied in layers, each via an instrument of a different colour or tone. The lower layers had mostly faded, almost obscured. More current marks could more clearly be made out. Messages leapt out at her on careful inspection, like one of those magic pictures that conceal a three-dimensional image.

Must never forget, deserve to remember… Forgetting is cheating, not yours to take… Yours is remembering, always… Forgetting is stealing, don't take anymore… Unforgivable to forget, don't deserve it… Stop cheating, not yours… Take what you deserve…

Similar words and phrases echoed throughout the scrawl. Forgetting, remembering, cheating, deserving. Hieroglyphics to her would have held more meaning. Her face fell slack. Luke hadn't moved but he had detected her presence. He shifted his head until she could see the side of his cheek and his neck. The dusky glow continued to shift at her periphery. The aesthetics at his window lingered in her mind; the soft mauve ambience, creamy figures in silver attire, motions like underwater reefs in a soft sea current. By contrast, Luke's dark looming figure made a lurching motion upon one foot as he shifted balance. He planted his hand upon the wall. The mattress pitched as he turned and faced her. In small motions, his gaze shifted across. His sights alighted on hers. Sweat pasted his forehair to his brow. His chest heaved. The lower buttons of his shirt, otherwise open had been fastened askew, exposing his chest to his abdomen. Black hair gathered at his navel and the centre of his chest. One of his nipples protruded at the seam of his shirt. She averted her eyes to encounter coarse hair at his legs, orientating and thickening towards his groin. She shifted her sights again and realised she was looking at the large and nobbled feet of her voyeur. Standing on the bed, Luke appeared oversized and resentful for his downward gaze, although his expression remained still. The weight of his eyes squashed her out of existence. Half-naked and upon a platform like an exhibit, she could decipher his humiliation. He could not shirk away, he could not erase the scrawl, he could not dress himself. He could only watch and wait it seemed for some articulation of repugnance, a scream perhaps, a scurry from the room.

Gemma clutched at her duffel coat and realised Luke could interpret this as indicative of distaste. In the silence, his eyes resigned, did not change. In a bid to release herself from the moment, she turned away and immediately rued the compulsion. The diptych burned her eyes again. Fox was kissing the cake mixture from Cat's abdomen. Cat arched her back in apparent ecstasy, her fingers gliding along Fox's forearms. Cat's other hand rested against the barstool, her elbow jutting demurely. Fox kissed, Cat licked; they rocked together. Gemma burrowed her fingernails into her palms in anguish. She was an intruder upon a male fantasy, on the wrong side, watching those like herself undertake tasks that should remain invisible except to him. An unnerving self-awareness crept over her. Luke was not watching. The drapes obscured his view but he didn't have to see. The show was his, he carried the diptych in his head; he must have seen this sequence or something like it a hundred times. He was watching her watch *Domestic Bliss*.

Gemma could no longer bear to see the candy-coloured figures engaged in staged erotica. What was it but a three-hour presentation of pretty lesbian flat-mates forever in the mood? The sexuality was not the offender, nor the participants, but the fakery of it, the flightiness. She resumed her gaze and experienced a visual backlash – Luke's dark bulk, taut on the bed, half-naked, disheveled, disgraced in front of his ugly scrawl on the wall. The words pulled her attention. *Remembering, forgetting*: Awake, asleep. *Must never forget*: Must never sleep. *Deserve to remember*: deserve to stay awake. *Take what you deserve*: Forever awake.

Hadn't she once thought that sleeping was like forgiveness?

Her phone pierced the silence. Her sights jerked towards his eyes. Luke did not flinch. His chest continued to heave beneath his shirt. Gemma ferreted through her coat pockets and lifted her mobile to her ear. Her voice shook. 'Hello?'

Ben's small utterance floated back to her. 'Mum?'

Gemma's chest took a jolt. She turned to face the wall. 'Ben…oh, God!'

'Mum, I'm at Patti's.'

Gemma shut her eyes against gathering tears. 'Where have you been? I've been looking for you.'

'I know.' Ben's voice faltered. 'I went to the mall. I sat there for hours. I…I didn't' know what to do with myself.' Ben's voice thickened with anguish. 'Mum…I'm so sorry.'

The room fell into a spin. 'It's all right, Ben. I'm just glad you're safe.'

'Mum.'

Gemma sniffed noisily. She gritted her teeth. 'Yes, Ben.'

'I love you.'

Gemma's lower lip trembled. 'I love you too, Ben.' Gemma swallowed a salty lump in a bid to steady her tone. 'I'm coming home soon…we can talk. I promise things will be better for us, Ben. I promise.'

Ben's voice lowered into a half-whisper. 'Okay.'

Gemma waited for Ben to cut the line and then the corner of her lip curled of its own free will. She switched her phone off and slipped it in her pocket. She wiped a damp streak from her cheek onto the back of her hand. Gemma had forgotten herself. She looked upon Luke with a new foreboding. Now was the time to leave, never to say anything. But a question loitered, insistent upon expression.

'Why is there blood in your hall?'

Luke's right eyelid wavered before blinking heavily. His voice emerged gravelly. 'Someone broke into my flat.' He resumed his steady appraisal. 'I showed him the door.'

Gemma clutched her coat ever tighter. 'And…and the photograph in the hall. Who is it?'

Luke swallowed dryly. 'My son.'

His reply hung in the air. The uncanny resemblance to Ben remained an unspoken acknowledgment.

And then Luke added, 'Charlie.'

A name she had considered for Ben. Classic. Timeless. 'Where is he?'

Luke seemed suddenly weary. 'In a box.'

Gemma feared she had understood him correctly. The words *forgetting* and *remembering* behind him kept jumping out from the scrawl.

His gaze shifted momentarily. 'I backed into him one day…on the driveway. I was in a rush and I didn't check the mirror. I didn't see him.' Luke's tightened his grasp on his pencil. 'He couldn't get out of the way quick enough…Later that day, he died in hospital.'

Gemma could see that Luke was mistaken. Charlie was not in a box. Charlie was dead. Luke was in a box, a box that looked out onto a lie that could never obscure his scrawl of shame. Gemma's voice came thickly. 'Where is his mother?'

Luke did not blink. 'She left.'

Gemma's wrath this afternoon came back to haunt her. She'd called him a creep. She'd wished eternal wakefulness upon him, to live in this box forever. She tried to contain her shaking. 'You attacked my car,' she blurted not meaning how that sounded. Her breaths jerked. 'The accident happened six years ago, is that right?'

Luke's non-response confirmed the fact.

Collective recall bombarded her; her feet grew restless. The way he'd watched Ben in assembly, the Wii fit gift for Ben. *He is a very special boy*, he'd said. *You are lucky to have him*. Gemma wanted to run out of his flat, she wanted to hide. 'Why didn't you tell me about him?' she cried. 'I thought…*you know what I thought!*'

Luke growled at her, 'Get out!'

Gemma backed away. She turned and saw Fox offer a finger-dollop of icing sugar to Cat. Cat lowered her head and sucked slowly at Fox's offering.

'I said, *get out!*'

Gemma's head jerked away.

She sped from the room.

Chapter 35

IF GEMMA had encountered an earlier version of herself gazing at the scratch marks on his door, her present self would have been unable to articulate what she'd seen. Her hands grasping the railings at the top of the stairs mottled crimson and white. Someone opened a door. Gemma withdrew into the shadows. The door closed. Trudging footfalls echoed on the landing. The sounds retreated down the stairs.

Gemma had the option of going the same route. Ben awaited her at home. She could run him a warm bath, soothe his aching joints, get his clothes ready for school and then cuddle up with him on the sofa in front of the TV. Ben liked a hot chocolate before bed now and again. She could make him marmalade on toast, a favourite accompaniment and then they might talk. A phone call conveying his one syllable had brought this world back. An instant before, Gemma thought she had lost this world forever. Worlds chasms apart annexed by Ben's small utterance. This emotional depth-of-field nauseated her like the view of Fell Reservoir from the rim. Her mind pulled back into shape from extreme contortion, as shattered as her car.

Gemma steadied herself and viewed his door through blurred vision. The sensation of losing Ben continued to stalk her. She would have blamed herself. Her loss. The minefield of blame: she should have reported him to the police like Stacy had; she should never have fallen asleep this afternoon; she should have met Ben straight from school; she should have driven faster, moved quicker.

Gemma approached his doorway. She wrung her hands, hesitating. Her bare feet padded over his blooded doormat. A rain of blameful retrospections peppered at her as she stepped over the bloody atolls in his hall. She approached the photograph of Ben smeared with blood, merely pausing. She entered Luke's room. *Domestic Bliss* arrested her briefly. Fox lounged on the bed like Venus in a reproduction Gemma recalled her mother possessing as a jigsaw – Velazquez's *The Rokeby Venus*. Cat presided like the winged Cupid holding the mirror. She clutched body oil instead. Gemma glanced across. Luke still on the bed had backed up against the wall, his profile aligned with his right shoulder and his eyes closed. Humiliated and deserving pity yet the sight burned her. Why hadn't he removed the blood from the photograph? Why hadn't he bolted the door from the inside? *Why hadn't he told her about Charlie?* Other whys joined their former shoulds and together they jabbed against an internal organ she'd acquired upon Ben's birth, as real and bloody as her liver and kidneys. The floppy matter would have plopped to the floor had her belly been slashed. The answers to either should no longer matter but whether they did or not differed by a hair's breadth. Her innards, afflicted with contusions, surged, slipped and grasped desperately for internal moorings.

Gemma stepped onto the bed. The mattress' sudden pitch alerted his attention. He dropped his pencil. But his alarm did not last long, his brows knitting to the bridge of his nose and his mouth taking on a grimace. 'I don't want your *pity!*' he hissed.

His assumption affronted her. 'This isn't about pity,' she uttered. She planted the palms of her hands onto his shoulders. He smelled of moss steeped in fresh sweat. She gathered the fabric of his shirt into her fingers for anchorage. His damp warmth radiated through. She bore down. Believing she was pulling him towards her, he extended his arms and pushed at her hips. Mouth knitted, he maintained her distance at arms' length. The edge of the bed encroached at her heels. Gemma decided she was conceding no more territory to him, even if this meant toppling backwards off the bed. He would have to join her on the floor via her clutches. Her legs, communicating her resolve offered him no choice but to prize her fingers from his shoulders despite his superior physical strength. In this endeavour, he released his grasp from her hips which enabled her to step closer and push harder. Luke squeezed his eyes shut and grappled at her right hand. '*Get away from me!*' he snarled.

'You *owe* me,' Gemma affirmed and with this declaration a new resolve overcame her. 'You hurt Ben,' she seethed.

Luke kept his eyes shut preoccupied with his mission to burrow his index finger beneath her right palm and prize her fingers open, but her hand, balled into a fist, permitted no room. 'I never touched him,' he hissed.

'Yes, you did,' Gemma seethed. 'There's blood on him. I saw it on the photograph. You took him away from me!'

Luke's other hand sought purchase on her coat with little to grab onto. He licked sweat from the flesh above his lip, the bed squeaked. Their grappling embrace was the antithesis to *Domestic Bliss* playing out through the window, not smooth, not elegant, but dark, unwieldy.

'*Let go of me!*' he snarled. He shook her. The room pivoted at the hinge joint of her clutches. She staggered briefly. Gemma feared he could never submit to her will by her strength alone. His knees resisted gravity without effort and he had a height advantage. Part of him had to give in to her purpose. Gemma now committed, compressed the fabric of his shirt. 'Get down on your *knees!*' she grunted.

He didn't respond. Through the fronds of his eyelashes his gaze could just be discerned but all expression had slackened. She kept vigilance however. His hands now grasped the flanks of her coat as though to administer a decisive shove. Gemma's fists shuddered, locked into a spasm. The fabric of his shirt scrunched within her clasp. The contagion spread throughout her body, her chest lurching and her ankles trembling. Gently, Gemma opened out her fingers into shells, fully aware he had his chance to push her off the bed. Lightly she urged his shoulders downwards. His knees juddered as though jabbed from behind. His body canted to one knee. He endeavoured a recovery but his legs seemed to have forsaken all will to support his weight. His narrow gaze vanished behind closing eyes. He collapsed onto his knees in one lumbering motion. As though overtaken by a brief lapse, Luke drew hastily away as a frantic drowner, his surrender a boiling sea. Gemma decided this was no way to seek redemption and embraced the back of his head. She pulled him towards her until the end of his nose prodded at her blouse just below her breasts. He wrenched his head aside. She clutched his hair. Sweat came away in her hands. She held fast, easing his face into her belly. His fists wrung at her coat, prospecting for leverage. The bed pitched violently. Undeterred, she clasped her hands snugly around the back of his head. Her wrists resting upon his shoulders pushed down. He could move in no direction without her counterforce. He gave a muffled groan.

Domestic Bliss' candy-glow flickered impassively upon the far wall. He pawed at her coat. He groped at her pockets, buttons, her elbows. He pulled at her forearms. He exuded hot snorts against her blouse. They rocked on the bed as one, clutched together ultimately by the notches at her fingers. His hands slid uselessly against her wrists. Heat pulsated from the top of his head with his efforts. His hand grappled at her skirt beneath her coat. He bunched the fabric. Hot gales ebbed against her abdomen. He became still, but his fists began to shake. Her skirt pulled tight against her knees. He drew cool air through her blouse in a protracted and jerky inhalation before letting forth a choked sob. Gemma relaxed her hands, overwhelmed with compunction. The blooded photograph of his son sat heavily behind her. She did not have to look to see the boy's arched eyebrows, his grimace, his crooked front tooth. Abstractedly, she drew a thumb through Luke's hair. Luke now seemed to gain comfort from the seclusion of her blouse, his face buried deep within the folds. His shoulders jerked violently in a back-tide to a forceful lament that made her cheeks burn. He sounded like a child at a lower frequency. He spread his fingers though her skirt, tips hooked. Her blouse now felt hot and damp. Gemma rested her hands at the back of his head.

In repose.

Gemma lay beside him watching his profile at rest wondering how a scene so tranquil could captivate her so much. His face was slack; his eyes closed yet his eyelids twitched intermittently. A tear had escaped his eyelid and was making a slow rivulet across his cheek. She dabbed the moisture onto her index finger. Gemma had clutched him to her until the room resumed silence. She had lowered him onto his side believing him to be asleep when he straightened his legs to the foot of the bed. She lowered his arm onto his side and observed his torpor from over his shoulder. He lay still for over a minute and then suddenly rolled onto his back. He gazed up at her. His eyelids immediately drifted downwards. Whether he would remember seeing her she could not be certain. *Domestic Bliss* came to an end. The lights opposite went out, rendering his profile into a silhouette. Before leaving quietly, she whispered two words into his ear.

Chapter 36

SHE had seen what a creep he was, peeked out of his hide-e-hole, read his twisted scrawl, looked upon his sweaty, disheveled form. Had she darted out, never to return, his humiliation would have been complete.

She had been cruel, looked upon him as an offender, demanded he fall to his knees and beg for her forgiveness for something he had never done – a bestowal worse than pity. His knees had betrayed him; he loathed the notion, believing such a deed self-effacing, but an inner shadow desired it sneakily, greedily, more than air. Suddenly, his knees could no more support him than a baby. He fell into her clutches. She had instantly swaddled his face into her blouse. Held him in place. Wanted him there, needed him there. Housemaid's arms engaged in her purpose. Her linen smelled of showers before an Atlantic blow. Never had he needed someone so horribly. Never had he given himself so completely. His face pressed into his own tears, soaking her blouse, sobbing like a child. No one had looked upon him with disdain, judged him, his father now indistinct, no longer towered over him, his dark face looming over his starched collar, his token of power, now merely formal wear. No longer was Luke caught between the belt and self-loathing or penance and guilt. Only the smell of her linen and her cool hands cupping the back of his head arrested his senses. Swathed within the folds of her fabric made no matter of how an emotional sledgehammer contorted his face, his eyes squeezed shut, his teeth clenching, his nostrils flaring. Her fabric did not judge, only caressed, provided sanctuary. Events of his son's death tore away from the inner cascade, so overplayed in his mind, they appeared sun-parched. Late for work, reverses at full throttle, his car lurches, his window down, permits the whiplashing crack beneath the engine's roar. Engine dies, Luke drifts from his car, stench of gasoline and oil. A broken form beneath the wheel axel, legs of gesso chalk pushed out of true. Shin-bone punctured flesh, a bloody gash. A foot twitches, a crutch pinned beneath – its counterpart on the grass. Luke jacks the car, breaths hitches, chest throbs, moans. Calls an ambulance, hands shaking, son's inert form lays undisturbed. Luke prizes the boy's glasses off, his final fatherly duty. One lens cracked, eyes closed, blood on tarmac. A juddering ride, a drip-feed, painkillers, a neck-brace. The boy's eyes never open.

The house dies. Alison denies him. She wishes Luke had taken the boy's place. Tear-stained, gaunt, her face frozen. She has nothing else to say.

Luke falls out of the event leaving glutinous black syrup. Severed from the memory, the fever pushed through his windpipe, his ears, his nose, his every pore, forcing sweat and tears in an upward surge. Luke didn't think his body could withstand the force. His flesh surely would rent. A wall of the substance rammed him from his core like a supernova. Her hands held him in place, his only mainstay.

Penance and guilt. He saw a third option. She'd uttered the words before he had tumbled into the ocean. 'Sleep now,' she'd said. Forgiveness. Sleep now. Forgive yourself.

Luke grew dimly aware she had left the room soon afterwards. He wished for once that his sleep had abstained. He wanted to share consciousness with her if only to look. But sleep insisted in a non-compromise. Sleep would have its way. His eyelids had closed with the force of gravity. He wished to return to the folds of her blouse, to bury his face there. He wanted to be still, for time to postpone.

Luke came-to at nine. Exhaustion palled over him like a sickness. He rang in absent and then contacted Philip to postpone again. Luke unplugged and switched off all modes of contact before he got the third-degree from any quarter. Luke withdrew into her fabric, imagined his pillow smelled of her linen left out in the rain. He never wanted to leave this sanctuary again but did so to visit the bathroom. His right eye appraised him through the mirror. No longer disdainful, merely lazy, had it always been that way? Disdainful or not, he would remember her last utterance. He could do so if he wanted.

He surrendered the lease to six Templeton Court. The flat remained empty for a week before young female students moved in. Was Luke guilty of peeking? Well, he'd spotted a buttock or two, although not through his binoculars. Of course Luke hadn't objected but he had always sought out her blouse when retiring to bed. Only her soft linen smell carried him over the threshold. But he regretted his sleep time encroaching upon his conscious imagination. He wished to lie within her scent a little longer, to press his face against her hot abdomen, her arms in repose around him. One day he fancied he would actually kiss her scar. She would close her eyes in surrender as he had done so in front of her. He had wanted her since that day in the garden. Like a fool, he had followed her to the supermarket and Fell Reservoir, had blundered in finding a way into her world. Instead, his sleep onset grew shorter, almost out of contrary smugness. Had he beaten his insomnia through a double-bluff as well as through a surrender of self?

Poor Philip couldn't accept his notice without a full explanation. Why? he'd kept demanding. It seemed Philip had grown quite attached to his *Domestic Bliss*. Having taken on many commitments around Stratford and London, money could not have been a concern. Luke could have told him the reason lay in seeing himself in Christian Lovett after the weasel had blackmailed his way into an impromptu viewing of *Domestic Bliss*. Luke knew who'd broken in the instant he saw the locks had been tampered with. Christian had the impudence to take offence at Luke's foresight, believing Luke owed him for 'allowing' him have the flat, calling him a bastard, threatening to report him to the police for loitering outside the school gates again. Luke's suit at this point had been immaculate in the wake of smashing her car on the conviction the slippery clutch may deceive her whilst Ben happen to skirt the rear bumper. But Christian's nasal blood had now spotted Luke's right cuff as Luke's fist's connected with Christian's cheekbone. All tension had dropped from Luke's face at that moment, his gaze steady, full of purpose. Blood surged from Christian's nose as though a faucet had been released. Red syrup made a runnel down his chin and the front of his silver shirt. Christian looked upon Luke, at first stunned, and then outraged yet gratified. 'You fuckin' broke my dose,' he'd croaked, at which point Luke belted him again for soiling his cuff. Luke had already conceded his other suit to bird excrement, the fabric at his collar flattened beyond repair. Christian fell against the door with undue emphasis, assuming the victim role with relish. Luke belted him through the hall for such clownish display. Luke would explain if the police came knocking that he'd had a very bad day; he'd been called a creep in front of his work colleagues, he'd had no sleep in three days and had come back to find his locks tampered with. Christian had stumbled into the upper landing where Luke promptly slammed his door in his face. Having heard nothing for days, Luke assumed Christian had finally got the message.

But, no. It wasn't strictly Christian's display on that day. *Domestic Bliss* had never seemed the same since Gemma had put on her fat suit. Philip's arrangement now seemed a parody of itself. Minus the lust, ambience and music, what were the routines but a lightweight pleasantry?

Without conscious decision, Luke prepared his flat for a transition. The time had come to put his detached in Berkham on the market and he needed to make space here. He'd always fancied one of those Victorian semis just outside Warwick. The divorce settlement had now been paid off and he owned the place outright. He could do well despite the turbulent economy. Luke picked up the photograph of Charlie. He hadn't looked at it properly since moving into the flat, the image failing to convey the real Charlie: his compulsion to roll his tongue against his canted tooth whilst cogitating, the manner in which his brows gathered at one of Luke's corny jokes, his trill-like chortle. Luke now held a series of coloured-pixels that happened to make up Charlie's image. Luke trembled as he wiped the blood from Charlie's leg with a damp cloth. Resentment prickled at such an unfair exchange – the real thing for a two-dimensional replication. Luke hadn't spent enough time with his son, this deficit surging in significance since the opportunity to put this right had been snatched away. Watching Ben in assembly showed him what he'd missed. The sight of that boy narrating his lines had pinched through his heart. Never had Luke attended parents' evenings, sports days, or assemblies when Charlie had been alive. Alison took over such tasks, assuming her mother role with abandon, almost possessively. Luke's time with Charlie had come second-place, delegated to a dispensable aspect to the family structure. And Luke was equally culpable, allowing his work commitments to take precedence. Alison needed to be needed, to be loved by everybody. What more could she have wished for than a disabled son? She had been faithful, loyal and dutiful, but she had never truly been his. Luke carefully replaced the photograph.

Luke took down the aerial picture of Warwick. He'd never seen his scrawl in daylight before. His chest prickled at the full ugliness of his outpourings. Gemma had seen it, yet she had returned to his room. Luke scalpeled a neat square into the wallpaper. He teased the words off. Syllables split away from one another: *forge…ember…serve…cheat…ways*. Luke experienced the final cascade of a conviction like a virus breaching a computer programme. The peeling off was exacting, time-consuming, for Luke wished to maintain neat edges, free of tears. Once finished, Luke was left with a perfect square presenting bare plaster beneath. Luke stared at the blankness. He could only compare the experience to staring at a straight horizon expecting to see an aberration. Luke saw nothing.

Luke had a paper-shredder but wouldn't be needing it. Tearing the defaced wallpaper into tiny pieces the old fashioned way had been gratifying. He replaced the aerial photograph of Warwick on the wall once he had finished.

The moment he did so, a sweat overtook him. The air in the room bunched up against his chest. He fled into the bathroom, filled the sink with cold water and submerged his head. The shockwave bleached everything out. He closed his eyes, let his lungs protest. He could feel her hands clutching the back of his head, pulling him out. Trapped bubbles fizzed against his skin. He exhaled forcibly, submitting again to her insistence. He withdrew gasping. Insomnia's embrace had finally given way only to be replaced with another kind of imperative. He wanted to push his tongue into her mouth; he wanted to dwell on her, taste her at leisure. A potent drowsiness overtook him. Luke slept nose buried deep within her blouse. He slept soundly, deeply for nine hours.

Chapter 37

GEMMA had not needed her smashed-up car to get home to Ben. She had walked in the dark relishing every step. She could have walked forever. Ben was waiting for her in a new way. Ben was not the boy in the picture. The blood had never been his. She closed her eyes and sniffed woodsmoke from smouldering bonfires.

Luke could have lifted her up.

She opened her eyes with a start. He could have lifted her from the bed and carried her off. Of course, in his fevered state, such an idea had never occurred to him but still. She kept thinking about it. Luke lifting her up, him carrying her, her arms encircled about his neck, him lowering his head and ensnaring her upper lip gently in his mouth. She forced the thoughts away. Not long ago, she had been her voyeur and a pervert. She had just forced him to his knees in front of the photograph of his dead son. Her face burned at the names she'd called him at his place of work, only to see how unjustifiable her outburst had been. She sought consolation he was now unconscious. The way she felt now, she never wanted him to regain consciousness again. He most likely was glad to see the back of her. A transit of time might temper her shame. Their paths may never cross again.

Ben hadn't wanted to talk much after all, tired after walking around for hours, pale and hollow-eyed. He had snuck out of school early to pack his things and find somewhere to stay, fully aware his granddad would have returned him to his mother's. Ben hadn't realised Gemma was in the living room asleep until he came down to leave his crutches behind. The things would have burdened him more than his tendinitis alone, apparently.

Once in Birmingham's Palisades, Ben had nowhere to sit, the benches taken. Shopkeepers kept telling him to move on. He bought a KFC yet his stomach kept gnawing. Despite the influx of people, nobody noticed. Nobody cared. His dad wasn't coming back and nobody cared. He'd cried.

Once the shutters had come down, Ben begged the bus driver for a free ride home, preferring not to submerge himself within the stern silence of her car. The house was locked and he didn't have a key. He'd gone to Patti's.

Gemma had crushed him against her the moment she had arrived. Patti seemed gratified at the reunion. She wore a ribbed housecoat and fussed about her modest kitchen enclosing a folding table and four lathe-back chairs. She'd served tea from a pot sporting an illustration of Blackpool Tower. Once home, languor hit Ben hard. He didn't want marmalade on toast or a hot chocolate in the end. But tucking him into bed had been Gemma's most anticipated task.

Sleep deserted her, haunted by Luke's box looking out onto a fabrication, his floundering scrawl. In another world, was there a version of her without Ben, where she resided in her own box? What would it be? He had been on the other side to where she is now. He had lived through the unthinkable. In the other world. He had surrendered to her will. He had forsaken the opportunity to push her off the bed whilst her palms had flattened out. The moment before falling to his knees, he had peered at her through eyelashes in a skulking manner. She didn't have to read his scrawl to comprehend his desperation, his features sweaty and slack as though a palpable hand of guilt was squeezing at his windpipe. He would seek her forgiveness. To him, the only way out. Falling before her could not have been easy for someone with such self-composure and who always got his own way. In his need, he had given himself to her. More so than in sex. Only on a quiet moment like this could Gemma relive that moment. In giving to her, she had given to him.

Gemma took leave from work and allowed Ben time off school – a bad cold, she'd told Mrs. Matthews. During his lie-in, Gemma went to town early and brought herself a new laptop with Colby's refund. She spent the day setting it up. At last, she was able to catch up on her finances. She let Ben open a Facebook account and message with Zack. It was then that Gemma realised her Fiesta was still parked at Templeton Court. She tried not to dwell on whether he still watched *Domestic Bliss* and pore over other women. Her chest ached anyway. *So*, she wanted her voyeur to look only at her now? The idea was absurd seeing as it was no longer her business who he looked at anymore. She telephoned breakdown to have the car towed to the scrapyard and learned it had already been dealt with. *He had given himself to her*. She knit her mouth. He could move on now and so could she.

Gemma went upstairs to find her car details. She happened to look out on passing and spotted a black Jaguar coupe at the bottom of the road. The sight snagged her to the spot. She darted behind the curtain. The oblique glass distorted the view but she could make out his figure inside, his shirted torso. He raised a hand and loosened his tie. How long had he had been sitting there, she couldn't be certain but he appeared restive, constrained. He curled his hands around the steering wheel and kneaded. Her mouth became dry. She entreated inwardly for his form to emerge, to walk her way yet feared the prospect more than anything. What would she way to him? Her words would come out a jumble, or get stuck. She turned away in a juvenile panic, gathered her hair which had yet to see the comb since getting back and affixed a clip. Ben was still downstairs. She cursed inwardly. At least her cat mask was hidden away in her wardrobe this time. And she could concede her laptop to Ben, suitably diverting at a time like this. She would have some serious explaining to do for Ben afterwards though.

She looked out again. Luke was walking towards her house. A prickly ball pushed up her chest. She would offer him a cup of tea, that's what she would do; maintain lightweight chitchat, if that was possible. Take things slowly. Had to. Her mind had been dragged through the mire. She needed time to adjust, to see him in a new light.

Afternote

The locations portrayed within this novel are a combination of actual and imagined places. Warwick and Kenilworth are actual places in Warwickshire; however the Prospect Business Park and Southsbury are fictional, as is Brynton Sands.

A writer's plea

Oh, the joys of reading a book,
I hope you're glad you took a look.
I've written some others, if you didn't know,
But a lack of reviews, makes selling them slow.
So buck the trend if you want something to do,
Go to your computer and write a review!
Thank you!

Other novels by Charles J Harwood

The Shuttered Room

Little do they know their captive holds a deadly secret.

Jessica Fraser would appear to have everything: money, a devoted husband, a healthy son and a fulfilling career. But her life takes a dramatic turn when she is taken hostage and incarcerated in an upstairs room by three thugs demanding a huge ransom from her rich father.

Jess manages to draw attention to the house in a failed escape attempt. But her captors preserve their cover by feigning a family setup to keep the police off the scent.

In desperation, Jess cuts a hole in the bedroom floor with a cutlery knife. From there, Jess observes the three of them going about their everyday business.

But Jess has a secret. She is no ordinary captive. Jess's view into their private world becomes a portal into her own dark past. Her spying grows in obsession until she finds herself drawn into a dangerous psychological game with her abductors. With no one to save her, Jess must rely upon her wits to escape. But will she escape with her sanity intact?

Book's dimensions: 5inx8in, 290 pages and 87,000 words approx.

A Hard Lesson

A teacher takes on the pupil from hell only to learn what treachery means.

Sarah, a fledgling teacher haunted by the memory of her dead brother embarks a relationship with old school-friend and rogue, Frank. She feels a misfit when she meets his tightly-knit gang, headed by charismatic Kurt.

Sarah is soon abandoned at the hands of Frank's commitment to his cause. Her sense of inadequacy deepens when she takes on the pupil from hell, Josh. But Sarah's wounded pride drives her onward despite Josh's tough trials and the revelation that he is dyslexic.

Little does Sarah know the implications of the assignments she sets Josh on erotic art. Slowly, Sarah gets drawn into the dark secrets of his family and the inner workings of Kurt's tightly-knit circle.

Can Sarah survive the ultimate test of facing her greatest fear in the face of a psychopathic leader and his cohorts?

Book's dimensions: 5inx8in, 285 pages and 85,000 words approx.